PROLOGUE

"I'll see you in the morning, Ceres. I love you. Happy Birthday. Thirteen! I seriously can't believe how old you're getting."

Looking up, I saw my mother had poked her head into my room to say goodnight. The voices, The Oracle as they called themselves, came to life in my head. They wanted to read her, but I put up my mental block.

"Okay, Mom. Thanks. I love you, too."

She wasn't aware of the voices that had plagued me since childhood. No one was, except for one of my aunts. I had prophesied to her when I was a young child in order to save her life. She thought I was a total creep because of it and avoided me at all costs. That was the first and last time I delivered a prophecy. Mostly, I kept my mental walls up around people at all times.

The Oracle urged me not to tell people about their whispers in my head. The voices insisted the more people that knew about my gift, the easier it would be for "him" to find me.

I looked back at my tablet, finding the spot on the page I was reading. Soon, though, the words blurred together as my lids ached to close. I laid the tablet against my chest, sighing as I rubbed my eyes. Maybe I would read just one more chapter.

Thunder clapped, deafening, as if a storm cloud was sitting right on top of the house. A subsequent lightning strike flickered across the walls of my bedroom like a thousand clicks of a flash camera. Stunned, I looked around the room. My tablet, still open to the book, crashed to the floor. I must have fallen asleep.

But I sensed something wasn't right. The hair on the back of my neck stood up, and I glanced around again, searching for the source of my discomfort.

As the lightning struck, my gaze fell on my balcony doors. I froze, sucking in a sharp breath. A figure stood there, a black silhouette outlined by the white electricity of the storm. Its hand lifted and grasped the doorknob.

As long as I could remember, the voices warned me that "he" was searching for us. That "he" would find us. Who "he" was, they either wouldn't tell me or didn't know. Instinct warned me it was him at the door. I knew I'd finally been discovered.

My heart quickened in my chest, jumping against my ribs like a rabbit trapped in a snare. I knew I'd never get to the bedroom door in time, so I scrambled from my bed and ran to the closet. As I clicked the door shut, I heard the small squeak that always accompanied the turn of my balcony door hinges.

For several seconds, I could hear nothing except my shallow breathing and the rush of blood in my ears. I covered my mouth with a shaking hand, struggling to stifle the sound of my ragged gasps. There was only silence outside in my room. No footsteps, and no movement.

Another loud crash of thunder roared through the room, absorbing the sound of my scream as the door whipped open. A tall, muscular figure in an ethereal white robe loomed over me. His face was concealed, and he smelled strange, like freshly tilled soil and cinder.

I opened my mouth, ready to scream again, but his hand caught the sound. Silenced, I kicked at him, determined I would fight to the death. I was no match for his strength, and he easily snaked his arm around my waist and pulled me into him.

His arms clamped around me like an iron vise, holding me firmly against his chest while he cooed, "Hush now, Pythia. I've been searching for you."

CHAPTER ONE
Ten Years Later

"It's time to rise now, Pythia. The master is coming for a reading, and you need to be prepared."

Prepared. Bathed, plucked, waxed, painted, dressed, and then drugged. You'd think they would be kind enough to give me the drugs beforehand.

I groaned and stared at the ceiling.

Finally, I turned my head to Keilah and sighed. "I told you not to call me that. I have a name."

Well, several names. Ceres, the name my mother and father had given me at birth. The master had taken that name upon my arrival here. He'd strictly forbidden anyone to speak it because it was associated with the Goddess Demeter, and he didn't want to draw her attention.

I hadn't heard it out loud in years. I kept my given name close to my heart, a tendril of the life that I had lived before the master had taken me from my family over a decade ago and imprisoned me in this golden cage he called a temple. I'd convinced myself it was preferable that no one knew that name. It was mine. A part of my parents that I didn't have to share.

Instead, I was to be called by my official title. To the people here I was the Pythia, the Oracle of the Gods. I belonged to the master—Apollo, God of Sun, Medicine, Prophecy, and many other things. Although I could not call him by that name, only master.

I hated the official title, and I didn't like being a nameless girl, so Keilah and I had fixed it the best we could. We changed the spelling of Ceres and kept only Cere. In private, Keilah would call me by that name, pronounced *Sa-ree*. That way, I had a name, and we weren't at risk of drawing unwanted attention from Demeter.

"I'm sorry, Cere. But we are running late. I've let you sleep too long."

Sitting up, I pushed out a long and exasperated sigh. Keilah fiddled with my wardrobe and selected the right pieces for my ceremonial outfit. The main garment was a rich scarlet, the only color of dress the Pythia could ever wear, and a scarf of dark mustard embroidered with gold thread that would wrap around my shoulders.

Keilah turned, fixing me with a stressed smile. She was my handmaid, one of three people who had been allowed to touch my skin over the last ten years. The other two being the overseer of the temple, and my physical trainer, Laurenth. Master placed great emphasis on my *purity*. I wasn't to be touched by unworthy hands, lest I lose my gift.

Keilah was my guardian, and I loved Laurenth like a sister, so she also called me Cere. It had worked well, and it had been our fun little secret until the overseer had learned of the nickname. I'd been punished, and he used it now, too, if only to mock me.

I didn't return Keilah's smile, choosing to sulk instead.

"Don't be childish," she scolded, her lips dropping into a frown. "It just makes the day drag on longer."

I huffed but stood and allowed her to fuss over me. I didn't know specific details about Keilah's life, or about anyone at the temple. The rules were clear. I wasn't to speak unless spoken to, and I wasn't ever allowed to ask questions. Following rules was never a strength of mine, even before I arrived here, so when I was alone with Keilah, I asked a lot of questions. Most of the time, she wouldn't answer, or she claimed she didn't know.

Even though she was always aloof with me, I felt a fondness for her. I loved her. The feelings may not be mutual, but she was my constant, my caretaker, and my best friend.

As I often did, I stared down at the golden locket around her neck. I'd asked at least a thousand times what was in it, but she insisted that her life before this was over, and it was none of my business. She looked haunted whenever she clasped her hand over the locket, and I sensed if she ever did tell me the story, it would be a tragedy. Part of me understood her detached behavior was due to her own trauma and had nothing to do with me.

Keilah, I would guess, was in her fifties or sixties. Her curly black hair held a growing number of gray strands, especially at the temples, and her mouth and eyes crinkled with lines that showed she loved to laugh. I could only assume that applied to her life before she arrived here, because our strict, monotonous lives left little space for laughter.

She always tied her thick hair back into a low bun at her nape, and her skin was a rich honey color that I envied. It differed from my pasty complexion. My freckled, pale skin held a flushed pink undertone, making me look at all times as if I'd just finished running a mile.

Keilah's eyes were a beautiful rich chocolate that held a sage tenderness, but they could also grow as sharp as a whip if she felt I needed a scolding. Mine were similar to those of my mother, but where hers were a soft hue of pure gold, mine were brighter, some would say yellow. I knew many found them unsettling.

"Let's go," she clucked. "The bath, hurry now."

I shuffled behind her to the adjacent door. She opened it and allowed me to pass beside her. The room was a decadent display of luxury that would make most people squeal with happiness.

I removed my night slip, which was also red, and walked down the steps of the bath. The tub was enormous. It was the size of two king-sized beds lying side by side and adorned with rubies and gold. I never understood why such a large bath was necessary when I was the only one who used it.

As always, they had filled it with smelly oils and various types of flowers. Sometimes the scents were so strong that my nose would itch the rest of the day, overwhelmed by the onslaught of perfumes. I was thankful today wasn't one of those days, and found the smells were dominant but not overpowering.

Pleasantly warm water embraced my legs, and I melted into it, sighing. Turning on my back, I floated and gazed at the tall ceiling. As I often did, I wondered at how they had covered the entirety of it with a magnificent ivy vine. It was threatening to move from decor to infestation as giant tendrils of the plant hung down, nearly brushing the floor. I'd asked Keilah before, but she didn't know how they did it either.

"No time for games, Cere. We need to bathe you."

I hated it, but I'd grown to understand after years of fighting that Keilah just did as she was told. She was under the strict control of the master and the overseer, too. I could bathe myself, but she insisted she had to do it. A few years ago, I had finally convinced her I could take care of my body, but still allowed her to wash my hair.

Her firm fingers pushed against my scalp and scrubbed the dark amber locks with yet another strongly scented soap. The soft waves were long, having not been cut since I arrived here, and they brushed the bottoms of my thighs when left untied.

Keilah hummed a gentle tune, as she always did while I was in the bath. I closed my eyes and listened, halfheartedly washing my legs and arms. She dumped a pitcher of water over my head, shocking me, and I yelped.

When I looked at her, her lips twitched as if she wanted to smile. She teased me like this sometimes and I splashed her with a swipe of my hand. Moments like these were how I knew she cared about me, even if she was only here because it was her duty.

A knock on the door stole her small smile, and she hastily pulled the curtain across the tub, concealing me from view. I knew to stay and wait. If anyone saw me indecently dressed, it meant severe consequences for me—and even worse for them. That I'd learned the hard way.

"Come in," she called.

I heard the tinkle of a tea cart alongside the scurry of feet. They exchanged no words, and when Keilah withdrew the curtain, the room was empty again.

I could smell the steamy cup, a rich bergamot—my favorite. Keilah toweled my hair, squeezing the water from it, and then ushered me behind the gold and red silk screen. I sat and prepared myself for the onslaught of tweezers and wax sticks—this was one of the worst parts. And it was something else I didn't understand. No one ever touched me. Why did I need to be tortured with hair removal?

When she finished, I was as smooth as the day I'd been brought into this world. Keilah covered my tender skin in the mint balm that soothed some of the sting.

Grinning, I finally snatched my cup of tea and sipped greedily. On ceremonial days, tea and water were the only things I could ingest before the reading. Fasting increased my piousness, or so I was told.

I sat still while Keilah painted my face with makeup. Black coal shadow on my eyes and deep red stain on my lips. Yet another thing I didn't understand because I performed the reading behind a wooden screen. What did it matter if my face wore make-up?

"Lovely," she said, clicking the palette shut.

Her adept hands braided my hair, only pulling once when I tried to sip my tea. That had earned me an annoyed click of her tongue. After just a couple of minutes, one large braid that started at my forehead and traveled down my back took form, and she tied the end with a red ribbon.

My handmaid glanced at the clock on the wall and huffed. I saw the time and a beat of anxiety shot through me. The master did not like it if I was late, and I didn't want Keilah punished on my behalf. Again.

Working together, she helped me don the restrictive scarlet dress that covered every inch of skin aside from my hands and my face. The neckline even climbed high enough to brush the underside of my jaw when I spoke.

Now considered decent, I was able to leave my chambers and walk down the hallway. My guards awaited—six of them—and flanked me on either side. I clasped my hands in front of me at my waist, and we started our procession.

I couldn't complain about the luxury they had thrust me into as the Pythia. The halls had tall ceilings held aloft by intricately carved pillars, all white marble lined with gold and rubies. Beautiful art hung on the walls, paintings I had never even gotten to examine closely, for it was improper for me to loiter in the hallways. In an alcove to my left, a grand fountain bubbled, and its song was the only other sound besides the falls of our feet.

Despite the luxury I lived in, I still considered myself locked away. In the ten years I'd resided here, I hadn't left this temple aside from my regular walks through the expansive garden outside. And while it was all beautiful and grand, it was still a prison. If you catch a bird and lock it in a cage, does it really matter if the bars are made of gold or iron?

As we walked, servants stopped in their tracks and took extraordinary measures to get out of the way. Pressing against the walls, they fell to their knees with their foreheads on the floor. I stared straight ahead. I had learned it was easier for them if I didn't unsettle them by glancing their way.

A slight commotion in an alcove on my right caught my attention, and I craned my neck to see what was happening. Between the cluster of servants and my guards, I could only catch a small glimpse.

But it was enough.

An older maid laid on her back, and her blank eyes stared at the ceiling. Her right hand still clutched her left arm, and a mask of pain twisted her features. The air seemed strange, and I thought I smelled a floral scent, like lilies.

The amount of people gathering jammed the hallway, and we had to stop for a moment. I winced when the guards started yelling—hitting and pushing the servants in our path. They scattered like mice trying to get out of the way, and I got a better look at the scene.

"Move on," Keilah whispered fiercely to me. She knew the overseer was cruel and would seek any excuse to dole out punishment.

Nothing out of the ordinary ever happened, and curiosity seized me. Despite my better judgment, I found myself asking, "Gods. Is she dead?"

"That's not our concern," she snapped, pushing me softly on the back.

I forced my eyes forward, wondering what had befallen the poor woman.

"What do you think happened?" I gushed with macabre excitement, knowing I was being much too loud.

"Pythia," she warned, glancing around. "Hush now, please."

She always used my official title in front of others. I knew they could punish her for being informal.

I clamped my mouth shut, sensing some sideways glances from the guards that flanked us. My heart dropped. I knew the overseer would find out and I would face discipline for speaking when I shouldn't have.

The arch of a grand doorway came into view, bordered by pillars, and crested by the emblem of a golden snake. I pursed my lips as a beat of apprehension coursed through me.

It was time.

CHAPTER TWO

Keilah hurried me into the door, pulling me towards the right where I would enter the ceremonial chamber. Stopping, she retrieved the sacred laurel branch from her robes and handed it to me.

I clutched it in my clammy hand as a cold sweat broke out over my body. Thoughts of the dead woman in the hallway dissipated, and I focused on breathing the fresh air while I could.

I had to do this once a month, the reading for the master, but it felt like far too often.

Keilah's eyes were pools of sympathy as she gazed up at me, our height difference almost comical. I was tall for a woman, and she was shorter than most.

"Just go on," she whispered, squeezing my hand. "It will be over quickly, and I'll take you to the garden. I'll have the baker send some lemon pastries."

I swallowed the tense feeling in my throat and nodded. Lemon was my favorite.

"Thank you, Pythia," she continued, running her thumb over the back of my hand to comfort me. "We all know how important you are to The Cause."

The Cause.

They had pitched it to me since I arrived. I was being kept locked away for the greater good. My prophetic visions were helping the allies of light fight away the darkness that threatened to encompass the mortal realm. The master had shown me he was only seeking to end unnecessary suffering in the world.

I knew he told the truth, for I had seen the unimaginable darkness in my visions.

Steeling myself, I pushed open the door and entered the chamber. A single three-legged stool sat at the center. Surrounding it were iron pots emitting vapors that filled the room and stifled my ability to draw breath. I resisted the urge to cough, having learned it just forced more of the acrid air into my lungs.

My gift of sight was random. Sometimes I would receive only images, or only whispers. At rare times, I might see and hear both. However, most times when I let my walls down around others, I got nothing from them.

The master knew how to remedy that. These vapors exacerbated my visions, making them clearer and more intense. I felt like I was choking on acid, and I truly hated every moment, but I tried to remind myself that I was saving lives.

"Pythia," his voice sneered from the other side of the wooden screen. "You're late."

I hurried to my seat, mumbling, "I'm sorry, Master."

I clutched the laurel branch as tears ran down my cheeks in response to the burn in my lungs. The vapors invaded my mind, forcing away the block I always had in place.

The voices sprang to life. Some whispered, some shouted, and I had to resist the urge to clamp my hands over my ears, like I had as a small child.

"What do you see?"

I focused on the master, trying to sense his future. The same images I had seen before flared to life. Through his eyes, I witnessed people lying in hospital beds. Dying.

The sensation of the Oracle overtook me, and when I opened my mouth, the voices spoke with me—through me.

"Malevolence lays ruin to the Earth realm. An unnatural plague brings the end of the dominance of humans, killing all in its wake. The rest of the mortal world follows at their heels."

It was the darkness we were trying to stop. This vision was one of the reasons why I had stopped fighting and quit trying to escape. I had loved ones out there somewhere in the mortal realm. My parents, my twin brother, and my little sister. If I had to be a scarlet bird caged in gold to save them, then so be it.

New images filled my mind, ones I hadn't seen before, and I gasped in horror

"What do you see?" he insisted.

"The plague sours. Some die, but some do not. The undead walk. They starve, hungry only for the flesh of others, but they are never sated."

I saw images of them, people that were no longer people, transformed into mindless fiends. Their skin turned the color of smooth pearl and their eyes blacked out like open pits. They ripped at the flesh of others, their teeth like razors and their jaws stretching wider than should be possible.

I clutched my stomach, whimpering and trying not to be sick. They were eating their victims, feasting on the flesh and bone. I was thankful my visions weren't accompanied by sound.

Tears streamed down my cheeks at a faster rate, the vapors overtaking every part of my senses. My heart hammered against my chest, so heavy it felt like it was made of lead.

The master hissed in a breath behind the screen, but I didn't know what emotion warranted the reaction. I'd never laid eyes on him. I didn't know what his face looked like, and I'd only ever seen the white outline of his robe.

"See, Pythia? The damage that is being caused."

"I see," I choked.

"Now tell me who? Who do I need to worry about?"

He always asked this question, and usually no images filled my head. It was always a disappointment. I wanted to see who was responsible, so he could stop them.

But today was different. I gasped again. *Eyes.* I saw purple eyes glaring through the darkness.

I could feel the tension in the room increase. "Who?" he demanded, sounding more aggressive.

"Two forces rise against you. First, violet and shadow will take your sight. Without it, you won't see the beginning of your greatest enemy, the child born of shadow and sun."

"Who?!" he roared, startling me. "Give me a name!"

The image dissolved, and I saw nothing.

"I-I don't know. I don't see."

He snarled, and the inhuman sound filled me with dread as he smacked his hand against the wooden screen. My eyes whipped open in fear, and confusion blossomed in my muddled mind. Wasn't it good I'd seen something? Now we had a clue.

"Who?!"

I closed my eyes again, purposely inhaling the vapors. I wanted to know. I wanted to see.

But only blackness filled my vision. The traitorous voices remained silent.

"I don't see." My voice was barely a whisper, wrought with panic. But he would still hear it. He was a God. "I'm sorry."

I heard the door on the other side of the screen opening and then slamming shut. I stood and stumbled to the exit, desperate to get out. I'd never upset him like that during a reading before.

I fell out of the door into Keilah's arms. She caught me, her body stiff with shock while I sucked in the fresh air.

"What? What Ce—Pythia?" In her concern, she'd nearly used my real name.

"I couldn't see what he wanted. He's angry."

Her body was rigid, but she stroked my hair in a soothing, motherly way. "It's okay. We'll go lay in the garden now."

I shook my head and whispered in her ear, as I should've done earlier, to prevent others from hearing me, "I'd just like to go to my room first."

She nodded, and I walked next to her on shaky legs back to my bedchamber. When we got inside and were free of the guards, she asked, "What happened?"

"I don't know," I answered, grateful as she helped me remove the heavy dress. "I saw something when he asked who he should worry about, but the image was vague. I couldn't tell him who."

She helped me slip into a silk nightgown, frowning in concern as she did. I was unsteady—woozy and clumsy. My head pounded, the throb growing more aggressive by the second.

"You've inhaled more vapors than normal."

I nodded. "Yes. I was trying to see."

"We'll go to the gardens tomorrow. You should rest."

She helped me into my bed and rubbed my bare arm for a few minutes, and I wondered for the thousandth time if she'd had children before she came here. She smoothed my hair and hummed a song for me. An ache formed in my chest whenever she acted this way, because it made me miss my mother.

CHAPTER THREE

Vile nightmares drove me from sleep early the next morning. I saw my family being struck by the plague and turned into those monsters. Into whatever those creatures were that I'd seen in my visions yesterday. Things that used to be people, but now had sunken black eyes and fangs that tore at the flesh of others in a frenzy of crazed blood lust.

As I did every morning, I pictured the faces of my mother and father. I didn't want them to fade with time, but the images were blurring. I conjured the image of my twin brother Henry, who looked so similar to my father, and my little sister Jillian, who favored my mother.

Today was worse than others though, as I felt I'd failed them when I was unable to identify the eyes from my vision. I needed to save the mortal realm. My family may not be human, but I knew the plague would eventually find them as well.

What if the master couldn't stop it? The sickness would spread because I couldn't see what I needed. Everyone called the sight a *gift*, but I thought it was a burden. It was vague and unhelpful. By the time a prophecy made sense, it was usually too late to change fate.

I sighed, rubbing my eyes. The headache had softened, but still beat like a small drum in my head. It wouldn't keep me in bed today, though. I had training this morning with Laurenth and I refused to miss it. Days with her were the highlight of my mundane, lonely life.

Standing, I stilled for a moment. I thought maybe the vapors were eating away at my brain, because I swore I'd smelled that floral scent again—lilies.

Keilah entered as if she could somehow sense I was awake and started busying herself by drawing the curtains.

"Do you smell that?" I asked.

"What?" She sniffed, looking at me.

I shrugged. I couldn't smell it anymore, either. Maybe I had just imagined it.

"Are you up for training this morning?"

"You know the answer to that." I chuckled. I was always up for training.

She searched my wardrobe, producing my leather tights, my red fighting dress, and my only pair of boots. Once I was dressed, she braided my hair.

I grabbed my dagger, glancing down at it as I sheathed it. I remembered the day Laurenth had brought it to me, telling me I'd advanced enough in my training to earn a weapon of my own.

It was thirteen inches from the top of the handle to the tip of the blade. The steel was Damascus forged, which caused beautiful ripples of design to roll through it. The rosewood handle and brass blade-guard fit perfectly with my fingers, and Laurenth told me they had forged it with the knowledge that a woman's hand would wield it.

I strapped it to my thigh underneath the dress. My training dress was easy to move in, but I still felt like it was a nuisance. I wanted to wear fighting clothes like Laurenth did, but that would've been improper for the Pythia.

Besides that, Laurenth insisted I wear it because if I ever faced a realistic threat, I would have on a dress. Training to fight meant nothing if you didn't take real life obstacles into account.

We left my room, flanked once again by my guards. I didn't think the master originally planned to teach me how to use a weapon. That changed when I was fifteen. A man broke into my bedchamber and attempted to kidnap me. I fought him desperately, more than he was expecting, and made enough of a ruckus to draw Keilah from her room. We'd learned he was a guard of the temple who planned on selling me for a handsome price. I wasn't sure what happened to him, but I had no doubt it was bloody and gruesome. The master was not a kind man, and the overseer was worse.

After that, they had given me to Laurenth three days a week to learn "basic self-defense." Thinking about the master using that phrase made me smirk, because she'd taught me a lot more than that. I was efficient with my dagger, a short sword, and a bow. I didn't think I'd ever need to wield the latter two, but it didn't hurt to learn.

Laurenth also taught me to fight without a weapon, hand-to-hand self-defense. In her world, nothing was off limits. Eye gouging, groin strikes, and even biting were all things she encouraged.

When I first started training, I had impressed Laurenth with my natural ability. At that time, I didn't trust her, so I didn't tell her that my father had already taught me the basics of wielding a blade.

We arrived at the training hall, and the guards filed in around me. They were to stay with me at all times when I wasn't in my bed or bath chambers.

Laurenth clicked her tongue, as she always did. "At ease, fellas. As you know, she's safe with me. You can wait in the hall."

They looked unsure, as usual, and she placed her hand on her hip. Giving them an annoyed nod of her head, she hissed, "Get out."

This time they shuffled into the hallway, not wanting to invoke her wrath. Although she was shorter than I was, Laurenth had an attitude that exuded confidence and authority. People listened to her. She was a natural born leader with the skills to back up the words.

I found her quite beautiful, even though I'd heard the guards comment her features were too sharp. She had severe green eyes that seemed to catch every movement. They were always scanning the room as though she never stopped checking for a hidden threat. Her hair was as black as the ravens that sat amongst the grapevines and styled in a dramatic layover to one side. She shaved the other half of her head, giving her an intense appearance.

I kind of suspected she was, or had at one time, been a fierce warrior. She was a master of weapons and could wield them all with expert precision. Sword, spear, and even the mace. Her tanned skin covered ropes of lean muscle, and she always donned the same look—a tank top and fighting breeches.

On her waist she wore a leather sheath, and inside it was the most beautiful weapon I'd ever beheld. It was Mastix steel, which she had informed me was the only material in existence that could disable a God. Pierce the heart or sever the spinal cord, and *lights out*, as she liked to say. The blade pattern was similar to Damascus steel, but the ripples shone in various shades of pigmentation, adorning it with a beautiful kaleidoscope of colors.

The handle was wood of the olive tree, which I was told was sacred. Over the years, I had questioned her enough to learn Laurenth was a demigod, the offspring of a mortal woman or man and a god or goddess. She wasn't immortal like a god, but her lifespan was extended, and she could only be killed by Mastix steel. Her father was Ares, the God of War himself, but she despised him. I believed she'd called him a "psychotic prick" when she'd described him to me.

"How are you?" she asked, looking concerned.

She'd heard about the reading yesterday, no doubt. I knew she was closer to the master than anyone else—respected by him, even. I'd tried to breach the subject with her several times, but she flatly refused to answer questions regarding him. When I'd pestered her too much, she'd threatened to stop training me.

"I'm fine," I answered, looking down at a loose thread unraveling from the seam of my dress and picking at it.

"Good, then I won't take it easy on you."

I smiled. Of everyone, Laurenth treated me the most like a normal person. "Wouldn't want you to." There was a beat of silence, and then I couldn't stop myself from asking, "Is he mad?"

"He is. But not *at* you. At the prospect that someone could thwart all of our hard work. He knows that's not how your gift works. He knows how important you are to The Cause."

I nodded, but my mouth felt dry. "I just hope next time I can be more helpful."

We practiced with daggers today, hand-to-hand combat. I thought it was fun, even if she nicked me twice. With her being a demigod, a mortal like myself would never best Laurenth. Her speed and strength were insane—unfair. But I felt having an unbeatable opponent made me better. If I ever had to fight someone that wasn't a demigod, I knew I could beat them.

Pushing my dagger forward, I stabbed at her, but she blocked me. I moved my leg to make her think I planned to trip her, and she lowered her arms just enough to expose herself. I couldn't go after her with my blade, but I punched her hard in the chest. Using my core just like she taught me, the blow landed with force and her breath pushed out. We stopped, and I grinned at her as sweat dripped down my face.

I opened my mouth to say something, but I stilled, looking around. I smelled it again—those lilies. The hair on the back of my neck prickled with goosebumps while my instincts screamed I was being watched. I already knew we were the only ones here, but I glanced around anyway.

"Damn Cere," Laurenth said proudly, bringing me from my thoughts as she rubbed the spot. "You might be a warrior after all." She pinched my upper arm and teased, "Even if you should eat more."

I shrugged. She was always calling attention to my lanky appearance. Behind us, the door closed, and Keilah clicked her tongue. "All she does is eat, that I can promise you."

"Well, you need to feed her more protein and fewer lemon tarts," Laurenth scolded.

I rolled my eyes at them both. "I'm just naturally slender. Like my mother."

They both hesitated, glancing at each other.

The rules forbade me from discussing my past life. I was to dedicate myself completely to The Cause. I was the Pythia—not Ceres.

"Sorry," I mumbled.

"Don't worry about it, it's just us," Laurenth answered, patting my shoulder.

I didn't understand her sometimes. She seemed as devoted to The Cause as anyone, but also the most forgiving when I broke the rules. In the past she'd brought me things I wasn't allowed to have, particularly books. Sometimes educational magazines, most of them about animals. When I was done with them I had to burn them in the fireplace in my room. I hated doing it, but they could never be discovered.

The books were usually young adult fiction, but once a gushy adult romance novel snuck its way into the stack, and it was one of my greatest treasures. I hid it behind the baseboard of my bed, and not even Keilah knew of its existence.

The things she brought were my only connection to the real world outside, and they kept me sane. Maybe Laurenth did it because she wouldn't face the same punishments as others. I knew no one would dare try it—not even the overseer.

"Do you still want to visit the gardens today?" Keilah asked. "And eat lemon tarts?" She gave Laurenth a pointed look, and a small smile played on her lips. Laurenth shook her head, but chuckled.

"I'm afraid she won't be going to the gardens," a deep voice interjected. "The overseer has summoned the Pythia to his office."

Turning, I found the commander of the guard. I thought his name was Clintock, but no one had ever introduced us. He was a tall, thick man boasting an untamed black beard and piercing eyes that seemed too small for his broad face. I wondered if he was a demigod like Laurenth as he had that same confident air about him.

"No," Keilah said quickly. "She needs to rest."

The guard arched his eyebrow at her. Speaking out like that could earn her a strike by his hand.

"What's this about?" Laurenth asked, stepping in front of Keilah. She may have some respect for the master, but Laurenth despised the overseer. However, here in this temple, his word was law. She could do nothing to help me.

The guard frowned. "Even if I knew I wouldn't tell you."

She glared at him, a red flush of anger crawling up her neck. "Well, I'm not done with her yet."

"Well, I don't care," Clintock snapped, his beady eyes sharpening. "She is to report to his office, immediately."

CHAPTER FOUR

Dread settled in my gut, like I'd swallowed an iron weight. Had he found out about the failed reading? Was I being punished because I couldn't tell the master who the violet eyes belonged to? Or maybe it was speaking out in the hall when I walked past the woman who had died—a transgression I knew the guards would report.

I straightened my back, determined not to portray the fear I felt. The overseer's office was a place I avoided at all costs—yet it was where I found myself often. He handled my *discipline* if I acted out of line. And he enjoyed it a little too much. He capitalized on the tiniest mistakes, and all the servants and guards were in his pocket. I suspected they may receive a reward if they reported even my smallest blunders.

Saying goodbye to a fuming Laurenth, I marched alongside Keilah and the guards, led by their commander. My handmaid looked physically ill as we approached the double doors, the shine of their dark wood much too clean for what happened behind them. Keilah had also suffered punishment from the overseer, but neither of us ever discussed what happened inside.

The guards stepped aside, and I passed by them with my head held high. They all had some idea of what occurred when I saw the overseer but were most likely powerless to stop it. Or they just didn't care.

I knocked hesitantly and then opened the door. My hand was slick and clammy against the golden knob. I stepped into the office, taking in the extravagant decor of supple ivory leather and rich red mahogany. The overseer faced a window, looking out over unending acres of grapevines. An enormous vineyard surrounded this temple, and it seemed to have no end and no beginning.

Once, when I was younger, I'd escaped through the garden. I didn't understand that escaping the grounds meant nothing when there was no direction to go. No way to get out. I'd traveled for hours through the grapevines, panicked and sure I would die out there. I couldn't see anything when I was in them, and a claustrophobic feeling had overwhelmed me. Finally, I'd seen a break in the distance. I remember the elation I'd felt, running to my presumed freedom.

But I'd walked right back into the temple's garden and subsequently into the wicked hands of the overseer. Memories of that night always elicited a shudder from me.

"Cere," he purred, slapping me with the name he had no right to use. "Please come in and sit."

I did as I was told, sitting on the small leather foot stool across from his desk. My "seat" whenever we had these interactions. It was low to the ground, forcing me to look up at him.

"My lord," I greeted him.

He turned on me, a delighted sneer curling his lips.

I knew some women would find him attractive. Maybe I would if I didn't know what hid beneath that flawless, shiny veneer. His short, neat platinum hair gave him the appearance of false innocence. It was styled to sit under the gold dragon circlet that adorned his head. Bronzed skin handsomely complemented his sharp aqua tone eyes, and I shuddered under their gaze—they should be beautiful, but they were cold and unfeeling. There was no consciousness living in those pools of brilliant blue.

His face was always clean shaven, so I could see his pointed chin and high, defined cheekbones. As always, he donned a white and gold tunic adorned with brooches, as well as extravagant bejeweled rings on both hands. It was gaudy overkill in my opinion.

I could tell by the look in his eye that I was definitely in trouble.

"I'm disappointed to inform you that a transgression has been brought to my attention."

I doubted it disappointed him at all. My lips clamped shut. I didn't want to admit guilt when I wasn't even sure why I was being punished. I could talk myself into more trouble. I had done it before.

"That's unfortunate, my lord," I answered, choosing my words with careful consideration.

He stared at me, a predator watching its prey.

"Are you aware of what you've done?"

"I am not. But it must be something important as you would not summon me for no good reason."

Except he would.

The way I spoke didn't sound as docile as I'd hoped. It was more of a challenge, and I bit my tongue. My hand traveled discreetly to my thigh, where my dagger sat waiting. Not that I would ever use it. I didn't even want to know what the master would do if I stabbed his overseer through his disgusting, icy heart. But that didn't stop me from imagining it—several times a day.

He clicked his tongue. "I think you're lying. And I'll take that into account when doling out your punishment."

I tried not to react as he stared at me again. His icy eyes traveled down my body, and despite being dressed as modestly as possible, I still felt exposed to his gaze.

"You've blossomed into such a beautiful young woman," he drawled, making me feel like I had acid in my throat. "It's too bad your poor attitude doesn't reflect that."

I resisted the urge to glare at him. My poor attitude could get a lot worse. But I once again said nothing. He had provoked me into accidentally creating greater punishments for myself before, and I was old enough to understand his game.

"You spoke in the halls. It upset many of the servants. The circumstances were unexpected, with the maid passing, but you know that is unacceptable."

A sigh of relief nearly escaped me. I knew I would still receive a punishment, but it wasn't because I couldn't give the master what he wanted from my reading.

"I think three lashes will suffice," he said.

I heard the tinkling of pens as he grabbed his weapon of choice. He removed a ruler with one steel edge, which I guess was some kind of sick play on a disciplinary school marm. One wouldn't think of it as an intimidating weapon, but I knew the pain it could inflict. It wasn't the original one. He had to get new ones often because he struck my back with such force the wood splintered.

"And," he added coolly, making my body stiffen. "That handmaid of yours made you late again yesterday. She will receive her punishment as well."

My heart sank. Keilah and I had *barely* been late. If that poor woman hadn't been lying in the hallway, we would've been on time. But I knew he knew that. It's not like he would be sympathetic or accommodating. Anger flashed hot in my chest, and I was quick to defend her.

"It was my fault," I blurted. "She shouldn't pay for my mistakes."

His eyebrow arched, and I knew he was pleased to hear those words.

"Well, it can't go unpunished. The master was not happy."

He was sauntering around the room as he spoke, and now stood behind me. The action made me feel like a caged animal—even more so than normal. I had to suppress a shudder as I felt his eyes sear into my back. My fists clenched, and I focused on the pain of my nails digging into my hand.

"Then I will take her lashes as well," I ground out through clenched teeth. "*My lord.*" As soon as the words left my mouth, I knew he'd pounce on them. His hand fell on the back of my neck. Even through the material of my dress, his touch made my skin crawl.

"That sounded like defiance in your tone. That can't be what I heard—is it?"

"No, my lord," I answered, my tone flat.

"Good. Then I'll only add five lashes."

I gasped in surprise. Eight lashes? Five just for being late? It was a higher number than I was used to, although the night I'd tried to escape, he'd exacted fifteen across my back. The soreness had lasted days.

When I was a younger girl, he frightened me. Any minor infraction turned into a punishment like this, but as I got older, I felt less fear and more annoyance bordering on ire.

And as I'd matured, his gaze had changed too. He looked at me now with what even I could identify as lust. I knew he wouldn't dare go too far; my purity was too important. But he went plenty far enough. I wondered if the master knew what happened in this room. A sad voice in my head told me he surely did, but did nothing, just like everyone else.

"Don't you think that's fair?" he asked.

"Yes," I hissed.

"Yes, what?"

"Yes, *my lord.*"

It wasn't really a question, and I knew not to argue my case. It never resulted in fewer lashes. He moved around in front of me, and my blank stare studied the weave of the fabric of his tunic.

He gripped my chin and pulled my face up to look at him. A vicious, delighted sneer twisted his features, while his thumb caressed my lips in a way that I imagined a lover might. I closed my eyes, restraining myself from biting him. My stomach churned, threatening to spill over into my throat.

"Such a shame," he purred. "A lovely little flower destined to never be plucked."

Gods, I didn't want to know what he'd have planned for me if I wasn't the Pythia. I focused on the breath entering and leaving my body.

"The lashings, my lord?"

He laughed, dry and emotionless. "Desperate to get started?"

I wanted it over with so I could go. Lashings were one thing, but to be subjected to his sickening caresses was another form of torture—one that I couldn't withstand.

I stood and walked to his desk, placing my hands on the cool wood. I bent forward slightly, giving him my back as I felt him approach behind me, pushing against me with his lower body while his hand slowly unfastened the clasps of my dress. My eyes squeezed shut, and I tried to quell the horror rising in my chest.

Pushing harder against me, he said, "I do hope someday you learn to behave." The breathless, raspy sound of his voice made my stomach clench again. I doubted very much he hoped for that.

He pulled roughly at the dress, parting it and exposing my bare back. To my dismay, he did something he hadn't done before and also pushed it down my arms, exposing my chest. My cheeks flamed to life, and I had trouble drawing breath.

I was sure he would touch me, but to my surprise, he didn't. He walked around until he stood across from me, staring for several seconds. I knew he was looking at my bare breasts, but I studied the natural detailing of the desk. I counted the whirls of the wood and traced them with my eyes.

After what felt like forever, he moved back behind me, and I steeled myself. The side of the ruler cracked across my back, and I bit into my bottom lip to contain the scream that rose in my throat. I'd stopped screaming a long time ago—I knew he enjoyed it. Pain seared at the spot, traveling down my back and into my arms.

The second blow fell, and I squeezed my eyes shut, trying to leave my body and go somewhere else. Pain blossomed—hot and stinging. My hands moved to the edge of the desk and clamped down on it. It was my tether to the real world, and I focused on the feel of the smooth wood under my hands.

After several seconds, I realized the third blow had not come. My eyes fluttered open, and I dared a peek over my shoulder. What I saw forced my adrenaline to a whole new level of intensity.

We weren't alone anymore. A tall, hooded figure, clad in a tattered black robe that hung to his thighs, held the overseer by his throat. I looked down to see his feet were at least six inches off the ground.

The overseer made disturbing choking sounds as he whipped the assailant's hand with the ruler, but it didn't seem to have any effect. It snapped in half with a loud crack as the scent of lilies exploded in the room, filling my nostrils.

CHAPTER FIVE

The black-robed figure had a wicked Mastix steel scythe secured to his back, and I thought he might reach for it. But he didn't. Instead, he squeezed the hand around the overseer's neck until his blue eyes bulged out of his head and his face colored to the shade of a ripe tomato.

My hand fell to the dagger on my thigh, but I made no move to help. Shock, and if I was being honest, sick satisfaction, held me in place.

I shrank back as black tendrils floated from the hood of the figure, traveling the space between the two of them. The ribbons of shadow moved like smoke at first, drifting, and then as they neared the overseer's nostrils, they surged. I watched in horror and intrigue as the blackness filled his mouth, nose, eyes, and ears. If he could have screamed, he would have, but he couldn't make any sound with the hand at his throat. Blood poured from the orifices of his face, running down in streaks and dripping from his chin onto the floor.

After what must've been seconds, but seemed like hours, the hooded figure dropped the overseer's limp body to the floor at his feet.

He turned to me, and I tried to climb backwards over the desk, yelling, "No! Leave me alone!"

His face was concealed in darkness behind the hood and in those smoky shadows, leaving me to wonder his intentions.

He moved towards me, and I kicked out at him, finding his shin. I hissed in pain, as it felt like I'd kicked the marble wall of the temple. His hand grasped my left arm as I gripped the dagger in my right hand. I thrust it forward, straight at his heart. I knew without a doubt it wouldn't kill him. That thing had to be a god.

I felt it push through flesh and bone, and a small grunt of pain passed from the hood. No way—I'd stabbed him in the heart! A strange part of me wanted to take a moment and celebrate. Laurenth would be so proud.

I glanced down and realized that I hadn't quite found the target I was intending. His hand had blocked the strike and taken the blade clear through to the hilt. He wrapped the fingers of his impaled hand around the guard of my dagger and ripped it from my hold. I thought about punching him, but the hollow blackness of the hood unsettled me. What was under there?

My hesitation passed, and I decided to find out.

I threw a haymaker at him, but he moved quicker than anything I'd ever seen. His hand caught my fist and then he used it to pull me against him. I gasped as his arm wrapped around me and lifted me against his chest. His hold was like a steel vise—absolute and unmovable. I kicked and screamed, trying to make even an inch of space appear that I could work with. Reaching over his shoulder, he grabbed the scythe with his hand that was still impaled by my dagger.

Oh gods, this was it. I was going to die.

He swung the weapon, and I closed my eyes, expecting to feel the impact of it. But it never came. When I opened them again, I realized the weapon had made a slash in the very fabric of reality. A black void opened, and he stepped through it without hesitation.

The world fell away, and my stomach dropped to my feet. The hair that was free of my braid lifted around me as we plummeted into oblivion. A scream ripped through me, echoing around us as I closed my eyes and prayed I would somehow survive.

He landed with a blunt thud of his boots. I opened my eyes and found he was looking down at me. Glancing around in horror, I realized the overseer's office was gone, as were the vineyards and the temple.

"Where are we?" I whispered.

"The Underworld." His voice was deep and calm—strangely soothing.

We'd landed on a dilapidated cobblestone road in an area that appeared deserted. It looked dead, the trees were charred like a recent fire had burned through here, but I didn't smell any smoke. They were blackened ghosts hidden in a heavy fog, and the sky was a dower gray color. I saw no clouds, and I couldn't find the faint outline of the sun anywhere in the haze.

A horse stood here waiting for us, and I couldn't help but stare. It was the biggest equine I'd ever seen, standing well over seven feet tall. I gaped at the animal, realizing it wasn't at all normal. Its skin looked like oil, dripping and swirling across its skeletal structure. Like its master, it had wings, but they were not feathers or skin. They consisted of the same dark shadows that had leaked from the figure's hood.

I realized he was still holding me, and I pushed my hands against his chest. "Let me go!"

He hesitated and then turned his head to the right and set me down. "Don't run. I'll catch you."

I immediately felt the cool air against my chest and realized my dress was still open, the material of the bodice bunched at my waist. Was he trying to be polite? My face burned a thousand shades of red as I scrambled to pull it on, but they designed my clothes with Keilah's help in mind, so I couldn't hook the clasps by myself. When I tried, the sore skin on my back pulled and I sucked in a pained breath.

The robed figure was busying himself with the buckles of the bags tied onto the behemoth horse, his back to me. I reached for my dagger and then realized that he had it.

"Who are you? You're a god, aren't you?" I demanded, shifting nervously from one foot to the other.

"I am a god, and I have many names," he said, as if that was sufficient.

"Well, throw one out for me," I snapped, feigning bravado that I did not possess.

He hesitated again and then decided to answer. "I am the God of Death. The Reaper of Souls."

My blood stilled, cooling in my veins.

"I'm dead?"

"No, you're very much alive." He paused, and then asked, "Are you dressed?"

My chest was no longer exposed, but I'd only managed to get the top clasp closed, so I muttered, "Yes. Mostly."

He turned back to me and seemed to look at me for a long moment, as if he didn't know what to do. I couldn't read his expression because his face was still concealed in the impossible darkness of that hood.

Seeing what he held in his hand I straightened my spine. "I want my dagger back. It's mine."

He turned it in his hand.

"Since I pulled it from my flesh, I think it belongs to me. You *actually* stabbed me." His tone was dripping with shocked admonishment.

I gaped at him because he sounded both offended and amused at the same time. He tucked it away in some inner fold of his tattered robe.

"You were kidnapping me! Of course I stabbed you."

"And here I thought I was saving you."

I thought of the ruler and the overseer and I felt my face redden again.

"Well, you weren't. I had that handled just fine."

"I see. So no thank you should be expected?"

I glared at him. "No thank you will ever be uttered."

He clicked his tongue. "You *wound* me."

I stared at him, incredulous. Was he serious?

"Are you going to ride willingly?" he asked.

"On that thing? With you? No. I want you to take me back."

He sighed, long and loud. "You will not be going back."

"Then I'll fight you every moment we spend together. *Death*."

One second he was several steps away from me, and the next he was inches away, gazing down at me. This guy was tall, and I had to crane my neck to look up at him. No wonder he needed such a massive mount.

I punched him in the stomach and almost cursed. Pain exploded in my hand, and I shook it.

"Gods! What are you made of? Rock?"

"You are a vicious little thing, aren't you?"

Vicious *little thing*?

"You have no idea," I hissed. "But you're about to find out."

He made a sound, and I realized he was chuckling. I glared at him and tried to kick him as he grabbed me like a parent would seize an overreacting, screeching child.

"Let me go! How dare you!"

He turned me around and held me to his chest facing away from him. I kicked out but couldn't make contact with anything. The way I flailed was very undignified, but I wasn't going out without a fight.

"You are making this much more difficult than it needs to be," he said, his casual tone informing me of how little effort it took for him to hold me.

"Good! I want to make things difficult for you."

"I meant for yourself."

Anger flared in my chest, and I increased my efforts. I even tried to bite his forearm that held me, my teeth clacking with the attempt.

At that, he chuckled again and leaned down. "What exactly are you?" His voice was sultry and cool, and I blushed from the tone of it.

His hood brushed my cheek and I realized how close his face was. I gritted my teeth and threw my head back as hard as I could. It connected with his mouth and chin, and he grunted in surprise as hot pain skyrocketed through my skull. His grip on me didn't falter, but I glared over my shoulder at him.

"How was that for vicious? You old creep—" My voice trailed away because I realized his hood had fallen back off of his face. I strangled the gasp in my throat and stared in surprise. I was expecting an old terrifying skeleton man or something, but that's not what he was.

His violet eyes gazed down at me intently, a small frown pulling at the edges of his lips where a spot of blood trickled from the split I'd caused. To my surprise, it was not red but gold. The wound healed incredibly fast, the flesh knitting together right before my eyes.

"That was a rude thing to say."

A beat of recognition spiked through me. His eyes. I knew my vision had been realized. He had taken me and set into motion the events of the prophecy I'd delivered yesterday.

I didn't know how to respond to him because my brain had stopped working. He was quite beautiful. Strands of tousled blue-black hair fell forward over dark brows and into his eyes, which were framed by thick lashes. The features of his pale face were sharp, like he was sculpted from marble. My eyes traveled over his cheekbones, high and angular, and down to his mouth, where his lips were pulled in a firm line.

Every dormant female instinct I had hummed to life, and I became incredibly aware of each place our bodies touched—shocked by his very hard, very male chest resting against my back. Aside from the overseer, Keilah, and Laurenth, I hadn't been touched by another person in years, and now a very handsome man held me against him. I gulped, trying to swallow the sudden dryness in my mouth.

"You're—you're not old," I sputtered like an idiot, and then cursed myself for speaking.

"I certainly am old," he answered. "But I am not a creep."

"Just a kidnapper," I snapped.

"I thought we decided I was a rescuer."

"*We* decided nothing."

His lips twitched, like he wanted to smile, but he lifted me off of the ground and climbed onto the winged black beast. Unsettled as I was, I didn't fight back.

He placed me sitting side-saddle in front of him, but I quickly swung my leg over. It had been a long time since I'd ridden—my mother had loved horses—but I still remembered how.

I didn't realize that the action would push me back, molding me against his body. We both tensed in surprise as the coolness of his skin leaked through our clothes and I bit my lip, feeling hot despite the rush of cold. Was I so deprived of touch that I would react this way to our greatest enemy? I hadn't forgotten my vision from yesterday, and the threat he was to The Cause.

This is the God of Death, Cere. Get it together.

He was rigid as my back pressed up against him, and he dropped the split reins over the knob of the saddle. I didn't understand what he was doing until I felt him fiddling with the back of my dress, pulling the clasps together. I winced as the fabric brushed the two fresh welts on my upper back.

His hands stilled. "Do you want me to leave this part open?"

I thought for a moment, unsure. I should have him close it for my purity's sake. It would hurt, but I'd certainly endured worse. That he'd touched me this much was impious enough, but the wounds felt better when they had space to breathe.

I just nodded, still biting my lip and chewing on it. I jumped in surprise when his hand flattened against the still bared skin. As cool as he was, it felt like someone had placed ice on the welts as Keilah sometimes did, even though she wasn't supposed to.

I stopped breathing and tried to calm my thunderous heart. I felt like he, too, was holding his breath, as he had gone completely still behind me.

After a few moments, he snatched his hand away and grabbed the reins again. He kicked the horse into action, and I listened to the clop of its feet against the cobblestone.

"Where are you taking me?"

"To see the king."

I furrowed my brow. "You aren't the King of the Underworld. You're Death, aren't you?"

"I am Death. But I do not rule the dead. That right belongs to Hades."

CHAPTER SIX

"What's going to happen to me?" I asked.

"I don't know, that's why we're going to Hades."

"What do you think he'll do?"

"I don't know."

"Well, what's he like?"

He sighed. "Do you always ask so many questions?"

"No, I'm not allowed to. And when I do, I don't get any answers."

"So it's just me then, that is going to be subjected to this death by a thousand questions?"

"If it kills you, then I promise to continue."

"That's rude," he said, clicking his tongue. "So vicious."

The teasing tone of his voice made me consider throwing my head back again, but I was certain that it hurt me more than it hurt him.

"You seem to inspire those emotions in me," I muttered.

Okay, so I often had rude thoughts, especially involving the overseer, or if I was being honest with myself, the master. I had a lot of pent-up rage, but he didn't need to know that.

"I saw you training earlier. You certainly are a vicious little mortal."

I stiffened and glanced over my shoulder at him. "You were there. I smelled your—flowers. And you were in my bedroom too when I woke up!"

The corner of his lip curled, and I knew I was right.

"How long have you been watching me? You are a creep! Did you see my bath yesterday, too?"

His eyebrows shot up in surprise. "No, I did not. Because I'm *not* a creep."

My cheeks flared, and I turned so I was facing forward. It should repulse me. I should be absolutely offended. So why did I feel neither of those things? I felt mortified. Gods, what had he seen? I often got bored in my room and did really stupid, embarrassing things. Two days ago, I'd sung what words I could remember of an obnoxious pop song and used the rounded post of my bed as a microphone. If he had witnessed that—I swore I would die of shame right here. Embarrassed to death by Death.

I squirmed, both from the discomfort of my position on the saddle and the burst of anxiety that was running through me. He slid back, creating more room, and then his hand snaked around my waist and pulled me into him.

I tensed at the contact. My breath abandoned me again, and my fingernails dug into the leather of the saddle horn. A shiver ran through me, and I guess he took that as I was cold, because his cloak fell around my shoulders, and it brought me even closer to him. With the cloak gone, there was just his shirt and my gaping dress between us. I quivered, completely unnerved by the contact.

"Are you cold?" he asked.

"No—um. I'm not allowed to be touched. I'm not used to being touched."

"Curious."

"Why?" I realized I was whispering. The air here was so still. So quiet. It felt wrong to disturb it.

"Because I'm not used to wanting to touch anyone."

My mind went to whirring at that proclamation. And what? He wanted to touch me? Something deep in my belly stirred, a feeling I'd only felt before when I read my paperback romance novel. All ten thousand times I'd read it.

"And it looked like the one you were with didn't feel the need to keep his hands off of you."

Bile rolled in my gut. Had he seen all of that? "How much did you see?"

"Enough."

"He-he is allowed," I stuttered.

"He was vile."

I didn't answer because he was right. The overseer was vile. And he hadn't been able to take things too far with me—I often wondered how he punished the servants, or even Keilah.

Death tensed and then sighed, and I looked over to find a small golden sparrow fluttering next to us. It twittered at him, and he ignored it. It was not perturbed, and flapped incessantly around Death's head, making a shrill noise. For several moments, I just stared ahead, unsure of what to do.

Nothing made sense outside of the temple. A horse with skin made of oil. The things I was feeling at a simple touch. Now, this psychotic sparrow.

Death spoke, making me jump. "I'll get there when I get there. There was an unforeseen distraction."

The bird tweeted a response, and I realized they were speaking to each other.

"No, that is *not* why she's sitting in my lap."

I blushed, looking down at the saddle horn and picking at the thread that held the worn black leather together.

The bird seemed to answer, and if I didn't know better, it sounded sassy. Death sighed in annoyance and then I felt his muscles bunch just before his hand around my waist snapped out from his robes. It was so fast, I barely realized what was happening. I heard a humored tweet as the bird just escaped being caught and crushed. He swirled around our heads a moment longer, and then buzzed ahead of us, cresting the upcoming hill, and disappearing out of sight.

"What—who was that?"

"You'll meet him momentarily," he said, the words riding on an exasperated sigh.

The black horse climbed the hill, and I let my curiosity win as I reached up and touched its broad neck. The skin there was cold, like Death's, and it didn't feel at all like a horse. It was rubbery and strange under my fingers.

"What's its name?"

"Her name is Nychta."

"Nychta?"

That was a strange name. Hearing it, the mare turned and looked at me over her shoulder. Her eyes weren't normal either. They were obsidian black, with irises that looked like dancing fire. She nickered low in her chest and then faced forward again.

"It means night. She was a gift from my mother."

I couldn't imagine what the mother of Death might be like.

"Oh. That name suits her."

We topped the hill and all thoughts of the horse drifted away. I gasped and sunk back against him.

"What is that?"

"Welcome to the Palace of Hades, Pythia."

My heart skipped a beat. I didn't realize he knew who I was, although I should've figured. If he knew, then what did he mean when he asked earlier what I was?

Wonder coursed through me at the sight of the expansive estate that sprawled out in front of me, covering the desolate gray land like a slash of dark paint. It was an opulent castle made of cinder black stone. The front entrance boasted a spectacularly tall, thin, pointed archway, and the open area under the arch was adorned with an enormous stained-glass window that depicted a three-headed dog.

On both sides of the entrance, identical, thinner arches decorated the entire expanse of the building. Many of the long, ornate windows were stained glass, and several wicked looking gargoyles sat atop the spires of the structure. It was breathtaking and intimidating all at the same time.

"He likes his dog," I commented, staring at the large window. "Does it really have three heads?"

"Yes."

At some point the cobblestone had turned to smooth black pavers and Nychta's hoofbeats sounded slightly different. She carried us around a humongous fountain crafted from black glass and embellished with gold. We rode under the massive archway and came to a stop at the bottom of some stairs that led up to two hulking doors.

A man waited for us, grinning.

"Brother! You've arrived. We were starting to worry. And you're not full of shit like we all thought. You really found the Pythia. We didn't tell you we thought that, of course, just talked about you behind your back."

Death sighed and didn't answer. Brother? I glanced between the two men, a little surprised. They looked nothing like each other.

The man descended the steps, his eyes on me. I felt strange under his scrutiny and my cheeks heated. The need to duck and hide somewhere burned across my skin, but there was nowhere to go. People didn't just *look* at me. It was unnerving.

Where Death was, well, darkness, this man was the opposite. He had shoulder length hair the color of moon beams, and skin bronzed as if he spent every day in the sun. His eyes were a pastel blue, so light that the color was almost indistinguishable from the whites. He wore a royal blue, knee-length, one-sleeved tunic that was secured with a gold medallion. On his head there was a wreath of red poppies sitting on top of what I thought was a crown, but when I looked closer, I realized it was two golden wings that sprouted from just behind his temples and curled around towards his forehead.

"You're the sparrow," I guessed as he stared up at me.

"I am. Hypnos, God of Sleep, pleasure to make your acquaintance."

He said it with a wicked grin and a strange drawl, that made me shift uncomfortably. He extended his hand to me, and I stared at it with my nose wrinkled until he withdrew it with a furrowed brow.

"Aren't you married?" Death grumbled as he slid from behind me.

Hypnos huffed and ignored him as Death tried to help me down off of the horse. I shrugged off his attempts and dismounted myself—no small task considering the size of the mare.

When I was standing next to Hypnos, he offered me his arm. "Come on, don't be shy. Hades is *dying* to meet you."

I stared at him, truly at a loss for what to do. I should try to run, or fight, but I was weaponless and stuck in a strange land. It would be wise to bide my time and make a plan.

"Careful," Death warned. "She's vicious."

Hypnos quickly dropped his arm, eyeing me with suspicion. "Really?"

"She stabbed me."

I flushed, glaring at him. "You deserved it."

"Yes, how dare I save you?"

"You *kidnapped* me."

"Well, I like her already," Hypnos interjected. He motioned for me to walk up the stairs and I fell in stride beside him.

Death kept pace behind us, his footsteps silent. I considered how I could get away and back to the temple. I needed to help the master save the world—save my family. The scythe came to mind. It seemed to be a tool that could travel between dimensions. Maybe I could get my hands on it and escape.

"So tell me, what do you know of our king?" Hypnos asked.

I shrugged. "I watched the *Hercules* movie when I was little. You know, the animated one."

Death coughed behind us, and a grin formed on Hypnos' face. "It will *thrill* him to hear that, I'm sure. Such an accurate representation of him."

I barely remembered the movie. My recollection of my life before the temple was spotty, and I wasn't sure why. Maybe it was just my mind trying to cope with the fact I would never see my family again. Maybe the vapors had eaten away at my brain. Maybe it was a combination of both.

But if what I remembered from the movie was accurate, I didn't think Hades was a good guy.

When we arrived at the doors, they drifted inward soundlessly. I noticed the knockers were also representations of the three-headed dog.

We entered a grand hallway with vaulted ceilings. It was open and tall, making me feel tiny. Black granite floors and pillars made of solid gold dominated the room. There were resplendent paintings framed in gold and diamonds hanging on the walls. As we passed them I realized they were all of—the three-headed dog? Hades really had an affinity for his pet.

There was one grand painting, the largest of them all, prominently displayed in the middle of the wall above the next set of doors. It depicted a red-haired woman in a field of tiny white flowers. I assumed she was someone important.

"Who's that?"

"The Queen of the Underworld, Persephone."

"She is beautiful. Will I meet her?"

"She's topside right now, as usual, until winter is upon us, then she'll return."

Hypnos was certainly more forthcoming than his brother. I glanced around, surprised by the number of people here, all hustling around as if they had specific jobs that pertained to the house. I wondered if they were gods or mortals. They all wore black slacks and black shirts; whether they were male or female didn't make a difference.

"Who are these people?"

"Citizens of Hades."

"I thought the king was Hades?"

"He is. Both he and the Underworld are referred to as Hades."

I furrowed my brow. "Well, that's odd."

I watched people bustle about, noticing that they gave us a wide berth. Their eyes were either glued to or diverted from the God of Death. He walked behind us, seemingly unbothered by the attention.

"I just thought it would be more…dead."

Hypnos shook his head. "A common misconception."

"Where do these people live?"

"In town."

I furrowed my brow again, finding that hard to believe. "There's a town in the Underworld?"

Hypnos turned to his brother. "She's a curious one."

"She promised to murder me with her questions."

The God of Sleep's eyebrows shot up in amusement. "I like a woman with some homicidal tenacity," he said. Turning to me, he added, "You'll fit right in here."

I frowned at him, unsure what that meant.

"Later, I will do my best to answer everything you want to know," he promised. "But we've arrived."

The double doors in front of us opened of their own accord, and we entered a throne room. There were two thrones that appeared to be made of black glass, one smaller that was currently empty, and a larger one.

A beast of a man sat in the latter, his fingers pressed together in a steeple. When we entered, he sat up and scrutinized me. His long black hair fell over his shoulders, defined by one large white highlight at the front. He peered at me with eyes that seemed to be staring into the endless black abyss I had fallen through earlier. He wore the same type of one shoulder robe as Hypnos, but it was longer and gold. The sparkling hue beautifully complemented his deep, ebony skin. A Mastix steel weapon, like a pitchfork but with two prongs, sat at his side.

Atop his head sat a crown of deep onyx, its tall spiky peaks reminding me of the castle's spires outside. I felt his heavy aura, stronger than any I'd ever endured, and I marveled at the way the power rolled off him in stifling waves.

He needed no introduction.

"Thanatos," he boomed. His voice was loud and clear, dominating the room. "You found her."

"I told you it was her. Although I heard you all thought otherwise."

Hades gave Hypnos a pointed look. "That was mostly your brother. I absolutely believed you."

The God of Sleep scoffed but didn't defend himself further than that.

Death's name was Thanatos. He mentioned he had many names. I guess we had that in common.

"So," Hades went on. "This is the Pythia. And we're the ones who found her. What luck."

"How did you find me?" I asked Thanatos.

"The maid that died of a heart attack. I was reaping her soul when you walked by."

Of course. I had smelled the lilies then, too. I said a silent prayer of thanks that he did not find me in time to witness the karaoke session in my room.

"What did you find out about where she was being held?" Hades asked.

"It was strange. It took me all night to find it again after I reaped the maid's soul. Someone powerful must have created it. They tucked it in between the Earth and Olympus dimensions. No wonder Apollo hasn't been able to find her. It was sheer luck I did."

"Well, he's not getting her from us, either. We found her so she's ours."

"Apollo?" I asked in confusion.

They took my question to mean I didn't understand who Apollo was.

Hypnos answered, "The God of Sun and like a thousand other things. He's *amazing*, just ask him."

"Then this is a misunderstanding. I was with Apollo."

They all glanced at each other in surprise.

"No," Hypnos said, arching his brow. "You weren't. He's been looking for you for years."

I stared at him and then huffed, crossing my arms. "No, that's not possible. He told me he was Apollo. I am very important, and I need to go back to him."

Thanatos spoke behind me. "Whoever had you lied to you."

"No," I shot over my shoulder. "That's not true."

My heart felt like it would explode. They were liars. They had to be. The master *was* Apollo, the God of Sun and Medicine. We were working to end the plague.

Hades looked at me. His eyes had turned a strange silver color and seemed to swirl. "What a mystery we've stumbled upon. Regardless of who he was, you won't be going back. Welcome to your new home Pythia."

CHAPTER SEVEN

I stared at him, toying with a thread on my skirt. He wanted me to stay here?

"I have to go back," I pleaded.

"Why? It may look a little depressing at first, but I promise the Underworld is the best of all the realms to live in."

I pursed my lips, refusing to answer. I needed to go back and aid The Cause. But I didn't know if the plague involved Hades, and I couldn't risk revealing any vital information.

"It is a bit nicer than the movie," I commented instead, looking around at the grandeur of the palace.

Hypnos snickered next to me, and Hades frowned. He pinched the bridge of his nose, sighing, "I'm never going to live that down. Thanatos, will you watch over her? I'm too busy. The festival is almost here."

"I'm confident my brother would love nothing more," Hypnos answered in his stead.

I glanced at him in confusion, but he didn't elaborate.

"Good, and don't lose her. Few are brave enough to come down and try to steal from me. Those who have foolishly attempted such a thing have faced dire consequences—but let's try to keep her concealed until the festival is over. I don't want Apollo snooping around down here during the most important event of the year."

"No one will take her," Thanatos said, inclining his head. He sounded sure of himself.

No one would take me, but I would escape. I had to.

I was bursting with a million questions but quelled them knowing that Hypnos would answer them later. We turned, but Hades stood.

"Thanatos, anything else to report regarding our other problem?"

"Fifteen more over the last two days."

Hades had been benevolent until this point, but his features twisted with rage. I watched his eyes shift again, turning white, which was somehow more unsettling than the voids of black. "When I find out who is trying to cheat me out of the souls I should be collecting, I will tear them apart."

A small spike of fear shot through me, and Thanatos guided me towards the door. My traitorous heart quickened at his hand on my back—but it was just me reacting to being touched after all these years. I assured myself I would have the same reaction to anyone.

We left, leaving Hades to stew over whatever upset him. The walk out of the house was silent, and I assumed the brothers were lost in their own thoughts.

"We're not staying here?" I asked, looking back at the doors.

The God of Death shook his head. "This is not where we live."

Nychta still stood where we had left her, and I figured we would ride her again.

"No, that takes too long," Hypnos complained. "Pick that pony up and I'll just flash us there."

Pick her up? *Pony*? She had to weigh well over a ton by the size of her. Thanatos took a coin from his pocket and flipped it over the horse. He grabbed it in the air and slammed it against the saddle. In the blink of an eye, the horse disappeared. He tucked the coin back into his pocket and looked at his brother.

"That was," I started, staring at the space where the horse had been. "Wow."

"For someone who has lived amongst the gods, you're easy to impress. The ol' horse in the coin trick. Pretty basic," Hypnos said, looking curiously at me.

"I've just never seen anything like that."

"Well, if you liked that, check this out."

He grabbed my upper arm and Thanatos' at the same time. I stiffened against his touch, gasping. It felt like my body was being pulled by an invisible string tied to my belly button and the world blurred around me. I squeezed my eyes shut, but it only lasted a couple of seconds.

"There, much quicker. What'd you think of that?"

I turned away from them and emptied my stomach of the measly remnants from my breakfast. The world was slowly coming back into focus, but that had been awful.

"Hmm. Mortals. Such weak stomachs," he said dismissively.

"I don't want to do that again," I mumbled.

The icy hand laid on my bare back again and I found Thanatos looking down at me.

"I'm okay," I added quickly, blushing as I wiped my mouth.

When I turned, Hypnos was giving his brother an odd look, his head tilted to one side.

"This is your house?" I asked, breaking the strange tension.

Hypnos furrowed his brow, but finally followed my gaze. "Yes. Home sweet home. The Cave of Hypnos."

It was another castle, much smaller than Hades' though. This one seemed to be made of the same black glass that the king's throne was crafted from, and it glinted in the greenish gray light of the Underworld.

The structure was built into the side of a mountain, so it was an intriguing combination of black glass and dark stone. It was surrounded on one side by a strange green lake, and the beach butted up against an eerie forest that formed a seemingly impenetrable wall. The leaves were all an odd purple color, and the trees themselves were black and bent, reminding me of stooped old men.

The spires of this castle were sharp and ragged, giving it a tall, dominating appearance. I didn't understand why it was named for Hypnos because it reminded me more of Thanatos.

We walked across the beach to the entrance, which was not a door, but the mouth of a giant cave. Around the cave grew a field of red poppies, exactly like the ones Hypnos wore on his head.

I looked up in awe as we passed under the overhanging structure and lip of the rock. In the upper parts of the building, a person would be several stories off of the ground.

It was cool and dark in the cave, but lanterns were lit, guiding us toward a spiraling staircase. Hypnos went first, and Thanatos followed behind me. I was careful with my steps, as the stairs were the same slick black glass as everything else, and if I fell flat on my face in front of these two, I'd never forgive myself.

"You told me the movie was an accurate representation of Hades," I said to Hypnos' back. Hades hadn't seemed to think so, and I felt embarrassed for mentioning it.

"My voice was dripping with sarcasm when I told you that! I didn't think you'd actually bring it up—I'm so glad you did though, that was amazing."

I flushed, biting my lip.

"What, did they keep you locked in a basement or something? You can't recognize sarcasm?"

My heart pinched at the words. He had no idea how close he was to the truth.

"Hypnos," Thanatos warned behind me. Obviously, he understood what I was thinking, as he had a peek of my life firsthand. That brought about a fresh wave of humiliation.

We ascended into an open foyer, and I toyed with the thread on my dress again.

The God of Sleep glanced between us. "Holy shit—no way. Were you really locked in a basement? I'm so sorry. I didn't know."

I looked up at him and opened my mouth to answer but closed it again. Embarrassment flooded my veins and paralyzed my tongue, so I just shrugged.

"See you at dinner," Thanatos cut in curtly, leading me around his brother toward a split staircase.

We took the left side, ascending the glass steps. The house was incredible, like nothing I'd ever seen. An enormous chandelier that looked to be crafted from diamonds hung in the foyer. It glittered magnificently, casting a pattern that the black glass absorbed. The reflection produced a dramatic effect that made it look like we were walking on stars.

He led me into a room. The powerful scent of lilies graced my nose, and I knew it was his bedroom. I tensed, stopping in my tracks.

"I'm not staying here."

He looked surprised, arching an eyebrow at me. I reminded myself again that he was the enemy. He had something to do with the plague or knew something. I had seen it in my vision.

"I'll take a cell if you have one," I hissed.

The surprise shifted to amusement. "Really?"

I scowled at him. "What kind of woman do you think I am?"

"That—is a good question," he answered, as if he were trying to figure it out himself. "But you're not staying in here, and I would not ask you to."

I opened my mouth to argue, but realized he'd been agreeing with me, so the only thing that came out was, "Oh."

He was rummaging around in a chest, and I heard glass tinkling as he did. I glanced around the room. It was spacious but sparse. A fireplace was lit, burning low, and I wondered if he ever felt warm considering how cold his skin was.

There was a large four poster bed pushed into the corner of the room flanked by a small bedside table. Aside from that, an ornate dresser with a large mirror, and the wooden chest were the only items in the room.

"It's empty in here," I commented.

He grabbed a glass vial of something and turned to me. "Well, my wardrobe doesn't change much, so I don't need a lot. It's this black robe. Every day."

I wrinkled my nose. "Gross. I hope you launder it."

He looked at me, stunned, and his lips twitched. "I assure you I do."

Heading back towards me, he walked around to face my back. I stiffened as my mind flashed to the overseer's office. I didn't like people behind me.

"What are you doing?" I demanded, whirling to face him.

He had the vial open. "Putting oil on your welts. It will help with the pain, and they should heal faster."

His compassion surprised me. They'd offered no type of pain relief before at the temple. The overseer wanted to make sure I experienced every moment of my punishment.

"Oh, um. I'm really fine. I've had much worse."

That answer did not please him, and his lips pulled into a deep frown. A flash of anger danced through his eyes and the violet color clouded with blackness for a moment. I took a step back, surprised by the sudden change.

He sighed and walked around behind me. I allowed him to this time, even though I knew I shouldn't. I felt him lift my braid and move it, brushing his fingertips over my shoulder as he did. Even through the fabric of my dress, I had to fight the involuntary shudder that wanted to dance through me.

His fingers worked at the top clasp, and then it opened. I bit my lip, feeling exposed. A flurry of emotions danced through me, and some of the shameful ones shocked me. I felt the coolness of his fingers against the top welt. Despite my best efforts, I hissed out a pained breath.

"I'm sorry," he muttered. "I returned for just a moment to consult with Hades about—taking you." He at least had the decency to sound ashamed. "I didn't know what was going to happen in that office, or I wouldn't have gone without you. I wouldn't have allowed it."

My breath hitched in my throat. *Wouldn't have allowed it.* Like everyone else had, including the master. The guards, Laurenth—they'd all allowed me to be treated like that and done nothing. I should've shoved my dagger through the overseer's heart when I had the chance.

"Why was he striking you?"

I cleared my throat. "I spoke out of turn in the hallway. It's forbidden. I was also late to an important…meeting."

After several moments of silence, he spoke again. "I'd kill him again if I could, but I promise his soul went to Phlegethon, the River of Fire, at my request. Where he'll be for a very long time."

I didn't know what that meant, but it sounded like bad news for the overseer. Good. He was a cruel and sadistic man.

"Thank you," I mumbled, hating it but knowing it needed to be said.

He chuckled, and the throaty sound made my traitorous heart twirl. "I thought no thank yous were to be uttered?"

"Don't get used to it," I retorted. "And for the record you still kidnapped me."

He said nothing else, but I felt his hand on my other welt. I thought he was certainly taking his time, as it should've been a rather quick application. I wasn't about to complain. His cool skin was nice against the hot pain. And that was *definitely* the only reason I wanted him touching me. It had nothing to do with the small sparks that danced under my skin at the contact.

The amount of sacrilege that had already taken place today was astronomical, so I didn't think receiving a little oil on my wounds was that big of a deal.

"And I'm sorry for Hypnos. He doesn't understand that not everyone enjoys hearing him talk as much as he does."

"It's okay, he couldn't have known."

He stuck the lid back onto the vial and refastened my dress. I once again felt he lingered longer with his fingers than he needed to, a thought that elicited a strange heat in my blood.

Gods, I'm pathetic.

"Now to your room," he said, leading me out into the hall and to the door right next to his.

I arched an eyebrow at him.

"I promised to keep you safe. And I will. Nothing like what I just witnessed will ever happen to you here."

He opened the door and led me in. Compared to his room, it was beautifully furnished. Everything was decorated in a deep plum color that complemented the black walls and floor. Besides the similar furniture that he had in his room, there was an expansive wardrobe and a plush sitting area in front of the fireplace.

"The bathroom is through there," he said, pointing at a closed door. "This wardrobe will present you with items made to fit you. Whatever you want."

My eyes widened, and I looked at the ornate piece of furniture. "That's amazing."

"I know you're probably hungry, so I'll have dinner prepared and then I'll come get you."

"I'll have dinner in my room," I declared, wondering if he would let me make the choice.

He did, nodding and saying, "Of course. That's fine."

With that, he left, the soft click of the door confirming I was alone. Hurrying to it, I slid the lock closed, and then my gaze darted around the room. I inspected everything—what exactly I was looking for I didn't know—and then I opened the balcony doors.

I leaned over the railing and looked down. We were only on the second story, and I was sure I could escape this way if I needed to. Although between the water on one side and the forest on the other, I didn't know where I could possibly go.

Glancing to my right, I realized his balcony was only about eight feet away from mine. Maybe I could get into his room and take the scythe while he slept.

There, at least I had a plan. I would wait a few days to lower suspicion, and then I would take the scythe.

CHAPTER EIGHT

I stayed in my room for the next two days, refusing to come out. I only saw the God of Death for brief interactions when he brought my meals, and he was very polite. No one else bothered me.

At my request, they laundered my clothes, and I only wore them—even to bed. I didn't know if it would be improper to wear something else from the magical wardrobe. The oil Thanatos had used on my welts had worked miracles, and I could now button all but one clasp by myself.

As the third day drew to a close, my boredom and curiosity were winning out. I felt if I spent one more minute here, I'd go crazy. They did not lock me in. Thanatos didn't even post a guard at my door, which was already an exciting change from my normal existence.

Cautiously, as if someone caught me they might throw me over their shoulder and carry me back to my room, I slipped out into the hall, noting the many doors. Assuming they were private rooms, I didn't open any. I returned to the double staircase and descended. This house was silent, making it feel like every one of my footfalls made a monstrous sound.

I found the open foyer, still in awe of the twinkling chandelier, and chose a random door to explore. I found myself in a kitchen with silver and black appliances. It was surprisingly modern, as was the rest of the house. I didn't see any televisions or similar entertainment yet, so I wasn't sure how caught up they were with technology. I thought longingly of my tablet I'd left on the floor of my bedroom back at home over a decade ago. I doubted the Underworld had Wi-Fi.

Stepping further into the kitchen, I started poking around through the utensil drawers. I was desperate to find a weapon. Any weapon.

I thought I was alone, but a walk-in fridge door opened, and I froze, panicked.

A tall lanky man wearing a chef's uniform ducked out and faced me. He looked surprised, and then a warm smile spread across his face. It made the aging skin around his eyes crinkle and exposed one golden tooth.

"You must be the Pythia. I was told I might be seeing ya. I'm Glendyl."

"Yes," I answered, backpedaling. "I'm sorry, I didn't know what this room was."

"You can stay if ya like. I'm just starting to prep for dinner."

I watched him warily for a few moments, not missing the Mastix dagger at his waist. Maybe I could steal it.

"Ya know how to run a peeler?"

I blinked, finding his eyes again. "I'm sorry. What?"

He presented a vegetable peeler and a bag of potatoes. "I could use the help, if yer willing." He held up hands with knobby fingers. "I've got some nasty arthritis."

"Oh," I answered, glancing around. "Okay."

I accepted the peeler and the bag. "Where should I peel them?"

"Over that sink'll work."

Finding the sink he suggested, I removed a potato and started peeling. I was clumsy at first, not knowing or remembering if I'd ever done this, but I caught on quickly.

Glendyl whistled a lively tune as he worked, preparing what looked like a beef roast. He didn't speak, and neither did I, but after a couple of minutes, I felt my shoulders relax.

I focused on the skip of the peeler and nothing else, allowing my mind to calm. It surprised me when I reached for the bag and found it was empty. Glendyl came over and stood by me.

"Yer pretty skilled with a blade, Pythia. I'd hire ya. We need to rinse 'em though."

Glendyl reached for the potato I held. Realizing he was about to touch me, I recoiled and dropped it into the sink.

Embarrassment flooded my face and chest. "I-I'm sorry."

His eyes were curious, but he didn't pry. "That's alright, my lady."

Glendyl gathered the peeled potatoes and took them to another sink to rinse them. Afterwards, he diced them while I cleaned the sink out. The cook was nice, and I was oddly comfortable here. I found myself asking, "Do you need any more help? And, please, call me Cere."

He gave me a few other things to do, and I helped him finish the dishes. I didn't have an opportunity to snatch his dagger, but I tucked one of the smaller kitchen knives into my boot.

When we finished, the cooking food created a mouth-watering aroma.

"It smells good," I told him.

"Well, thanks to you I've got time to spare," he said, grabbing a book and plopping down in a large chair in the kitchen's corner. "I appreciate yer help. When ya eat tonight, you can feel proud of the work." He winked at me and then opened his book.

I let myself out and walked down another hallway. It was so strange to walk alone—no guards and no Keilah. I worried for her, hoping she was okay.

I noticed a cracked door, and I peeked in, being nosey. I stilled when I realized Thanatos was in the room. He was relaxing on a leather loveseat. I was surprised to see him working on what looked like a puzzle in a book. He was filling numbers into boxes, but I didn't understand the reasoning.

A light music played, and I listened to the dance of the piano keys. The back of my eyes burned with emotion. I hadn't heard music in a long time.

"Here to kill me?"

I jumped in surprise and thought about bolting. Instead, I stood there awkwardly, caught snooping.

"You can come in."

He gave me a choice and I should've taken the opportunity to leave. Of course, I didn't, which called in questions regarding my sanity.

Curiosity flooded me and I hesitantly pushed the door open. It was a plush looking office, with a desk and several shelves. My fingers itched looking at all the books housed there. I wanted to touch them. Devour them. And I didn't even have to burn them afterwards.

Thanatos was in the sitting area, where an overstuffed loveseat and two chairs flanked a square table.

"What are you doing?" I asked, indicating the number game.

"A Sudoku puzzle," he said, sitting up. "Would you like to try it?"

"I don't know how."

"I'll show you."

The pads of my fingers found a thread on my dress and fiddled with it. My lack of education embarrassed me. I'd read every single book that Laurenth brought me, but I had done nothing math related in a long time.

"Okay. But I didn't finish school. I read while I was in the temple, but I didn't do any math."

His expression remained neutral. Either he wasn't surprised, or he was good at hiding it. "Can you count to nine?"

I flushed. "Of course. I didn't go to the temple until I was thirteen."

"Then you'll be able to do this puzzle."

My body was stiff as I sat down, unsure. He flipped to the front of the book, where many of the numbers were already filled in.

"The goal is to fill the nine-by-nine grid with numbers. Each row, column, and three-by-three section must contain the numbers one through nine. You don't want any of the numbers to repeat in the rows, columns, or three-by-three sections."

I stared at the page, biting my lip, and then he pushed the pen into my hand and handed me the book. With him, I didn't have the reflex to pull away like I had with Glendyl. His fingers were gentle as they brushed mine, and butterflies sprung to life in my stomach.

The blank boxes glared up at me, making me feel like an inadequate fool. I hadn't held a pen in so long, it felt foreign in my hand. My brain worked to dust off the old memories of writing stored in the far corners of my mind.

"So three there," I said, writing it. My number looked childish, but I was satisfied with his answer.

"Yes."

We were sitting very close, and my body was aware of everywhere he touched me. He was a patient teacher and told me several helpful strategies. I went slowly at first and he had to correct me twice, but I got the hang of it and was soon smiling down at the completed page. My hand felt tired and achy when I set the pen down, and I flexed my fingers.

"That was fun."

"You can keep that book, I have more."

"I didn't expect Thanatos, God of Death, to play book games," I muttered, glancing at him. "I expected you to be, you know, killing people all the time."

He looked amused. "I'm an escort for the dead. I don't kill people as a hobby. When I was younger, I enjoyed exercising my control over life and death, but that was a long time ago."

"So you play puzzle games instead?"

Shrugging, he ran his finger over the worn corner of the book. "I liked it when it came out in the eighteenth century, and it's become a favorite of mine. Life becomes incredibly dull when you're immortal. If I don't find things to do, I will lose my mind. Hypnos knits."

I gawked at him in disbelief. "He does not."

"He does. And you can call me Thaos. I know my full name is tiresome."

"How old are you, Thaos?"

Sharp chips of violet stared back at me for several moments before he responded. "How old is death?"

His answer confused me. "I don't know…that's why I asked."

"I should be clearer. How old is the act of dying?"

My brow furrowed. "Well, people have died as long as people have lived."

"I'm that old."

"But… that's hundreds of years."

"Thousands."

I averted my eyes, looking back at the book in my hand. The information was unexpected and overwhelming. I was already a nervous mess in his presence, and the revelation only exacerbated those feelings. I wasn't sure how to react.

"Wow. You look great for your age."

I clamped my mouth shut as soon as the words slipped out, and my cheeks erupted with heat. Gods, of all the things I could've said, why would I choose that? I braved a glance at him and saw the corner of his mouth had curved up.

"There are benefits to being immortal."

"You claim you don't kill people, but you killed the overseer," I pointed out, desperate to change the subject.

A muscle flexed in his jaw. "Yes, I did."

"I wish I would've done it," I whispered.

His eyebrows shot up at my disclosure. "If you'd ever like to kill anyone else, I would be glad to assist you."

His eyes were on me, a hard look filling them that assured me he was being sincere. This was odd, sitting here with him discussing homicide, but it somehow felt nice.

"I'll let you know," I mumbled, offering him a lopsided smirk.

"You should come down for dinner tonight. I promise no one here will harm you."

"You must take me back to the temple," I insisted, grabbing his forearm. "It's vital I go back."

He tensed and looked down at my hand, then back up to search my face. "Why?"

Not sure what had come over me I snatched my hand back and clenched it in my lap. "I can't tell you that."

"Well, I can't take you back. I'm sorry."

"You can't or you won't?"

"Both."

"What do you want from me?"

He ran his hand through his hair. "I want nothing from you. I only want to keep you safe."

"For Hades to use me."

The corners of his mouth turned down, but he didn't respond.

I sighed but didn't argue anymore. I planned on attempting to steal the scythe tonight, anyway. But I was beyond curious about the God of Death, and I thought there wouldn't be any harm in eating dinner with him tonight.

CHAPTER NINE

I stood in the shower, loving the way the water felt against my skin. I hadn't ever showered at the temple because there wasn't one in my bathroom. There were several rich smelling soaps, not feminine scents, but still nice. I had to admit that I did not miss the overly scented oils of my regular bath.

The events of the last three days ran through my head. The overseer was dead and now destined to suffer for eternity. A dry chuckle escaped me. I found so much joy in it.

Maybe I had some issues.

And I had the God of Death to thank. I wasn't sure what kind of picture I had of Death in my head, but it didn't involve the tender care of my wounds, Sudoku puzzles, or the sparks that danced on my skin when he touched me.

Sighing, I felt confused and saddened. I wanted to go back—I had to. But I would be a liar if I said I wanted to don that red dress and inhale those vapors again. The thoughts of not going back made me feel selfish. I needed to accept my fate and deal with it. My destiny was to remain pure and help the master stop the plague and discord that was threatening to bubble over into the world.

I ran the tendrils of my russet-colored hair through my hands as I washed it, realizing these last three days were the first times Keilah hadn't done it for me in years. How empowering it was to wash my own hair. My throat tightened at the odd thought.

I had taken a long time, so long that the water wrinkled the pads of my fingers. Back out in the bedroom, I noticed someone had brought tea and set it in front of the fireplace. That unnerved me a bit, but at least I knew they had a key to my door.

Wrapped in a towel, I walked to the wardrobe. I decided I would use it, but Thaos hadn't explained how it worked. I stared at it, wondering if I needed to push a button or something. Shrugging, I opened the door. I gasped in surprise as it was full of dresses of all different colors and designs. It was a stark contrast from my wardrobe at the temple, which had only held red dresses and mustard-colored sashes.

I pulled several of the more casual pieces free and laid them on the bed. Not a single one I liked was red. Was it wrong of me? Should I just wear one of the red ones?

No one would ever know if I didn't.

I selected one. It was a lovely royal purple, and I held it up to myself. Glancing in the mirror, I took a deep breath and decided to live. Just this one night. This one dinner. I could pretend to be a real person. I would eat around other people, talk freely with them, and I would wear purple.

It was still modest enough, with long sleeves and a nice, high square neckline. The skirt was asymmetrical though and fell just below my knee in the front. *The scandal.*

It was at that moment my awesome brain reminded me that the God of Death had seen my bare breasts, anyway, so modesty was a fruitless endeavor. I flushed just thinking about it and wondered for a moment if I even still had my gift. Those at the temple had drilled into me the knowledge that I would lose the sight if I wasn't pure and worthy. Who judged my worthiness, I didn't know.

I braided my long hair, chuckling as it took me a few tries to get it right. I had grown so used to Keilah doing it for me.

A soft knock sounded at the door, and I jumped. This was all so strange. Foreign and new. And I was ashamed to admit— *exciting.* I hadn't been excited about something in a long time. As long as I could remember.

I opened the door to find Thaos. My eyes drifted to my target, the scythe, still attached to his back, and wondered with a slice of panic if he ever put it down. The thought conjured an image of the God of Death curled around his weapon in bed and I had to suppress a smile.

For the first time, I noticed a small hourglass set into the top of the handle. It seemed to be housed in some kind of spinning mechanism, with two gold circles surrounding it.

To my surprise, he'd removed the robe and now wore a fitted tunic, slim leather breeches, and boots. They were all black, and I doubted that he had any other color in his wardrobe. The fashion was behind in the realms of the gods. I hadn't ever seen anyone wear jeans here or at the temple. Leather breeches or leggings and tunics or robes seemed to be preferred.

I tried to focus, but my eyes wanted to wander down his body. The way his clothes fit drew my gaze. My cheeks burned at the thought, and I forced myself to stare at his face. His handsome face. As if that was any better.

"Hi," I breathed.

I balled my hands into fists to keep from slapping myself. *Hi?*

His lips twitched, and I wondered if I would get to see a smile before I left this place, and him, behind. A strange heaviness settled into my chest at the thought.

His gaze drifted to my dress for just a moment and then snapped back up to my face. "That color suits you."

A playful light seemed to dance in his eyes and only then I realized that of all the dozens of colors of gowns in that wardrobe I'd chosen purple. A shade very similar to his eyes, too. I tried to stop my cheeks from flushing. Why had I done that? When I picked it I had just found the color to be beautiful. Very beautiful.

"Where's your robe?"

The corner of his mouth turned up. "I told you I have it cleaned occasionally."

"Don't you have another one?"

I didn't know why I couldn't stop asking questions. My heart was hammering. I was so nervous, and I couldn't stop my tongue from moving.

"I prefer that one." His eyes were light and sparkling with what I thought was amusement. "Are you ready?"

"Yes. How many people will be there?"

"Tonight it's just the three of us. I figured the questioning you're going to endure from Hypnos is enough for one evening. But, I'm sure you'll meet his sons soon."

"Doesn't he have a wife?"

He shrugged. "She might stop by sometime."

"That doesn't sound like a very loving marriage."

I thought of my parents. From what I could remember, they were deeply in love.

He regarded me with open curiosity. "What do you know of love, Pythia?"

My brow furrowed. "I suppose not much. My mother and father were in love. At the temple, I read a romance novel that I wasn't supposed to have." Before I could stop the words I gushed, "I read it probably a thousand times."

His eyebrows arched and the corners of his mouth turned up. My face burned with a new flame of heat. Gods, what was wrong with me? The words were like vomit. I couldn't hold them back.

I turned the question to him. "Well, what do you know of love?"

He stared at me for a moment before answering, "I am Death. I do not know love."

"Oh. I'm sorry."

"I'm not. Love always turns into weakness. If you love something, people can use it against you."

"Well, that's very bleak. And don't call me Pythia," I snapped. "I have a name."

He nodded in understanding. "Regarding my brother's marriage, you'll find that there are very few instances where unions between Gods have anything to do with love."

"That's depressing." I felt bad for anyone being forced into something they didn't want for the sake of duty. I was an expert on the subject. "How many sons does he have?"

"Three."

I hesitated. "And—you? Do you have children?"

He tilted his head, as if the question surprised him. "No. I do not. And if you're going to proceed with your quest to kill me with questions, I'd like to do so while we're eating."

That made my lips curl into a small smile. He offered his arm to me, as his brother had done when we'd first arrived, and I surprised us both by taking it. He led me back to the split staircase.

"Is that chandelier made of diamonds?" I asked, looking around at the twinkling sparkles that filled the entire room.

"Yes. We have a lot of them."

We entered a dining room, where Hypnos was already sitting. The black wooden table was large for only three people, and I wondered if they had guests often.

Hypnos' eyes fell on us, where our arms connected, and then the same curious look he'd given his brother crossed his face again.

"I'm hurt," he said. "You'll hold his arm, but not mine?"

I blushed, unsure of what to say, and snapped my arm away. I took the seat across from him and Thaos sat between us at the head of the table.

There was an abundance of food. Way too much for three people. I wasn't allowed very much meat at the temple, something Laurenth had always complained about, so I took it easy on the roast. I didn't want my stomach to react badly. Glancing at the steaming mound of mashed potatoes, I smiled, finding Glendyl was right—I felt proud.

"So, Pythia," Hypnos started.

"It's Cere," I interjected. His eyebrows arched, and I added, "Please just call me Cere."

"Okay. It's much lovelier anyway, isn't it?"

I didn't know who he was asking, so I said nothing.

"It is," Thaos said, earning a curious look from both of us.

Hypnos' gaze shifted to me again. "So, Cere, I find you so interesting. Tell me about your life."

"Like what?"

"Like I sense you're a mortal, but not a human. What are you?"

I was surprised. Most people didn't know, and I rarely shared the information. Sometimes I even seemed to forget.

"My parents are shifters. Wolf shifters. But I'm not, I don't understand why, but I never got my wolf."

I remembered that painful time when I'd turned eighteen and expected my wolf to manifest. When she hadn't, I'd hoped I was off a few days on my birthday and waited desperately for the next full moon, praying I would have my first shift. Nothing had happened. That night was the last time I had allowed myself to really cry.

"Interesting. A daughter of Artemis is the Pythia."

I knew who Artemis was. The Goddess of the Moon and Hunt. Sacred to my people. We also knew her as Diane, which was my middle name after my father's mother.

Hypnos went on. "Tell me about being locked in a basement. I'm dying of curiosity."

"You're nosey and intrusive," his brother scolded him.

"It's okay," I said. "They did not lock me in a basement. I was just led to live a very pious and pure life in a temple. A beautiful temple with fountains and flowers and art—certainly not a basement."

"And who? Who led you to live this life?"

I hesitated. Four curious eyes scrutinized me. I didn't know how much I could reveal to them, so I was careful with my words.

"Apollo. Everyone referred to him as the master. I only saw him when he came for a reading. And even then, he was separated from me by a wooden screen. Other than that, I had a handmaid. She was in place to ensure my purity remained intact. A trainer who taught me how to protect myself and my purity. And then the overseer, who ran the temple and took care of any—" I glanced at Thaos, who seemed particularly aggressive with the piece of beef he was cutting. "—discipline issues, if I violated any rules. There were others, too. My guards and the servants that cared for the temple."

"So your *purity*? What does that mean? You're a virgin?"

I was beginning to agree that Hypnos was very nosey, but I also felt a little surprised they wouldn't already know this about me. I was the Pythia. Wasn't it common knowledge that I must remain pure?

"Of course," I answered. "It's impious enough that I'm even talking to you. And I shouldn't have touched any of you, either. I'm not supposed to be touched. If I'm not deemed pure, my gift will be taken. I thought you would know. Surely Hades knows, and you're his minions."

"Minions?!" Hypnos threw back his head and laughed. "He is a minion," he said, indicating Thaos. "I just help people sleep or make them not sleep if I feel like being a dick. Which is often."

My cheeks flushed softly at his language, and I cleared my throat. "Well, I must remain chaste. That's all I'm saying."

They exchanged a curious glance.

"What?"

"Nothing. I just hadn't heard that about the Pythia. Also, as far as I know, my brother is the only one you've allowed to touch you. Besides when I flashed us, and that wasn't even a second."

I stared at my food, realizing he was correct. I had even been careful when helping Glendyl that I'd never touched his skin.

"And since everything we're doing right now is sacrilege, how do you know if your gift is still intact?"

I stilled. That was a good point. I had trained myself to keep my walls up at all times, so I wouldn't know I'd lost it until I tried to use it. I glanced at Thaos again. He had seen a lot of my flesh that first day and I'd allowed him to touch me. Feelings, inappropriate ones, had blossomed from his touch.

A beat of dread shot through me. What if I'd already violated too many rules? Had someone already deemed me unworthy of the sight? I tried to ignore the tiny bit of relief and hope that sprang up inside of me. If I didn't have the sight, I wouldn't be of any value to anyone and I could go home. Just in time to watch the plague spread. Guilt blossomed in my chest and replaced anything else I was feeling. I certainly was unworthy of such a gift if I was so relieved at the aspect of it being gone.

I looked at Hypnos and tentatively pulled my walls down. The sensation that accompanied the sight rushed through me and the whispers invaded my senses. I could not stop it, and the disembodied voices forced their way out.

"You have an important role to play, God of Sleep. When time chimes, use the candlestick."

I threw my wall back up and blushed, clamping my hand over my mouth. They both stared at me, and Hypnos boasted a giant grin.

"Oh my! Was that my first reading? That was exciting. *Use the candlestick*. What does that mean?"

"I don't know. None of it ever seems to make sense until it's actively happening, and by then it seems too late to change anything. Sometimes I see images, sometimes it's just words, and sometimes it's both. If we knew what vapors they had me inhale at the temple, I could tell you more."

The brothers exchanged another glance. "Vapors?"

I didn't see any harm in revealing the information. "Yes. I had to hold the sacred laurel branch and inhale the vapors. My visions were exacerbated that way."

"Curious," Hypnos said, more to Thaos than to me. "Apollo does do that. And the red dress."

A frown pulled my lips down. "I told you it's him. The master is Apollo."

He nodded, but I could tell he wasn't convinced.

There were a few long minutes of silence and then Hypnos asked casually, "So you're a virgin? Does that mean you've never…hmm, had an orgasm? Is that a no-no?"

The God of Death grabbed his wine and tipped it back, imbibing like someone would if they were lost in the desert for a month and stumbled upon a glass of water. His brother watched him, clearly amused.

I blushed again. Was this how dinner conversation always went? It had been so long since I'd eaten with anyone aside from Keilah, and we would never discuss such things. Before that, I'd lived in a pack of wolf shifters, and they were very open about sex and nudity. One of my uncles was outspoken enough to ask such a personal question.

My upbringing had caused me a lot of torment. I was raised to view sex as a beautiful, normal thing. When I arrived at the temple, they had drilled it into me that sex was shameful. The feelings often tumbled together in a tornado of conflict, and I wasn't sure how to feel.

I considered Hypnos' question and supposed such a blunt question warranted an equal answer. Even if it was shameful, and if anyone at the temple knew—I shuddered. The overseer would enjoy that disciplinary lesson.

Would have, I reminded myself with a wicked beat of satisfaction. He was burning in the river of fire.

"Well, no. I mean, I have. Myself. I've given myself one." My ears burned, and I felt this was very inappropriate. "And my gift still works, so I guess it was okay."

Thaos was choking now, coughing like he'd inhaled the wine instead of drinking it. Hypnos stared at me with a delighted humor in his eyes.

"You are very interesting," he said, laughing.

I blushed deeper, confused. I was sure my face was as red as the overseer's had been when Death was squeezing the life out of him. Was that answer—wrong? It must be. I knew seeking sexual pleasure was wrong when I had done it. I blamed that stupid romance novel.

"Don't be embarrassed," Hypnos said, still grinning. "We all do it. Ask him. He's the God of Death and Masturba—."

"Stop talking," Thaos ground out, glaring daggers at his brother.

The God of Sleep was laughing at us both when the doors pushed open and two women and two men, all dressed similar to those who served at Hades' house, entered to clear the table. I was thankful for them and felt relieved to have a break in the stressful conversation.

Another server came in after them and placed a silver platter on the table. My heart jumped and then my gaze slid to the God of Death. Curious violet eyes watched me, gauging my reaction.

The plate was stacked high with lemon tarts.

CHAPTER TEN

I closed the door to my room and pressed my back against it, taking a deep breath. Well, that had been *intense*. I had many things to mull over. Embarrassment burned in my chest, and I knew my social skills left much to be desired. Gods, I was awkward, and it was mortifying. I did not know how to be a real person. Luckily, Thaos had said nothing about it while he walked me back to my room.

I was taken from the real world on my thirteenth birthday. Since then, I'd been allowed to talk to four people. Half of those relationships weren't positive, and the other half were forced by duty. Sure, I had read a lot of books but reading about life and actually living life were starkly different, as I'd just discovered.

How was I supposed to know what was inappropriate dinner conversation? Especially with Hypnos, who seemed to have no shame with his questions.

And the lemon tarts. What was Death's intention? I didn't understand why someone would do that. An exasperated sigh parted my lips because I didn't seem to understand anything at all.

A jittery energy pulsed through me as I removed the dress and found a red nightgown in the wardrobe. I didn't feel confident in my plan to steal the scythe, but I had no idea what else to do. It seemed it was the only way I could get out of here. I doubted that the Underworld was open to come and go as one pleased.

But I didn't know how to use the weapon. In the overseer's office he'd just cut the air and it had worked. Was it that easy? I supposed it would have to be a quick learning curve.

Plus, it looked like a heavy weapon. I wondered if I could even make the jump back with it in my hands. With that in mind, I unlocked my bedroom door. I could come back in that way if I needed to.

What if he woke up? The thought caused a shudder to pulse through me. Would it anger him?

Probably.

I should be frightened, and I was, but I was determined too. If he woke up, I would just accept the punishment. I'd been disciplined often in my life. What was once more?

Although, I was sure the God of Death could deliver something worse than being switched with a ruler. I thought of the tendrils of shadow that suffocated the overseer. But, for some reason, I had a hard time picturing Thaos as cruel. I was an idiot, surely. He was Death. He didn't even know how to love. Of course he could be cruel.

I sat in front of the fire and stared at the flames. When I heard the neighboring door click shut, I knew Thaos had returned to his room. I glanced at the clock. It was eleven, so I would wait a couple of hours and then sneak in and grab it.

I touched the silver teapot, yanking my hand back in surprise when I found it was still hot. Was it magic like the wardrobe? I poured myself a cup and thought about never receiving my wolf. Maybe if I ever met Artemis, the Goddess of the Hunt, I could ask her why.

Being raised in the supernatural world, I had always known vampires, fae, animal shifters, witches, and even dragons were all real, living in the mortal realm of Earth. It wasn't until the master brought me back to the temple, though, that I realized gods were physical beings as well. They could walk among mortals, and some enjoyed meddling in their lives.

It was also when I finally learned the answer to the questions that had plagued me my entire childhood. Who was I? *What* was I?

I was the Oracle of the Gods called the Pythia. Destined to be reborn over and over as a mortal woman. I was an important and sought-after tool of Apollo's. Many wanted to possess me, so I had to be protected. He locked me in that golden cage for my own safety.

But his cage had failed—infiltrated by Death. Though, I didn't feel in danger no matter where I was. As far as I knew, no one wanted me dead. They wanted to use me. I was sure the King of the Underworld and his *minions* were no different.

I thought about the curious look between the brothers when I told them about my purity. Did they not understand, or not believe? It was all they had ever taught me at the temple. I figured it would be common knowledge.

After more mulling and pacing, I glanced at the clock. Ten minutes past two. My waiting was in danger of becoming stalling.

Taking a deep breath, I went to the balcony. The sky was strange in the Underworld. There was no sun, moon, or stars. The sky just darkened pitch black at night. During the day, it was always that strange gray color. An iridescent glow cast the beach below in a pastel green, the water below shining like the nightlight of the Underworld.

I drew another deep breath and focused, starting at the far end of my balcony and sprinting as fast as I could. Vaulting to the rail, I pushed off of it with my foot and closed the gap. I landed on the rail of his balcony, scrambling for a moment to gain my balance. A small grin pulled at the corners of my mouth. My wolf may have never appeared, but I knew I was still faster and stronger than a normal human.

I looked at the closed doors of his room and the darkness behind them. This was crazy. Maybe the worst idea ever. If he locked his doors, I'd just have to call it quits and go back. Part of me prayed they wouldn't open.

I turned the knob as silently as possible, trying to ignore the tremors in my hand. It clicked, unlocked, and I pushed the door. The hinges were blessedly silent as they turned. Maybe luck was on my side.

The fireplace was still lit with a low flame, casting a soft light. My eyes adjusted, and I scanned the room. I caught sight of Thaos, and my adrenaline spiked.

He was in his bed, his right forearm hitched up over the top half of his face. The blanket was down around his waist, and I watched the slow rise and fall of his chest.

Okay, I *stared* at his chest. He was shirtless, and it was the most I could ever remember seeing of a man. My eyes traveled over him, taking in the dips and valleys of his muscular physique. I blushed, feeling bad, but then reminded myself he'd been in my room at least once while I slept, so now we were even. Or now, maybe I was the creep.

Beside him, between the bed and the wall, I saw my target. The scythe leaned up in the corner. To get it, I'd have to crawl up the length of the bed and grab it, then crawl back down. The idea seemed risky because the bed was certain to shift with my movements. My other option was to lean over him and snag it. I opted for the latter and tiptoed to his side of the bed.

It was silent aside from the pulse of my heart, which felt like a rabid butterfly trying to rip its way free of my chest. I took deep breaths as quietly as I could. It was now or never. I couldn't just stand here all night and stare at him. Although that shameless part of me, whose voice seemed to grow louder the longer I was away from the temple, admitted I wouldn't mind it.

I set my knee as gently as I could on the bed, cringing as it dipped. I stared at him, watching for any sign of movement. When there was none, I leaned over him.

My fingers were close, but I longed to place my left hand down to stabilize my body. I underestimated the distance, and I quivered with effort to hold my balance. But if I just leaned a bit more—my fingers brushed the wood handle. A little closer and—

A cool hand snapped up and grabbed my wrist. "Looking for something?"

I yelped and reacted out of instinct, trying to break the grasp with a defensive blow from my other hand. It did nothing, as I should've expected.

I was already off balance, and he pulled. As I fell forward, I tried to lift my knee and hit him, well, where no man wants to be hit. Something Laurenth told me was very effective, albeit not very honorable.

He turned his leg, so my knee connected with his. Gods, I might as well just bash my knee into the metal railing on the balcony. A hiss of pain slid past my lips as I fell forward onto his chest.

He glared down at me. "That was almost very rude."

"You grabbed me!"

His eyes widened with shock. "You're *scolding* me, as you attempt to sneak into my room and steal from me? That's bold of you."

"I wasn't stealing. I was borrowing."

He scoffed. "Unbelievable."

I returned his glare, faltering when I realized our faces were mere inches apart. And our bodies were zero inches apart. Those tingles erupted and danced with the strange coolness of his skin. My body was an absolute traitor.

"You should let me go," I hissed, fighting his grip on my wrists. "This is very inappropriate."

I saw his eyes shift between us where our chests connected. They widened and then snapped back to my face. "Is it? I find it inappropriate to sneak into someone's bedroom in the middle of the night. Scantily clad."

My face burned, and I glanced down at myself. The nightgown was cut lower than anything I would ever wear outside of my room, and the contact pushed the swells of my breasts up between us. I should've worn a robe or overcoat, but I feared it would stifle my ability to jump. I hadn't planned for, well, *this*.

My body was humming with awareness of him. His strange coolness permeated my skin, which I welcomed because my blood felt like it was on fire. I squirmed for a moment and then stilled, like someone had struck me. I felt something else, too. Was that—?

I stared down at him in shock, blunt with my question, "You're aroused? Why?"

His eyebrows arched. "Maybe because an incredibly beautiful, scantily clad woman has broken into my bedroom and is lying on top of me."

A nervous gasp I was going to attribute to surprise left me. "I'm only lying on top of you because you pulled me down."

Beautiful? No one called me that except the overseer. And when he did it, it made me feel sticky and gross. I did not find that to ring true in this situation.

Thaos was shifting his weight. The movement was so quick I didn't understand what was happening until I was underneath him. Pinned.

"I'm more inclined to call this inappropriate," he said, his voice huskier than it had been before.

"That's because it is. Very inappropriate." I struggled until I was out of breath, getting nowhere. He just watched me, his face unreadable.

I glared at him, giving up. "What are you doing?"

"Seeing how long you're going to continue. I'm finding I enjoy feeling you writhe beneath me."

My next breath of air was so sharp it sliced its way down my throat. That might be the lewdest comment anyone had ever made in my presence. I should be offended. I *wanted* to be offended. So, of course, I wasn't. Not completely anyway.

Instead, a strange wet heat flooded my body. It bubbled like a boiling pot in my stomach. I willed the feeling away, but it would not go.

The sensation left me breathless. "That is *obscene*."

"You asked."

"Well, I didn't expect the answer to be so vulgar."

He snorted. "Strange coming from a woman who talks of her purity and then pleasuring herself in the same breath of conversation over dinner. An admission from which I'll never recover."

I gaped at him, my mouth opening and closing twice before any sound came out. "He-he asked! I thought. I don't know. I don't understand what to say, because well...you know." I stopped, arching an eyebrow at him. "What do you mean you'll never recover?"

He looked inquisitive, staring down at me with a penetrating gaze. "You've been oddly sheltered, and it makes you much too interesting. Maybe the most intriguing person I've ever met."

Well, I didn't believe that for a second. He'd been alive thousands of years. It also didn't escape me that he ignored my question.

"I am not intriguing. If anything, I'm dull." Aside from being the Pythia, there was nothing interesting about me. The life I led was boring compared to most people.

A frown pulled at his lips. "I disagree. You're innocent, some might say naïve, yet bold and vicious. All at the same time."

I gasped. "*Naïve*? And I am not vicious. I can't believe you told Hypnos that I was."

"Naïve does not mean stupid, so don't take it that way. And you just attacked me in my bed." His eyes held that glint of amusement again, earning a fresh glare from me.

"I did not attack you, but I'm going to if you keep teasing me."

"That's another intriguing thing. I am Death. But you seem to have no sense of self-preservation or regard for your own safety. You're actually *threatening* me. I believe you would attack me again if I let you go, and you have no chance of winning. But you'd do it, anyway."

I digested those words. I knew he could have killed me when I stabbed him. That he could kill me right now. It would be as simple for him as it was for me to squash an insect. I knew enough about the gods to know they were far from kind. Even the lighter gods had a cruel streak and probably wouldn't take kindly to being threatened. And he wasn't one of them—he was darkness. Yet, I didn't feel fear, not like I should have.

He was right, there was something wrong with me. I wondered if he knew a good therapist because I needed psychiatric assistance.

"Do you want to know what I think?" he asked.

I sighed in annoyance. "Not really. But I expect you're going to tell me."

"You knew this plan was reckless and held no chance of success. And you went through with it anyway. Why?"

I swallowed hard, feeling uneasy and staring up at him. I had known that. And here I was. "Well, I thought I had a tiny chance of success."

He considered me with genuine curiosity. "What did you think would happen, little mortal, when you entered the bed chamber of the God of Death?"

"I did not think this would happen. I knew I might get caught, but I thought you would punish me. Not—whatever this is."

I saw confusion pulsing in his violet eyes. "Why aren't you frightened of me? I can name no other being that would enter my chambers intending to steal from me. Do you not value your life?"

"Just because I don't fear death doesn't mean I don't value my life. And I am afraid. But I need to go back to the temple. I *have* to."

"Why?"

I scoffed and pursed my lips. Like I'd reveal anything to him.

He shifted on top of me, and my heart fluttered again. I felt heat traveling up my neck into my face. My gaze dropped to his mouth. His lips were full. Gods, they looked soft, too. Somehow, I found myself wondering what it would be like if he kissed me. When I drew my eyes back up, I knew he'd noticed my stare.

"Why are you really in my bedroom in the middle of night, Cere? Why are you looking at me like that?" He still sounded curious, but the change in the timbre of his voice sent another involuntary pulse of desire through me.

I gave a halfhearted pull at my wrists. "You should let me go."

"That's what you want?" he asked, his voice smooth and smoky. "Because I'll give you what you want."

I opened my mouth and then closed it again. *What I want.* I couldn't remember the last time someone asked me what I wanted.

Thaos' head dipped and his lips brushed my cheek, making my chest constrict in excitement.

His body tensed and he jerked away almost as if he'd surprised himself, too. Then he shifted, like he was moving off of me. "As long as you promise not to attack me again."

A silly, stupid, shameful part of me wanted him to kiss me. What if I returned to the temple and the rest of my life was as it had been before? This would be my only chance. I could live as Cere, not the Pythia, for just a moment. Just a taste of life. That couldn't be so bad, could it? Tonight I could wear purple and be kissed. And tomorrow I could be pious.

"Wait."

He stopped, looking back down at me with expectant regard. I thought I saw a tense excitement in his gaze, but his expressions were difficult to read.

I closed my eyes, taking a deep breath. "I don't know what I want."

His face was suddenly near again. He brushed his nose against my cheek and my heart leapt. "Don't you?"

I sighed. "It's against the rules."

"I promise I won't tell." Echoing my own thoughts he added, "Tomorrow we can pretend nothing ever happened."

I opened my eyes again, surprised to see tendrils of black twisting in the purple of his irises. I bit my lip, considering him a moment longer. His eyes fell to my mouth, watching my nervous habit.

"I want you to kiss me."

Guilt crashed through me. I had to be the most unworthy Pythia of all time. I hadn't even been out of the temple for a full week, and I was asking a man to kiss me.

Except he was not a man. I'd seriously just asked the God of Death for a kiss.

I felt his weight on me increase, and then his lips brushed over mine. The shock of the contact rippled through my body, as if he'd thrown a rock into a calm pool.

A slice of panic cut through me, but it dissipated into something else. Something hot and bubbly. I froze, unsure of how to act. I was hardly breathing, and I couldn't tell if my heart was beating too fast or not at all.

His lips pressed against mine, and he *kissed* me. The touch seared into me, despite his cool skin. It was only a moment before he pulled away and gazed down at me. I opened my eyes, and they locked with his. The heated look he wore pierced all the way into some untouched part of my soul. He was searching my face, seeing how I would react.

"I liked that," I blurted.

"My pride enjoys hearing that, but I have to be honest and tell you that was barely a kiss."

I was overcome with shameless, reckless want. I *wanted* so badly. To kiss him. To live and be a normal woman for once.

I tugged at my hands, still held by him, and he let them go. Wrapping them around his neck, I pulled myself to him. We'd already crossed the line, and I wanted my kiss.

"Well, are you going to show me?"

A shudder traveled through him as his head dipped. When his mouth met mine, I felt his smile on my lips. For a moment, I thought of pulling away so I could see it. I had a feeling it was rare for him.

"So bold." His voice was thick with humor and something else. Something that made my heart skip before returning to its wild dance with newfound excitement.

He pressed his mouth to mine again, harder this time. My lips parted under the pressure, and I jumped when his tongue touched mine. This kiss differed from the first. It was passion and heat and promises of all the things that happen after two people kiss like this.

I copied his movements, angling my head and deepening the contact. He trembled again and his arm pushed around my waist, pulling me closer to him.

He tasted good. A rich, sweet flavor that I was struggling to draw a comparison to.

My flimsy nightgown was doing a poor job of acting as a barrier between us, and I felt every spot where his hard body molded into me. His weight caged me, pressing me into the bed, and it was *thrilling*. Wanton heat flushed through me, settling between my legs in a heavy, vicious ache.

His left hand traveled down my body, my heart leaping as his thumb brushed the side of my breast. He stopped at the hem of my nightgown, and then his cool fingers pushed up the length of my bare thigh. A strangled sound escaped me, a moan and a gasp. What he was doing frightened me, and not because I wanted him to stop, but because I *didn't*.

His hand rested on the top of my thigh, and the kiss faltered.

"We should stop," he whispered against my lips.

"Why?"

"Because I don't want to. I want to do so many things to you, and I don't want you to regret me in the morning."

I shuddered, and I opened my eyes to meet his heated gaze. He was acting responsibly, something I should at least attempt to mirror. It shouldn't go any farther than it already had. And I honestly didn't know if I would stop him if we continued—if he didn't stop.

Thaos leaned back and looked down between us, his breath catching. I followed his gaze and my cheeks flared when I realized the stretchy material of the nightgown had pulled down and to the right, exposing my breast. Arousal tightened it, and it was pert and wanting. My hands were free. I could and should cover it. But I didn't move, and my own brazen behavior stunned me.

When he realized I wasn't moving to cover myself, shock spread across his features. He looked to his right at the empty room. The black and purple swirled in his eyes while his jaw flexed several times. He appeared to be having a debate with himself and I noticed a muscle next to his eye tick. I watched him, curious about what he was thinking.

A shocked gasp left me as he quickly dipped his head. His mouth clamped down around the apex of my breast, and I felt a sharp, heady pull as he sucked on the bud of my nipple.

The action forced a foreign sound from me. It was a strange, embarrassing moan, and my fingers clasped into his hair. I thought I had ached before. This unfamiliar sensation ignited the pulse of desire in my core, and I became acutely aware of how close his hand was to where I wanted it to be.

I wondered if his thoughts were the same as mine because his grip on my thigh tightened. My hips moved of their own accord, pushing into him. He groaned and then lifted his head, pulling my nightgown back up.

"I definitely shouldn't have done that. I'm sorry," he muttered. "Not that it's an excuse, but I am usually in much better control of myself."

"I liked that too," I gushed.

A hiss of a laugh left him. "I noticed. And that's even more concerning."

"Why?"

"I have to go."

"What? How come?"

A flood of embarrassment coursed through me. Had I done something wrong?

"It's not you. It's the dead. I was sleeping before *someone* broke into my room, and I've put the souls off too long. Normally, I go right after I wake up."

"How do you do it? There's got to be so many."

He looked at the scythe. "That hourglass allows me to manipulate time. When I use it, only minutes pass in the real world, while I travel for hours in the void. If a soul accepts death, they travel to the Gate of Hades alone. The ones that fight their fate are my charges. I also have help. My sister, Keres, escorts those who die during battle." As he spoke, his thumb caressed my collar bone in small circles. It was a sweet, intimate touch that I hadn't been expecting.

"And, by the way, the scythe only works for me," he added with teasing admonishment.

A sheepish smirk spread across my lips, and I asked, "Do you choose who dies?"

"I only help people cross over if they're fighting the inevitable. I end their suffering. So, no, that would be my sisters, the three Goddesses of Fate. Aside from Hypnos, I tolerate them best. Death and Fate are intertwined. Our purposes depend on each other, so we feel connected in a way."

"How many siblings do you have?"

The corner of his mouth lifted in an almost smile. "Many. I'm sure I don't even know them all. My mother is productive. But I am closest to Hypnos because we're twins."

My mouth fell open. "Really? I'm a twin, too. My brother's name is Henry."

"Then you know the bond."

I frowned and broke his gaze. I did not cry anymore, and I wouldn't right now. Not in front of him.

"How long has it been since you've seen him?"

"About ten years."

He tensed, and the circles on my collarbone stopped. "I'm sorry."

"I just hope he's okay. That they all are."

He was quiet for several moments and then leaned up again and brushed his lips over mine. I gasped, resisting the sudden urge to pull him back to me. He sat up on the edge of the bed and ran his hand through his hair. I noticed the light outline of his wings.

"Where were your wings at dinner?"

He glanced over his shoulder at me and clicked his tongue. "So curious."

I blushed. I asked a lot of questions, but it was so different to have them answered instead of ignored. "Sorry."

"Don't be. Sometimes it's hard for me to understand a mortal life, where everything is fresh and new. When you live as long as I have, life becomes quite boring." He started pulling on his boots. "My wings are made of shadow. They appear when I want them to, or sometimes when my emotions are heightened."

I thought of the overseer's office. They'd been large and swirling with power then. They weren't like that now, but they were there.

"Are you wanting them to appear now?"

"No, I did not ask for them."

I wrinkled my brow. "Then why are they here?"

He looked over his shoulder at me. "Because you are not boring."

I stared at him, unsure of how to respond.

"I'll be back in a few minutes," he murmured, running his hand through his hair again. "You can wait for me. You don't have to go."

I tensed in surprise. He was asking me to stay? Fear, anxiety, and something much more shameful crashed through me. What would happen if I did? Now that I had somewhat returned to sanity, I knew how far I'd stepped over the line. He'd put his mouth on my—*Gods*. Heat flushed my face.

I couldn't stay. I couldn't sleep in Death's bed with him, even if nothing happened. He's the enemy. Although, I hadn't been thinking about that a few moments ago.

Thaos stood and pulled on a shirt and his robe. He returned to the bed and leaned over me to grab his scythe, my long-forgotten objective. He brushed his thumb over my cheekbone and then turned, cutting a slash in the room like he had before and disappearing. The black hole fused closed behind him, and all was quiet except for the crackle of the wood in the fireplace.

My knees wobbled as I stood, and I straightened my nightgown. I peeked out into the hallway and then hurried to my door. When I got inside, I sank to the floor with my head in my hands.

What had I just done? I would have to verify tomorrow that my gift was still intact. He had kissed me because I'd asked him to. And I had blatantly enjoyed it. I'd even told him so. My body still hummed with the memory of his contact, and that needy ache his touch had ignited wasn't going away. It had settled deep in my chest and my core, and I wondered if it would always exist there.

I played the events over in my head after I crawled under the covers of my bed. Something stood out above all else. When he'd said we needed to stop, it was because he didn't want me to regret him in the morning. He didn't say "because you'll lose your gift" or "because you're chosen," like I would've expected. Something about that made me feel strange, warm and cozy in a way I never had before.

Why couldn't he just have told me to go? Why did he ask me to stay? I wondered how he would react when he returned and found I was gone. Did he really care?

I told myself it didn't matter. Things could never go past where they had tonight. I needed to get back to the temple. To The Cause.

CHAPTER ELEVEN

The next morning, a knock at my door made me bolt upright. I cracked it open, expecting to see Thaos and unsure how I felt about that. Instead, I found a woman carrying a tray. She wore black slacks and a black polo shirt. Her short hair was a sandy blonde color, and she had a dusting of freckles underneath round, green eyes.

"Hello?"

"Hi. I'm Aeryn, I was told to bring you tea this morning." Her voice was shy and quiet, and she looked to be my age or maybe younger. I felt she was mortal, probably human.

"Oh. Come in, please."

I opened the door, and she set the tray down for me. I glanced at the clock. "It's later than I expected. Did I sleep too long?"

"Too long for what?"

"I don't know."

"Then I don't think you did," she said, giggling. "Hypnos usually has a late breakfast. You'll probably find him in the dining room."

"What about Thaos?"

Her eyebrows arched, and I realized it might be because I'd used his shortened name. "I believe he's already left this morning."

A guilty weight set on my chest. I was sure he had.

Unable to resist, I asked, "You are allowed to call them by their first names?"

Her forehead wrinkled. "Why wouldn't I be?"

"Aren't you a servant?" I thought of what consequences the servants at the temple might face if they ever called a guard something so casual.

She giggled. "No! I'm not a servant. I'm an employee."

"You get paid?"

"Yes, I do, and handsomely, so don't be afraid to call on me if you need anything. I am happy to help."

"Oh. Okay. Thank you, Aeryn."

She nodded and then left. I went to the wardrobe and opened it, shocked when I found the dresses from last night gone and leather leggings and cotton shirts instead. When I went to it, I'd been hoping for something comfortable.

Smiling, I took a pair out and slipped them on over the underwear I'd already pulled out. I found a bra and a simple t-shirt. I frowned when I noticed the shirts were all purple. That didn't feel okay since I'd left when he asked me to stay. Well, he didn't ask. He said I *could* stay. Was that different?

I opened and closed the wardrobe again, willing shirts of other colors to appear. They did, and I chose a scarlet red, feeling guilty that I wanted to wear the baby blue one. I reached to my thigh, wishing my dagger was there. I only had the small kitchen knife, and I tucked it into my boot.

When I finished dressing, I wandered down the hall, remembering my way to the dining room. Hypnos was there, as Aeryn had expected, and Thaos was not.

"Ah, Sleeping Beauty, good morning."

It took me a moment to realize Hypnos was talking to me. "Good morning. Did I sleep late?"

"Who cares? I'm a big fan of sleep."

I sat and gathered a few items on my plate.

"So, what do you do as the God of Sleep?"

"I spend a lot of time in the mortal world. I help people sleep and I take sleep away. It depends on my whims and how I'm feeling on that particular night."

"Is that why you talk so normal? I expected you to sound old."

"Yes, I try to keep up on the changing mortal world. Most gods do."

"Does Thaos?"

His eyebrows shot up, and he scrutinized me with an intense curiosity. "*Thaos,*" he said enunciating his brother's nickname, "couldn't care less, but I suppose I rub off on him."

"So, your brother reaps souls, and you…help people sleep? No offense, but that doesn't seem nearly as impressive."

He frowned, arching an eyebrow at me. "Every mortal spends half of their life asleep. I own, exclusively, half of the life span of every person on Earth. They need me. They worship me. They beg me to visit them. Where other Gods have fallen to the wayside, I am still much loved. There's even a song about me. It's catchy too. No one begs for Death to show up in the middle of the night."

I contemplated that, nodding in agreement. "Maybe that is *somewhat* impressive."

He clicked his tongue. "I see. You're into the broody, emo type. Like my brother."

I blushed, images of last night replaying in my head. "I'm not into any type. I'm pure."

He furrowed his brow again, looking like he wanted to say something. After a moment, he sighed. "Okay."

"Hypnos? What did Hades mean when he said people were stealing souls from him?"

"It's complicated."

"So you won't tell me?"

"I didn't say that." He looked contemplative. "Someone is meddling with death. They're doing something to people, and it's unnatural. They don't die, at least not completely. When Thaos goes to collect their soul, he finds a bloodthirsty monster. And they're strong, too. They've hurt him before, and that isn't a simple thing to do."

My eyes widened. I knew what he was talking about. I'd seen them, too. "Who is it? Who is changing them?"

"We don't know. But their souls are trapped in their bodies until they're dispatched with a blow to the spinal cord or brain. That means Hades hasn't been getting the souls he's supposed to have. His biggest character flaw is that he's incredibly greedy regarding his souls and his riches. Whoever it is, we don't understand what they're doing. Or why."

"Do you think it has something to do with the plague?" I asked, probing him for information. I already knew it did.

His eyes flashed for a moment, conveying his surprise. "You know about that?"

"I've seen it."

"What else have you seen?"

"Nothing that I can make sense of," I lied.

I wasn't about to tell him about seeing Thaos' eyes. I considered the prophecy of a baby born from shadow and sun, but I didn't mention that either.

"I see," he said, arching a brow. I sensed he knew I wasn't being honest.

The door banging open interrupted us. There were loud male voices laughing and talking up the hall, and then three young men entered.

They all looked the same, but different. The first had dark skin and features. His hair was as black as coal and hung in tight curls to his shoulders. Onyx eyes matched his hair, and he had a soft-featured, handsome face. I noticed he, like Hypnos, had wings on his head that looked like a golden crown.

The next brother, because it was obvious they were, had bronze skin and brown eyes. His face shape was identical to the first brother, and he had the same golden wings crowning a head of wavy medium brown hair.

The last brother had the same color of hair as Hypnos, like moonlight, and it was perfectly straight. He was a copy of Hypnos all around, with light golden skin and blue eyes. It was like they were duplicates of each other, although each one was slightly different.

Even a naïve fool like myself could figure out these were the sons of Hypnos I'd been told about.

"Father? Who is this?"

They sauntered to me in a way that made me blush and look at my eggs like they were the most interesting thing in the world. They all seemed to move as one, even though they were three different people.

"Cere, this is Morpheus, Phantasos, and Phobetor. My spawn. Collectively, they're called the Oneiroi—the Gods of Dreams," Hypnos answered. To his sons he added, "And she's free, but you'll have to fight your uncle for her if you want her."

My head snapped up. Gods, did he know about last night? Betrayal cut through my chest like a sharp blade. Thaos promised he wouldn't tell.

"Which uncle?"

Hypnos looked at them as if they annoyed him. "The one that lives here."

"What? No way. He doesn't like women. He doesn't like anyone."

"Well, go for it and find out if you don't believe me."

My eyes grew larger, and I looked at the three of them. They stared at me as if I'd turned from a woman into a poisonous toad. After exchanging weary glances, they shuffled to the seats across from me. I watched with baited horror and respect as they consumed more food than I would've ever thought possible in one sitting. Maybe this was why the table was always stocked with enough food to feed a small army.

"Where's your mother?" Hypnos asked.

"In town, you know Mom. Life's a party."

"She's supposed to be the Goddess of Relaxation, but she doesn't seem to do much of that," he complained.

"The Goddess of Relaxation *and* Hallucinations. She's everyone's favorite party guest."

"Did you tell her I'd like to see her?"

"We did."

"And?"

They all snickered like schoolboys. "She says that you are more than welcome to find your ex or a nymph if you want to get laid. She's not the jealous type like Hera."

I noticed that they all talked in turn, one after the other, and somehow seemed to know what the next brother would say.

My face flushed in embarrassment for Hypnos and his mouth fell into a deep frown. "Maybe I will then."

They giggled again. "We will make sure and tell her that."

"Is there anything else you want? Or did you just come to eat my food?"

"The food," they all said in unison.

After several beats of silence, Morpheus asked, "So who are you?"

I glanced up and realized he was speaking to me. "I'm Cere." My eyebrows furrowed in confusion. We'd just been introduced.

"We know your name. Who are you?" the next brother said.

I stared at them with my mouth slightly open and my eyes slid to Hypnos. He seemed distracted by his own sullen thoughts.

"I'm Ca-ree," I said again, enunciating my name this time. Was something wrong with them?

They all giggled, and my face flushed in confusion.

"Who are you to our uncle?" the third asked, more tenderly this time, as if he understood they were confusing me.

"I'm no one to him."

"You must be. He's never had a woman here before."

"I'm here because Hades wants me to be."

"Why?"

"None of your business," Hypnos interjected. He didn't want them to know Hades had the Pythia stashed here. Did he not trust his own children?

They all tipped their heads, scrutinizing me with the same expression on their faces.

"Interesting," the second brother commented.

I cleared my throat. "So, what do the Gods of Dreams do exactly?"

Hypnos sighed, pinching the bridge of his nose. I didn't understand. I was only trying to be polite. Was that wrong?

The Oneiroi grinned at me with the same wolfish smile painted on each of their faces. Morpheus sat forward.

"We make your wildest dreams come true, love."

"What does that mean?"

They all snickered again. The middle brother, Phantasos, cooed, "She's so sweet."

The third agreed. "Innocent."

"Let's just say we're a team. We do everything together. *Everything*," Phantasos said, lifting his eyebrows twice in a gesture I didn't initially understand.

It took me a moment, but realization dawned on me. My face flushed all the way to the roots of my hair.

"Gods," I blurted. "How does that even work?"

My question caused a beat of stunned silence to echo through the room. When the Oneiroi recovered, they burst into a fit of laughter.

"Maybe not so innocent!"

Morpheus leaned forward, reaching for my hand, but I pulled it away instinctively. He looked offended for a moment, but his expression shifted back to humor. "Well, I'll explain. See, you would—" He started motioning with his hands and I titled my head, curious.

"Okay," Hypnos interrupted, drawing out the word. "That's enough. She doesn't need to know because it's never going to happen."

Their heads all turned to their father, glaring. "You're no fun. That's why we like Mom better."

He returned their look and then lifted his hand with his middle finger extended.

They all chuckled and stood with impressive synchronization, seeming to tell the truth about only wanting food. I realized their plates were empty. That had to be some kind of record.

"Well, Pops, we will see you when we see you. Hades has us doing many things to prepare for the festival."

"I'm *so* looking forward to it," Hypnos said, picking at his plate with his back curved in a pouty slouch.

"That was sarcasm," I announced proudly.

Hypnos' lips curved on one side and the Oneiroi looked at me like I was very odd, and I supposed maybe I was. Saying nothing else, they piled down the hall.

I watched them go, still wondering how that would work. "I have so many questions."

Hypnos looked at me with raised brows. "I refuse to explain that to you. I'll admit I have fun provoking you, but foursomes involving my own children is where I draw the line."

"That's rude. You shouldn't enjoy provoking someone."

He shrugged. "I'm thousands of years old. I'm bored and apathetic."

"Fine, if you refuse to answer those questions. Then what's the festival?"

"A celebration we have to mark the return of Persephone, our queen. She lives in her mother Demeter's realm for half of the year. It's the only grand party we have down here. The Olympians even grace us with their presence."

I nodded in understanding, but another question burned on my tongue. "So—" I bit my lip, picking at my silverware. "He told you about last night?"

He sat up, livelier than he'd been all morning. His eyes whipped towards me in excitement. "Who? Told me what about last night? What happened last night?"

I froze, feeling like an absolute idiot. "Nothing happened."

"Liar!" he hissed. "Oh my *Me*, you can't do this to me. What happened last night?"

My cheeks flushed, and I stood. "Thank you for breakfast. Is there a library here?"

I wanted to read while I was here. I needed to find out everything I could about the gods before I returned to the temple. I had to confirm that the master was Apollo. I had to prove they were all wrong about him.

"I'll tell you where it is if you tell me what happened last night."

I rolled my eyes. "I'll just ask Aeryn."

He threw up his arms in exasperation, yelling at my back as I rushed from the room. "You are killing me, Sleeping Beauty!"

Aeryn was helpful, as I expected, and introduced me to a massive library. More so than I could ever have imagined. It made me wonder what Hades' library looked like. I selected several books that interested me and padded up to my room, terrified that if I stayed, Hypnos would corner me for the truth about last night.

Pouring some tea, I read until my head hurt. I now understood much more about Apollo and his relationship with the Pythia. Apparently, a long time ago, he'd defeated an enormous serpent at the temple of Delphi on Earth. There he established his own temple with the Pythia, an oracle that famous people, mortal kings and various other leaders, had visited from all over the world.

Now, he had his own realm in the Olympus dimension that he'd also called Delphi. The Pythia usually lived there with him.

Had that been the temple they had kept me in? Thaos said it was strange, and that it wasn't in Apollo's realm. Plus, I didn't think the master resided there, but it wasn't like I had freedom to walk the grounds alone and explore.

To celebrate his victory, Apollo also created the Pythian Games, which still happened in his realm every one hundred years, even though humans didn't officially celebrate them anymore. The Pythia, me, was to attend the games, and had for centuries. Or at least the past versions of me had. We were now five years overdue for when the last games should've been held.

If Apollo had me, why hadn't we just held the games like normal? Why was my life such a secret? Maybe the master was Apollo, and he was keeping me more protected than usual in that strange, in-between realm. Or he had lied, and Hypnos and Thaos were telling the truth. Maybe the person I'd been with wasn't Apollo.

The thought made my stomach churn. Being away from the temple made me realize I'd been kept in a constant state of obscure understanding during my time there. They only gave me small snippets of information. Even the name of our movement, The Cause, was vague.

Closing the book, I sighed. I had uncovered plenty, but it only created more questions.

I took a deep breath to center myself like Laurenth had taught me and went to the balcony. The lake was more like a very strange marsh. It seemed dead, which was fitting for the Underworld. There were no animals that I could see, such as birds or small mammals. I thought maybe I'd glimpsed a fish, but I wasn't sure.

On the other side of the beach, the forest was eerily beautiful. The leaves were purple on one side and black on the other. Their color scheme made me think of Thaos, and I glanced at his balcony with a blush.

I bit my lip. I was tired of being cooped up inside, so I wandered until I found the spiral staircase. I knew there were a few employees here, but I didn't run into anyone.

The cave was dark and damp, smelling of the deepest earth. I walked along the beach of the marsh for a small stretch, but I didn't touch the water. Every instinct I had told me that was a bad idea.

A breeze drifted through the trees behind me, making the leaves whisper. I turned and walked towards it, curious because I hadn't felt any wind in the Underworld. The forest was dense, and I couldn't see more than ten feet past the tree line. I reached up to touch a leaf as it spun in the wind.

Feeling bold, I stepped into the trees and walked a few feet. I wondered if I could get through this forest and emerge somewhere where I could find a way out of the Underworld. Hypnos mentioned there was a town somewhere. I looked over my shoulder, contemplating.

I needed to get back to the temple. Apollo or not, the master had to stop the plague. The forest may be dangerous, but I had my little knife, and I knew how to use it.

I kept going, surprised when a cold breeze danced against my skin. It seemed the wind only blew here in these trees.

I hadn't made it very far when a woman stepped out of seemingly nowhere. She wore a sparkling, magnificent golden gown. Her hair was nearly white and so long the braid brushed the ground behind her. I gaped at her beauty, stunned by her abrupt appearance. Snapping back to reality, I quickly reached in my boot, snatching the knife, and holding it towards her.

"Who are you?"

Her face was strained, like she was in pain. "I'm not supposed to do this, but you're following the wrong path."

"What's that mean?"

I glanced around the forest floor. As far as I could tell, I wasn't following any path.

"Your true fate lies behind you. You will only find your death in these woods. That's all I can say. Don't tell anyone you saw me."

I blinked, and she was gone. Just ahead of me, I heard a strange, eerie howl. Being smart enough to heed a warning that was thrown right in my face, I turned on my heel and ran. My adrenaline spiked as I was overcome with the feeling of being chased. I swore I could hear the breaking of sticks behind me but didn't dare a glance over my shoulder.

I burst out of the tree line and onto the sand of the beach, stumbling the last few steps. I whirled, expecting to find something right on my heels and was astonished to see nothing but thick forest. I tried to calm my ragged breathing, stoked to life from panic and exertion.

"You shouldn't be out here."

I yelped in surprise and turned to find Thaos behind me. His hood was up, concealing his face. I hid my blade in the sleeve of my shirt, hoping he hadn't seen it.

"What?"

"Did you go in there?" I could hear the shock and admonishment in his tone.

My fingers found a loose thread on my shirt. "No."

"I truly hope you never have to lie to save your life because you are terrible at it."

My hands balled into fists at my sides. "What do you care if I was in there or not?"

"This forest is full of things from your worst nightmares. And they'll all kill you, slowly and painfully. Then they'll eat you, bones and all. It's not called the Woods of Woe for nothing. Don't *ever* go in there."

I wanted to tell him I could take care of myself and that I couldn't care less about his scolding. I wasn't a child.

But, I chose the *mature* thing and changed the subject. "Where were you today?"

"I had things to do."

"What things?"

He pushed his hood back. "I got you this."

He held up a ring, a simple silver band. When I looked closer, I saw it had an inscription engraved on it in a language I didn't recognize.

"What is it?"

"It will keep others from recognizing that you're the Pythia. Another precaution to keep you safe."

He gently took my right hand and slid it on my third finger. I watched intently, surprised by the intimacy of it. He reached into his robe and removed my dagger.

"And this. It's yours."

"You're giving me back the dagger that I stabbed you with?"

"Do you plan on stabbing me again?"

I hitched up one shoulder. "I don't know. It's possible."

The corner of his lip curled, and I took it from his hand.

"You should go back into the house, Cere. I have to go."

He took the scythe off of his back and cut a doorway.

"Thaos," I said, suddenly shy. "Um…about last night."

He tilted his head, expression unreadable. I didn't even know what I wanted to say. I bit my lip, trying to find the words.

Finally, he spoke instead. "What about it? I told you. It never happened."

I watched him turn and go, and then the doorway disappeared. A blossom of discomfort opened in my chest, even though I knew it shouldn't be there.

CHAPTER TWELVE

Aeryn knocked on my door again the next morning, and when I opened it, I found someone else in the hall with her. He was a strong looking young man with dark hair and red-brown ochre skin that seemed to be blessed by the sun. The man was dressed in a plain but substantial leather fighting cuirass. The sword strapped to his side caught my eye. It was Mastix. A long sword, most likely to be wielded with two hands.

"Cool sword," I told him while Aeryn readied the tea behind me in the room.

He looked surprised. "Oh, yeah. Thanks."

"And—who are you?"

His brow furrowed, and he shifted on his feet. "Didn't he tell you? I'm your guard, Ulther."

"Excuse me?"

"Uh, I'm supposed to guard you."

I offered him a tight smile. "I don't need a guard, but thank you anyway."

"Sorry, my lady, but Thanatos said I am to stay by your side. And I'm more scared of him than I am of you."

"Well, that is unwise of you," I huffed, slamming the door.

Aeryn was behind me, trying to conceal a giggle.

"I don't need a guard," I told her, as if she could do something about it.

"It's just an extra precaution. But I believe you when you say you don't need a guard."

"Am I a prisoner now?"

She balked. "Of course not! You are still free to go wherever you like. Ulther just has to go with you. Don't worry, he's nice." A soft blush colored her cheeks when she added the last comment, but I was too angry to acknowledge it.

I crossed my arms as she walked by me and left the room. How dare he? I didn't need a babysitter. Was this because I entered the woods yesterday?

I dressed faster than I ever had and went out into the hall, huffing again as Ulther followed me. Stomping into the dining room, I was pleased to see Thaos seated next to his brother this morning.

I glared at the God of Death, not missing Hypnos' raised brows.

"What is this?" I asked, hands on my hips.

"What is what?"

I stepped aside to present Ulther, who stood in the doorway looking uncomfortable.

Thaos crossed his arms, leaning back in his chair.

"Your guard."

"I don't need one."

"I disagree."

"I don't care."

He stared at me, and I didn't miss the shock that appeared for a breath of a second. Hypnos looked to be somewhere between a burst of laughter and a heart attack.

"Well, he is your guard, and you're only making it harder on him because he will do as I say."

"I refuse to be treated like some—some prisoner here. I don't need to be escorted around the house."

"You aren't a prisoner."

"Is this because I went into the forest?"

"So you admit you lied to me?"

My cheeks reddened.

Hypnos gasped, chuckling. "The Woods of Woe? You're wild, Sleeping Beauty."

"Well, now that you've told me they're dangerous, I won't go in them."

"Why don't I believe that? We both know you're reckless."

My eyes widened because I knew he was referring to the fact I'd broken into his room. Hypnos glanced between us, appearing delighted by this interaction.

"You know nothing about me," I hissed, my face heating.

"I know enough. And I'm supposed to keep you safe. That's what I'm doing."

My hands balled into fists, and I offered him the most withering glare I could muster. "I dislike you."

His eyebrows shot up, but I turned on my heel, shoving past poor Ulther, who was looking at me like I'd lost my mind. I fumed my way to the library. My guard stood vigil all day while I read books and cursed Thaos under my breath.

Aeryn brought me lunch at midday, and I noticed there was a lemon tart. I didn't eat it. As if he could sway me with pastry.

When it was getting dark, I stomped back upstairs and went to my door.

I leveled a glare at Ulther. "You're standing out here all night too? Don't you have to sleep?"

He either didn't notice or ignored my look. "No, my lady. I'm a demigod, son of the Goddess of Day, and I require very little sleep."

"If you're the son of the Goddess of Day, why are you down here?"

I had learned all twelve Olympians and Hades each had their own realms, similar to this one, with cities and land of their own. Lesser Gods of similar power usually chose to live in whatever realm suited them best. Ulther should be in Apollo's realm.

"I like it better down here. My uncles leave me alone and let me do what I wish."

It took me a moment to compute what he was saying. "Hypnos and Thanatos are your uncles?"

He nodded. "My mother is their sister, Hemera, Goddess of Day."

I gave him a clipped nod and then closed the door. Feeling guilty, I opened it and mumbled, "Goodnight, Ulther. I'm sorry." It wasn't his fault that he had to be here.

"Goodnight, my lady. And it's okay, he told me you were vicious." His lips twitched, and I could tell he wanted to smile.

Oh my Gods.

My temper flared again, but I reminded myself it wasn't Ulther's fault. "Just call me Cere, okay?"

He nodded, and I closed the door again. I showered and then slipped into a nightgown and robe. The fireplace must be magic as well because it always burned low.

I drank my tea and stared at the flames. I contemplated whether I should tell the brothers more about my visions involving the undead and maybe the child of sun and shadow. Hypnos had seemed genuine in his confusion when we discussed the creatures, and I couldn't imagine why Hades would be involved if he wanted their souls.

I looked up and realized it was well after midnight. I didn't feel like sleeping and instead went out to my balcony. Looking over, I half expected to see Thaos there. He wasn't, and I assured myself it did not disappoint me in the slightest.

I stared at the marsh, gasping as the water changed. Bursts of glowing color came to life. Yellow fluorescent flowers, maybe? I wanted to go look, but I didn't want to make Ulther walk all the way down there. Not that I thought he'd mind. I watched them for over an hour, marveling at how even the land of the dead could be so beautiful.

The next two days went by similarly. I always started breakfast with Hypnos, and I was sure if I continued spending time with him I would soon be a master of sarcasm.

Then it was the library for most of the day, but the amount of mythology for me to read was intimidating and I had to pace myself.

I helped Glendyl with dinner both days, and I enjoyed those moments the most. It felt nice to do something for myself. It made me feel accomplished even if it was only peeling and mashing potatoes. Plus, the old cook comforted me. Most of the time, we worked in silence and when we spoke, he taught me about food and seasonings. He treated me like a normal person and never pried into my life as the Pythia. It seemed so ordinary compared to everything else.

Ulther followed me diligently, and I felt bad for him, as it had to be dreadfully boring. I didn't see Thaos at all, and I tried and failed to convince myself that it didn't matter if I did.

I was used to living a mundane life. Doing the same thing over and over. At the temple, I'd accepted it was my fate, but now after only a few days I was growing annoyed and restless. I wanted to see more. I wanted freedom while I had a chance.

It was late, and I was out on the balcony again, sitting with my legs hanging through the bars of the railing. As expected, the yellow lights flared under the surface of the water. They always started around midnight, and I'd watched them from here both nights since I'd first spotted them.

I decided I was going to see them. Up close and without Ulther. I grabbed my dagger and strapped it to my leg, just in case.

Using my sheets to make a rope, I climbed down the balcony, falling to the sand below with a soft thud. I only had my nightgown and robe on, but I wouldn't take long. Walking across the beach, I wiggled my bare toes in the sand and grinned.

On closer inspection, the lights were as I suspected. Fluorescent flowers. Up close, I could see that they were white. Five pointed petals opened when they bloomed, and the insides glowed gold. I watched with a grin as a tiny fish swam into one and then—I jumped back in surprise as the petals snapped shut. It took me a moment to realize that it was eating the fish. I sat in the sand and watched, amazed.

Behind me in the Woods of Woe, I heard a disturbing noise. Jumping to my feet, I turned, and my hand drifted to my dagger. As I listened, I noticed the surrounding air on the beach was deathly still, but the leaves on the trees danced.

"Help! Please!"

It was a woman's voice, followed by the distinct cry of an infant. It sounded just inside the tree line. I started running and then faltered. I shouldn't go in there. I should get Ulther or Thaos. Turning, I started back towards the mouth of the cave, but then I heard it again. The voice was frenzied and panicked.

"Oh Gods, please! My baby! Help!"

My adrenaline surged, and I ran in. It might be too late if I tried to get help. I ducked under the first low-hanging branches and into the woods, feeling the powerful cold tendrils of fear crawling up my spine. Ignoring them, I pressed forward.

My breath was shallow, and I looked around as the cool forest floor soaked into my bare feet. I couldn't see anything for more than a couple of yards. I'd never known trees to grow so close together, my body having to bend and weave just to get through. A strange mist hung between the trunks, stifling any visibility I might've had. Wincing, I bent and pulled a splinter from the bottom of my foot.

The wail of the infant picked up just in front of me. I stepped carefully, but quickly. Looking back over my shoulder, I noticed I couldn't see the beach anymore. I flashed back to running lost in the vineyard at the temple, and I had to suppress a new wave of claustrophobic panic that surged through me.

The woods broke, and I walked into a large clearing. An awful feeling came over me, making the hair on the back of my neck stand up and tingle with ominous warning. The grass, like the leaves, was an odd shade of blackish purple. It floated in the breeze that seemed to only exist inside the tree line. I swallowed hard. What lay in the middle of the clearing had my heart seizing and telling every sane part of me to run and not look back.

An infant's cradle sat alone, rocking in the breeze. The soft creak of the wood whined with every forward and back motion. I walked to it, my panicked eyes flicking across the tree line. It was so quiet that I could hear only my breath and the gentle, steady groan of the cradle.

I reached for the pink blanket that covered it. My quivering hand refused to steady as I grabbed the material, and part of me was stunned at how soft it was. Ripping it back, I found the cradle was empty except for a doll and a rattle.

My lungs gulped for air, my heart plunging and flipping in my chest. The doll had two sticks stabbed into its eyes, and one through its mouth. The air chilled, becoming so cold that my next breath produced a small cloud of steam.

I heard it then, just a whisper of a sound. My neck hair sprung to life again, and the goosebumps traveled down my back. Someone, or something, stood just behind me. A sound rolled through it, a popping crackle of a growl that made a violent tremor of dread course through me. The smell of rot invaded my nostrils, so vile that nausea churned my stomach. I gripped my dagger, not wanting to turn, but knowing I would die if I didn't.

I whirled and found the clearing empty. The stench remained and out of the corner of my eye, I caught a shred of movement. Ducking, I narrowly escaped having my head torn off by—by the most nightmarish creature I'd ever seen.

I couldn't even scream as my eyes fell upon it. Only a strange fearful groan escaped me. I stumbled back, looking up at it. It was twice my size, standing well over ten feet tall. The body was humanoid, but disgustingly gaunt. Sick looking dark green skin was stretched tightly over its skeleton like a torn latex suit. The ragged bones jutted out, as if the creature hadn't eaten in years.

My stare settled on its mouth, repulsed but too frightened to look away. Jagged teeth, blackened and rotting, were framed by bloody, tattered lips that hung in pieces like it had chewed them to shreds. Its eyes and nose weren't there. I stared into the black pits, searching for any kind of human emotion and finding none. What hair it had looked like strands of oil and some parts of its scalp were bare, so the tendrils hung in strange, irregular chunks.

It opened its mouth and a long black tongue fell well past its chin, drool dripping from it. I'd never felt fear like this before. It hollowed out every place in my body and I felt like a solid block of ice. The terror rendered me unable to move, scream, or think. My breath erupted in tiny, rapid puffs of steam as if the mere presence of this creature brought winter to the clearing.

It turned its head to the side and screeched, a sound so disturbing I knew it would haunt me for the rest of my life. Which was shaping up to be only a few more seconds.

It lunged at me with such speed I could only react by hurling myself out of its path. My instincts from training with Laurenth kicked in and I stuck out my foot, tripping the fiend. It only stumbled a moment and then turned on me again, lurching forward with its mouth open and ready, intent on feasting on my flesh. I avoided it and swung out with my dagger, catching it in the chest. The blade sliced its tight skin, and I felt bile rise in my throat as maggots poured from the wound.

It screeched in pain and anger, turning and slashing its claws across my shoulder. Wearing only a nightgown and robe, the razor-sharp tips sliced through my flesh like a knife through an over-boiled potato. A flurry of pain erupted from the wound, and I blindly thrust my dagger towards its hand. I met resistance and then heard three small thumps. Looking down, I realized I'd severed some of its fingers. Maggots poured out of the nubs on the ground.

Its other hand slashed at my face, and I reached up to block it, like I would in a regular fight. It hit me with such power that it took me off of my feet and flung me to my back. The landing was forceful, smacking a painful huff of air from my lungs.

I didn't have time to recover as it was on me, jumping over me and landing with its feet on either side of my rib cage. It slashed at me again and I struck with my dagger. I managed to impale the creature's hand, but it ripped the blade out of my grasp.

The monster wailed in pain and then stepped onto my chest. Tremendous pain blossomed, and my eyes bulged with the pressure. It held me there, and then bent so it was inches from my face.

Drool from its tongue dripped onto my cheeks and lips, and then it licked me from my collar bone to my forehead. I smelled its rotting breath as it made an animalistic sound—a disturbing chortle of pleasure. I clawed at its leg, trying to move it so I could draw a breath, but I came to the stark realization that this was it. This thing was going to rip me to pieces as it consumed me alive.

I closed my eyes, clawing at its face with every bit of tenacity I had left. I heard a strange squeal, and I hoped maybe I had inflicted some kind of painful wound in my frenzy.

But when I looked at the beast, a blade protruded from its chest. Someone had stabbed it in the back. The creature lurched forward, and the blade pulled free. Maggots rained down into my face and I gagged. The creature's hand impaled by my dagger dropped close to my head, and I grabbed the handle, ripping it free and then sticking it into the empty right socket where its eye should be.

It sprang back off of me, wailing and clawing at the handle that now protruded from its face. I rolled to my side, and a hand clasped my arm and yanked me to my feet. I smacked at it, panicking and thinking the fiend had me again. When I felt the cool grip, I stopped.

Desperation drove my actions as I wiped at the maggots, trying to get them off of me. I couldn't tell if I succeeded, because my entire body crawled with the sensation of the tiny wriggling larvae.

Angry violet eyes met mine, and I felt my cheeks burn. A very prideful part of me wished the creature had eaten me alive.

"I know you can't be serious," he hissed at me. "Not even *three days* after I tell you not to enter the Woods of Woe, what do you do?"

"Well, it's past midnight, so technically you told me that four days ago," I whispered.

His eyes widened in shock. "You are—"

He wanted to say very rude things to me. However, the monster intervened on my behalf, and Thaos had to turn and face it again.

I could sense it was unsure now, as it stalked around Death. I could feel the hunger rolling off it as it watched me, apparently only interested in feasting on my flesh.

"Why doesn't it want to eat you?"

He shot me a look of exasperation. Yes, I was going to ask a question right now.

"I'm too old," he said, straight-faced, but I sensed he was being sarcastic.

"Probably bitter, too," I hissed.

He glared at me, but I thought I saw amusement hiding in his eyes.

My dagger still stuck from the creature's eye socket, and moved in the direction it was looking, giving away its intent. The handle shifted to Thaos as it launched an attack. I watched with my mouth hanging open as the two exchanged aggressive blows.

Laurenth, to me, had been an extraordinary fighter, and I realized she would stand no chance in a duel with the God of Death. If she had the element of surprise, then maybe she could inflict some damage, but it was a firm maybe.

I understood how insignificant I was and why I should fear Thaos. I couldn't believe I'd stabbed him. A small sense of pride bloomed at the fact I'd even managed it, but I tamped it down and scolded myself for thinking such horrible things.

The beast lunged and Thaos made a defensive move, compounded by an offensive one. The scythe sliced through the flesh and bone of the fiend's upper arm, severing it. Maggots sprayed everywhere, hitting me in the face again. I blinked rapidly in shock as a fresh wave of nausea washed over me. The creature wailed and then retreated into the woods. Thaos turned to me, eyes burning with fury.

I had my hand clasped over my upper arm where my flesh lay open like a gutted fish. With the cold air gone, I felt the blood pouring more rapidly through my fingers. He was in front of me now, and his hand clasped over mine to add more pressure. I bit back a scream of pain and my wide eyes found his glare.

"Move your hand," he ordered.

I did as he asked and he put his hand directly on the wound, squeezing. I couldn't stop the cry of pain this time. The cool touch of his skin was trying to stanch the blood loss, but it wasn't enough. Lines of tension bracketed his mouth, and I noticed the black tendrils of shadow overtaking the violet of his eyes.

"*What*," he growled, "are you doing out here?"

"I thought there was a baby."

He shook his head in disbelief. "There was no baby. It was a trick."

"Well, obviously," I mumbled, earning a look of admonishment from him.

Maggots wriggled on his shoulders and in his hair, and I felt them on me, too. I closed my eyes, feeling woozy and thinking I might vomit. I heard the slash of the scythe and then realized he'd opened a tear in reality again.

"Oh no," I said, tensing and trying to back up. I didn't want to experience that free fall again.

"Oh yes. That creature is not the only thing that calls these woods home. Your blood will bring them all."

He grabbed me and stepped through into the void. I slammed my eyes shut. My stomach jumped like I'd missed the last two steps on a set of stairs, and then I vomited as we stood in the cave's entrance. He kept his hand on my arm as I revisited my dinner and late-night tea. I was still present enough to feel mortified that I had thrown up twice in front of him now.

My head was spinning when I finished, and I tried to fall to my knees, but he held me up.

"I'm okay," I slurred.

"You're losing too much blood." I noticed the anger had left his tone, and he sounded concerned.

I tried to say something else, but only an unintelligible mumble of sound came out. He cursed and then picked me up as I succumbed to the blackness of unconsciousness.

_____

When I woke up, Hypnos sat next to my bed. He was, in fact, knitting a sweater and when my eyes found him, he glanced up at me.

"Sleeping Beauty, the slayer of beasts, awakens," he said, grinning.

I brought my hand to my injured shoulder and winced as I palpated the large bandage there.

"Yeah, it was a doozy. I am so glad you came to live with us, though. You don't know how boring things are and then you show up and it's like I'm on the edge of my seat wondering what's going to happen next. Is she going to yell at my brother, Death, in front of other people, something no other would dare do? Or is she going to take on the wendigo of the woods her first week in Hades? In her jammies, too! Why not, right? I'm loving it, honestly. Sleeping Beauty with a hint of psychopath."

I glared at him. "I thought there was a baby."

His face pinched with mock sympathy. "Yeah, fell for the ol' wailing infant trick. That's a little embarrassing."

My cheeks flushed. "It sounded so real."

"Well, yeah. Do you think they're going to get gullible idiots to wander into the woods with a subpar fake baby?"

I glared at him again. "Maybe I'll stab *you* next."

"There's our homicidal psycho," he cooed. I looked around for a weapon, glowering at him.

The skin around his eyes crinkled with a broad smile. "Hey, it's happened to all of us, right?"

"Really?"

"No. No, definitely not. I was just trying to make you feel better, but I'm terrible at it."

"Yes, you are," I said, a small smile cracking my lips. But, maybe he wasn't.

"I heard you cut off some digits and crammed that little pig sticker of yours in its eye. Pretty impressive for a mortal."

"Thanks." I'd only stuck it in the eye because Thaos had arrived. Thinking of him, I glanced at the door. "Is he mad?"

"I mean, a little. I believe his exact words were 'this woman is insufferable.'"

I giggled because his impression of his brother's flat, cool voice was spot on. But the words made me wince, and I put my head back against the pillow. "He hates me."

"Oh, he far from hates you. And he hates that."

"What?"

He just smiled, his blue eyes shining with amusement.

"What was that thing out there?" I asked.

"It's called a wendigo. That's what humans named it, anyway. It's the personification of greed. They say the most selfish people turn into them after they die, and they have insatiable appetites for mortal flesh. They always feel like they're starving and are never full no matter how much they eat."

"I didn't know things like that existed."

Hypnos tilted his head and shrugged. "Most of the things humans tell stories about exist."

I shuddered, remembering its sunken black eyes. And the maggots. "Why doesn't someone just kill it?" I was pretty sure Thaos could.

"Oh, old Wendi," he said, waving his hand dismissively, "He makes a great guard dog. As long as our guests stay out of the Woods of Woe."

I stared at him, trying to figure out if he was serious. As far as I could tell, he was.

I pulled back the bandage and my eyebrows creased. Four large pink slashes glared back at me, but the injury should be much worse. I knew they would heal fast thanks to my shifter blood, but not that fast.

"How did this happen? They're almost healed."

His expression shifted to mirror my own curiosity. "You should ask Thaos that question. I don't feel it's my place to say."

CHAPTER THIRTEEN

I took it easy for the next two days, making sure the wound healed as thoroughly as possible. Feeling as good as new, I sat down at breakfast on the third day, finding Hypnos there and wondering if he ever left this table.

"Your brother is avoiding me," I said, leveling him with an annoyed frown.

He looked up from his knitting, and I wanted to slap the amused expression from his face. "Good morning to you as well. And no comment."

"It's very immature."

"Maybe it is. He'll come around. He can't resist you."

My eyes widened, but I didn't ask him to elaborate. "Have you heard anything else about the undead?"

"No, we have found nothing new. As strange as it may seem, a lot of resources are being devoted to Persephone's festival."

"That seems silly."

"It's a big deal for Hades. Their love story is...odd."

"You mean how he kidnapped her, so her mom tried to kill the world with famine to get her back. And was somewhat successful in doing so. Now Persephone spends spring and summer in Demeter's realm, but autumn and winter down here."

"You've been studying. But, yes, it's a *grand* event."

"How does Persephone feel about Hades then? Is it like your marriage?"

He looked like I'd slapped him, and I realized I'd overstepped.

"Sorry," I mumbled.

"No, it's okay. It must be bad if a socially inept, silly little mortal like you can tell."

I frowned at the insult, but let it go, considering I was rude first.

"As far as I know, Persephone enjoys being the Queen of the Underworld. Demeter, her mother and his sister, still resents him though."

I choked on the piece of fruit I was chewing. "Persephone is his niece?"

He chuckled. "Yes, twice over. Her father is Zeus, brother to both Hades and Demeter. Welcome to the world of the Gods."

I wrinkled my nose, and eyes still wide from that revelation I asked, "Can I go to the festival?"

"Uh, no. The chances of that happening lie somewhere between slim and none."

I frowned. "Why can't I go? Aren't other mortals allowed to go?"

I was aware I was whining, but I wanted to see a festival.

"They are. But they aren't being sought out by Apollo. And it's possible whoever had possession of you before us wants you back."

Possession. That word scratched over my skin like a wool sweater.

"Apollo had me before," I said, but even I knew I sounded unconvinced. The more I thought about it, the more I suspected it hadn't been him. There was just no reason he would hide me.

Hypnos sighed and looked at me with sympathy. "Look, Sleeping Beauty, I know you want to believe that, but he didn't. Someone had you, and it was not Apollo. He likes his Pythia, and he has been desperate in his search for you. Throwing a fit about it, really."

"What will happen if he finds me?"

"He will claim you. He is the one who established the Pythia at Delphi. Since you've been reading, I'm sure you know he shot a gigantic serpent a bunch of times and killed it. The serpent actually had a name, but I can't remember it. You can't believe how much you can forget when you live this long." He looked pensive, as if trying to remember, and then shrugged. "Anyway, establishing the temple at Delphi is a nice way of saying he stole it."

"From who?"

"The serpent guarded that temple for Gaia, a Titan and the Goddess of Earth. Apollo stole the temple and the Oracle. So, it is his right to have you."

His right.

"I'm tired of being treated like a possession," I hissed, stabbing at my food.

"I'm sorry, but in the world of the gods, a mortal woman is one."

"It's horrible," I said, feeling annoyed and depressed. "I still feel like I don't get to make any choices of my own."

"You have more freedom than you did before, right?"

"Yes," I admitted. "But it only makes me want more."

"Well, let's just get through the festival and then maybe we can figure something out."

"I would still like to go."

He sighed. "I'll see what I can do, but Thaos won't go for it."

"If he ever speaks to me again, I guess I'll ask him."

"He will speak to you again," Hypnos answered, a wry smile pulling his lips. "I told you he can't stay away."

After breakfast, I spent the day in the library again, but ended up napping most of the afternoon on the couch. When I woke up, I looked at Ulther.

"Why didn't you wake me?"

"Was I supposed to?"

"I guess not."

I glanced at his sword. "Ulther, would you like to train with me? I used to train several times a week and I miss it."

My body was growing accustomed to these lazy days in the library, and I needed to stay in fighting shape. I didn't know when I might need to defend myself.

Ulther looked unsure. "You mean train with weapons? I'm a demigod. I wouldn't want to hurt you. Thanatos would kill me."

"Why are you so afraid of him? He's your uncle."

His eyes widened. "Bold talk from a mortal. Why *aren't* you afraid of him? He's terrifying. Can't you feel his aura? It's crushing."

I frowned. He didn't seem to have that effect on me. "I don't feel anything."

He looked at me like I was insane. I knew what Thaos was, and I knew he was deadly. But I didn't fear him, and I didn't know why. I'd never felt like he would hurt me, and he was kind to me.

"Well, then something is wrong with you," Ulther said plainly.

"I can't argue with that," I mumbled. "Come on, Ulther, I need a weapon if we're going to spar. I guess the wendigo gets to stare down my dagger for all time and eternity."

It saddened me to lose the weapon. It was like an old friend and Laurenth had gifted it to me.

He sighed and followed me out of the door. We scrounged up a sword—and by scrounge, I mean I stole it off of a mantlepiece while Ulther kept watch— and then we went out to the beach.

Ulther was an excellent fighter, and being a demigod, he had an extraordinary advantage. However, I disarmed him twice.

"You are better than I expected," he said when we finished and sat together on the sand. "I thought I would feel embarrassed for you."

Sweat poured down my body, and I wiped at it. I felt amazing. Snorting a laugh, I glared at him with mock offense. "Wow. Thanks a lot."

"We can practice every day if you like. You must've had a very competent teacher."

I smiled. "I think she is. Her name is Laurenth."

He tensed, making me glance at him in surprise, and ask, "Do you know Laurenth?"

His eyebrows knitted together. "Well, I know of a Laurenth, and she was skilled. A first commander that served Athena, Goddess of Wisdom and War. But she was discharged dishonorably and cast out."

"Why?" My heart had quickened. It couldn't be the same person as my Laurenth.

"She and several others were part of a plot to overthrow Zeus, the King of Gods. He was almost deposed."

"They tried to kill him?"

"No one can kill Zeus. He and his siblings, Hades included, are true immortals. Mastix steel would hurt them, but not kill them. Their only hope would've been to incapacitate him and lock him away like he did with the Titans."

"Why would they want to do that?"

"Not everyone is happy with the King of Gods and the way he rules. He favors his own children and hands out strict punishments for some while giving light sentences to others for more serious crimes. Some people want change, a new ruler. I know Athena pleaded for Laurenth's life and that's the only reason Zeus spared her. Many of the others weren't so lucky."

My heart was beating loud in my chest. Laurenth? Why would she want to take down Zeus? Maybe it wasn't my Laurenth.

"Do you know who her father was?" I asked.

"Well, yes. Many know that was why she was so capable on the battlefield. Ares, the God of War, is her father."

That night I had trouble sleeping. I couldn't understand how Laurenth fit into all of this, and not being able to put the puzzle pieces together was driving me crazy.

I was restless in my room, and I went out to the balcony. The flowers were blooming again, so I climbed out of my room using my sheets. As I walked to the water, I spared a shuddering glance at the Woods of Woe. Twenty thousand crying babies couldn't get me to step foot in there again.

I sat and pushed my toes into the sand, watching the flowers devour their prey.

"Your lack of concern for your life is starting to unsettle me."

Jumping in surprise, I looked over my shoulder to find Thaos behind me. He must have been sleeping because he didn't wear his robe or a shirt, the same as the night I'd tried to steal the scythe. I frowned and stared back at the flowers.

"What unsettles you is not my problem."

"Do I need to take your sheets from you?"

"Go ahead. I'll just find another way."

He clicked his tongue in annoyance. "You should've brought Ulther with you. He wouldn't mind."

"I don't need to bring Ulther."

"Once again, I disagree."

"Wow, I'm shocked," I snapped, and smiled at my adept use of sarcasm. Being around Hypnos had its perks. "Why do I need him when I've got you watching me all the time?"

He was quiet for a moment. "I'm not always watching you. And it's dangerous out here. As you discovered."

"I promise I'm fine. You can go back to bed."

"I'm not giving you a guard as some punishment, Cere. It's so you're safe when I'm not here."

"You mean when you're avoiding me," I mumbled, unable to stop the words and cringing once they passed my lips.

He said nothing and my heart dropped. If it wasn't true, he would've said so.

"You don't understand," he answered after a long while.

"I may be naïve, but I think I understand just fine."

"I promise you don't."

"Then explain it to me."

"I don't know how."

I scoffed. "Well, there are bigger things going on and I'd like to be able to talk to you about it, so I would be pleased if you would stop avoiding me because we kissed. I don't know why you even did it. Maybe you pitied me because I've been *locked in a basement for ten years*." I set my chin on my knees. "It's okay if you don't want me but things don't need to be awkward."

It disappointed me, the thought of him not finding me attractive despite his claim of my beauty that night, but it was okay. It would be easier that way to deal with the strange feelings he awoke in me. But, I needed to talk to him about my visions of the undead. And I'd like to do it without this weird tension between us.

I stood, intending to climb back up my sheet rope and go to my room. When I turned, I gasped in surprise. He was right behind me, and I hadn't even heard him move.

"I hate when you do that."

I moved around him and took a step in the house's direction.

"What do you mean, bigger things?"

I sighed. "The undead. The ones whose souls you can't reap."

"Hypnos told you."

"Yes, but I knew about them already. I saw them in my visions when I breathed the vapors. It gets worse. They're a byproduct of the plague that envelopes the entire mortal world. It's the end of humanity. That's why I have to get back to the temple." I turned on him. "Take me back. I'd like to go. Now."

"You're not going back to that place," he said, the black tendrils of shadow appearing in his irises.

"I have to. The master may not be Apollo, but he was working with others to stop whatever is happening. I was a big part of it. Was my life the best? Maybe not. But I must save my family. That's all I have focused on for years. It's how I survived."

"No. I'm not taking you back to be humiliated in an office behind closed doors for talking too loud in the hallway."

My face burned at the reminder of what he'd seen. "Well, you killed the overseer so, it's fine, Thaos. Take me back."

"Another would just take his place. And if your former *master*," he said, saying the word like it disgusted him, "thinks you are so valuable, he should've protected you. I would never take you back."

I opened my mouth to argue, my hands balling to angry fists at my sides, but he cut me off. "Even if I could, it's gone. I went back to see what else I could find out and *talk* to all the other wonderful people that stood by while you were abused. The realm has been destroyed by whoever created it."

"What?" My blood ran cold. How could I ever find them again? How could I save my family?

My eyes burned, and I swallowed hard. "And when were you going to tell me this? That I no longer have the chance to help save my family and everyone else."

"When I deemed it necessary."

I frowned up at him. "I would like to stab you again."

I was serious. I wanted to. To keep this from me? He should've told me as soon as he found out.

"That doesn't surprise me. Too bad your dagger is stuck in a wendigo's eye socket," he answered, looking amused.

Little did he know I had my borrowed kitchen knife strapped to my leg. I felt bad because Glendyl had been nothing but kind to me, but there was no way I was going to be unarmed.

"But I promise I'll do everything I can to help save your family. I already am. Whoever is doing this is interfering with death, and that's not acceptable."

"Then you'll include me. And tell me things."

"Possibly."

I huffed. Now I really wanted to stab him. I went to push by him, but he held my arm.

"We're not done."

I shrugged him off. "I think we are."

I walked forward, and glanced behind me, stunned to see he was gone. *Good*—only to run into him again when I turned back around. I growled in frustration.

"We still have an issue to discuss."

I scoffed. "We have a lot of issues. None of which I want to discuss."

"You suggested I find you unattractive, and that I kissed you out of pity. How can you even think such things?"

I blushed and looked away. "It doesn't matter. But maybe because you've been avoiding me for days."

"I'm avoiding you because I *am* attracted to you. Too much. I want to touch you for no reason, and I don't understand. I shouldn't want to, and I don't want to hurt you."

My eyes slid back to his face, and I tried to find the lie in his expression. A coil of heat twisted to life in my stomach, and I swallowed the nervous lump in my throat.

I cursed that wicked thread of desire. Even if the temple was gone, it changed nothing. I couldn't sacrifice my purity, my *gift*, just because I wanted things. I could still help as long as I had the sight.

"Please. Those are just words. I imagine you say similar ones to every woman that warms your bed for a night. And like I said, it doesn't matter. I still have to remain pure."

"And I'm assuming your gift still works after the other night?"

"Yes, it does." I had tested it on both Aeryn and Ulther. Nothing in their futures warranted a spontaneous outburst from me, but I heard some unintelligible whispers.

He stepped closer to me. "So if I kissed you again right now, do you think it would still work tomorrow?"

I swallowed and looked up at him. His expression was full of promise. A warm flush ran through me, followed by guilt. The first time had been the only time. It couldn't go past that one night. Even though I'd imagined it a thousand times only to be left with this awful, heavy ache in my chest—and lower.

I shouldn't even entertain the thought of doing it again. I should step around him and walk to my room.

So, of course, I did the opposite.

"I think it would," I answered, the words thick on my tongue.

My weak resolve was a continuing source of disappointment for me.

CHAPTER FOURTEEN

His speed was incredible. I felt his hand wrap around the nape of my neck, pulling me to his chest, and then my back was pressing into the sand. He laid down beside me, propped on his elbow so he could look at me.

I gasped, trying to find my bearings.

"And I do only speak those words to women who warm my bed," he said, holding my gaze. "Because you're the only woman who's been in my bed in a long, long time. And as I recall, you're the one who left when I asked you to stay."

"I couldn't stay. We know what would've happened."

He looked surprised and then offered me a mischievous chuckle. "Tell me, Cere, what would've happened?"

I blushed, ignoring that. "And you didn't *ask* me to stay, you said I *could* stay." I'd convinced myself that there was a big difference between the two.

"I wanted you to."

My heart tripped over itself.

"Why? I stabbed you. I tried to steal from you."

I studied his face while he answered. It annoyed me how alluring he was. His eyes searched, like he was trying to find the right words. "You don't understand. I've never wanted to touch someone so much in my life. In fact, I avoid touching people. But you." He ran his fingers across my collarbone as if to finish his thought. My skin sprouted goosebumps there, reacting to the coolness of his fingers. "You fascinate me. And the way you react to my touch. You want me, too, and *that* I can't understand."

My breath was shallow, a whisper. "Why?"

His eyes flicked to meet mine. "Because no one ever has."

I didn't understand how that was possible. He was the most attractive man I'd ever seen. Desire fluttered to life in my chest, joining the frenzied dance of my heart. I didn't understand how I could find him so handsome. He was the God of Death. That alone would perturb a normal person.

Plus, he infuriated me with half answers and withheld information. Yet, it did not extinguish the flame. It burned hot. Hotter with every second I was around him. He made me feel alive, which had to be some kind of macabre irony considering he was Death.

His head dipped, and he kissed where his finger had just touched with lips that were cool and hard and soft all at the same time.

"And yet you tell me I find you unattractive. When all I've thought about for every moment since I kissed you, has been kissing you again."

I closed my eyes and tilted my head back into the sand, exposing more of my skin to him. The warm feeling returned in my stomach, sparking flutters of breathless energy through me.

"When all I've thought about is your breast at my lips, and how I loved the sound you made when I pulled it into my mouth." He was kissing down the valley of my chest, parting the robe. I froze, not trusting myself to stay in control if I let go. My pulse somehow quickened again, and I bit my lip when his hand started pushing up my thigh. "And I think about how close my fingers were to you. How I should've pressed them further and found out if you were as wet and tight as I imagined."

My eyes flew open, widening. These words were wicked. Yet, they acted like another caress against my body, heating me and teasing me until I couldn't breathe.

His lips came back to my ear, and he ran my earlobe through his teeth. Shudders of pleasure rolled through me, and I gasped. "And then, when I can't stand it any longer, I take my cock in my hand and think of you some more."

I gasped, scandalized by that admission. "Really?"

"Really," he whispered. "But it's frustrating when I know I could walk ten feet down the hall to your room and have you wrapped around me instead. When I know I could bury myself so deep inside you that if you ever take another man after you would still think of me."

Gods I'd never blushed so fiercely, my face burned as hot as the rest of my body. His words caused a damp heat to form at the apex of my thighs and I felt his hand at the knot of my robe, pulling.

"I don't know why you do these things to me. I don't know why you *feel* so good when I touch you. But I do know I am very, very attracted to you, Cere, and I can't stand the thought of you feeling otherwise."

His lips were on mine, cool and pressing. Hungrier than before. I opened for him, a moan escaping me as I did. His tongue pushed into my mouth, and I felt the lash through every cell in my body. He shifted on top of me, and his weight pressed my back deeper into the sandy beach.

As I lay there, enveloped by his hard body and the light scent of lilies, I realized how unreal this all seemed. How a little while ago I wouldn't have been able to imagine this, even in my wildest, wettest dreams.

Thaos took my bottom lip and ran it between his teeth. I felt the sharp brush of his canines. They were sharper than normal.

Hypnos', Ulther's, and the Oneiroi's were too. They smiled often and I could study them.

The hand that was laced in my hair pulled my head back and his lips moved down my neck. He sucked at the tender skin, making me gasp. I pressed my hands against his chest and dug my nails into him.

His teeth brushed my neck, and for a moment, some insane part of me wanted him to bite me. The thought stunned me, drawing my thoughts. Was that the wolf part of me? I knew they could be rather bitey during intimacy.

But all thought soon left me again, because he was pushing my robe open, and I only wore the thin silk nightgown underneath. The coolness of his skin passed through the flimsy fabric as his left hand cupped my breast, and I felt my nipples pucker with the sensation.

His mouth covered mine again, and the kiss became a frenzy of passion. I was lost to it, wrapped up in my own want and taken by the heady thought of his desire for me. I could only hear us, our breathless chorus traveling across the barren beach.

Instinct guided me, my body understanding what it wanted even when my mind was at war with itself. I opened my legs, and he dropped against me. A shudder rolled through him, and I couldn't suppress the moan that left me, as the most sensitive part of me came into friction-rich contact with him. He pressed his hips into me, rubbing against me, and my fingers tightened on his back.

"Anything I do," he said, pulling back to look down at me, "if you don't like it, tell me and I'll stop. It's been a long time, and I could never forgive myself if I hurt you."

I shuddered. It was a warning that there was more to come, and I already felt out of control. It was more than just want now. I *needed*. All thoughts had abandoned me regarding purity, piety, and everything else in between. I was just Cere at that moment, and I let go.

He sat up and both of his hands traveled to the collar of the nightgown. I heard fabric tearing, and a beat of confusion passed through me. Air kissed my breasts, and a small groan rose from his chest. Only then did I realize what he had done. A flash of excitement bolted through me as he gazed down at my exposed chest.

"You are the most beautiful thing I have ever seen."

I flushed, fighting the urge to cover myself from his intense stare. His lips dropped to the apex of my right breast and pulled it into the cool heat of his mouth. I moaned, loud, and dared a peek, only to find his eyes were on my face. His gaze seared into me as he traveled across my chest and gave my other breast the same attention. I dropped my head back into the sand, the ache between my legs intensifying.

"Gods," I gritted out as I laced my fingers through his hair.

"Just one," he mumbled against my flesh. I stilled, realizing he was making a joke.

"What?"

My head snapped up as he rested his chin on my chest bone and grinned at me. I just stared, a smile tugging at my own lips. He looked so different, softer and younger. The expression took my breath away.

My heart pinched, and I wondered how few people had seen him like this. A terrified part of me told me this was turning into much more than kissing and touching, but I pushed the thought away. I *would* be able to walk away from him—it just couldn't happen any other way.

"There's just one god to praise for all this pleasure," he clarified.

"I understand the joke. I'm just stunned it passed your lips."

Lifting himself back up, his mouth found mine again. He kissed me, and time seemed to do strange things. I felt it had only been a few seconds, but when we broke apart, both of us were breathless. When my eyes opened, I noticed how plumped his lips were and I imagined mine looked the same.

His hand pushed up my thigh, pausing as he traveled over the kitchen knife fastened there. He clicked his tongue and his pupils pulsed in excitement.

"You little thief."

"I wanted a weapon."

"I find it incredibly alluring the way you wield a blade," he admitted, running his finger over the handle.

My eyebrows drew together. "Even if I wielded it against you?"

"Especially because you did. As I've mentioned, eternal life can be dull. Nothing surprises me anymore." His eyes still burned into mine, as he muttered, "Except you."

Then he went past the blade, shifting to his right and pushing up higher than he had before. My breath caught in my throat as his fingers glided over the band of my underwear at my hip.

"I want to make you come," he purred. "I know I left you aching last time."

His hand pushed all the way up and flattened against my lower stomach. My skin jumped and tingled under the touch, and the ache between my legs twisted with a sharp twinge.

"Even though it was your fault, if you would've stayed, I would've never left you in such a state. Although I've driven myself mad wondering if you were doing something about it on the other side of that wall."

I understood his insinuation and a furious blush colored my face. "Of course I wasn't!"

Another devilish grin cracked his lips. "You really are the worst liar."

"Oh, shut up," I sputtered, "or I'll make good use of that kitchen knife."

His grin widened and his hand inched lower. The heated flush spread until the tips of my ears burned. I grabbed his forearm, fear spiking in my chest, and he stopped. His gaze was on his hand against my stomach, and his eyes lifted to my face. One of his fingers moved in small rhythmic circles against my skin, sending continuous threads of sensation that traveled all the way to my toes.

I bit my lip. "I should tell you to stop."

"You should? Why is that?"

He already knew that answer, and I pushed out an annoyed breath. "You're so inappropriate."

"Am I?" he asked, as his lip twitched at the corner.

I was glad he found this amusing, all while his finger swirling on my stomach made it difficult for me to think.

"Did they give you any specifics regarding what counts as too far? Since somehow your sight is magically connected to you being…what? We know it's not being kissed, either on the lips or the breasts. The line isn't drawn at you pleasuring yourself. Where's the purity boundary? It would be helpful if they told you that."

"I-I don't know. They didn't tell me specifics. Just that I have to remain pure. So I *should* stop you."

"Should. But don't want to? That's what I'm hearing."

I swallowed and closed my eyes. I didn't want him to stop. I wanted to feel *that*, too. I'd felt so little aside from hurt and complacency for the last half of my life. I wanted to feel good, and he was incredibly talented at making me feel that way.

He stared at me for another long second and then started to withdraw his hand. "It's okay, Cere. If you don't want—"

I tightened my grip, my nails digging in and holding his hand there. He arched his eyebrow at me, the corner of his lips curling. "I'm receiving very mixed signals."

"I'm very confused," I admitted.

"I don't think you're confused at all. You know exactly what you want."

I stared at him, biting my lip and then I pushed on his forearm, guiding it down. He brushed the top of my panties with his fingers but didn't slide underneath them like I expected.

His fingers coasted over the top of them, gliding against the satiny material. They caressed the most sensitive part of my body, and my hips twitched in response. He moved his hand up and down, and the contact was barely there. But every nerve in my body was so heightened, so achy, that I felt every stroke.

He smiled again. Was that two or three smiles he'd given me now? His head dipped and his lips brushed mine, and then his mouth traveled to my ear and his sinful voice unraveled me again. The pressure of his fingers increased and moved in steady circles around the spot where the ache throbbed.

"How about you worry about should, and I'll tell you about want."

Oh, Gods. God. Oh, God.

"I think you want me to push this fabric away and find out how ready you are for me. And I want you to think about how that would feel, if nothing separated my skin from yours."

I did as he said and imagined what that would be like. The thought set my body on fire, consuming me with flames of desire. This was wrong. I knew it in every cell of my being. But it didn't feel wrong. It felt amazing and right. My hips started rocking, trying to find more contact. It was good, but I knew it could be better.

"You want more?"

"Yes," I moaned in response, and he pushed his fingers harder against me. A small cry left me, and my hips lifted more.

"You want my fingers inside of you, don't you? Maybe, you want me to taste you."

"Yes."

Gasps and soft moans crossed my lips, and I stopped trying to hold them in. His fingers and my hips moved together, and then his touch grew more intense, and I knew he'd been holding back.

"As good as your mouth tastes, I can only imagine…" His voice was a thick, raspy drawl that elicited an intense reaction from me as I imagined that, too.

My stomach and my core were tightening. The first small waves of pleasure pulsed through me, promising me there was something better just in reach. My eyes squeezed shut, and the sound of my moans increased. I forgot to care if anyone in the house could hear.

His thick, breathless voice caressed me again. "And what I want is for you to ride me like you're riding my hand."

The want in his voice was palpable, making him sound as desperate as I was for the physical touch of another.

I couldn't be ashamed of what I was doing. I didn't have the brain space for it, and I knew I was shamelessly, inappropriately, obscenely taking what I needed. Pushing my hips to his hand and chasing the pleasure he offered.

He pressed the pad of his thumb hard against me and my body lifted in a tight bridge of tension. My mouth fell open as my head fell back, and I thought I shouted his name, but I wasn't sure. The tension snapped, and then I was shuddering as waves of intense pleasure pulsed through me. I knew he was watching me the entire time. I could feel the heat of his gaze on my face.

As the shudders of pleasure ended, his full weight was on me again, and he pinned my wrists by my head. The weight of his lower body pushed into me, making me moan as satin panties and leather breeches did a poor job of concealing how hard he was.

I felt his teeth and mouth at my neck again, and then he stilled, his rapid breath fanning my skin. He took a long breath before placing a gentle kiss on my shoulder. Abruptly, he stood, pulling me up with him.

He held me against him, and I looked up at his face, feeling dazed. His eyes were closed, and I noticed tiny black cracks branching out of them. I blinked, and the cracks disappeared. I wasn't sure if they'd been there at all.

"What's wrong?"

His eyes opened, and they were violet. He looked confused or concerned. "I was about to go too far, and I thought you would stop me. But then you didn't. You would've stopped me right?"

"I don't know."

His hands tightened around my waist, and he groaned in frustration. "That's not helpful."

"I'm sorry." I knew I was being difficult and confusing. But that's how I felt inside. I was glad he was responsible enough to preserve my gift because I didn't think I would've stopped him.

He pressed his lips to the top of my head and a small gasp parted my lips. How did that feel more intimate and romantic than everything else he'd just done? I lifted my head up and wrapped my arms around his neck.

My lips found his again, and he answered my passion.

I felt like I should thank him or something for what just happened, and I felt bad about the tension that I could still feel straining his breeches against my stomach.

After the kiss grew too heated again, he broke away. "We're still trying to not take it too far, right?"

"I'm unworthy," I whispered. "I sought the pleasures of the flesh, and I can't even pretend it was just one time now, since it's been two times."

His hand stroked the long waterfall of my hair. "I think I'm just a bad influence."

"Yes, but I let you influence me."

I needed to get myself together. This was escalating at a dangerous pace. I put my forehead against his chest for a moment longer and then I pushed away and severed the contact between us.

He looked at me with wide, heated eyes, and the voice was a husky rumble. "You don't understand what you do to me."

I looked down and realized I was almost nude, the deep tear in my nightgown leaving very little to the imagination. Gasping, I grabbed the robe and wrapped it around me.

"You're the one who ripped it."

"I am. And I would do it again. It was in the way."

His wings were full, powerful, and pulsing with energy.

"Your wings."

"I'd say I've been experiencing a fair bit of intense emotion. Desire most notably."

I tried to touch one, but my hand just misted through. The shadow was as cold as ice and made my flesh tingle. As I reached out, he captured a lock of my hair in between his fingers.

"I like your hair free like this. It's beautiful."

I blushed at the sincere compliment, suppressing the desire to grin like an idiot. I pushed my hand through the tangled mess and shook it, and what seemed like a pound of sand fell out, making me sigh.

"I guess now I decide whether to climb back up or do the walk of shame in front of Ulther."

He grinned and then grabbed me, holding me bridal style, and carrying me back to the house.

"What are you doing?"

When we were just under the balconies, I felt his muscles tightening and he jumped, his wings somehow pushing the air even though they were made of shadow. I yelped in surprise as he landed on the edge of my railing, balancing on what could only be a few inches of slick metal. I looked down at the ground and then up at his face.

"That was amazing." I felt silly for being proud of the jump I had made between the balconies.

He hopped down from the railing and set me down. I sensed he was preparing to leave, which I knew was for the best. What did I expect? We shouldn't even be doing this.

To stall, and out of curiosity, I asked, "What's that flower called? In the marsh."

"She has a few names. Most commonly we call it the gillylily." I snorted. What a silly name. "It's real name is *asteri tou thanatou*, or star of death."

"It is lovely," I said, looking out over the lake.

"And vicious," he added. "It reminds me of someone I know."

My eyes slid back to him, and the way he looked at me made my heart skip. "I'm not that vicious, or that lovely."

"I'm going to ignore that last comment because I've just spent a good amount of time proving to you how lovely I find you."

I blushed, looking away from the heat of his gaze.

"And you are vicious. You told me you wanted to stab me less than an hour ago."

"You deserved it."

He smiled, shaking his head.

"That's the fourth or fifth smile you've given me in the same amount of time."

"You're counting?"

"Yes."

"And you've already lost count? At four?"

"I was...distracted."

"With what? Nothing too *inappropriate* I hope."

I blushed. He knew it was. Chuckling, he stepped towards me. "I have to go."

"Thaos? How did my wounds from the wendigo heal? Hypnos said I should ask you."

His expression twisted then, into something that resembled guilt. "I gave you my blood. Just a small amount, one drop, so it didn't consume you with lust for more. As long as Mastix steel didn't inflict the wound, a god's blood can help. But it's dangerous if done improperly, as it can be addictive. If you were a full human, I wouldn't have. They have a particularly weak resolve to it."

"Why would you do that? They would've healed on their own."

"I couldn't stand to see you bleeding like that." He cleared his throat. "I didn't like to see you in pain."

My heart did that annoying flip flop again, and I sighed, chewing on my lip. "Well. Thank you."

He arched his eyebrow at me. "Another thank you? I'm touched."

"Don't get used to it."

He looked humored but his face tightened. "We shouldn't do this again. It's not fair to you."

"Why?" I almost slapped myself. I should agree, but a strange ache formed in my chest at the thought. "Because of my gift?"

He stared down at me with an intense gaze. "Has anyone ever been able to stop one of your prophecies?"

"No," I admitted. "It's always too late to do anything by the time they make sense."

"Then, why would I care about hearing them? Fate is what it is. I don't need to know."

I was stunned. He would've shocked me less if he'd smacked me across the face. If he wasn't concerned with preserving my gift— "Then why shouldn't we do this?"

"Because you deserve better. I am Death. I could never give you what you would eventually want. What you deserve."

"What do you mean?"

"You deserve to be loved, Cere, and I can't do that."

CHAPTER FIFTEEN

I watched him go, and he leapt from my balcony to his with feline agility. For reasons I couldn't explain, I dropped my mental walls and looked at him as he walked into his doors. The voices screamed to life in my head, and an image formed, surprising me. That rarely happened unless I inhaled the vapors. The image was through his eyes, and it was more vivid than any vision I'd ever experienced.

It took me a moment to realize what I was seeing because it was dark, a tangle of limbs, but then I saw myself, and my eyes widened.

I was underneath him. My swollen mouth parted in ecstasy, and my cheeks rosy. We were—oh, Gods. My face heated.

The image shifted, and I saw my face, unable to make out any details aside from that. Thaos was walking towards me. My face twisted, changing from joy to panic.

I gasped, and the words poured out of me, even though I was the only one who could hear them.

"She'll have your heart, Death, for it belongs with her. But, once it's surrendered, the son will steal your life."

I clamped my hand over my mouth and rushed into my room. My breath was shallow as I closed the door. There was no way I could allow any of that to happen.

Who could the son be? The son of who? This was a perfect example of why I hated my sight. *The son* could mean any man in existence. Every single one of them was a son to someone.

My sleep was fitful, the images and prophecy playing on repeat in my subconscious mind. I was already up and dressed when the soft rap on my door told me of Aeryn's arrival. I greeted her, and her eyes immediately fell to my throat. Blushing, I covered it while she giggled. Even though I healed faster than a human, there was still a giant mark where Thaos had kissed my neck—aggressively.

She spared me by not saying anything, and I thanked her for the tea, still flushed. After she left, I asked the wardrobe for a turtleneck, relieved to see it covered the mark, though barely. I went to breakfast and found Hypnos reading a magazine called *Sports Illustrated*.

I thought about asking him if I could read it next. When I was younger, I liked sports. But the girl on the front made me reconsider. Maybe it was a different kind of sport.

"You're up early Sleeping Beauty."

I sat and filled my plate. After several seconds of silence, I asked, "Hypnos? Do Gods drink blood?"

"I love it. Every morning I sit here and wonder what you've come up with to ask me over breakfast," he said, grinning. "But yes, they can. Younger Gods especially crave blood. Luckily, there's usually plenty of willing participants. It can be a pleasurable experience for both parties if done correctly. Us old guys don't need to, but I know many still do. It's quite a rush."

"I see."

He regarded me with a curiously lifted brow that told me he was definitely going to pry. "Why do you ask?"

"I noticed you and your sons have fangs. And I noticed Thaos does, too. I wasn't sure if it was all gods or just your family."

"And how, I wonder, do you know Thaos has fangs? I know I'm all smiles over here, but my brother is very close-lipped."

Even though I willed it not to, my face heated until my ears burned. I looked away from him, but it was the worst possible thing I could've done. He gasped, and I realized the turtleneck had pulled away just enough to show the mark. Covering it with my hand, I winced as he tsked his tongue.

"I *knew* it. I guess he is very close-lipped unless it involves a certain *pure* mortal."

The way he said pure made me cringe, and I glanced at Ulther, who was doing his best to stay stone-faced. His twitching lips were the only thing that signified he understood what was happening.

I suspected Aeryn had told him what she'd seen after she left my room. They had a subtle, sweet relationship, and I often wondered if they were more than friends. It wasn't obvious, but when you're locked in a house with only a handful of people, you notice things like glances or light brushes of the hand. I wondered if he'd heard anything last night and thought I might die of embarrassment.

"The fifty shades of red your face just traveled through were *amazing*. Spill it, Sleeping Beauty. Or *not* sleeping, I guess."

I glared at him. Hypnos had no shame with his questions and took no issue with making me squirm.

I cleared my throat, smoothing my hands over my napkin. "There is nothing to tell."

"Oh, please. Has anyone ever told you that you suck at lying?"

Yes. Someone had told me that. More than once.

"I don't even know why I come to breakfast with you," I hissed, glaring at him.

"Because your choices for company are severely limited."

The door opened, and I thought someone had saved me, but I was wrong. Thaos entered, eyes searching and then falling on me.

He glanced at my neck and smirked, no doubt knowing what the turtleneck was concealing, and doing a poor job of it.

The heat in my face doubled, and I glanced at Hypnos, who still watched me with an amused, curious expression. I felt like an insect under a magnifying glass and the wielder was a cruel child holding me under that searing reflected beam of sun.

"Good morning, brother," Hypnos said smoothly. "I was just having the most fascinating conversation with Cere."

I wasn't sure if Thaos understood what that meant, but he ignored him and walked over to sit in the chair next to me.

"I brought something for you."

"Oh. A present?"

My heart skittered. I didn't get many gifts, and only ever from Laurenth.

"A *present*?" Hypnos echoed, maybe more shocked than I was. The way he looked at Thaos, you'd think he'd grown antlers.

"I retrieved this for you." Thaos pulled my dagger out of his black robe and extended the handle to me.

My lips parted in surprise, and I glanced up at him. "You went and pulled this out of the wendigo's eye?"

"He seemed relieved. And I think the chef would like his knife back." I blushed and glanced down at it. Not that Thaos didn't already know it was there. The memory of his fingers sliding up my thigh and finding it flashed in my mind.

I looked back up at his face and could tell by his expression that he knew exactly what I was thinking about. The heat in his eyes told me he was remembering the same moment. His gaze fell to my lips and my eyes widened. For a heartbeat, I thought he might kiss me in front of Ulther and Hypnos.

My eyes flicked to the God of Sleep. I knew he'd interpreted the same from his brother's expression, and he wasn't attempting to conceal his shock. His chin was practically in his lap.

"I didn't like being unarmed," I answered finally, looking back at Thaos.

Hypnos gave Ulther a pointed look. "I thought your job was to keep track of her? Yet, she's stealing all sorts of sharp things. Don't think I didn't notice the mantelpiece with a sword inexplicably missing."

I'd hidden it in my room under the mattress.

Ulther's lips twitched. "The lady wanted a blade. I wouldn't want to be unarmed either."

A small smile played on my lips. I liked Ulther more all the time.

"But simple steel won't do much for you," Thaos said. "So I found you this."

My eyes widened when he pulled another dagger from his robe and handed it to me. The leather scabbard was intricate and decorated by a swirling floral design. Looking closer, I realized it was depicting the gillylily and my heart erupted like an overdue volcano.

The blacksmith had crafted the handle from some kind of antler, the natural curve of it acting as a perfect hold. I laid my fingers into the four smooth indents and squeezed. It felt perfect in my hand.

"Don't stab me with this one though, it would hurt."

My eyes snapped to his face with a gasp. "No way."

I yanked the blade free and beamed. It was Mastix steel.

"Why are you giving me this? I could kill you with it," I blurted, drawing a startled cough from Ulther. I imagined few people openly threatened the God of Death.

"It's for self-defense, not homicide. Plus, having the weapon to kill a God and actually killing one are two different matters."

"You don't think I could do it?" I asked, narrowing my eyes.

"I think you would certainly try."

"That's not an answer."

"I don't know why I was expecting a thank you."

"Foolish of you," I said, and then mumbled, "But, thank you."

A lopsided smile lit his face and Hypnos looked like someone had slapped him, gawking at his twin. I returned his look, but my grin faltered where the words of my prophecy filled my head, and I tried to harden my heart. I would not soften to him anymore. Even if he had just given me the most thoughtful, stunningly beautiful present I'd ever received.

He stood. "And since we all know about it now, I will share that the undead creatures are forming at a faster rate. I've been doing my best to kill them, but there are simply too many for me to handle. At Hades' request, I captured one. It's in his dungeons right now. On closer inspection, it almost seems to be a vampire... but worse."

My brow furrowed. "What do you mean, worse?"

"Vampires maintain some semblance of their humanity. They usually know what their name is and can speak, even when they're brand new and overcome by thirst. These things are mindless beasts."

"You don't think Aphrodite is behind it this time, do you?" Hypnos asked.

My eyes widened. "Aphrodite? The Goddess of Love created vampires?"

"Love *and* Lust," Hypnos said. "She was envious of Artemis because she created shifters. When Aphrodite saw the devotion and attention Artemis received, she wanted her own race of supernaturals. But she went a little too hard on the lust part and ended up with Dracula. Now she tries to pretend it wasn't her, but we all know."

"It could be her. It could be anyone. No one is ruled out right now," Thaos said, looking at me. "Hades wants me to bring you and see if you can discern anything by reading the creature."

"Read the undead? I don't think it will work. What kind of future could it have?"

"He wants you to try."

"Okay." The idea piqued my interest.

"Then we should go if you're finished eating."

I stood and removed the kitchen knife, sheepishly setting it on the table. Smiling, I put my blade back in its spot on my thigh and then fastened the new dagger to my other leg.

"I'm not missing this," Hypnos said, standing as well.

They both looked at me. I didn't like the amusement that danced in both pairs of eyes.

"How would you like to travel there?" Thaos asked.

"Horse?" I asked. It was wishful thinking, but their expressions told me it wouldn't be happening. "So fall through the void or have my guts ripped out?"

"Those are your options."

"They both suck," I groaned. "But I prefer the void." At least it wasn't painful.

"What a surprise," Hypnos said dryly, giving his brother a peculiar look before vanishing.

"You can have the day off, Ulther," Thaos said.

"Oh. Yes, of course." He sounded disappointed to be missing out and then turned and left. I wondered if he would find Aeryn.

I watched Ulther go, feeling a cool hand snake around my waist. My pulse jumped, and I turned to find Thaos gazing down at me. He pulled me into him, holding me to his chest.

"I thought we weren't doing this anymore?" I said breathlessly.

"Doing what?"

"I could step through the portal myself."

"Do you want me to let you go?"

"I should," I whispered.

But I don't. The words hung unsaid between us.

The side of his mouth lifted, and he used the scythe to cut through the fabric of reality. We stepped in and everything fell away beneath our feet.

It wasn't as bad this time, and I kept my eyes open. It didn't really matter either way, as it was just blackness around us. The fall was kind of exhilarating if you were expecting it. I vaguely remembered riding a roller coaster once with a big drop. I'd been sitting next to my brother, Henry. Grinning a little, I suppressed a giggle.

We landed next to the doors of Hades' castle, and I was still smiling. My heart fluttered from the fall as the tingle of waning adrenaline coursed through me. When I turned to Thaos, he was watching me curiously.

Giggling, I asked, "Has anyone ever told you traveling like that is fun?"

"You would be the first."

My hand clenched the fabric of his shirt, so I unfurled my fingers and smoothed the material. My eyes drifted back to him, and I found he was staring at my mouth. I blushed, sensing he wanted to kiss me again. The images and message from my vision flashed through my mind, and I quickly stepped back.

He released me, and his expression gave nothing away. We stepped towards the doors, and they opened as they had before, revealing the grand entryway with all the dog paintings. Through my reading, I'd learned his name was Cerberus.

Thaos led me in a different direction than the first time, and we came to a stone staircase that spiraled into blackness.

Warily, I said, "It's dark down there."

I assumed he could probably see in blackness like that. I had some night vision thanks to my shifter blood, but it couldn't handle anything that dark. His icy hand wrapped around mine, and he pulled me forward.

"Don't be afraid. I won't let you fall."

The staircase seemed to go on forever, and I could barely see Thaos' figure in front of me. Our shoes scraped the stone as we went down, echoing in the empty chamber.

I was trying to focus, so I didn't trip, but he was being very distracting. After a few steps, he went from cupping my hand to pushing his fingers into mine and threading them. I could feel the calluses on his palm from wielding the scythe, and my heart skipped like a flat stone thrown across a smooth pond.

I saw the glow of a lantern up ahead and we finally arrived at the bottom of the steps. I pulled at my hand, but he held on.

"I can see," I said, confused. "Are you going to let go of my hand?"

He turned his gaze to me. The corner of his mouth curled, and he answered, "I should."

But I don't want to.

Was this our unspoken code now? We should and shouldn't be doing a lot of things, and I understood then that he was struggling with want, just like I was.

"We're not supposed to be doing this anymore," I reminded him and myself.

"What are we doing?"

"Whatever this is."

"I'm finding it is easier said than done."

After a moment, I whispered, "Yeah, so am I."

He released my hand slowly, his fingers brushing against mine, and I let out a breath I didn't realize I'd been holding. Somewhere up ahead, I heard an inhuman shriek.

"Is that it?"

He nodded and led me towards the sound. We rounded a corner and two figures waited for us in front of a cell. I immediately recognized Hypnos, who glowed slightly in the darkness. Hades stood with him, holding his weapon, which I'd learned was called a bident.

"See, I told you they were coming," Hypnos said when he spotted us. "He's just acting strangely."

Hades turned and greeted us. The circles under his eyes appeared more pronounced today, and I didn't know if it was the lighting or if I was imagining things.

"Thanatos. Pythia."

I didn't correct him with my real name but nodded a greeting. Thaos moved protectively to my left side, just as a pained wail ripped through the room from that direction. The undead creature smacked into the bars, and I heard teeth clacking as it bit down in wild, rapid succession. I gasped in surprise and stepped back.

It, well she, looked just like I'd seen in my visions. Her skin had turned a shining pallid white, it was pearly and boasted a strange sheen. She didn't wear any clothes and I could only tell she was female from the mounds of her breasts. Everything else was one smooth stretch of skin. Even her navel had disappeared.

Her eyes were completely black, no whites left at all, and her mouth opened much wider than should be possible for a human. I looked at her canine teeth, which were elongated, and listened to the flat tops of her other teeth clapping noisily together with each bite.

Curious, I moved to the other side of Hades and Hypnos. She followed me, pushing against the bars, and reaching her groping hand out to me. We passed by the two gods, and she completely ignored them.

That was interesting. "She only wants me. Is it because I'm mortal?"

"Possibly," Hades said. "I understand as much as you do."

"You know I can't read the past, right? I don't understand what I could learn from her."

"Please indulge my curiosity."

I shivered, holding myself. It was cold down here, freezing as if we'd walked into a winter night. Not exactly t-shirt weather. It surprised me that my breath wasn't creating steam. I heard a swish of fabric and then a lily scented robe fell heavily over my shoulders.

I blushed and heard Hypnos mutter to Hades, "See, I told you he was acting strangely."

I focused on the undead monster and dropped my mental walls. The connection between us sprung to life, and I stiffened, seeing only blackness. But for the first time during a reading, I *felt* what she would endure. Emotional agony ripped through me, and I clutched my chest, unable to draw breath. Involuntary tears rolled down my cheeks, and there was something else there, too. I experienced her insatiable hunger and groaned from the sharp throb in my gut.

Thaos' hand found mine again, and our fingers laced. My mouth opened of its own accord and the disembodied voices of the Oracle pushed out two words.

"*Pain. Hunger.*"

I ripped my eyes away, unable to bear it a moment longer. They accidentally rested on Hades and the sensation of sight took control again. I saw from his eyes as he watched his power drain away until he couldn't leave his bed.

My own legs failed me, and I grew unsteady on my feet. Thaos caught me and supported my weight. With Hades' power gone, malevolent monsters escaped the boundaries of the Underworld, emerging from what looked like a bottomless black pit, and started wreaking havoc on Earth.

First, figures clad in different colored robes that twisted the minds of mortals. The influence on those they touched was immediate. Their victims would be possessed by their corresponding plague. Greed, hatred, and pain were a few. I watched the vision unfold as wars erupted amongst the nations of the already suffering mortal realm.

Next, an enormous monster with the upper body of a man and the bottom half of a snake emerged. Black gossamer wings with tips like razors brushed the ground as the beast slithered forward. I felt fear and realized with a start it was Hades' feelings coming through the vision. This creature engaged in a fight with a God that glowed with soft light and had hair the color of clouds. He wielded a bolt of lightning in his hand. It had to be Zeus.

Finally, I watched a God ride out of the pit of darkness on a beautiful white horse that matched the ivory feathers of his giant wings. Rusted chains hung off of his black armor, the links warped like they'd been broken. I couldn't see what he looked like because a heavy black helmet concealed his face.

Dread and fear coursed through me as the person set eyes on Hades in the vision. The God dismounted and approached. Hades held up his hands defensively, but the God's hand snapped forward and pain blossomed in my chest. Hades was so weakened already he couldn't even fight back.

A cry of agony left me, and I grabbed at my own heart, the searing burn unbearable.

"Cere?" I heard Thaos say my name, but the vision was so intense it sounded like he was miles away.

I watched through Hades' eyes as the God pulled his hand away. In it, he held the beating heart of the King of the Underworld. Flipping the bottom half of the helmet up, the God brought the heart to his mouth and took a bite, chewing the flesh with a bloody grin.

My breath was quick and shallow as the vision ended and the voices surged forward.

"Death disrupted weakens the king. Tartarus unleashed signifies the end of the mortal realm. The drums of war beat on the horizon."

I quickly built my mental wall and stared at Hades, shocked. He mirrored me, and then hot rage filled his face.

"Is this true?" Hypnos breathed. "Are these things weakening you?"

Hades winced. "Yes. The inability to collect their souls is influencing me. People cheat death all the time, but it's not enough to create an issue. These souls are trapped. I don't know how much you pay attention to news on Earth, but the sickness is spreading rapidly. Reports of attacks by these things are coming to light in the human world, although they are still writing most off as conspiracies. When they bite another mortal, that person changes, too, although it can take over a week before the initial illness kills the victim. The more it happens, the weaker I am."

I listened, saying a thousand silent prayers that my family was still unaffected.

"What does it mean Tartarus unleashed?" I asked, looking between the three of them.

The king looked somber, sucking at his teeth before he answered. "Tartarus is the prison of the Underworld. It holds ancient evils that haven't been seen since the beginning of Zeus' era. The Spirits of Plague released from Pandora's box, and the Titans, for example. My strength is the power of Hades. If I fail, it will unleash horrors that the mortal realm hasn't witnessed since the beginning of time."

"I saw them," I said, my voice barely a whisper. "The Plagues and the Titans."

Hades nodded and opened his mouth to say something, but I cut him off.

"There was someone else, too. I thought he was a God. Clad in black armor and broken chains. He rode a white horse and had white feathered wings." I looked at Hades, clearing my throat. "He, um. He ripped your heart out." The king's eyebrows shot up, shock rippling across his features. But I wasn't done. "Then he ate it."

All three men stiffened, the air filling with a thick tension. Hades looked furious. His aura that had already been stifling me became even more suffocating. I glanced between them, wanting an elaboration on who this person was.

Hypnos put his head in his hand. "Oh, boy. This is bad."

"Who is it?" I asked, annoyed I seemed to be the only who didn't know.

Thaos tightened his grip on me. "Apollyon the Destroyer. The end of times is said to ride at her heels if she were ever to escape Tartarus."

The revelation that she was a woman stunned me. I'd just assumed it was a man. "Well, you can stop her, right?"

They exchanged unsure glances.

"The Olympians and Underworld together could," Hades finally answered. "But getting them all to unite for a common cause is not as easy as it used to be."

Dread settled in my gut. "So, you're saying someone is starting an apocalypse?"

"It appears that way."

"To what end?"

Hades pushed out a breath. "I do not know. And it seems to be at the cost of the entire mortal realm. Every single person on Earth will surely perish."

My heart dropped, and I thought of my family. "We have to do something," I blurted. "All those innocent people."

"We will, Pythia. I will go now and contact Zeus and Poseidon."

"Don't tell them she's here," Thaos said, stepping protectively in front of me.

Hades furrowed his brow. "I might have to."

"No. Zeus will tell Apollo. He'll want her."

"I have bigger problems, Death."

"Look how helpful she's already been. We need her."

Hades seemed to consider that. "For now, I will keep her existence a secret."

Everyone made movements to leave, but I glanced at the forgotten creature in the cell. She snarled at me, her hand still extended through the bars, grasping the air.

"Wait," I said. I noticed for the first time she had recently manicured nails, now dirty and broken. My heart pinched in sorrow. "This is—was—a person. And she's in pain. She's already dead, right?"

"Yes," Thaos answered me. "But something about this form keeps her soul trapped in between life and death."

"Well, we need to end whatever this is. She's living in torment."

Without argument or warning, Hades picked up his weapon and shoved it into the undead woman's throat. I knew his brutal strike was precise and that one prong had severed her spinal cord.

I watched her slide to the floor and felt an overwhelming burst of sadness. As her head lolled to one side, I spotted something on the back of her neck.

"What's that?" I asked, pointing.

Thaos reached through the bars, twisting her head, and pulling her neck into the light of the lanterns. We all crouched, looking closely.

"It's a brand," Hypnos said. "But I don't recognize it."

Thaos looked at me and sighed. "I do."

My eyebrows knitted in confusion. "No...I don't understand."

It was the same snake that adorned the doorway in the temple that I walked through when I was doing a reading for the master.

"A snake. Great," Hypnos said sarcastically. "That narrows it down."

"There's something else too," Thaos muttered, scratching his finger over the back of her neck. Small white flecks broke away from her skin.

I wrinkled my nose. "Are those scales?"

"Yes. The rest of the skin is smooth, but there is a small patch here."

I knew many gods used snakes as one of their symbols, so it didn't point to anyone specifically.

"The one you called the master," Thaos said. "Is there anything else about him?"

"I know nothing about him. The day he took me, he smelled of soil...earth and cinder. He wore a white robe every time I was around him and had the hood pulled up. He was using my visions to stop this." I nodded to the dead creature, but my voice trailed off as I stared at the brand on her neck. I finished my thought with a whisper, "At least that's what I was told."

"This is all curious and disturbing," Hades said, and his sharp black eyes regarded me with suspicion.

"I had nothing to do with this," I blurted. But I didn't even know if it was true. Disturbing realizations were dawning. Had the master been trying to create these monsters, not stop them?

Hades glared at me, looking unconvinced. "I guess we will see."

Fear spiked in my chest, and I turned away from him, unsettled. I stared down at the dead creature, feeling emotional about her plight. This poor woman.

"So, she's okay now? She's at peace?"

"Come," Thaos said, standing and pulling me up by my hand through a hole he'd just cut with his scythe.

CHAPTER SIXTEEN

The world melted away until we were standing in the void. A blonde woman sat on the ground with her knees pulled up to her chest. She was sobbing.

"It's her," I whispered, realizing we were staring at the soul of the undead creature Hades had just ended.

Her head whipped up when she heard me, and Thaos released my hand.

"Who are you?" she asked him, eyes wide with terror.

"I'm here to escort you."

"To where?"

"The afterlife."

His voice had taken on a strange, melodic tone. It was hypnotic and soothing, as was his presence. His wings were full, and I noticed with intrigue that several black and purple butterflies fluttered around him.

"I'm dead," she answered, and then a sob left her. "Finally." Her eyes drifted to me, and recognition formed in them. "I know you. You saw me."

My eyes widened, and she stood. Thaos offered his hand to her and said, "It's time."

She smiled and took it. He grabbed my hand as well, and the void fell away. We stood at an enormous black iron gate. I was only a spectator, standing behind them.

"I'm going to hell?" she asked, a tremor in her voice.

"It is not hell, it's Hades. Where you go is not for me to decide. The Three will judge you."

She glanced at him, hesitating only a moment, and then he released her hand. Walking as if she weighed nothing, she floated to the gate. It parted for her, and she disappeared into a blinding light. The gate shut behind her as Thaos returned to my side. Emotion choked me as I spoke.

"Why did you bring me?"

"I thought you would like to see."

"I did."

He wrapped his arm around my waist and pulled me against his side. When he grabbed his scythe, I asked, "Why are you so kind to me?"

The gift of the daggers this morning, now this. His thoughtfulness overwhelmed me.

"I am not kind, Cere. I am Death."

"I think death can be kind," I argued. "It was for her. Sometimes death is the kindest thing for someone suffering."

His gaze slid to me, and I saw his surprise. I noticed his wings had grown larger and roiled like smoke does when you run your hand through it. "You never answer the way I expect you to. Everything you do is unexpected."

"Is that bad?"

"No. You're—"

"Reckless? Vicious?" I interjected with a small smile.

"And many other things."

He opened the void, and we fell through. I shamelessly clung to him more than necessary. I thought of how he'd looked when he wanted to kiss me, and I wished I had let him.

I reminded myself about purity, and about the vision I'd had. But a silly, weak piece of my heart sighed. *"It's just one more time."* One more kiss couldn't hurt. My sight still worked after last night, and it had been so much more than a kiss.

I felt his feet land against solid floor and realized we were in the library. I offered him a questioning look.

"This is where you spend most of your time, isn't it?" he asked.

I nodded. We could let each other go now, but neither of us moved away.

"Your gift," he said curiously. "I didn't realize you could sense emotion."

"How did you know?"

"You cried when you read her. I did not like it."

"It's never happened. The images were intense, too, more so than they've ever been without the vapors. I actually experienced her agony. And I felt how Hades felt, too, as he grew weaker in my vision." I wavered, touching my chest. "I felt his pain as Apollyon ripped his heart out."

His lips turned down. "I didn't like that either."

"Is that normal? Do the Pythia's gifts evolve?"

"Not that I've ever heard."

I frowned. That was an interesting development. "Things are bad, aren't they?"

"Today's revelations were unsettling. We'll see what Zeus says, but I imagine he's going to try and cover it up. I want Hades to cancel the festival, but I know he won't. I don't like all the Olympians coming down here while he's weakened. For all we know, it could be one of them plotting this."

His thumb on my hip drew small lazy circles on my side, like he was doing it without thinking. Sparks of distracting pleasure erupted as he did, and I did my best to ignore them.

"I wish my visions were more precise." I grimaced, thinking of the master smacking the wooden screen when I couldn't tell him who he should be worried about.

"What is it?"

"The person who had me. He always asked me who he needed to be worried about, and I always saw nothing. Until last time. I saw you, but at the time it didn't make sense. He was mad I couldn't elaborate."

Thaos seemed to mull this over. "It meant I was going to take you. What else did you see with him?"

"Always the same thing. This plague. The last time, the images of the undead surfaced. There was something else, too. A baby born of shadow and sun, foretold to unravel his hard work."

"Interesting. Can you tell me anything else about him?"

"No. I'm sorry. I hardly ever saw him."

His gaze remained intense and thoughtful as his hand continued its loose pattern of swirls. The touch was tender and intimate, and my eyes fell to his lips as I thought about kissing him again. Just a kiss. It didn't have to get as heated as it had last night. The thought led my mind down that path, and then I was thinking of the beach and his hands—

"Don't look at me like that."

My eyes snapped back to his. "Like what?"

"Like you're thinking about *obscene* things. I find it very inappropriate," he teased, but his voice was huskier than it had been just moments ago.

I flushed and smiled. "Is it inappropriate if you're the one who did the obscene things I'm thinking about?"

"I would hope that's what you're thinking about. The only other available man you've been around is Ulther, and I like him. I don't want to kill him."

My eyes widened, and then I understood he was joking. Maybe?

"You're supposed to be the responsible one, and here you are looking at me like you want something from me," he said.

"I am terrible at being the responsible one."

"I've noticed."

"It's just kissing."

"Unless it's not. I did a lot more than kiss you last night."

My blood heated. "Well, you're the one who's touching me and making me think inappropriate things."

"What, this?" he asked, his hand stopping.

He lifted the hem of my shirt and flattened his hand against my bare stomach. His pinky finger pushed just under the top button of my pants and started drawing the circles again with his first finger, this time around my navel.

"Is that better?"

"No…and yes," I said, breathless.

"We decided less than twenty-four hours ago that we weren't doing this anymore, as you reminded me twice earlier today."

"I was feeling responsible then."

"And what are you feeling now?"

"Like I could try to be responsible again tomorrow."

He turned me the rest of the way into his chest, and I pressed up on my toes to meet his lips. My hands fisted the front of his shirt and I pulled. When our lips met, I could feel him smiling. Our heads both slanted, and the kiss deepened.

His hands folded around my waist and drew me tight to his body, and I felt a tug at the tail of my braid, followed by his hands working through the strands. He freed my hair, fisting it and pulling my head back. His mouth traveled to my neck and sucked hard, making me gasp. It didn't escape my attention that he left the mark well above where any turtleneck could cover.

The coil of desire twisted to life in my stomach, and my hips pushed against him. He was contesting the collar of my shirt now, trying to push it down.

"This is in the way," he grumbled.

I tried to reach for the hem, but then I heard the fabric ripping. Cool air swept against my chest and stomach. He shoved my shirt and his robe down my arms until they collected at my feet.

"I could've just taken it off," I gasped.

He chuckled against my collarbone, and I felt the point of one of his sharp teeth scrape against my skin. A shot of exhilaration flashed in my chest, accompanied by a wave of heat. He picked me up and carried me to the couch. As he sat, my legs parted, so I straddled him.

I felt the hard length of him beneath me and my instincts guided me as I thrust my hips against him. He groaned and clamped his hands on my waist.

"I think you overestimate my ability to control myself," he hissed against my lips. "Because you're acting like you want to do a lot more than kiss."

"So are you. You just ripped my shirt off."

My breath was shallow as I thrust my mouth against his, distracting him. When I felt his hands relax, I instantly dropped my hips down again, moaning at the friction I created. Another chuckle danced over his lips, but this one was dark and mischievous.

"You are a fearless little mortal."

"I have no idea what you're talking about," I said, feigning innocence as I increased the movement of my hips.

Something like a growl resounded in his chest as he caught my bottom lip with his teeth and tugged. The kiss became rougher, more desperate, and his hands clutched my waist. They encouraged me to move against him, helping me maintain a steady rhythm. The friction of our movements elicited wicked pleasure, shooting shards of intense heat through every cell in my body.

I was reckless, and I was shameless, and I was *alive*. My body hummed with life, every nerve firing with the satisfaction of touching him. Maybe I was the most undeserving Pythia that had ever lived, but I didn't care. The temple was gone. I didn't know who or where the master was, or if anything he'd ever told me was true.

I was making my own decisions now, and I was choosing this. I just wouldn't let it go too far. I still needed my sight if I was going to help save the mortal realm.

In an instant, Thaos lifted me and spun me around like I weighed nothing. My back pressed into his chest, and then he was kissing my neck, slowly sliding the straps of my bra down my shoulders. I snaked my arms through, and he shoved the cups down so the material gathered at my waist. My hand lifted and my fingers threaded in his hair as he took both of my breasts in his hands and kneaded them. I moaned, dropping my head back against his shoulder.

While his left hand settled at my breast, his right moved down to the button of my pants and pulled at it. He pushed underneath and cupped me, making me gasp. Hot desire burned through my entire body, stopping and coiling into a throb beneath his hand.

"You want more?"

I nodded, not sure if I could find my voice.

"Say it."

A shaky breath passed through me. "I want more."

I felt his breath on my cheek, his lips pressing a swift kiss to my jawbone. "Do you trust me?"

"With what?"

"I want my finger inside of you, but I promise to be gentle."

I closed my eyes and gave a small nod. "I trust you."

"We'll talk about your poor judgment of character later," he teased, his deep timbre vibrating through me. After a moment, he whispered, as if he was in awe, "But thank you."

His hand moved, pushing my panties aside, and suddenly he was touching me with no barrier between my skin and his. I cried out, overwhelmed by the intensity of the direct contact. His finger ran up the slit of my core and he moaned deep in his chest.

"You are so wet for me." His voice was thick, and I spread my legs further apart in response.

The hand still on my breast squeezed and the competing sensations overwhelmed me. He touched the bud at the apex of my core first, swirling gently with his finger. I said his name, like a broken plea of submission, as my body writhed against him. The coil of desire was tightening, and the promise of release was building. I felt him sliding his finger down and then pressure against the softness of my center as he pushed inside of me.

As he promised, he was gentle, and I was the one who moved my hips, seeking more.

"Fuck," he hissed as I did. "You're too much."

"More," I rasped, surprising him and myself.

His chest rumbled again, and he sucked on the delicate spot between my neck and my shoulder. His thumb caressed me at the same time as his finger moved inside of me, and I felt myself coming apart. When teeth scraped my skin again, I purposefully pushed my shoulder up.

I moaned when the fangs pierced my tender flesh, just barely. He tensed, all of his movements stopping. I felt the erratic rise and fall of his chest beneath me. His mouth was still there, and I felt his tongue flick across the sensitive marks. He moaned, louder than I'd ever heard him, and then he sucked hard at the bite. Pleasure erupted from the spot and cascaded through me in a rush of pure sensation. My voice grew louder, and his hand started moving again—more aggressive this time.

My back arched, and the pleasure caught me in that second of standing on the edge. The pad of his thumb rolled with more pressure across my sensitive bud, and I fell, losing myself to waves of bliss. I shivered against him, astonished at how this climax compared to last night. The first one shattered my world, yet this went far beyond that.

It felt like I took a lifetime to recover, my eyes finally cracking open. The first thing I saw was the library door, and I remembered it was unlocked. I blushed, thinking of what someone would witness if they walked in right now.

Thaos' free hand still roamed my body in a lazy caress, and I felt his shallow, irregular breaths on my cheek as he withdrew his hand from me. I didn't realize what he was doing until I heard him suck on his finger. My face and body heated when he groaned in pleasure.

"You are so sweet," he praised, lips pressed against my ear. "I've tasted nothing better." I knew he was referring to my blood, too. "But I didn't mean to bite you and I'm sorry."

He sounded anxious, catching me off guard because he hadn't ever been anything but confident in front of me. He thought it would disturb me, and I twisted in his arms to face him. As I expected, he looked guilt ridden.

"I pushed my shoulder up," I admitted, blushing again, but not wanting him to blame himself. "I wanted your bite."

He stared at me, the black tendrils of shadow leaking out of his pupils and into the surrounding violet.

I started babbling, feeling self-conscious. "I noticed you had fangs and Hypnos said gods did that and, I don't know why, but I wanted you to do it on the beach, too. I couldn't help it, I just—"

His head dipped, and he placed the softest of kisses on my lips. My arms wrapped around his neck in an immediate response. The sane, responsible part of me warned that this was quickly becoming alarmingly natural between us. Being in his arms. Kissing him. Wanting him.

I was in his lap, nearly nude again. Even though I hadn't expected it to go farther than it had on the beach, it had escalated well beyond that. And, once again, I'd voiced that I wanted it to. In fact, if anyone was the driving force behind what had just happened it was me, not him.

Withdrawing from the kiss, he pushed out a rough breath. "What am I going to do with you?"

I knew it was a serious question, but I didn't even know what to do with myself

CHAPTER SEVENTEEN

I stood and dashed to the door, sliding the lock into place.

"Seems a little late for that, no?"

"Someone could still walk in," I said, pulling my bra straps back on, "and since I no longer have a shirt to wear…" I picked up the tattered remains of the turtleneck and sighed.

He didn't look sorry at all, reclining on the couch in a relaxed position that was devastatingly sexy. "I prefer you shirtless."

I glared at him, but I felt my cheeks heat slightly. I enjoyed being shirtless with him. "You *are* a bad influence."

His eyebrows shot up. "Me? You're the one who looked at me the way you did."

"You're the one who was touching me."

"Well, I'm proud that my hand on your hip can elicit such a response from you."

"We just can't be alone together," I offered. Obviously, I couldn't trust myself at all to behave sensibly around him. Even with the knowledge I had from my reading of him.

"That might be the first thing we've ever agreed on. My inability to control myself with you is…unsettling. Even now."

His eyes roamed over me, and then he stood and closed the distance between us. His hair was messy, spilling over his forehead and brows. I recalled having laced my fingers through midnight tendrils, and how soft they had been. My eyes fell to his lips, and I shivered.

"All I can think about is kissing you again," I conceded.

He forced out a breath as he stopped in front of me. His hands ran up my bare arms, the cool roughness of them making my skin tingle.

"I'm thinking of much more than that."

Sighing, he pulled his shirt over his head. He offered it to me, and I took it, slipping it on. It might as well have been a dress. I had to roll the sleeves several times to find my hands again.

He sucked in a breath and shook his head.

"What?"

"I was foolish enough to expect that would make it better but seeing you in my clothes is seductive in its own way."

I placed my hands on his bare chest. "And now you're shirtless, so I don't think it helped at all," I whispered.

"Well, we're both being saved by the dead calling me. I must go."

He caught my hand and placed a kiss on my wrist, right on the pulse point. The action surprised me, and I felt my heart clenching. I flattened my hand against his cheek, and he leaned into my touch.

"This is the last time we're doing this," I said, not sounding confident at all. "Right?"

"It should be. Because one of these times I will end up on top of you. Inside of you… and not with my fingers."

I swallowed hard, remembering precisely what that looked like from my vision. My body had a needy, visceral response to the image, and I had to shove it away.

"Can I come with you?"

Surprise crossed his features. "To reap souls? Why?"

I wasn't ready to return to my room and read or do nothing. If I was being honest, I wasn't ready to leave him, either. I shrugged. "I just want to. Please?"

"Please?" He smiled, pulling his robe back on. "That's an expression I didn't think I'd ever hear from you. You are very persuasive when you want to be. But I thought you just said we can't be alone together."

"I'm feeling responsible again."

Although him standing shirtless with only that robe on was quickly dissolving that resolve.

He held me with an inquisitive gaze. "No one has ever asked to go before."

"Then I can come?"

"If you really want to, you can." His eyebrows furrowed. "It's not enjoyable. It just must be done. Most of the time, it's very sad."

"I'm sorry you have to do it alone."

He blinked twice, staring down at me as a flurry of emotions I didn't understand danced across his features. Thaos didn't answer me but grabbed his scythe and draped his arm around my waist.

We plunged into the void for just a breath of a second and then landed in his room, where he grabbed another shirt and put it on. When we entered the blackness again, he tapped the hourglass, and it started spinning in the mechanism that held it.

Our feet hit solid ground, and I realized we were looking at the scene of a car accident, although we were still concealed in the void. A man stood just in front of us looking down what seemed like a tunnel towards where I could see his physical body lying on the pavement. Paramedics worked desperately to save him, but he was mangled and bloody.

Thaos let me go and went to him. The butterflies were back, and the scent of lilies drifted heavier than normal around us. The man turned in astonishment when he sensed someone next to him.

"Who are you?"

"I'm here to escort you to the afterlife." Thaos' voice was so strangely soothing when he was speaking to the dead.

"I can't go," the man said with a sob. "My daughter is in that car. I have to know if she's okay."

"She is," Thaos assured him. "Her injuries aren't severe."

The man looked back down the tunnel. I heard a paramedic yell in desperation, but I couldn't discern the exact words.

"You're sure?"

"I am," Thaos said, offering his hand. "But you cannot stay. It's time."

"Okay."

The man took his hand, and the void shifted. It was the first time I was falling through it without Thaos holding me and I almost yelped. I was glad I didn't though because this moment seemed so raw and sacred.

We landed back at the iron gate, and as the woman had done, the man tensed in fear.

"I'm going to hell?"

"This is Hades. I don't determine where you go. The Three will judge you beyond those gates."

As if that was the only explanation he needed, the man walked forward into that shining light. It was as emotional as the first time I'd witnessed it. I couldn't believe Thaos had done this alone all this time. Millennia. Thousands of years of sadness. And I thought being burdened with the sight was bad. His calling was heartbreaking, and it would last for all time and eternity. At least I would find peace in death.

"What do your butterflies do?" I asked when he returned to my side.

"Their presence soothes the souls. My voice has the same effect. Without it, people would fight me much more than they do. That man didn't want to leave, but he had to. If I wasn't able to calm him, he would've held on and suffered."

I nodded in understanding. "And his daughter was really okay?"

"Yes." He was looking at me again like I was the most intriguing thing he'd ever seen in his life. "Do you want to stay with me? I can take you home if you'd like."

Home.

I knew he meant nothing by it. It was his home. But it made my heart flip strangely in my chest and I felt confused. It wasn't my home.

Or was it? I didn't really have a place to go back to now. The temple was gone. There was my family to consider, but to appear there after all these years? The thought terrified me. What if my presence put their lives in danger?

I leaned into him. "I'd like to stay with you."

The corner of his mouth lifted, and he pulled me to him. I watched him work for hours, enthralled with the tragic beauty of it. I didn't understand how the hourglass worked because he was always there at the exact moment someone needed to cross over. It was magic I just couldn't comprehend.

He came to me as the most recent soul crossed into the light beyond the iron gate. I was trying to hide the yawn that threatened to take me, and I caught a shift in his expression.

"What's wrong?"

"Almost all of these have been deaths because of the plague. It's spreading faster than we predicted."

"What does that mean? Hades will weaken quicker than we thought?"

"Yes. And the mortal realm is descending into chaos," he said, sighing. "We've got one more."

I nodded and folded my arms around his neck so I could lean my head against his chest. Although he appeared calm, it stunned me to feel his heart beating like a snare drum.

"Do gods have faster heartbeats than normal people?" I asked, leaning back to look at him.

A smile tugged at his lips. "No. Usually they're slower."

"Yours is so fast right now."

He gazed down at me with bright eyes. "I told you. You don't understand what you do to me."

We dropped into the void, but I barely felt the fall. My mouth was parted in shock. He was suggesting I caused his heart to race? That stupid, silly part of me felt flattered, and I grinned like a fool.

Our feet landed, and he immediately cursed. He pushed me behind him as I heard a familiar shriek that I recognized from Hades' dungeon. My blood chilled and my hand snapped to my weapon. We were in the midst of a pine forest somewhere and Thaos let the void fall away.

I peeked around him and realized that a person had just died, and they were changing. The man was crawling on all fours, squealing in agony. He fell and flopped to his back and his body flexed into a pained bridge, his toes and the back of his head the only things still touching the ground. I covered my mouth in horror as his tan skin started peeling away.

The man's screams ripped through my ears as he tore at his clothes. When he was nude, he didn't stop desperately clawing at himself.

"Oh, Gods," I whispered, covering my mouth with my hand.

He was tearing his own skin away from his body. It sloughed off like he was shedding it. Underneath, he was revealing the pearly alabaster complexion identical to the woman in the dungeon. Like her, the new skin didn't boast human characteristics like hair, a navel, nipples, or genitals. It was just one smooth covering of glossy white flesh.

He shrieked to life, turning on us with obsidian eyes burning with hunger. Thaos stalked forward and removed his head with one quick, unforgiving swipe of his scythe.

Around us, I heard several more howls. He glanced around and then hurried back to me.

I peered up at him. "How many?"

"Too many."

I scanned the tree line where they were emerging and counted at least ten more creatures.

"I can help," I said, raising my dagger.

He didn't have time to argue with me as they advanced towards us. I noticed he tried to take the brunt of them, still blocking me, and I moved from behind him. One creature clamped down on his forearm and he hissed in pain, but his focus was still on me.

"Cere," he warned through gritted teeth. "Run. I'll find you."

My annoyance spiked, and I ignored him as a creature rushed me. The way they moved was disturbing—running on all fours instead of upright. It lunged at my throat and my training instincts kicked in. Jamming the dagger underneath its chin and up into its skull, I ended its misery.

I glanced over at him. "I can do this."

He shoved out a breath, but muttered, "I know you can. Do not let them bite you. Mortals get sick and die or turn."

His back was to me the next moment, and he was fighting with that graceful ferocity that I could only dream of possessing. He still stepped in front of me, trying to hold them all back, but I realized they were fighting to get around him. They shrieked in desperation, trying to attack me.

One slipped by and rushed me. I crouched, diving slightly to my right and tripping it as it flew by. It fell face down, and I leapt on its back, pushing my dagger into the soft spot at the base of its skull.

I turned and found another one almost on top of me. I kicked out with my foot, catching it square in the chest. Its teeth snapped at my ankle and a beat of panic coursed through me. Reacting, I thrust my dagger into its temple. A shriek died in its throat, and I pulled my blade free.

I realized I was hearing the ring of metal against metal and turned to find Thaos in a fight with someone who was certainly not undead. They wore a brown hooded robe pulled up around their face. It had to be another God or Goddess because they were nearly as fast and agile as Thaos.

Movement caught my eye, and I saw the remaining two creatures rushing towards him. I ran before I even understood what I was doing.

An irrational rage overtook me at the thought of him being harmed, even though they were interested in me. I jumped in, close enough to feel the wind whistling off of the whirling blades. Dispatching one creature with a thrust to the eye, I turned and pulled the blade free. I sidestepped the final beast and spun, shoving my blade through its neck and into its spinal cord.

I felt a sudden chill and turned to find shadows pouring out of Thaos and engulfing the one who was attacking him.

"You're not going anywhere," he said through gritted teeth.

The brown-robed figure was flickering like a dying lightbulb, blinking and then reappearing the next second. I realized they were trying to travel similarly to Hypnos, and the shadow was preventing them.

"Who are you?"

They giggled. "A new order will rise, Death. There's nothing you can do to stop it."

It was a woman's voice. She raised her sword and plunged it through her own heart. I gasped in shock at the quick and violent act, glancing at Thaos, who seethed with anger.

The shadows pulled back, and her body collapsed to the ground.

"She's dead?"

"Yes."

"A Goddess?"

"No, but she's immortal. A dryad. A woodland nymph. An old one, too, she was powerful."

Thaos pushed the hood back from her face, revealing a beautiful woman with strawberry red hair. She didn't look a day over twenty. Leafy vines laced into hair and eyebrows, framing blank forest green eyes that stared forward into the sky.

"I've never heard of them. Dryads," I said, studying her.

His eyebrows furrowed in confusion. "I haven't seen one in so long. I didn't know if they even still existed."

"Why did she attack you? This was a trap?"

"It was, and it's not the first. I think they want to kill me so I can't reap souls. If that happens, Hades will weaken beyond help."

"Where did her soul go? Maybe we could interrogate her in the afterlife?"

"While I enjoy your ingenuity," he said, and I swore I saw a flash of desire in his eyes, "she accepted her death, so her soul did not call to me. She's probably deep behind the iron gate now, beyond even my reach."

He searched her robe and pockets but found nothing.

"Her robe pin," I said, pointing.

It was the same golden snake that adorned the temple archway. The same symbol that was branded on the neck of the creature in the dungeon.

Standing, he walked to me, looking me over for injuries. "Are you hurt? Did they bite you?"

"No. I'm doing better than you."

The wound on his forearm was seeping blood and didn't seem to be healing. "I shouldn't have brought you," he said, still looking at me with concern. "But I'm glad I did. That would've been interesting without your help."

CHAPTER EIGHTEEN

He took us back to his room and started putting the same oil he'd used on me across his forearm.

"You won't get sick?"

"I haven't yet," he said. "They've bitten me before."

I shuddered. "That man changing was the most disturbing thing I've ever witnessed. What will you do now?"

"I'm sorry you had to see it." He sounded sincere in his apology. "I've got to go back and reap those souls, then I'm going to try to persuade Hades to cancel the festival. Most likely I will fail."

I cleared my throat, wanting to ask something and not knowing when I'd have the opportunity again.

"When is the festival?"

"It's two weeks from today." He arched his eyebrow. "Why?"

"And everyone is going?"

"Yes." Sensing my intent, he continued, "Everyone except you. And Ulther. I would stay with you but if someone is plotting to attack Hades, I need to be there."

"I want to go."

"No."

"Please," I whispered.

His eyes flashed, and he frowned. "Don't do that to me."

"Do what?"

"Make me feel bad for wanting to keep you safe. Not only am I suspicious of an outside attack, but Apollo is attending as well."

"I can defend myself. And you said with the ring on no one would know it's me."

"Yes. Most likely. But I don't know for certain. Especially him."

"Then I should be able to go. Please. I'm going crazy here. I want to leave this house. I know we were out today, but I'm talking about a day with other people. It's been so long."

I grabbed the upper sleeve of his robe, well aware I was begging. He looked sympathetic, running his thumb over my cheekbone, but I knew he wasn't going to give in.

"Do you want me to get you something? More books? Or that, what do humans call it—*Netflix*?"

"I don't want anything," I argued, feeling my anger spike. "I want out. I'm tired of being locked up. That's all I've ever been."

"I'm sorry," he said. "It's not happening."

"It's not fair."

"You're right, it's not."

I huffed at that. "Will it ever end? Me being treated as some precious item that everyone wants to hoard or steal. It's revolting."

He hesitated. "It is and I'm sorry."

"That's all you can say?"

"I don't know what else to say. I agree with you, but that doesn't change the fact that you can't go."

I gritted my teeth and glared up at him. "I am so tired of being a possession and not a person."

His expression changed to something softer, and I realized it was pity. My gut churned at that. I didn't want pity. I wanted freedom. Today had sparked something inside me. I could fight. I could protect myself.

He reached out to touch my cheek again, but I pulled away. Turning on my heel, I left and didn't glance back.

———————

The next morning I paced in front of the fireplace long before Aeryn was due to knock on my door. Thoughts of the undead and their origins disturbed me too much to sleep.

A dark voice of reason told me what I knew as The Cause was not fighting to stop the undead. It looked like they were connected with the appearance of the creatures.

What else could the snake brand mean?

I was struggling to accept it. The master and the overseer I could consider having ulterior motives, but Keilah and Laurenth? There was no way they devoted themselves to something that would devastate the mortal realm. Millions of people were going to die.

The mystery of it was driving me insane, as were thoughts of other things. A certain God of Death who seemed to make me forget myself and my priorities without even trying.

I glanced at his shirt that was lying on the wardrobe. If it didn't have some blood on it, I would probably still be wearing it.

Even if I was angry when I left yesterday, I knew he was trying to keep me safe. However, I was also so tired of being "kept safe." I just wanted to go to a stupid festival and experience something normal. It irritated me thinking about how natural it was for other people to just live, while everything they took for granted was unobtainable to me.

A knock on the door told me Aeryn had arrived. She was dressed casually today in a dark green day dress and black leggings. When she realized whose shirt was on the wardrobe, her eyes widened, and I saw pink flood her cheeks.

"Oh," I said, flushing. "We didn't—it's not."

She giggled, her gaze falling to my upper neck where he'd sucked on my skin, and then my shoulder where I knew the small puncture marks were still visible.

"You don't have to be embarrassed."

I nodded. It was nice of her to say but my face still blazed.

"But you should get ready."

"For what?"

Her eyebrows knitted together. "He told us, Thanatos, that we were to take you to see the town today. Didn't he tell you?"

I stared at her and my heart swelled. "He's having you take me out?"

"Yes. Ulther and I. And Hypnos wants to go."

"To do what?"

"Whatever you want. He instructed me to get you anything you asked for."

I blushed again, and I noticed she did too. "He's very taken with you," she commented.

"What do you mean?"

She shrugged. "He just acts much differently with you."

"Oh." I didn't know what else to say.

"Now," she said, clapping her hands excitedly. "What should we have the wardrobe make for you?"

I chose a white dress with small yellow flowers and brown leggings. I liked the fact I could hide both of my daggers this way. Aeryn helped me tie my hair half up and half down instead of braiding it, complimenting me the entire time about how long it was.

I looked at my freckles, which came from my father, and I tried to picture his face. My heart dropped because I forgot more all the time. I wondered if someday I wouldn't be able to conjure the image at all.

Staring at myself in the mirror, I did something I hadn't done in a long time. I dropped the shield and tried to read myself. When I was young, the voices had warned me every day that the master was coming for me, but they'd never offered me anything else concerning my own future. This time was no different. The voices were quiet.

I sighed and shielded myself again. I didn't particularly like my gift. Most of the time it didn't help at all and then at rare moments it did. But it didn't seem to have rhyme or reason to when it would be useful.

I went back out and joined Aeryn and Ulther in the hall. We found Hypnos in the dining room, and to my surprise, he'd donned an aqua blue fitted shirt and dark brown leathers today. It was the first time I'd seen him in anything except his robe.

"You look handsome," I said, drawing a smile.

"Yes, well, I may see my wife today and I was hoping to catch her eye."

Their relationship was strange, and I really didn't understand it at all. I still hadn't met her or seen her at the house, and she seemed to cause him a lot of stress.

"Well, sorry to tell you Sleeping Beauty, but I've got to flash us there."

I frowned and glanced at the food on the table. "I'll skip breakfast then."

We stood in a circle, joining hands. I held Aeryn's and Hypnos', and when I glanced at where Aeryn's hand connected with Ulther's, I saw his thumb drawing small circles against hers. My lips curled in a tender smile.

The awful sensation pulled at my stomach, and then the world blurred around me. It was over just as quickly as before, and we stood at the head of a large Main Street. People bustled about their business, and I noted many wonderful smells permeating the air.

Streets of black cobblestone spider-webbed around me, flanked by sidewalks of pure gold. The buildings all reflected this color scheme, and the architecture was strange and asymmetrical. The shops almost looked cartoonish, tall and thin, with curved bows for walls instead of straight edges. I noticed green, purple, and white were the only other colors that were thrown into the landscape, providing some interesting contrast.

Intricate lampposts topped by small golden statues of none other than Cerberus himself held hanging baskets of flowers. I recognized one plant as a type of white lily, and I smelled it. The familiar scent made me smile like a fool.

"Not what you would expect from the Underworld, is it?" Ulther asked.

"No," I said, looking at everything. I was suddenly overcome with blunt emotion. This was the first time I'd been out in public in a decade, walking among other people like a normal person. No one knew who I was. They didn't stare at me or dive out of the way as we walked. In fact, Hypnos was the one who earned sideways glances and whispers.

"Who are these people? How does a person come to live in Hades?"

"The demigods are most likely in the same track of mind as I am," Ulther said. "Not everyone enjoys the shining white political mess of the Olympic realms. Most of the mortals probably had ancestors that served one God or another and found their way down here at some point. Hades is calmer. No one bothers the King of the Dead, and he generates enough fear that hardly anyone has ever tried to infiltrate his realm. Those who did paid dearly."

Hades was scary. He had a powerful aura, and when his eyes turned white—yikes. "The king must be fierce."

"They say he can turn people to dust with just a touch, but I've never seen it."

"That's horrifying."

"It is. Thanatos too. They say he can kill someone with shadow. It comes from his mouth and suffocates the person. But I'm not sure if that's true, either. They call it the kiss of death."

He talked like a little boy in awe. Whispering like it might be scandalous to mention such things.

"It is true," I said.

His head whipped to me, mouth open. "You've seen it? Gods, wait until I tell my friends it's real. What was it like?"

I thought of the overseer's face, and the blood leaking from all orifices. "It was… intense. Maybe disturbing. But the man on the receiving end deserved it."

"Wow," he said, beaming. "I hope I get to guard you for a long time. Maybe I'll see it too."

I snorted a laugh, and then Aeryn grabbed my hand. "What would you like to do, Cere? The day is yours. What do you want to see?"

I looked around at the various shops and attractions. "Everything."

We did as much of everything as we could. I loved every second of it, and the people were so kind. Hypnos had disappeared after we'd arrived, and I hadn't seen him since.

After visiting several stores, we sat at a small sidewalk cafe eating pastry and drinking my first ever cup of coffee. It was bitter, but the cream in it made it smooth, and I liked it very much.

"What is the story with Hypnos and his wife?"

Aeryn looked around, as if checking for him, and then whispered, "I don't think she cares for him. But he seems taken by her. It's sad, but it happens a lot with the Gods and Goddesses."

"Then why are they married?"

"She was gifted to him by her mother Hera, Queen of Olympus. He did a favor for her."

"Must have been some favor," I remarked. "That's appalling." The thought of being gifted to a man by your own mother made my chest ache.

She shrugged. "It happens a lot in this world. It's how things are done. Women, many times, are viewed as possessions for trade instead of people. It's one reason I prefer the Underworld, although Hades isn't innocent in the practice either, unfortunately."

"Why are you here Aeryn? In the Underworld. You're human right?"

"I am. My ancestors served Ares, the God of War. It wasn't a pleasant calling. Some of the gods allow citizens freedom to come and go as they please, but Ares is not one of those."

I nodded in understanding. "His own daughter told me he was terrible."

She offered me a tight smile. "When my mother found out she was pregnant, my father risked his life to defect and sneak her down here."

"And now they live here? In town?"

"My mother does. My father didn't survive to see me born free."

My face fell, and I shocked myself by grabbing her hand. It was the first time I'd initiated contact with anyone besides Thaos.

"Oh no. I'm so sorry."

She shrugged and offered me another sad smile. "I just try to live the best life I can for him. When I'm not working at the Cave of Hypnos, I help my mom in her bakery. I'm the one who makes your lemon pastries. Glendyl is an incredible chef, but he doesn't have enough patience for baking. Someday maybe I'll own the cake shop myself." Her eyes had lightened talking about the future. They drifted away from my face, and then a happier smile crossed her features. "Excuse me a moment? I see a friend of mine."

She called out to a girl with smooth cocoa skin and beautiful curly hair that was standing by a fountain. They embraced and then started chatting, too far away for me to hear the conversation. I noticed Ulther's eyes followed her the entire way. While she'd spoken of her life at the bakery, he'd been beyond smitten.

Not one to hold back a question, I asked, "Are you in a relationship with her?"

His face flamed to life, the deep flush spreading across his already red-toned skin all the way to the tips of his ears.

"Of course not."

"Are you lying to me?"

"No," he said, looking sheepish. His eyes found her again. "We are more than friends, but nothing more than that. However, I would very much like to be in a relationship with her."

"Then ask her." I felt it was obvious she shared some feelings for him.

"I have. She doesn't want to be with me," he explained quietly.

My eyebrows knit together. "Why?"

"Because she's human and I'm a demigod. She'll grow old and die much sooner than I will, and I'll be able to do nothing but watch it happen. She says she won't do that to me."

My heart pinched. How tragic that seemed. My thoughts drifted to myself and Thaos. The same would be true between us. I would age and he would stay the same. Not that we had a future together, I reminded myself.

"I'm sorry, Ulther, that's terrible."

"At least when I'm guarding you I get to be around her more often." He smiled. "Maybe I'll win her heart."

My lips tugged up, and I sipped my coffee. I hoped he did.

There was so much going on around me, and my eyes wandered to the busy street. They connected for a moment with a woman who was walking by. The eye contact forced the walls in my mind down, and I tensed in surprise. That had never happened before.

Images filled my mind of one of the undead attacking her and tearing at her throat. I could feel her pain and her panic. Gasping, I realized it was going to happen right here next to the fountain.

I shot to my feet, grabbing the woman's arm. She glared at me with confusion.

"You need to run," I said, gripping her shoulders. I looked around in a panic, yelling at everyone close to me. "Run! Run!"

The woman pulled from my grasp and stared at me like I should be committed to an institution, as did several others.

Ulther laid his hand on my shoulder. "Cere? What's happening?"

My eyes searched around the fountain, and I cried, "We need to get Aeryn!"

A bloodcurdling scream sounded over the noise of the street. Ulther drew his sword and my hand drifted to my dagger.

"Run!" I yelled again, hysterical, and this time people listened.

"Oh, Gods," Ulther whispered.

I followed his gaze as people started stampeding past us down the street. A wailing screech filled the air, inhuman and chilling. One creature, an undead, was on the street. It launched itself on the poor man closest to it and tore at his throat. Crimson blood poured from the wound, and the screams erupted louder.

Panicked faces whipped by me, and I searched the crowd.

"Aeryn!" Ulther bellowed in a panic, climbing up and standing on the table.

"There!" I cried, finding her hunched over the body of her friend, who had been trampled in the chaos.

He looked at me, unsure. Confusion made me pause, and then I realized he was trying to choose between his duty to guard me and Aeryn.

I blinked in surprise, shocked that he would think I would have him abandon his love for me.

"Well, let's get her!" I shouted, surging forward in her direction.

He jumped down and took the lead, throwing people aside as we fought against the crowd. I clasped the back of his leather cuirass, so I didn't lose him. My skin crawled in discomfort at so many bodies touching mine, but I told myself to get over it.

We broke through the edge of the wave of people and onto the empty, disordered street. I searched for Aeryn, crying out in panic when I spotted her. There were six undead now, three of them busy eating. Bile rose in my throat—they were eating fallen people. The sounds were nightmare fodder, slurping and crunching that made my stomach turn.

The fourth headed for Aeryn, who covered the body of her friend with her own. Ulther pulled away from my grasp and ran towards her. The two remaining creatures sniffed the air, the sound sucking into the black pits where their noses should be. When their eyes set on me, they stopped.

They wailed and jumped from the platform, rushing towards me with speed. As they had last night, they moved on all fours like deranged animals. Momentarily unsettled, I stepped back in horror. Thaos wasn't here this time.

The icy fear filled me again, as it had when I'd faced the wendigo, but I pushed it away and took a deep breath. Time seemed to slow down, and I drew my dagger up. The first one lunged at me, and I sidestepped, allowing it to pass. I caught its upper arm as it went by and slammed the dagger into the base of its skull.

The second was right behind and I spun, trying to use the body of the dead one as a shield. The creature rammed into me, knocking me down with the dead one between us.

It was howling, crazed, and snapping its teeth, trying to get around the head of the fallen one and seize my throat. I gagged at the smell of its breath, like rot mixed with the embers of a dying campfire. I reached up and grabbed it by the throat, trying to hold it back. It was incredibly strong, and I pulled my head to the left as it dove forward. I heard its teeth clack just beside my ear. I was barely saved by the space the dead body was putting between us.

I slammed my palm against its forehead, and a scream of effort left me as I pushed with everything I had. Its head snapped back, and I jammed my dagger into its throat. Black blood spewed from the wound onto my face, and I turned my head away, stunned that the blood was cold and thick. I sliced with the dagger, drawing it across the creature's flesh as violently as I could.

Chokes and gurgles left it, but when I opened my eyes, it astonished me to see it was still trying to bite me even with its throat flayed open. I withdrew the dagger and then sank it into its neck again, finding the spinal cord this time. The creature finally stilled, and I grunted with effort as I tried to move out from under the weight of both of them.

Ulther was there, helping me. He carried Aeryn's unconscious friend on his shoulder and was muttering every curse word in existence, which startled me because he never swore.

I heard more wailing and shimmied out from under the beasts. I popped to my feet, wiping the blood from my eyes.

Ulther had killed the one that almost had Aeryn, but three more had emerged. They galloped at us, that unholy gait covering the ground between us at incredible speed. Ulther set the unconscious girl down again and took his weapon in both hands.

"I am very relieved you can handle yourself," he quipped. "Or I fear I would experience the kiss of death firsthand."

I snorted a laugh, and he smirked at me.

They were upon us now and I stepped to the first, going on the offensive and slamming my hand against its shoulder as it rose to its feet. Although aggressive, they had no sense of fighting. I stuck my foot behind its leg, pushing and tripping it at the same time. It fell to its back, and I pounced, shoving the dagger into its neck.

Ulther had dispatched the other closest to us, leaving just one. He kicked it in the chest, and it flew back towards me. I dodged to the left and then whirled, grabbing the back of its neck with my right hand, and sinking my blade into its eye with my left. Pride and adrenaline surged through me. I'd just done that.

A new confidence took root in my chest. I *could* take care of myself. I didn't need to be kept safe.

I found Ulther with a grin, and he returned it. We looked like two kids that always sat on the bench and finally got to sub into a game. But his face paled, and he gazed over my shoulder with wide eyes.

I whirled, thinking there was another beast but finding Thaos flanked by twenty soldiers in full armor. The suits were beautiful, black with gold embellishments, and their crested helmets made them appear much taller than they really were.

"Why am I not surprised to find you here?" Thaos hissed from the dark shadow of his hood.

"It wasn't Ulther's fault," I blurted. "I ran in, and he followed."

"As if I would actually think it was Ulther's idea. Ulther is not reckless."

I squared my shoulders, setting my jaw in defiance. "They were killing people. We had to do something."

"I would've handled it when I got here. You should've waited for me."

"I didn't know you were coming. And several more people could've been harmed if we hadn't intervened. It's not my fault you were so slow."

Ulther made a choked sound, and several of the soldiers shifted on their feet. Thaos stepped towards me, so our chests nearly touched. I refused to back away, glaring up into the black of his hood. I knew he wouldn't harm me, no matter how many scary shadows he wanted to project.

"You vex me."

"Good. You know I can wield my weapon just fine. Quit treating me like a child."

Hypnos suddenly appeared, looking dreary and intoxicated.

"What'd I miss?" he slurred, glancing around at the carnage. "A lot apparently. Whoops. Good job though, team, you didn't die. Except for her...she looks close. Do we know her?"

He was staring at the girl on the ground where Aeryn leaned over her and held her hand.

"She's not," Thaos said. "She's just unconscious."

"Good to know," Hypnos answered, his tone indicating he couldn't care less. "Well, Sleeping Beauty, how was your first day out?"

"It was lovely," I chimed, still glowering up at Thaos. It really had been, too, until the monsters showed up. But even fighting with them had been slightly exhilarating. I wondered if Laurenth would be proud. "If no one had been hurt, I'd give it five stars."

"I'm glad you two find this amusing. They could have killed you, Cere. Or bitten you. Then you would turn into one of these beasts."

"But I wasn't killed or bitten. And several other people weren't either because Ulther and I were here. You could just say thank you."

Hypnos guffawed.

Thaos turned to his brother, whose mouth snapped shut. "Take her home."

He turned on his heel and walked through the soldiers, shadows billowing around him. They were quick to move out of his way and offer him a wide berth.

I considered following him and continuing the argument, but I glanced down at the creature next to me. It was the first one I'd killed, the one that saved me from being bitten by the second.

It was devoid of all clothing like the rest, but I could tell it was female. A necklace still hung down to its collar bone. Somehow it avoided being torn away when the creature shed its skin.

The world tilted beneath my feet. It was a heart-shaped locket I would recognize anywhere. I'd seen it every day for ten years. Blood rushed to my ears, and my heart beat suddenly louder than anything else around me.

I fell to my knees by the body and grabbed the locket, opening the latch and finally looking at what I'd never been allowed to see. It was Keilah in one photo, but she looked much younger. She was smiling in a way I'd never seen in all of our years together. A true beam of joy and happiness. The picture was of her and a handsome young man. They gazed into each other's eyes, and I realized she was wearing a white veil. A wedding photograph. The other half of the locket was a picture of two little girls, their features a mixture of Keilah and her husband.

My eyes tracked to the creature's face. It was so hard to tell with no real discernable human features, but I looked at the rise of her cheekbones, and I knew it was her. This thing was Keilah. I turned her head, being as gentle as I could. The snake brand was fresh on the back of her neck.

"Oh, no. No, no," I whined, a sob choking me. I pushed it down, not letting the tears fall.

"Cere?" I realized it was Ulther speaking to me. His hand was on my shoulder again. "What's happening?"

"I know her. She was my handmaid at the temple."

I immediately looked up and scanned for Thaos. Despite the words we'd just exchanged, I wanted him. But he wasn't there anymore and had probably gone to see Hades.

I leaned into Ulther, who tensed in surprise and then wrapped his arm around my shoulders. My eyes found Hypnos, who looked down at me with pity.

"She was my friend," I whispered. "Please make sure her body is taken care of properly?"

CHAPTER NINETEEN

After we stayed long enough that I was sure Keilah's body, as well as the rest, were being cared for like they deserved, Hypnos brought us home. I was told they would be cremated to ensure the infection didn't accidentally spread. After some thought, I'd left her locket with her. It was hers.

Ulther and I ascended the stairs toward my room, and he was stealing strange glances at me.

"What?" I snapped, annoyed.

"I am so sorry for your friend," he said sincerely. "But you really are reckless, you know."

"Ulther not you, too. We had to help—"

"I don't mean fighting the beasts, I mean Death. I don't understand how you get away with speaking to him like that. In front of the King's Knights, too."

I realized with a shock that he sounded worried for me, like he thought it was dangerous for me to talk back to Thaos. I remembered how he spoke of the kiss of death, like a child in awe.

"He won't harm me, Ulther. I'm too important to Hades. I just hate how he treats me like a child. I can handle myself just fine."

"I believe you can handle yourself, and I think he does too, but I don't think he worries for you like a parent does for a child."

"Worries? Please. He's only protecting me because he was instructed to do so."

"I know that's not true, and I think you do as well."

My heart dropped slightly. "What are you saying?"

"I think he worries for you like, well, I would worry for Aeryn. Like a lover would."

I paused, glancing at him. "That's not true, Ulther, he's assured me that death cannot know love. We are *not* lovers."

His eyes fell to the mark on my neck, and I flushed, while he chuckled. "If you say so. Plus, lovers aren't always in love, but they certainly feel something."

"How much trouble do you think we're in?" I asked, shifting the subject from that area of discomfort.

"It would probably be less if you hadn't antagonized him."

I sighed, feeling guilty. I had acted badly, worse than normal.

"I should apologize," I muttered. "And I'm going to hate every second of it."

He didn't answer but fought a smile trying to turn his lips. We stopped outside my door, and I looked at him. Like me, he had the blood of the creatures on him, and it smelled like rot and ash.

"You can go shower, Ulther. I think I'll be okay in my room."

"You want me to abandon my post after what has already happened today? I don't want Thanatos any angrier than he already is. I think I'll wait until I can at least leave you with Hypnos."

Nodding, I went in and showered quickly, trying my best to repress what I'd just seen in that courtyard with the fountain. I didn't want to break down and cry, afraid I'd never stop. Afterwards, Ulther walked me to the dining room where I found the God of Sleep. He looked worried, bordering on disturbed.

"I'll go shower now," Ulther said.

"What's wrong?" I asked Hypnos, suddenly frightened something may have happened to Thaos.

"I don't think it was a coincidence those things showed up on the day you happened to be in town."

"Me either," I answered, the guilt returning. "But I don't understand how they would've known I was there. I feel terrible that those people died because of me."

He put his head in his hands. "I think it was because of me."

"What?"

"I went and saw Pasathea, my wife. I may have been too forthcoming with information."

I gasped. "You told her who I was?"

"No! No I swear I didn't tell her you were the Pythia. But I used your name, Cere."

My mind whirled. This revelation confirmed things I'd been trying to deny. The only people that knew me as Cere before I came here were the ones at the temple, and the master.

"I was using my sight to aid the enemy," I whispered, as the truth I'd been denying barreled through me. "That whole time, all of those years I thought I was helping. But I was confirming for him that whatever he was doing was leading to the creation of those things."

The realization crashed through me, and my eyes burned. I felt physically ill, my stomach churning. Even if I hadn't done it purposely, I'd played a direct hand in the deaths of many and the future deaths of many more. In Keilah's death. I squeezed my eyes shut as images of her ripping her skin off filled my mind.

"It's not your fault," he said softly. "You were a child. He manipulated you."

"I was an idiot," I spat in disgust.

He leaned back in his chair and rested his head in his right hand. "So was I."

"Your wife," I realized. "She's a traitor?"

"Possibly. But we weren't in a completely private area. Anyone could've heard."

"Hypnos," I gasped, stunned by his carelessness.

"I'm sorry. She's the Goddess of Relaxation and Hallucination. You don't know how persuasive she can be."

Despite my irritation I felt sorry for him. I knew he desired her affection and attention.

"Why are you married to her? She doesn't love you."

I didn't say it to be rude. I said it as a friend, and I had no doubt he would be as blunt with me if our roles were reversed.

"She doesn't," he admitted. "But I love her."

"Why? I don't understand."

"I don't either. I just can't let her go."

"You're a lovesick fool."

Hypnos jumped in surprise, and my eyes found the source of the voice. Thaos stood in the door. He could be very sneaky when he wanted to be, and his tone had been pure acid.

"Fuck," was all Hypnos said, not lifting his head from his hand.

"At least we know now that the people who had me before are the ones responsible for the creatures," I said quietly. "They're the only ones who would recognize my name. And one of the creatures...I knew her."

It was getting more difficult to hold the tears at bay. The shock was wearing off and reality was threatening to break through. I couldn't reconcile Laurenth and Keilah with those types of people. They had to be unaware like I had been. I knew they couldn't possibly know the truth of The Cause. I wondered how much of everything had been the truth or lies.

"I'm going to go see if Glendyl has more wine. Or something stronger maybe," Hypnos said, standing.

He left, exiting through the door that led into the kitchen. I looked at Thaos, who turned on his heel and walked back down the hallway.

I followed, almost running to catch up. He entered the office where I'd found him playing Sudoku. It seemed like it had been so long ago. I felt like a completely different person than the one who had peeked through that cracked door.

"Hey," I said, pushing the door in. "I need to say something."

He looked at me pointedly but didn't answer.

"I'm sorry," I mumbled.

His eyebrows shot up in surprise.

"Not for killing the creatures, I'd do that again in a heartbeat." He sighed in annoyance, and I added, "But I acted—" I huffed, hating it as much as I thought I would. "I acted like a brat and I'm sorry."

"A *brat*," he said, arching an eyebrow. "That's a good word."

I frowned. "Only I get to call myself one when it's warranted."

I thought I saw a shadow of a smile on his lips.

"But I was acting that way because I can handle myself just fine and I felt like you were treating me like a child."

"I'm supposed to keep you safe, yet you seem to want to do anything in your power to prevent me from doing that. I knew before I even got there I'd find you right in the middle of it, and you didn't disappoint."

"I know Hades wants me for my sight and you need to protect that for him, but I am a person, and I can make my own choices. Especially if it means helping people."

He looked frustrated. "I don't like the insinuation that I only want you safe because you're the Pythia."

That was not what I expected him to say, and I stared at him in a state of shock. He, too, looked surprised that the words had passed his lips.

"What's that supposed to mean?" I asked, finally finding my voice.

He stared at me for a moment and then pushed his hand back through his hair. "Nothing."

Several long seconds of awkward silence settled between us until I cleared my throat. "Well, uh, I'm just saying I'm capable of defending myself."

"I know you're capable. I saw it last night and today, and even with the wendigo. But capable people are killed every day, trust me."

"Well I'm still not sorry I did it."

"I'm not either. You did save people and I'm glad for that. I just wish you were more cautious, and not quite so brave. It would make my life easier."

"I'm just trying to make sure you're not bored," I said, smiling. "And since I'm already here apologizing, I might as well utter yet *another* thank you for having Aeryn and Ulther take me to town. It really was amazing to be out."

"I'm glad you enjoyed it." His lips tilted. "You should be careful, or you may make a habit out of thanking me."

I found my hands were restless, wringing each other at first and now playing with the hem of my shirt. I wanted to touch him, and I shouldn't. My emotions were threatening to boil over, and I felt myself desiring not just his kiss, but his company. I wanted him to hold me through the storm of grief that was threatening to consume me. But, I hadn't cried in five years, and I didn't plan on starting now.

"I should go," I whispered.

He nodded just barely, but I saw the same conflict in his eyes that probably filled mine. I didn't want to go, and he wanted me to stay.

I turned, opening the door.

"There is one more thing," he said.

When I turned back around, he was standing behind me, right next to me. I gasped in surprise and glared up at him. I hated that. He grinned down at me, knowing I did. I watched him lift my wrist to his lips, kissing the pulse point there.

"Is this the one more thing?" I asked, my heart fluttering as I flattened my hand against his cool cheek.

"No," he said, his voice soft. "Don't ask to go because I can't take you right now. It's not safe for you or for them. But I found your parents, your brother, and your sister. I didn't interact with them, but they seem fine. I just thought you should know that. I thought maybe it could bring you some peace."

I stared at him in disbelief. "You saw them?"

"Yes, and they're safe. Untouched by plague. The fae are the ones at the border dealing with the undead that are leaking over from the human world. For now, they're doing a sufficient job."

"How did you find them?"

"I've been looking since you told me that first night. I have my ways, but it still took some time to find the right Henry."

Well, so much for my resolve to remain tearless. His face blurred as my vision swam. Thick, hot tears spilled over my lashes and ran heavy down my cheeks. I pressed my forehead into his chest and a sob choked me. His arms wrapped around me, and he held me while the tears of joy and relief for my family, as well as sorrow for Keilah, and guilt for the role I played in her demise, streamed down my face. It was a long, ugly cry, and I had no idea how he would ever find me attractive again afterwards.

Hiccuping and sniffling, I clenched my fists in the material of his shirt. "Thaos, I have to tell you something."

He held me back from him and cupped my face, brushing the tears away with his thumbs.

"I read you, that night we were together on the beach. I saw—"

"Don't," he cut in, frowning. "I don't want to know."

"But—"

He stopped my words by pressing his lips to mine in a soft kiss. I responded, grabbing his wrists and pulling myself up to him. This kiss didn't carry the same heat as the others, but rather a sweet tenderness that frightened me even more.

I broke away from him. "We can't do this. That's part of what I saw. You *can't* love me."

He let me go like I'd physically shocked him, straightening and looking down at me. His lips formed a thin, emotionless line.

"Then it should be fine because I told you I never will. I'm not capable and I'm not willing. Look at my brother who has jeopardized everything trying to earn the love of a woman who will never feel the same way about him. It's foolish."

His blunt words stung, but also brought some relief. "As long as you promise that's the truth then my vision won't be realized."

"I promise it is."

"Okay, good," I said the words even as my chest burned uncomfortably. "I'm glad."

This attraction between us was undeniable, so strong and irresistible. But it was also foolish, as he said. He would never love me, and I couldn't ever give myself fully to him for fear of losing my sight.

The air grew tense around us, and I sighed. "Thank you for checking on my family. I really should go."

I turned and left, feeling confused and like I suddenly carried a lead weight within my heart.

CHAPTER TWENTY

That night I existed in that awful place of awareness that I was having a nightmare, but I couldn't wake up. The things I'd seen all meshed together into a horrific kaleidoscope of images.

First, it was Keilah, smiling like she had been in her wedding photo. But the dream soured, and I watched, screaming in horror, as she pulled her own flesh from her body like the man in the forest had done.

As my nightmares always did, they shifted to prey on my love for my family. The same movie played out. We're all together, laughing, and then they were screaming in agony and ripping their own skin away. The pearly white flesh appeared, and they howled from their too-wide mouths. I was backing up in terror, but I couldn't move fast enough. My feet felt like they were stuck in honey, and I couldn't get away. Terror seized me and I screamed as I felt their teeth clamp down on my flesh—

"Cere, wake up."

The voice startled me, and I bolted upright, my chest heaving. A sheen of sweat covered me, and I could feel that my face was wet with tears. I gasped in fright when I realized someone was next to me but sighed in relief with my next breath because of who it was.

"Thaos," I breathed. "What are you doing?"

I was coming back to reality. My bearings returned, and I realized I was in the plum-colored bed at the glass castle. I pushed out a shaky breath and tried to calm my thundering heart.

"You were crying."

I glanced over and realized my balcony door was ajar. He must've entered that way.

"It was an awful nightmare. Maybe one of the worst I've ever had."

"About your handmaid?"

I nodded. "Hypnos told you who she was?"

"Yes. I'm sorry."

Tears filled my eyes again at the thought of Keilah. "She was my companion all those years at the temple. The closest thing I had to a friend… to a mother." A tear sprang free, and his hand lifted to my face. His movements were so quick, I didn't even know he'd reached for me until he was wiping it away. "I saw my family, too. They were all changing into those undead creatures."

He moved the covers back and laid down in the spot beside me. His arms snaked around me, cool against my sweaty skin.

I opened my mouth to ask what he was doing, but I closed it again. I didn't want to give him a reason to go. So I laid my head on his chest and listened to his heartbeat. It was fast again, like it had been the day I accompanied him to reap souls. His arms pulled me flush against him, holding me tight while his fingers toyed with the loose strands of my hair.

"You don't have to stay," I whispered.

He was quiet for a long time. So long I thought maybe he hadn't heard me.

When I accepted I wasn't getting an answer, he provided one. "I know. I shouldn't."

But I want to.

He kissed the top of my head, and then tilted my chin to find my lips.

He was gone when I woke the next morning, and despite the tenderness of the night, we only shared brief interactions over the following days. When we did, our behavior was polite and awkward. I knew it should be easier that way, but my heart ached, pounding against the icy wall that formed between us.

The nightmares visited every night, and he would appear. Very few words were exchanged during those times. He just held me. Sometimes we kissed until we were both overflowing with desire to do more. But it never went further than that. It was as intimate as it was confusing. The cold days and the warm nights blurred in a mess of conflicting feelings.

I tried once more to get him to let me come to the festival, but after the events in town, he'd doubled down on his refusal.

The event was tonight, and Aeryn had the day off to enjoy the celebrations. Ulther and I sat together on the beach, both sweating from training.

"I'm sorry you have to stay here instead of attending the festival tonight," I told him. I felt bad that he was missing it because of me.

"I'm not," he said. "Hypnos told me this morning I could go to the masquerade ball tonight because he's staying home."

"And Thaos knows about this?"

"He was there when Hypnos told me, so I guess he's okay with it."

"Well, good. I'm glad."

He gave me a half smile. "Maybe next year you can come."

I imagined Apollo would still be looking for me next year too, so I doubted it.

"Yeah, maybe."

"Well, I better head back," he said. "It's getting close to time."

I nodded, and we stood. Both of us gasped in surprise when we found the God of Death standing just behind us. Ulther gave him a tight nod and then walked to the house, disappearing inside.

"I'm going to the festival," he said. "I wanted to see you first."

I looked at his outfit, the same robe, breeches, and tunic as always. "I was told it was a costume party. Who are you going as?"

"As someone who doesn't care about costume parties."

"I see."

The awkward tension filled the space between us again, and to my surprise, he stepped forward and pushed a strand of my hair behind my ear. His hand lingered, and he brushed his thumb over my cheek.

"After tonight, there isn't any reason for you to have to stay here anymore. I've discussed it with Hades, and you'll be going tomorrow to live there."

"What? You're sending me away?" My heart pinched, a new blossom of hurt taking root in my chest.

"I'm not sending you away. I'm giving you freedom. You'll be happier there," he said, holding my gaze. "There're more people and you can go out easier. No forests or marshes to stop you. Ulther can go too—and Aeryn."

I frowned. What he said made sense. I knew it did. But as much as I liked Ulther and Aeryn, they weren't the ones I wanted. "You're not worried about my safety there?"

"Hades will keep you safe. And I'll be around. It's not like this is goodbye forever."

I looked down, tears forming in my eyes. "Well, it certainly feels as if it is."

"We both know it's better this way. Now you can live, Cere, like you should be able to. Fall in love and have the life you deserve. A husband. Children. The life I can't give you."

"So I'm just supposed to pretend none of this ever happened? All the things we shared?"

One side of his mouth curled up. "It's selfish, but I hope you'll always remember those things fondly. I know I will."

I nodded, understanding this was right. "I should want to go."

But I don't.

He bent and kissed my forehead. "And I should want you to."

But I don't.

"How will I sleep?" I whispered. "Without you?"

"Don't worry. I have a solution for that, too."

Before he could move away, I rotated my face up and pressed my lips against his. His hand wrapped around the nape of my neck, and I tried to absorb every moment of the kiss as it deepened and grew more intense. His taste, the feel of his lips, and the cool heat of his chest under my hands. I committed them all to memory because I felt this was the last time.

He broke the contact between us, but not before we were both breathless. "I've got to go."

"I know."

With that, he stepped away and walked into the void. I stared at the spot after he disappeared, trying to reconcile the icy chips of sadness in my chest with the reality that this was for the best.

I collected myself, going in and showering before grabbing my book. Hypnos slouched in the dining room reading a magazine and looking as sullen as I felt.

"I hate my life," I told him.

"Join the club, Sleeping Beauty."

I slumped into a chair, and he peered over the magazine at me. "He told you."

I nodded, reminding myself there was no way I was going to cry about this.

"It's for the best," I said.

"Is it?"

I glanced at him. "You don't think so? It's not like he and I could ever share a future. I can't even, you know, *give* him everything without losing the sight."

He opened his mouth to say something. After a moment, he thrust out a heavy sigh. "Of course."

I eyed him, suspicious. What was that about?

A flash interrupted my thoughts, and Hypnos' sons appeared. Their faces were all drawn in an identical scowl of annoyance. They were all dressed in costumes, but I didn't know what they were supposed to be. Their hats were magnificent—black, with large, wispy silver feathers adorning them. I felt a pang of jealousy, wondering what I would be if I attended. They were so lucky.

"The Three Musketeers?" Hypnos said with a dry look. "How cliché."

They ignored him, and Morpheus looked at me. "We hear you're having nightmares."

"What?" I glanced at Hypnos, who tilted his head, looking confused.

The middle brother clicked his tongue in annoyance. "Our uncle insisted we needed to leave the party we've spent months planning and come attend to his mistress and her nightmares."

"Although we are not to call you his mistress."

They were talking in turn again, and my cheeks flared to life. He'd sent them because he wouldn't be able to hold me at night anymore. I cleared my throat, trying to control the emotion gathering there.

Before I could say anything, they were all standing around me. They each pressed a thumb to my head, one on my forehead and the other two at my temples. I opened my mouth to protest, but a strange heat invaded my head and my eyes closed in response. Warm tendrils pushed into my mind like gentle probing fingers. They pulled the images I'd been seeing of my family, Keilah, and the undead forward.

Other segments of dreams I had burst to the forefront, too. Some involved Thaos, and I blushed all the way up to the roots of my hair as the Oneiroi snickered.

"Not so innocent," Phantasos confirmed, referencing our first conversation. I considered drowning myself in the vegetable soup because it had to be easier than this.

The tendrils selected the nightmares, and then the images were being tucked away far within my mind.

They removed their thumbs, and I was thankful, but mortified. I couldn't even look at them for fear I'd die of embarrassment. "Thank you," I mumbled.

"Our pleasure," Morpheus said. I didn't have to look at him to know he sported a wicked grin. "Good evening."

They disappeared as quickly as they'd arrived, and I looked at Hypnos, who was staring at me with a pensive look.

"What have you done to my brother, Sleeping Beauty?"

My eyes widened. "Nothing. I haven't done anything."

"Liar," he said, a sad smile spreading across his face.

I arched an eyebrow at him, trying to figure out what his deal was tonight, but he just looked back at his magazine. Sighing, I opened the book that I'd brought with me. It was a history about the Pythias of the past. With the strange way my gift was developing, I wanted to know if the others experienced something similar.

This section was more about Apollo being the founder of the Oracle and his claim over the Pythia. I was about to skip it, not wanting to read about being someone else's property when a word caught my eye.

Mistresses.

I read the entire sentence, tensing as I did.

Sometimes, but not always, the Pythia doesn't live full time at the Temple of Delphi because the God Apollo chooses her as one of his many mistresses. In those cases, she lives at his residential home.

I read it again, and then three more times. Blood rushed to my face, and I glared at Hypnos over the top of the book. I grabbed a dinner roll off of the table and threw it as hard as I could, hitting him in the forehead.

He looked up in shock. "What was that for?"

I seethed, rage erupting in every cell of my body. I couldn't ever remember experiencing anger this hot. "You knew. You both did."

"Knew what? What am I missing here?"

"You let me walk around here like an idiot for weeks talking about purity when it doesn't even matter!" I grabbed another roll and chucked it at him, followed by two more in rapid succession.

He caught them all with a cocky smirk. The look made my boiling temper erupt, and I lifted my hand, extending my middle finger like he had once done.

Stark shock crossed his features, wiping the smirk away. He glanced at the book in my hand, and I watched the realization dawn.

I was ranting, embarrassment and fury bubbling up in my chest and out of my mouth. "How could you? I thought you were my friend! I've beat myself up this entire time for wanting things I shouldn't. I've tortured myself. How *dare* you?"

I looked at the plate of rolls, considering throwing the entire thing.

"I'm sorry! You're right. Don't throw more bread at me. I'm intolerant to gluten." He was smirking again and teasing me like usual.

I didn't understand the jest, but I glared at him, funneling every bit of fury I was feeling into the look. I grabbed an entire plate of steamed spinach and chucked it at him. He flashed out of the way, appearing in a different chair as the dish shattered where he'd just been.

"Fine, make your jokes," I hissed. "I'm glad I'm leaving tomorrow."

He frowned, having the audacity to look hurt. "I'm not."

"Then why? Why would you keep that from me?" My heart ached, hot tears filling my eyes. Could I ever trust anyone? "I'm so tired of being lied to."

"Oh, please, for the love of *Me* don't cry. I can't handle tears. I'm sorry. Not to completely throw him under the bus, but I was specifically instructed not to tell you."

I stood, balling my fists. I thought of what Thaos had just said to me outside. *Fall in love and have the life you deserve. A husband. Children.*

Gods, if I had a shred of sense I would've realized he was telling me the truth right then.

"Why?"

"You'll have to ask him that."

I glowered at him. "Fine. I'm going to my room."

He scrubbed his hands down his face. "I'll share my theory, since my brother has glaring communication issues. I swear, I've said for centuries he needs therapy. This is only my opinion though. It's not like we discuss it. *You.* We don't discuss you. Not that I haven't tried."

I crossed my arms. "This better be good. No more secrets, or I'm throwing my fist into your face next."

He barked out a laugh, but then donned a serious expression. "He just wants to protect you."

"From what?"

He looked at me like I was missing something obvious. "From *himself.*"

"What do you mean?"

"How do you not understand? He's Death. You don't know how glad I am that I got Sleep and not his job. It's all darkness and tragedy all the time. For thousands of years. Everyone avoids him except me, Hades, and a handful of our other siblings. It's a miracle as a mortal that you can withstand his rather stifling aura of gloom. His aura doesn't bother other gods and goddesses, but they treat him like he's repulsive. I get invited to all the parties, and he doesn't, you know what I mean? His life is...*so fucking sad.*"

My heart pinched. I'd thought similar things before, lamenting how lonely and depressing Thaos' calling must be.

Hypnos continued. "Many people have one defining tragedy in their life, but his is just one big tragedy."

I nodded, but still didn't completely understand. "What does that have to do with me?"

"Then you show up out of nowhere and you're bright and alive. You can stand being around him. In fact, you seem to enjoy it. You're not afraid of him when most mortals piss their pants if he's in the same room. Judging from the diverse array of hickeys you've been sporting these last few weeks, you're quite the opposite."

My face flushed, and I picked up another roll and threw it at him. "I swear next time it's this steak knife," I hissed, holding up the blade.

He caught the roll and laughed. "Look, I don't understand why, but he's drawn to you. More so than anyone else ever in our existence, and I am not exaggerating. For him to willfully lay his hands on you is one of the most curious things I've ever seen. Not to mention the gifts. He's never even given me a gift! His own twin."

Hypnos feigned dramatic hurt, trying to get a smile from me. I frowned, rolling my eyes.

"He said he hasn't been with a woman in a long time. Not that he never has. Obviously he's been interested before," I countered.

"Well, yeah, I mean no one wants to be a thousands-of-years old virgin. But those women didn't want him, they wanted things from him. You don't understand the lengths people will go through to intervene with death, either for themselves or a loved one. Not that he can do anything about it anyway, he's just the escort, but that didn't stop them from trying."

"They seduced him to cheat death?"

"Yes, or with the assumption he could retrieve their loved one from behind the iron gates of Hades. He was young and naïve, but he still caught on quickly to that ruse. As far as I know it's been a *very* long time."

I pursed my lips and nodded, caught somewhere between sadness for his loneliness, and selfish relief that he had been telling the truth that night on the beach. My own jealousy stunned me. It's not like we were in a committed relationship, or that we ever would be.

Hypnos sighed. "Even having my sons come here tonight. He's never done things like that for anyone. Obviously, he is struggling with feelings he doesn't know how to deal with, and he doesn't want to hurt you. I have a theory he's convinced himself he'll ruin you somehow if things escalate."

"Why?"

"You're so young."

I opened my mouth to argue, but he cut in. "Trust me, twenty-three is unfathomable when you're our age. And, you're mortal. You'll die someday and he won't. If you two were together, you'd sacrifice your whole minuscule life for him. If I were him, I would feel guilty about that."

"I see," I said, choosing to ignore the minuscule comment. To him, my life was only a blink.

"But that doesn't change the fact that he wants you."

I still had questions, but they weren't for Hypnos. "I can't believe he didn't tell me." A small thorn of hurt spiked through the rage in my chest.

"He would've after you went to live elsewhere. When he thought he could do a better job of controlling himself around you. I seriously doubt it'll make a difference where you live. He can't stay away."

I was still glaring at him, the rage in my chest tampered but not extinguished.

"Don't be like that. Don't be mad. It's our last night here. Let's just sit here and be miserable together."

I turned away, unable to look at him.

"Come on, what'll it take to earn your forgiveness? I can't have you mad at me. I'm quite fond of you. Life was such a bore before you got here, and it's been so fun since you arrived."

An idea struck me, and I turned to him, grinning.

He sat back, looking like he regretted those words. "I don't like that look. Don't you dare ask—"

"Take me to the festival."

"No. No way. Do you want to get me killed? Is that what you want?"

"After you lied to me for weeks? Do you really want me to answer that?"

He put his hand on his chest. "Well, that's just hurtful."

"No one will know. We'll just go for a minute. I just want to see."

He stared at me, and I could see he was considering it.

"You owe me. Please. I'll cry! I swear I'll do it."

He sighed and closed his eyes. "I'm going to regret this. I know it."

"Really?!"

"Three rules," he said, putting up three fingers.

I nodded hard enough to suffer whiplash.

"One, if you see Apollo, you do not approach him or talk to him. In fact, leave the room."

"Okay. I don't know what he looks like."

"You'll know. He's hot, literally, and glows like the sun. You'd think he's Narcissus with how much he loves himself. Two, you will avoid my brother at all costs."

"Of course," I said. I didn't even know how to feel about seeing him after these recent revelations.

"And three, you'll do everything I say, and you won't leave my side. Got it?"

"Got it."

He ran his hand down his face and stood. "Alright, let's get ready. We can't go like this. It's a masquerade ball so you'll need a mask. The wardrobe can help you with that."

"Who should I go as?" I gushed. "It's a costume party."

He grinned. "Well, Sleeping Beauty, of course."

CHAPTER TWENTY-ONE

Hypnos helped me with my costume, putting way more thought into it than I expected. He asked the wardrobe for a gown from fourteenth century France, but with a contemporary flair. It produced a royal blue dress with gold accents. The collar was a slight vee, trimmed with gold fur that had a pattern of small black diamonds.

My shoulders were bare for the first time in my life, but I wore a golden circlet and veil that covered them and my back. The mask matched the colors of the gown and hid the top half of my face.

He even instructed me to braid my hair and pin it close to my head. I wondered how he knew so much about women's fashion in the fourteenth century, and he reminded me he'd been there for it.

Looking at myself in the mirror, I didn't think that even if Thaos saw me, he would notice me. I barely recognized myself.

Hypnos flashed away for a few minutes, returning dressed as Peter Pan. My heart trembled with excitement, and I felt jittery, unable to stop my hands from fidgeting.

"I can't believe we're doing this," I said, squealing a little.

"That makes two of us," he said. "Remember the rules and stay by me. It's going to be hectic. It might be a little too much for a basement dweller who hasn't been in a crowd like this."

I glared at him but had to fight to hide a smile. "Okay." I took a deep breath and gripped his hand.

I felt the pull of his magic and then my ears greeted the sounds of a boisterous party. We were near the stairs of Hades' house, and hundreds of people formed a crowd that poured out of the open doors, packing the street that was lined with booths selling various items from food to trinkets. It was strange to see the area so alive.

"I think we made it just in time to see the queen," Hypnos yelled over the music.

He pulled at my hand, and we shoved through the crowd. I quickly understood what he meant because I was dizzy as a sea of masked faces swirled around me in a hysteria. Most of them were smiling and laughing. Bodies pressed against me, thrusting me in different directions, and I clamped down hard on Hypnos' hand.

We made it to the stoop, where the crowd seemed to calm a little, and then finally inside. They had several platforms set up on either side of the hallway into the throne room. The platforms held pots of dead flowers, which I found odd.

A horn blared right next to us, and I covered my ears as it played a grand introduction. The hall grew quiet except for a few excited whispers.

"Here she comes," Hypnos said, still gripping my hand.

Workers ushered people out of the walkway, and then two doors across from us opened. A regal-looking woman appeared. She had smooth ivory skin and hair the same red hue as a summer fox. She stepped forward and turned down the aisle, everyone watching in reverence.

My mouth was open slightly because her gown was designed entirely from real flowers. They were small and white, but I didn't know their name. Cheers erupted around us, deafening, and she beamed, holding out her arms.

I realized Hades was waiting at the entryway to the throne room, a tired but joyous smile on his face. He wore a black dress robe tonight, and I thought the contrast of the queen in white and king in black was stark and beautiful.

Gliding down the corridor, she kept her arms out and the dead flowers resurrected and bloomed to life in a dance of colors. When Persephone got to where Hades stood, she took his hand and kissed him. They strolled together into the throne room and disappeared as the music kicked back up and people started gushing about the queen.

"That was amazing!" I said to Hypnos, who smirked at me.

He squeezed my hand, saying, "It is fun to watch you enjoy life. I've long forgotten what it's like to experience new things."

I squeezed his hand back, smiling sadly at his soft words.

We moved into a ballroom where hundreds of people danced. The music was a wide variety, with songs covering the centuries from modern to classical to ancient. Performers stood on pillars, some dancing with ribbons and others blowing blasts of fire. It was all so remarkable, and I grinned so much my cheeks ached.

Food and drinks from all over the world lined the walls, the smiling vendors handing out various samples. I tasted as much as I could, reveling in the different flavors.

Hypnos was a lax chaperone and obliged me to try whatever I wanted, even sips of alcohol. One in particular, a sweet rum, reminded me so much of how Thaos tasted that I indulged several sips. Hypnos stayed right next to me and allowed me to lead him around and view everything in wonder.

We slowly made our way to the throne room, where the king and queen sat in their places. I gasped in delight when I saw a monstrous three-headed dog sitting behind them. Cerberus was bigger than I predicted, bigger than Nychta, and one of his heads rested between the thrones where he happily accepted pets from Persephone.

There was a line to speak to them, and the queen dazzled with her smile as they spoke with their subjects.

I froze when I spotted a figure behind them next to Cerberus. I would recognize that black robe anywhere. My heart quickened, and despite what I'd just learned about my purity quest being a sham, I wished I was next to him. Either to kiss him or slap him, I wasn't sure which.

I tried not to stare, afraid he might sense me if I did. With his hood up, I couldn't see his eyes. His gaze could be on me right now and I wouldn't know.

"Thaos is in here," I told Hypnos, but his eyes trailed elsewhere.

I followed it and recognized he was staring at a beautiful woman, a Goddess, with caramel skin and long sparkling ashen hair. She pressed her lean body suggestively against a handsome man, who leaned down and kissed her neck.

"Who is it?"

His eyes snapped back to me and the hint of pain in them gave me a pretty good clue.

"My wife."

Tension bracketed his eyes, and when his gaze returned to her, I saw anger replace the pain. My heart ached for him, and I squeezed his hand in support. I hadn't had many friends in my life, but I considered Hypnos one. I didn't enjoy seeing him hurt, and I hurt for him.

"Go back to those benches where we were sitting, okay? Wait for me and I'll come get you. It'll just be a minute."

I nodded, feeling sorry for him, and he started their way. I watched as he confronted her and the other man. She was furious at his intrusion, raising her voice and drawing attention.

I hurried back towards the door, not wanting to be close to them if they caused a scene. A woman stepped in front of me, and I gasped. She wore a similar golden gown to the day in the forest when she warned me to go back.

"Ceres," she breathed with a sad smile.

I tensed in surprise, my eyes widening at the use of a name I hadn't heard in a decade. "How do you know that name?"

"I am Clotho, the Spinner of Fate. I know everyone. You are doing exactly the right thing. I'm sorry the path you are on has been difficult, and I'm sorry for what is still to come. It was the only way."

"What?"

She grabbed my hand and clutched it. Her eyes traveled to Thaos. "I tried to give you something to make it all worth it."

I glanced his way and my mouth opened, but she cut me off.

"We won't be able to speak again. Just know I chose you, but I won't blame you if you don't accept. If you do, remember this is all for the child. The child *must* live."

I was so confused, staring at her with my mouth hanging open.

"Tell no one we spoke," she finished, her tone full of ominous warning.

The next second she was gone, disappearing into the crowd.

Feeling unsettled, I pushed towards the door. The need to escape flooded me, as if I was being chased like that day in the Woods of Woe. I was almost at the exit when a large body stepped in front of me and blocked me.

My heart stopped when I realized who it was. As Hypnos said, I just knew. His skin was the color of rich sand and glowed brighter than anyone else. The tone matched perfectly with shoulder length curls that appeared to be spun from solid gold. I could feel the warmth of his body without even touching him, as if he were the sun itself.

"May I have a dance?"

He offered me his hand, and I froze, not sure what to do. Glancing back, I scanned for Hypnos, but I couldn't find him in the crowd.

My eyes shifted back to the extended hand, eyeing it as if it was a poisonous viper. "Thank you, but I'm here with someone."

I tried to step around him, but he stopped me. "They won't mind."

He caught my hand and dragged me towards the dance floor. I was speechless, glancing sideways to make sure Thaos was in his spot. Luckily, he was.

The song was an elegant, soft melody that should've been nice to dance to. Apollo pulled me flush to his body, one of his hands around my waist and the other holding my hand. He hissed in a surprised breath, and I immediately tensed, my skin prickling at the contact.

So far, Thaos had been the only person to touch me extensively, with slight gestures from Ulther and Hypnos. This God of Sun's hot skin felt like I was pressing against a simmering ember, making me feel uncomfortable.

"What's your name? I am quite drawn to you. Do you know why that might be?"

I swallowed past the dryness of my throat, looking up at him. "It's… Jillian. And, no, I don't know why."

I used my sister's name, unable to think of anything else. Curious sapphire eyes stared down at me from behind a white mask, studying me.

"Where are you from?"

"Um. Here. The Underworld."

He clicked his tongue. "Something so beautiful shouldn't languish in this dark hole."

I stared at him, unsure of what to say. My heart was erratic, and I glanced around, wondering how I could escape.

"You must know who I am? It's normal to feel star struck," he said with a sultry grin.

"Yes, you're Apollo the God of Sun and many other things."

His smile widened, and he spun me with expert grace, making me look like I knew what I was doing. While he did, my eyes caught on someone in the crowd. The person didn't fit in with everyone else. I could tell by their demeanor, the way they wore the hood of their brown cloak far over their face, that they weren't here for a party.

Something about the figure was familiar, and I watched them hoping they would look towards me. I would know the way their body moved anywhere. The figure turned and scanned the room, and my heart leapt. I only caught a glimpse, but I knew it was Laurenth.

Not wanting to lose her, I didn't even glance back at Apollo as I spoke, "Excuse me. Thank you for the dance."

He protested, but I pulled out of his grip and hurried after Laurenth. She disappeared down a long hallway and I saw her round a corner towards the left. I picked up my pace, jogging after her.

When I got around the corner, it was a dead end. There were five doors, and I opened the first one. It was a sitting room, empty, and I shut it. The second room was a small library with an intricate grandfather clock and a beautifully crafted stone fireplace. It was also empty, and I turned to close the door.

Someone grabbed me, pushing me inside. I spun, expecting to find Laurenth, but horrified to find Apollo had followed me. He shut the door behind him, and the click of the latch made me jump. My eyes darted around the room, panic rising in my chest.

CHAPTER TWENTY-TWO

"Now that I have your attention," he sneered, looking annoyed. "Who are you?"

"I-I told you."

"You're a terrible liar," he said, ripping my mask off of my face. I tried to wiggle free, but he tore my circlet and veil away as well. "I'm drawn to you."

He pushed me against the wall, his strength surprising me. I molded myself against it and he pinned me there. He pulled his mask off as well, and I realized he was truly handsome. Maybe the most flawless man I'd ever seen, but his perfect features were dipped in a tight frown as he glared down at me.

"Something is shielding you."

I gasped again as he grabbed the necklace I wore and tore it away, tossing it to the floor. The brooch that sat at the center of my chest quickly followed. As he grabbed my hands, I fought back, trying to keep him away from the ring. His strength was incredible, and he easily pried my hand open. I watched him pull the silver band from my finger and toss it behind him. It danced a tinkling melody across the floor to the other side of the room.

A breath of surprise left him, and then he grinned. "I knew it. My Pythia. I've been searching for you." He tilted his head, curious. "You're definitely my Pythia, but you're something else, too. What are you?"

"I don't know what you're talking about."

I ripped my hand from his grasp and tried to push him back, but he only chuckled at that and pressed harder against me. Another frown crossed his face, and then a sneer of anger, "But who's had you? I've looked for five years."

He put his face close to mine, so our noses touched. His eyes widened with surprise and fury. "I'd recognize that scent anywhere. Those lilies of Death. That's who stole you from me? Why?" His confusion was genuine.

I couldn't believe he could smell Thaos. I'd showered and brushed my teeth since we'd kissed on the beach. Apollo was looking at me expectantly, and I realized he wanted an answer. "No. He didn't steal me. He found me. Someone else had me before."

"But he didn't return you to me, and that's as good as stealing. You're mine. Everyone knows that. How dare he keep you from me? How dare he *touch* you?"

I could sense his anger, and I tried to move again. I felt claustrophobic, trapped here between him and the wall. My lungs struggled to draw air, and I only managed small choppy breaths. The feeling I had whenever I was in the overseer's office flooded through me and my wide eyes flicked around the room, desperate to find a way out.

"Let me go." I put my hands on his chest and tried to push him back again.

He grabbed my wrists and held them against the wall, not allowing me to pull away. His mouth pushed against mine and I tensed in surprise. I turned my head, breaking his kiss, but it did not faze him. His mouth lowered, and he moved down my jaw and to my neck. The heat of his lips seared through me, and I felt like I might be sick.

I jumped at the scrape of his pointed teeth against my throat and blurted, "No." It came out as a panicked plea, more than a demand.

He grabbed my chin and pulled my face back towards his. "No?"

The shock on his face would have been comical if I hadn't been so terrified. It looked as if no one had ever rejected him, although I knew that wasn't true. He hadn't taken it well the other times, either.

He gnashed his teeth together and raised my hands above my head so he could hold them with one hand.

"It's okay," he purred, as if to comfort me. "I've found you."

I squirmed, pulling against him until I was out of breath. His other hand grabbed the top of my dress at the vee and ripped it, exposing my breasts to him.

"Stop. Please don't," I gritted, my blood running cold with fear as I realized what was about to happen.

He leaned back to look at what he'd revealed, and it gave me just enough room to make a move. I lifted my knee in between his legs with as much force as I could, connecting with his groin. He grunted in surprise and fell to his knees.

I tried to run, making it three steps before his hand grabbed my ankle and tripped me. My hands smacked against the floor when I fell and I screamed for help as loud as I could, hoping someone could hear me.

I felt his body prowl up mine until his weight was on top of me. A fresh burst of claustrophobic panic erupted in my chest, and I screamed until my voice broke. His hand pushed under my head and clamped roughly over my mouth, muffling my cries.

"What, you're a whore for Death but not for me?" he spat, disgust and anger coating the words.

I felt him pushing my skirt up my legs and fought furiously, trying to buck against him. I realized he was laughing—having fun—and terror flooded me.

His weight had me pinned, and I felt him find my Damascus steel dagger. I heard the blade slide from the sheath, and then he brought it up by my face. It was so close to my eye that I froze in fear of being nicked.

"You're a fun, interesting little mortal. No wonder he kept you for himself."

He tossed the blade aside and then flipped me over, forcing my legs apart. My hand fell to where the other dagger was sheathed. It was my only hope.

His left arm caged my head, and the weight of his body pushed me flush against the floor. He pressed his lips to mine again, and I returned the kiss. He smiled against my lips and pushed his tongue into my mouth. I drew the dagger and then bit down hard. I thrust the Mastix steel towards his rib cage, hoping the bite would be enough to distract him.

He shouted in pain and pulled his head back. I thought for sure I had him, but I felt his warm hand clamp around my wrist. I couldn't believe it. How could he move that fast? Glancing down, I saw the tip of the blade had just pierced his skin. He twisted my wrist, ripping the weapon from my hand.

His chest was rising and falling in anger as he looked at the blade and then down at me. Apollo seemed in shock, and he reached up and touched his lip where a trickle of gold dripped from his mouth.

He smiled, his teeth laced with his own blood, but the look was cruel, and I pushed my head back into the floor trying to get away. "You'll be sorry for that."

He moved faster than I could comprehend and backhanded me across the face. I cried out in pain and my head snapped to the side. My ears rang at the impact, and I knew it was the hardest I'd ever been hit.

He pinned my hands again, and I blinked my eyes rapidly, trying to regain my bearings. His free hand pushed the rest of the way up my thigh, and I felt my skirt gather at my waist. His weight pushed between my legs and his hand traveled between us, unbuttoning his pants. I tried to pull away or move my body, but I was helpless, stuck underneath him.

The grandfather clock started chiming, counting the midnight hour as I continued my pointless struggle. My head turned, watching the secondhand tick on the clock in slow motion.

Apollo grunted in surprise, and I shifted my eyes back to him as another thwack sounded. He slumped forward against me, groaning in pain. I felt his body weight being rolled off of me, and then found Hypnos staring down at me in horror with a heavy marble candlestick in his hand.

When time chimes, use the candlestick.

The clock finished its song, and Hypnos reached down and grabbed my hand, pulling me to my feet. Apollo was already stirring, getting to his hands and knees.

"We gotta go," Hypnos told me, dragging me out of the door. "I'm the God of Sleep, so fighting isn't my strong suit. And he is going to be *pissed*."

My head spun, and I stumbled behind him down the hallway, clutching my dress closed. In my haze, it took me a moment to realize people were screaming. Shrieks of terror and panic bounced off of the walls in the throne room.

"What's happening?"

He glanced around, pulling me with the crowd towards the door. "Absolute party foul. Hooded people just started killing at random. I think some of those undead creatures are around here, too. It's chaos."

"Apollo," I choked through tears. "He followed me, and he tried to, he tried to—" I couldn't even say it.

"I saw what he tried to do," Hypnos hissed, still looking horrified. "Fuck's sake, this went about as wrong as it could have."

I nodded. "I kneed him in a not very honorable place, and I bit him, but if you hadn't come… there was nothing I could do."

The shocked tears rolled down my cheeks. I'd grown so confident in myself fighting the undead, only to be slapped with the reality that in the world of the Gods, I was just a mortal woman. I could be the most capable fighter in the world, and I wouldn't have been able to stop Apollo in that room with the clock.

"I'm so fucking dead it's not even funny," Hypnos said. "I'm so sorry, Cere." Then he muttered to himself, "My brother is going to rip my heart out and eat it. Then he's going to let it regrow and do it again."

I looked around the throne room, shocked at the violence occurring there. Brown hooded figures were fighting the King's Knights and undead monsters had people pinned, ripping at their flesh and eating. Cerberus was protecting his queen, biting and tearing enemies to pieces.

Hades held a brown cloaked figure by the throat, and I blinked in surprise as the person's face cracked like dropped porcelain. They disintegrated to nothing in his grasp, falling to the floor in a pile of white dust.

I couldn't see Thaos in the pandemonium and I prayed he was okay.

A banner hung from a staircase, a message painted on it in what looked like blood.

The True Heir Will Rise.

We were being pushed by the crowd towards the door, an ocean of terrified faces surrounding me.

"What about Thaos?" I yelled, trying to look back.

"He's the God of Death, he'll be okay. We've got to get outside, though. I can't flash from inside the house, it's a security measure."

I saw the door in front of us, but the crowd was parting. I heard the howl of the creature before I saw it. It leapt on a woman right next to us and started tearing at her. I reached for my blade, my heart dropping as I remembered it was gone.

Hypnos reacted, using his candlestick to smash it over the head. It snarled in pain and turned on him. One of the knights appeared out of nowhere and removed its head. The crowd surged forward again, and I lost Hypnos' hand, getting separated from him.

I had no choice but to move with the crowd unless I wanted to be trampled. I kept pace, stumbling with everyone else, and still holding the front of my dress closed. When we got outside, the crowd started dispersing, running to get away. I felt a soft hand on my arm, and it pulled me aside into the hedge.

"Aeryn! Oh, Gods. I'm so glad you're okay," I croaked.

"Me too. I saw you were alone! You're not supposed to be here."

Shame burned in my cheeks. "I know, it was so stupid of me to come."

"It's okay," she comforted, offering me a warm smile. "I know a place we can hide until it's safe."

She helped me to my feet, and we ran deeper into the tall hedge. I realized we were weaving through some kind of maze. It was dark, and a foreboding feeling thrummed to life in my chest. My mind wandered to the vineyard outside the temple, and that claustrophobic feeling strangled my breaths again. Soon, I couldn't hear the screams behind us anymore.

"Isn't this far enough?" I whispered.

"Just a little farther and we'll be in the garden."

She squeezed my hand, comforting me, and I followed.

We broke into a small garden with a fountain. My breath caught in my throat, and I yanked my hand from her grasp.

"Look out, Aeryn!" I stepped in front of her and faced down the man I knew to be the master. "Just stay behind me," I told her.

She giggled, and I stilled. The unmistakable jab of a blade at my back made me gasp.

"Aeryn?"

"Just don't move, little wolf. This is a silver blade," she warned. "We still want you alive."

I tensed but didn't move. I knew she didn't lie about the blade at my back as I felt the unmistakable burn of the fatal metal. As a shifter, silver would spell instant death for me.

"We did not expect you to be here," the master said, sounding pleased. "Such luck."

Another wave of shame crashed through me. Why did I have to be so insistent? I could be at the dining room table with Hypnos right now, commiserating in our misery.

"Who are you?" I was desperate to know. "You are not Apollo."

He barked out a laugh. "No, I certainly am not." He looked at Aeryn. "And if I ever start acting like that arrogant prick, I give you permission to end me right then."

She giggled again, and I had to remind myself there was a blade at my back because I wanted to whirl and punch her in her stupid traitorous face. My chest burned at her betrayal. I thought she was my friend.

"I have known him a long time, though," he continued. "I have hated him for a long time. So I stole his favorite toy, you, and used it to throw this entire world into chaos. I created a plague that he, the God of Medicine, cannot touch."

"So revenge? That's what this is about? The destruction of the entire mortal realm because you don't like Apollo?"

"Partly."

"That's millions of lives. Billions," I gasped, unable to wrap my head around that kind of destruction.

"Yes, and most of those lost will be humans," he sneered. "You won't find a shred of pity from me for those rats. The way they treat my mother—I hope every one of them dies."

"Your mother?"

I thought of my prophecy about Thaos. Was this the son?

He didn't answer, but I noticed his knuckles were white where he clasped his hands. His anger filled the space between us.

Instead of speaking to him, I said to Aeryn. "I trusted you."

"I know. Such a naive girl. At first I thought it may be difficult, but when I realized you were so desirous for companionship that you would crawl into bed with Death..." She snickered, and my cheeks heated. "I knew earning your trust would take very little."

The man in the white robe clicked his tongue. "Really, Cere, I know I sheltered you but, Death? How desperate are you?"

I bristled. "Shut up."

My attention was still on Aeryn. My friend that had baked pastries for me and was going to take over her mom's cake shop someday. I was reeling, trying to understand. It had taken next to nothing for me to trust her. I just did because Thaos and Hypnos seemed to.

"How did you get them to trust you?"

"They don't trust *me*. They trust Aeryn."

My eyebrows furrowed. "What?"

The one I had known as the master answered, "She's very special. A powerful shifter, long thought extinct. They used to call them skinwalkers."

"One of Aeryn's hairs was all it took," she explained. "And I was her."

She brought a short blonde hair in front of my face and dropped it. I heard skin sliding, and I knew she was shifting. I glanced over my shoulder to find a woman with long black hair and coal red eyes staring back. Her skin was far from anything I'd ever seen. It was textured, and a strange green color, making her look like she was covered in moss.

The master continued, "Between her blood, mine, and a powerful vampire count's, we created the perfect creatures. The undead. It took many years of trials and errors, but whenever we were on the right track, your visions would confirm it."

Fury and guilt rushed through my blood. I'd already suspected as much, but hearing it committed to words made me feel sick.

"This last batch was our strongest yet." He pushed his hood back, and I wrinkled my nose in disgust. He was bald, and his pearly skin was so pale I could see the veins of his face running like webs beneath the surface. Even his lips were barely colored, a light pastel pink. The creatures certainly did resemble their creator. "Do you want to hear about it?"

"That's enough." I looked to my right and found Laurenth walking towards us and, for a brief pathetic second, I thought she was there to save me. "She doesn't need to be tormented."

"Laurenth," I gasped. Fresh blood splattered her robe. "Did you kill people tonight?"

The master laughed. "Of course she did."

"It has to be this way, Cere," she said, no hint of shame in her voice. "Blood often paves the path to change."

I couldn't speak around the knot in my throat. When I finally found my voice, it shook. "Everything was a lie, then? I don't understand. Why did you lie to me about being pure?"

"Everything about your life at the temple was done for control," the master answered. "If you believed you could never love, that you could never leave, you would never try. Death obviously ruined that for me in more ways than one. It was fun. You were my little doll, and I was your master, bending you to my will."

I felt sick to my stomach, staring at his face. I imagined several scenarios where I could cut his head from his shoulders and shove the overseer's ruler down his throat.

"The overseer," I spat. "You knew what he did to me?"

I directed the question to Laurenth, but she looked away. At least she had enough decency to look ashamed.

"Yes, Oren," the changeling woman said. She sounded fond of him. "He had some sick predilections. Would it make you feel better if I assured you that your time with him was easy compared to everyone else? You were spoiled. Your poor handmaid and the other servants—" She clicked her tongue in mock indignation to finish her thought.

"It was a pleasure to watch him die," I hissed. "I promise it was slow and painful."

She growled, and the knife pressed into my back, biting into the skin.

The master's eyes, which were a strange orange-yellow, danced with amused satisfaction. He grinned a wide smile that looked as though he held too many teeth for the size of his mouth. "Did you like my last gift? I made it special for you."

"What gift?"

"For your big day out in town," he mocked, cackling like I was pathetic. "I thought you probably missed her."

It took me a moment to realize he was talking about Keilah. My eyes widened, tears welling in them. "You're sick."

He snickered and the thing holding a knife at my back did too. "I didn't have any use for her or any of the other temple servants after you left. They knew too much."

"I told you she didn't need to hear about it," Laurenth said, angry.

"How could you let them do that to her?!" I screamed at her, and my voice broke around the words.

She looked regretful and I glared at her. "I know you won't believe me, Cere, but I didn't know until it was too late. Keilah didn't deserve that. She was devoted to changing the world for the better."

The master rolled his eyes and laughed.

"You're right, I don't believe you," I choked through tears, staring at Laurenth, still unable to reconcile the woman I knew with the woman standing in front of me.

He grinned in delight. "Enough. We've spent too much time here. Bring her. We need to go."

I tensed and moved back. The blade pushed under my skin and burned.

"Move," the skinwalker snarled in my ear.

A strange glow overtook the garden, and the man whipped his hood back over his face and hissed.

"She is *mine*."

I recognized the voice as belonging to Apollo. The woman behind me gasped and turned to face him. I whirled as well, seeing he had a sword of blazing fire in his hands. Reacting quickly, I kicked her in the back, sending her towards him.

He didn't hesitate, slamming the blade through her gut.

The master bellowed, "No!"

The smell of charred skin filled the air along with her shrieks and a sick part of me enjoyed her agony.

I felt a hand on my arm and realized Laurenth was pulling me away from the fight that was about to ensue. The master cried out in fury as Apollo slid the blade from the woman and she crumpled to the ground.

Producing a blade of his own, the master attacked. The sound of metal clashing erupted in the quiet garden and echoed against the walls of the hedge. Both men were Gods, or something close to it, and skilled with their weapons. The fight was explosive and frightening.

"Let's go, Cere," Laurenth ordered me. "Pick up your gods damned feet and walk."

"Let me go!" I screamed, kicking her in the knee. "I'll never return to your gilded cage!"

Her grip tightened, and she raised her fist, most likely intent on knocking me out. I made a move to block, but I heard a dull thwack instead.

Hypnos was there, still wielding the candlestick. His eyes were wide, maybe a little crazed, and his face was badly beaten.

"You have impeccable timing tonight," I whispered.

"I'll tell you what," he drawled, holding up the candlestick. "Hades can send me the bill for this because I'm keeping it."

His hand fell on my arm, and he flashed us. My feet hit the floor of my bedroom and he and I stared at each other for several seconds in quiet shock.

CHAPTER TWENTY-THREE

To his surprise, I hugged him, throwing my free arm around his neck. The other still clutched my dress.

"Hypnos, how did you find me?"

He was stiff, but he returned the hug, and his gentle pats on my back were awkward but comforting. "I followed the God of Sun. With your ring gone, he can sense where you are if he's close enough."

"Will he come here? Apollo?" I asked, panicked.

"No, I don't think so. I don't think he's dumb enough to do that."

"Hypnos, I'm sorry. He made me dance with him, and then I saw a woman from the temple, the one you hit, and then I tried to follow her. I didn't realize he followed me. Then Aeryn—she's not Aeryn. He called her a skinwalker. Gods, I bet the real Aeryn is dead." I was rambling, my mind running to catch up to everything that just happened.

He pushed me back and looked at me with concern. "Don't apologize to me. Ever. I failed you, and I'm the one who should be sorry."

"What happened to your face?"

"Apollo got a hold of me for a moment, but I'll survive."

"We shouldn't have gone. Gods, it was so dumb."

"That attack was planned. It's not your fault," he assured me.

"Yes," I whispered. "I saw who I knew as the master. I still don't have a name for him, but I think Apollo may know."

"Interesting. One of his old enemies?"

"It seemed to be." Tears choked me again. "I hope Thaos is okay."

"Part of me hopes that, too," he said, "and part of me would be okay if someone bashed him on the head and he was in a coma for a while."

My eyes widened in horror. "What? Why?"

"Because he is going to murder me...maybe. He'll probably torture me for a century first."

I couldn't tell if he was joking about either statement.

He rubbed my arm for a moment. Then, lifting his weaponized candlestick, he said, "I'm going to go check what's happening. Are you okay to be alone?"

"I'm okay. Go help if you can."

He disappeared in a blink. I stood in the middle of my room for a few seconds, trying to process what had happened. I needed to shower. To be clean. I always felt this way after the overseer's office, too.

I had only just placed my hand on the bathroom door when I heard a swishing of fabric and then the thump of boots. I tensed, knowing it wasn't Hypnos.

"Cere," Thaos said. "I had to check and make sure you were here. There was an attack, and I thought maybe it was a distraction to get to you—"

I turned to him, and his eyes took in my costume. They clouded with blackness and his wings became thicker and started moving more noticeably. He was quiet for a few moments and then asked, "Is it even possible for you to do anything I ask of you?"

"I'm sorry," I whispered, new tears threatening to spill over. "You were right, it was a terrible idea."

I was staring at the floor, and I sensed he had moved closer to me. Gods, I couldn't even look up at him. I was ashamed of being so stupid and selfish. Ashamed of what had happened in the room with the clock.

"You're hurt," he said with concern, making guilt join in the crescendo of emotions crashing through me. "Did you get into a fight? This looks like someone struck you."

He lifted my face to his and then turned it, examining my cheek and jaw. I closed my eyes, and then I heard him suck in a breath. His hand fell to mine, where I still clasped my dress closed, and he pulled it away. The fabric gaped open, making it painfully obvious that I had been in a fight, but not like he was thinking.

"Who did this to you?" His voice was as calm as the dead green marsh outside, and somehow it was more frightening than if he'd been yelling.

He pulled my chin up. "Look at me."

I opened my eyes, staring up at him. The room was dark, like a moonless night, and I couldn't see the flame of the fireplace that was only a couple of feet away. The shadow poured from him, surrounding us in blackness. I could feel how cold it was, and I shivered.

Thaos' eyes had changed from purple to black, and lines of ebony flowed from them like spider veins across his face, making his skin look like cracked marble. Shadow leaked from the fissures, swirling around him. I'd never seen him like this before, but I imagined this was close to the last image the overseer witnessed.

"Who?" he asked again. His voice was strange, deep and terrifying. But he didn't wait for my answer, instead he leaned in to where Apollo had kissed my neck and inhaled a deep breath.

He tensed, the cracks widening as he looked into my eyes again. "Apollo?"

I nodded.

"What happened?"

I opened my mouth to answer, but a new sob choked me, and tears poured down my face. I shook my head. How could I ever tell him? Shame burned up from my chest and colored my cheeks.

His eyes widened, and the cracks in his face deepened more, branching down his neck and under the collar of his shirt.

"Did he—?"

I shook my head faster, feeling my hair that had been pulled from the braids dance around my face. "Hypnos arrived in time to save me." Then I added with a whisper, "But it was close."

Thaos stepped back. "Stay here. I'll be back soon."

I opened my mouth to tell him that so much more had happened, but he was gone. The shadows left with him, allowing the warm glow of the fire to fill the room again.

I peeled the dress off. Staring down at the ripped fabric, I felt fresh tears form in my eyes. Just a couple of hours ago I'd loved the way I looked in it. I'd been so excited to experience something. And it had gone so wrong.

Not wanting to see it anymore, I put it back into the wardrobe and willed it away. The wardrobe did as I asked and returned a soft cotton nightgown as if it too were trying to comfort me.

In the bathroom I studied my face. Loose tendrils of my hair shot out in every direction, and the tears had reddened my eyes. The bruise on my jaw didn't look half as bad as it felt, but I expected it to show its true colors tomorrow.

I showered, cranking the heat as high as I could endure and scrubbing until my skin was pink. Afterwards, I sat in one of the chairs in front of the fireplace and pulled my knees to my chest. The teapot was there, still hot, and I poured myself a cup. I tried not to think about the fact that Aeryn had been the one to bring it. But it wasn't Aeryn.

Another half hour passed before Thaos returned. The shadows billowed out across the room, wrapping us in near darkness again. He stood for a long time, with his hood up I couldn't tell if he stared at me or the crackling flame. I didn't know what to say, and my face was red with shame again.

"Do you know if Ulther is okay?" I asked.

"He is."

"How many people were hurt?"

"They killed thirty-six mortals. And one goddess. There are more injured."

I gasped. "Who?"

"Clotho, my sister. One of the Fates."

My mind whirled, and the floor seemed to drop out from beneath my chair. I had spoken with her just moments before her death. My mouth opened to tell him about it, but I remembered her warning.

Instead, I muttered, "I'm so sorry."

He said nothing, pushing his hood back and leveling me with an intense gaze.

"I shouldn't have gone, and I know that. I'm sorry." My cheeks burned, but I forced myself to look at him.

"I won't scold you," he said, his voice cool and soothing. "I think the consequences you've faced are more than enough. I'm the one who is sorry."

His compassion made my heart heavier, and I thought I would've preferred a scolding. I stared at the fireplace, feeling foolish. And lucky. I was so lucky it didn't escalate any more than it had.

"He took my dagger. The one you gave me." I sniffled. "I almost stabbed him with it, that's why he struck me."

His eyes flashed with anger again, the cracks of black erupting and then receding. "I'll retrieve it for you."

"Where'd you go just now?"

"To find him."

My eyes widened. "Did you?"

His grip tightened on the handle of the scythe, his knuckles blanching white. "No, he is wise enough to be out of my reach."

"Where?"

"He is on Mount Olympus with his father, Zeus."

"What were you going to do if you found him?"

"Kill him."

The stark promise that coated the words shocked me. "Wouldn't you get in trouble?"

"Yes. In their eyes, Apollo may treat you however he wishes. The Pythia is his. Zeus wouldn't understand me exercising such dramatic action over a mortal woman."

I considered asking why he would, but I wasn't sure if I wanted the answer, so I changed the subject. "I saw a woman from the temple tonight. She was with the brown cloaks. I thought she was my friend, but she killed people. Laurenth."

"Defector, daughter of Ares, and dishonored first commander of Athena."

My eyes slid to him. "Yes. How did you know?"

"I suspected she was one of Athena's when I saw you training together at the temple. Her name is well known because of her role in a plot to overthrow Zeus."

"She knew about all of it, including the creatures. She told me the destruction of the mortal realm is a casualty of change. I can't understand why she is helping them. She's a good person, I know she is." I clung to the armrest of the chair, desperate to get my point across.

"Rumor is that something similar to what happened to you tonight happened to her. But she didn't have an otherwise worthless God of Sleep to intervene."

Wincing at the admonishment of his brother, a sad gasp broke my lips. Poor Laurenth. That's why she'd gone beyond simple self-defense for me. Without her training I would've never been able to hold Apollo off long enough for Hypnos to arrive. I was thankful for her, even if I couldn't forgive her for what she was doing.

Despite her betrayal, my fists clenched, and I found defiant anger swirling in my chest. "Who did that to her?"

"Zeus. She is skilled, but he is the supreme. He would've overpowered her with little effort."

I swallowed my shock, feeling ill. "I guess I can understand her motives then. But it doesn't excuse their actions."

"Whoever is leading them is clever. They were there to kill one of the Fates tonight. I think they gave up on trying to kill me. They didn't attack Hades as furiously as I'd been expecting. Without Clotho to spin the threads of Fate, the system of the Underworld will break down. No souls will be collected. Hades might hold Tartarus for a few more days."

"The master was there," I whispered. "He almost had me again."

The thought scared me even more than what had happened in the room with the clock. To be in their possession again, locked up. I didn't think they would build the cage from marble and gold this time.

There was a strange recurring sound from Thaos' direction. I glanced over to see he was thrumming his fingers over the handle of his scythe. He moved suddenly and sat in the other chair.

"Did you know him? His name?"

"No, but Apollo might know. He showed up, and they started fighting. Laurenth tried to drag me away, but Hypnos saved me. The one I knew as the master called Aeryn a skinwalker. It wasn't the real Aeryn. She led me out to the garden so they could take me."

He stared at the flame. "Then I imagine Aeryn is dead."

"Poor Ulther." Shards of icy sorrow cut through me. "How could we have all not known she was an imposter?"

"Skinwalkers are powerful," he said. "They don't just take on appearance. They become the other person. I've even heard if they stay as someone too long, they can forget they aren't that person. I believed they were all dead. They were systematically hunted down and killed three centuries ago."

"Well, if she was the last one, they're all dead now," I mumbled. "Apollo ran her through with a sword of flame."

"What else did you learn?"

"That her blood, the master's blood, and the blood of a powerful vampire were how they made the undead creatures. He hates Apollo, and it sounds like he's obsessed with revenge. But he also claimed the humans deserved to die because of their treatment of his mother."

"His mother?"

I shrugged. "I have no idea what it all means."

We sat for a long time, and the quiet tension sizzled on my skin, making me shift in discomfort. Several minutes passed until I could no longer hold the question burning like acid on my tongue.

"Thaos?" I observed his face, watching every slight movement. "Why didn't you tell me I don't need to be pure? That it doesn't matter for my gift to work."

Surprise flashed in his eyes, and then anger. "Did Hypnos—?"

"No, I figured it out by myself. It was in a book. That's why Hypnos brought me tonight. He felt horrible for lying."

Thaos looked at the flames, choosing to remain quiet.

"But do you? Do you feel bad?" I asked, a fresh ember of anger burning in my chest. "You let me believe that. You let me walk around here feeling horrible for desiring you and guilty for the things we did."

"Honestly?"

I almost stood and slapped him. "That would be nice," I hissed through gritted teeth.

"Yes, I feel bad, and no, I don't," he admitted. "I despised it. But it was easier that way."

"What was easier?"

"Not being with you. When you had your own reasons for resisting, it was easier for me to resist. And even then I still struggled."

"Why don't you want to be with me?" The words sounded so desperate and broken that I cringed.

He ran his hand through his hair. "I do. So much I do. But it's wrong. No matter how much we desire each other, it's wrong. You're young, and mortal, and full of light and beauty. I'm Death. I'm old. Cere, I'm so old I can't even remember my exact age. Then there's my immortality, my inability to love, and that I'm the embodiment of darkness. I don't want to hurt you."

"I'm not that light," I said. "Even you say I'm vicious. And I stole things from you."

"Trust me, your soul is pure. That's why I can't keep my hands off of you, even when touching anyone else repulses me."

I threw my hands up, annoyed that everyone kept saying that, and I still had no clue what they were talking about. "What does that mean?"

"I can sense souls. I see the essence of them when I touch a person. The one you called the overseer had a soul of black tar and oil. It was truly vile. But you." His eyes turned to me. "You have a soul of ivory laced with gold. It drew me to you the moment I saw you in the hallway. Your soul is so pure and beautiful that it took my breath away when I laid my hands on you." He trailed off, his voice growing quieter. "It still does. That's why I chose to ride Nychta our first day together. We could've just traveled to Hades' house through the void, but I wanted to be near you for a few more minutes. I was trying to understand what you are."

"What am I?" I asked, my fingers fumbling with the hem of my nightgown.

He drummed his fingers on the arm of the chair. "I don't know. I've seen pure souls. I've reaped the souls of children and they are brand new… white and soft and untouched by the world." My heart broke at that, but he continued, "But I've seen nothing like yours. Your sheltered life has left your soul white and untouched. But the gold that flows through it. I don't understand what that is. It draws me. Calls to me and…" He trailed off, searching for the right words. Closing his eyes, I watched a shudder travel through him. "It warms me. I've never felt that before."

"You've never felt warm?" I'd wondered about that the night I broke into his room. Whether or not the fire warmed him.

"I've never felt alive."

His admission stunned me, and I couldn't find any words for a long time. I made him feel alive. I had thought the same about him, that he made me feel that way.

"Is it because I'm the Pythia? That my soul is unique?"

"No," he said, quick and sure. "I've reaped their souls in the past. They are the same as everyone else. I've never seen anything like you."

"Thaos—" I started, but his gaze whipped to me, so intense that I clamped my mouth shut.

"Tell me," he whispered. "How can I allow myself to take the most beautiful thing I've ever beheld and infect it with darkness? With me?"

I was shaking my head before he finished his sentence. "I think you're kind. And thoughtful." He had done nothing but give to me since I'd arrived. "I think you tell yourself you're dark, and maybe part of you is, but you're so much more than you claim." I shuddered, thinking of Apollo. "You're lighter than those who claim to be light itself."

"Cere, please. I am trying so hard to be an honorable man, and you make it so difficult." He ran his hand through his hair again and sighed. "I think they sheltered you from the world. From men. And I was the first one you encountered outside of that, and for that reason you want to make me better than I am."

He looked at me, his face set in sad determination. "I am sorry I lied to you. I'm horrible for that, too, but I didn't want to steal your light. I'm not right for you, and you should find someone else. Someone who is bright and who can love you. Someone who can give you the life you deserve." He stared at me while he said it, but tore his gaze away before adding, "I should go."

I watched him cross the room towards the door, and I stood, a small kernel of anger returning. "You should stop telling me how to feel or what's right for me. I can make my own choices. Maybe I *should* look for someone else," I said to his back. "But I won't because I *want* you."

He sighed, pressing his forehead to the door. "I can't love you, Cere."

"I know, and I'm not asking you to. In fact, I don't want you to. You promised you wouldn't, and I'm glad."

A secret part of my heart ached. Part of me wanted him to love me. But I knew he couldn't, and I knew it was for the best. Maybe someday I would move on and find someone else, but right now he was the only person I desired.

"Then what are you asking?"

I swallowed hard, my fingers returning to play with the hem of my nightgown as anticipation and desire coiled in my stomach. "I'm asking you to stay with me tonight."

His hand was on the doorknob, but he didn't turn it. "You know what will happen if I do."

It wasn't a question. We both knew.

"And still I'm asking you to stay. Please."

CHAPTER TWENTY-FOUR

With that, I heard metal sliding, and I thought he was turning the doorknob. My heart sank, only to rebound a second later when I realized he had locked it. My stomach fluttered to life, and he took his time before facing me as he laid his scythe against the wall. His wings were full, churning with whatever emotion he was feeling.

Turning, he stared at me for a moment before chuckling. "I thought you were supposed to be the responsible one?"

My hands trembled with restless energy, but I felt the coldness that saturated the air between us these past days melt away. "We both know I'm awful at being responsible," I said with a smirk.

"I'm worried your irresponsible behavior is contagious. I can't find the will to act sensibly, either."

I frowned and then asked, "You want this too, though, right? I don't want you to do this just because I'm asking."

His eyebrows lifted in shock. "I don't know how you can even ask me that. But yes, I want this more than anything. And while you deserve better for this moment, I'm going to be the one to do it, and that makes me happier than it should. You're choosing me and I can't stop myself, even if it makes me a selfish prick."

His words sent a shiver down my spine, and I went to him, unable to stand another moment away. I spread my fingers flat on his chest, feeling his wild heartbeat under my right palm. It seemed almost as frenzied as my own.

"Choosing you feels like the rightest thing I've ever done."

His hand cupped my right cheek, and I leaned into it. My head tilted, and I felt his breath on my jaw where I'd been struck as he placed a delicate kiss on the spot.

"I'm so sorry," he whispered. "I should've been there."

"You couldn't have known."

"It doesn't matter. I'll never forgive myself."

I turned my head and pressed my lips to his, but the soft sweetness only spanned the time of one more shaky breath.

His hands trapped my waist, pulling me to him. When our bodies pressed together, I felt like I was exhaling a stale breath that I'd carried for the last two weeks. Need crashed through me, and I laced my arms around his neck.

I had been nervous he would touch me, and I would only feel the God of Sun. That I would find myself back in the room with the clock. But that didn't happen. His cool hands chased those memories away, and I didn't think of them anymore.

The kiss turned into a fury of want and desire, lips and tongues clashing in a disjointed rhythm of lust. As it escalated, other things were happening quickly. I felt his robe fall and pool at our feet, and then I helped him pull his shirt off over his head. He strode forward, causing me to step back until the backs of my knees hit the edge of the bed. I expected to fall, but he was fast and graceful, guiding me down to the mattress.

He broke the kiss, and I heard the laces of his boots before he kicked them off. His fingers grasped the hem of my nightgown and lifted, pulling it off over my head.

I pushed out a shaky, breathless giggle. "I'm surprised you didn't rip it."

"I considered it," he said, his voice heavy with desire.

I was naked now except for panties, and I gasped in surprised anticipation when he hooked his fingers over them at my hips and slipped them down my legs. His gaze flowed up what he'd bared, the look luminous and full of lust. I bit my lip and shuddered when our eyes locked again.

"You are exquisite. I've never seen a more perfect woman, and I'm certain I never will again."

I blushed, finding that hard to believe for someone who'd lived so long in the presence of actual goddesses. But it still flattered me, and the way his eyes set on me made me feel more beautiful than I ever had before.

He leaned down and folded his arm under my back. It was a belt of cool steel holding me as he picked me up, moving me until my head rested on the pillows. He unbuttoned his leather breeches, and my body flushed with heat as I watched him undress. I thought maybe I should look away, but I didn't, staring with shameless interest and desire. The constant dull ache between my legs sparked with want, achieving a new heightened level of need.

"How inappropriate of you to gaze at me with such lust," he teased.

I blushed and looked back at his face, admitting with a playful smile, "I'm thinking very inappropriate thoughts."

His lips curled in a mischievous smirk as his lashes dipped, searing me with a half-lidded gaze. "That's good. Because I'm about to do very inappropriate things to you."

His weight pressed against me again, and then his lips crashed into mine. The fierceness of the kiss pulled a moan from me, and I thought of nothing except the way his body felt against mine. My heart leapt when I felt the length of him against my thigh, causing a flurry of desire to course through me. A strange part of me wanted to giggle. Gods, we were *naked*—together. Looming behind the warm feelings was a sharp pang of anxiety, but I embraced it, too.

I was ready. I wanted this, and I was making the choice to have it. My life was my own, and I would do with it as I wished.

We kissed until I thought of nothing else, and then he tore away from my lips and moved down my neck. He paused at the spot where his teeth had pierced me once before.

"You can," I breathed. "I want you to."

"I shouldn't."

But I want to.

"Why?"

A dark chuckle vibrated through him. "I fear I'm already in danger of becoming addicted to you."

Despite his words, I felt the sharpness of his teeth and then a slight pinch of pain. I moaned as it turned into ecstasy and blazed through my body like wildfire. My hips lifted against him, and his grip was rough on my thigh as a heavy growl vibrated through his chest. I felt the rumble of it travel past my skin and sink into my bones, making me quiver.

He nipped at my collarbone, his breath tight and uneven. "You don't know what you do to me."

Kissing down the valley of my chest, he left a searing trail of heat in his wake as he worshiped every inch of my skin with his hands, his lips, and his tongue. He slowed down at my breasts, taking his time, and my delicate moans echoed around the room.

Finally, he brushed the sensitive skin just below my navel. I was already breathless, but an astonished gasp escaped me. Instinctively, my thighs wanted to come together, a spike of embarrassment running through me. I felt his hands on the inside of each one, encouraging them apart.

"Cere," he purred, and I lifted my head up to find his gaze on me. I was positive they were already flushed, but my cheeks heated when he lowered his head without looking away.

The first lash of his tongue drew a strangled sound from me I'd never heard before. My hips raised to greet his mouth, and without thinking, I placed my hands on my own breasts and squeezed. The glide of his tongue was maddening, making me writhe against him, mindless as I sought more.

It was simultaneously too much and not enough, and the curling and twisting of desire in my core became a rampage of sensation. I stopped struggling to suppress my moans, and they bounced off the plum decor in a symphony of pleasure.

The times Thaos had touched me before, I'd been able to achieve a rhythm with my hips, following him in a sensible tempo. This time was defined by disorder, my movements irregular and choppy. The sounds he made, the small moans of satisfaction, rumbled against me and I couldn't believe how much I enjoyed that.

At last, my body pulled tight, hips arching as I languished one more second on the brink of release. I cried his name as the earth dropped away and I experienced the power of pure pleasure, the waves of electric heat barreling through me.

My eyes were still closed, chest heaving, as he moved back up my body. His lips pressed against mine and I could feel his wide grin.

"How was that?" he asked, sounding as breathless as I was.

Pulling at his bottom lip with my teeth, I teased, "I suppose it will do."

A deep laugh rumbled in his chest, and his tongue danced with mine again. A thought struck me. All these times we'd been together, he had offered me nothing but pleasure and asked for none in return. Feeling bold, as he liked to say, I reached between us and brushed my fingertips against the smooth hardness of his erection.

A sigh of pleasure escaped him, the muscles of his back tensing beneath my other hand. Emboldened by that reaction, I wrapped my hand around him, and he shuddered. The God of Death trembled at my fingers. The thought was seductive and intoxicating. It inspired me to tighten my grip and run my hand up and down the length of him.

"Why am I surprised?" he rumbled, hissing in a breath. "You never do anything I expect you to do."

"Am I doing okay?"

He laughed, and the sound of it was strained. "You're doing much better than okay."

My confidence increased, and I continued the up and down motion, in awe of the way his body reacted. His hand threaded into the hair at the nape of my neck, and he kissed me with rough need, a low groan of pleasure leaving him as his hips thrust into the movement.

"Are you ready?" he asked, his breath shallow.

I nodded, a spike of anxiety surfacing, followed by a flush of heat in my neck and face. My stomach twisted, the butterflies there feeling more like hungry birds of prey. The ache at the apex of my thighs reignited twice as hot.

Gods, I wanted him. I *craved* him.

He pulled away from my hand and settled his weight between my legs. His hand roamed down my stomach and I trembled. I couldn't stop quivering, my breaths shaky and uneven.

"Are you sure you're ready?"

I nodded again, even though he was looking down between us. Finding my voice, a trembling answer pushed its way out. "I am. I want you."

He glanced up, and I was surprised to discover a rather boyish grin on his face.

"What?"

He shook his head. "I'm just... relieved you said that. I'm not sure I would've survived if you had said anything else."

Smiling, I put my hand against his cool cheek. The tense moment lightened a bit with the humor.

My heart ceased when I felt something at my entrance, recognizing only a moment later it was his finger and not what I thought it was. I felt a slight pressure, and I pushed out a breath, and then a moan as another finger joined it.

He was watching me through heavy lashes, his lips parted. A groan left him, and he eased his fingers in and out of me, making my breath come out as light gasps.

"I don't think you could be any more ready," he said with a throaty drawl that acted like another caress against my body.

I blushed, but then his expression shifted to one of apprehension as he withdrew his fingers.

"What's wrong?"

"It just occurred to me that no one may have ever told you. But there will be pain at first, and I'm already sorry for it. I don't know what it's like, I've never..." His eyebrows knitted in worry as he finished the thought. "I've never been someone's first."

Oddly enough, that was one of the very last conversations I'd had with my mother. That day, the day of my thirteenth birthday, she'd subjected me to "the talk." I was pretty sure my brother Henry had experienced the same thing in his room with my father. The memory was vivid because, as a young teenager, it mortified me. Now I felt a twinge of emotion, and I was thankful to have heard it from her.

Breathless, I said, "I know. My mother told me."

He settled against me again. I felt his hand moving, and then what I knew was definitely not his fingers pushing against me. I pulled in a sharp breath and closed my eyes. His lips brushed my forehead, and then my cheek.

He moved, and the immediate pressure overwhelmed me. A moan passed through him, but the breath was ripped from my lungs. There was a resistance, a spot I didn't think he would get past, and then an abrupt, intense sting. I might've cried out, but my lungs were betraying me and refusing to draw breath. My eyes squeezed shut. The pain was more than I was expecting, and that traitorous coil of desire that had enticed me to this point seemed to abandon me. He was so still above me, I couldn't tell if he even breathed.

"I'm sorry," he rasped, and I could hear the guilt laced in his tone.

I drew a small gasp of air, the pain already lessening. A tense smile formed on my lips. "I'm not."

That was that. I never had to think of or speak the word purity ever again. It was like someone had removed shackles from my ankles and a heavy weight off my chest. I felt light. Free.

Taking another breath, I lifted my hips slightly. The sting was there again, but less intense. Thaos stayed still, his shallow breaths caressing my cheek. My stiff fingers relaxed on his back, and I didn't realize I'd been holding him so tight. I moved again, taking more of him, and he groaned softly in my ear. I moaned this time, too, and wrapped my legs around his waist.

After a long moment, I whispered, "I'm okay."

I studied him, noticing the blackness bracketing from his eyes. His lids were glued shut, and he pushed out a long breath.

"Thaos?"

As I said his name, the cracks disappeared, and he set his head against my shoulder. "My control was dissolving there for a moment," he said. "And I will not let myself hurt you."

"I know you won't." And I meant it. I knew he wouldn't.

His lips pressed against mine, and he advanced the rest of the way until he filled me. He was so gentle and caring that it made me emotional for a breath of a second. I didn't agree with what he'd said earlier because this wasn't wrong. This was right. Every fiber of my being told me it was.

There was still discomfort, but a pulse of pleasure echoed through me, promising me it was only going to get better. He seemed to sense the change as my body relaxed and I folded my hands around his shoulders. Only then did he start really moving, and I embraced the new overwhelming sensations that followed. The friction ignited a new thread of desire and it started pulsing with intoxicating bliss.

Things became more feeling than thought as the primal instincts that everyone has sprung to life in me. Moving with him, I felt his arm snake around my torso as the rhythm increased. My soft continuous moans drifted around us, and I could hear his deeper moans of pleasure meeting them.

I opened my eyes to discover his gaze on me, his lips swollen and his hair spilling forward down his forehead. It was darker now, the shadow of his wings pouring down and surrounding us like a blanket of night. The image was devastating. So erotic and beautiful, it was something I knew I would never forget.

He released my waist and grabbed my hip, pushing harder and faster against me. I heard a soft growl escape from him, and he bent his head to my neck and kissed me, sucking on the sensitive skin. His thrusts increased, and I felt his teeth scrape me at the spot where my shoulder meets my neck.

A needy spike of exhilaration erupted through me. I shocked myself, blurting, "Yes!"

My face flared, but he moaned my name in response, and I cried out at the piercing burn when his fangs pushed past my skin deeper than they had before. The pull of his mouth brought pleasure that was so acute, all I could do was cling to him.

I sank my fingernails into his back and held on as an unexpected climax rocked through me. I was stunned by the power of it, disbelieving that it could be any more intense than the one before, and then it went far beyond.

I felt him shuddering too, a moan vibrating against my neck, and then his motions slowed until the roll of his hips stopped. A stark quiet filled the room, and I listened in a daze to our chorus of shallow breathing. His fierce lips found mine, and I answered his intense passion with equal fervor. There was a different tanginess, and it took me a moment to realize I was tasting my blood on his lips. The thought excited me. It pleased me, and my happy sigh was caught by our kiss.

Thaos leaned back, studying my face, and I smiled at him, placing my hand on his cheek. How could I put into words that it had been more than I could've ever dreamed it could be? Even if we couldn't be together, and even if he couldn't love me.

"I'll never forget this moment."

He pushed out a breath, pressing a sweet kiss to my forehead. "Neither will I."

CHAPTER TWENTY-FIVE

I woke in the night's darkness, feeling the mattress next to me was empty. My heart sank, and a flutter of painful emotion seared through my chest. I'd fallen asleep in Thaos' arms and now he was gone. I sat up and glanced around the room, and the balcony door caught my eye. It was ajar, and I walked over to it feeling alarmed. I thought back to all those years ago when the master had taken me from my home.

I heard hushed voices and stopped, straining to listen. I realized it was Thaos and Hypnos on the next balcony over.

"I don't understand what you're doing," Hypnos whispered furiously. "You had sex with her tonight." I didn't hear a reply, but he added, "And don't lie to me about it, either. I may not have gotten laid a lot the last couple centuries, but I remember what it sounds like."

Gods.

"Don't listen at the door, then," Thaos said, and I thought my face would explode from the heat that surged.

"I came back to check on her. I'm glad I went to the door and didn't just flash into the room."

"Me too. She might've died of embarrassment."

I might die of embarrassment right now.

"So you admit it then?" Hypnos asked.

"Yes."

"I must also say that you're looking well. A nice rich color in your cheeks. Almost like, I don't know, you've been imbibing a bit?"

"I couldn't stop myself," Thaos admitted, adding in a husky voice, "She likes it."

My hand traveled to my neck, where I felt two tiny, perfect scabs. I should be ashamed, but I wasn't. My parents were wolf shifters. If I now believed everything at the temple to be a lie, then what I was told during my upbringing was my truth. Sex wasn't shameful, and neither was being marked by your mate.

My breath caught at the thought, and I scolded myself. Thaos was not my mate. What an idiotic thing to think. I didn't even have my wolf, so I couldn't have a mate. If I did, it would not be a God, it would be another wolf.

Right?

I could imagine Hypnos rolling his eyes to match the exasperated sigh he pushed out. "Well, lucky you. I'm sure he'll be thrilled to find those marks on her. They'll summon you. They'll make you deliver her. Apollo knows she's here and now he wants her."

"And whose fault is that?" Thaos growled, furious. "You brought her to that idiotic festival when that was the one thing I was firm on."

"I know it was bad, I do, but she was so sad. She threatened to cry. I felt terrible."

"I could forgive you for bringing her because I know how persuasive she can be." There was a blunt sound followed by a pained grunt, and I realized someone had been punched. "But I will never forgive you for letting him—" He hissed in an angry breath. "If you wouldn't have shown up and stopped him, I would kill you right now."

"I have been hit more tonight than in the last five centuries put together," Hypnos answered, pain straining his voice. A shot of guilt moved through me because I was the one responsible for all of those punches. "But I'll admit I deserved that. I can't forgive myself for what almost happened, either. I happen to like her, you know? Very much." The corners of my lips curled at that. "But whatever he was going to do to her in that room is nothing compared to what he's going to do to her now. She kneed him right in the safe deposit box *and* bit him. Then I clocked him on the head twice with a candlestick. He is probably so pissed right now. He would've killed me earlier if he hadn't been so obsessed with finding her."

"She tried to stab him too. With Mastix," Thaos added, and if I didn't know better, I'd think he sounded proud.

"That mortal is wild," Hypnos said, chuckling. They were quiet for a moment. "But you and I both know he'll want her now, and you don't have a choice but to hand her over. The Pythia always belongs to Apollo."

"She is a person. Not an object."

"Well, *fantastic*," Hypnos deadpanned. "I'm glad you're getting on board with women's rights and everything, but we both know that no one else gives a shit. If you won't give her up, then Zeus will make you. I'm sure Apollo is crying to him right now, and he won't want to disappoint the golden boy."

"Maybe Hades will—"

"Hades will do nothing. He's barely keeping it together now that Clotho is dead. There's no way he's going to bat for you on this one."

Thaos sighed in frustration. "I'm telling you right now, Hypnos, Apollo will not have her."

"And what are you going to do? Start a war between the realms for a mortal woman?"

"If that's what it takes. If I have to kill Apollo myself, I will. I would've done it tonight if I'd gotten my hands on him."

There was a beat of silence, and then Hypnos pushed out a breath. "Holy shit."

"What?"

"You love her."

"*No*," he said, defiant. "I can't—"

"Who do you think you're talking to?" Hypnos snapped. "It's me. Your twin brother. The person who knows you best. Please don't insult me by trying to push that emo *death can't love* bullshit on me. You are different with her than you've ever been with anyone else. I knew something was going on but..." He paused, sucking in a shocked breath. "Fuck's sake, you're in love with her. A mortal woman. A mortal that belongs to someone else."

There was a heavy silence, and my heart was beating so hard it hurt. He couldn't love me. He promised he wouldn't.

"She is special," Thaos said. "I care very much for her."

Cool relief rushed through me, at least he hadn't said the "L" word. Hypnos wasn't buying it, though.

I heard a dry, humorless laugh. "Tell me you love someone without actually saying the word 'love.'"

"I know we're not meant to be. She *is* a mortal, and she deserves a happy life. I can't have her for... too much longer. I know that."

"Really? Do you?"

"*But* I will not let her go to be used as an Olympian's plaything. I don't care about the consequences. We'll figure it out."

"*We*? I didn't sign up for this."

"Yes you did when you brought her to the festival."

Hypnos clicked his tongue. "I have a bad feeling about this, brother."

"I don't care. She's staying here. With m—" He paused, sighing. "With *us*. You would give her up? Let him take her? I thought you liked her."

"Of course, I do. It's just, this is going to piss a lot of people off."

"I don't care."

"What was it you spat at me? You're a lovesick fool? Wasn't that it?"

"You're testing my patience, Sleep. I thought you were tired of being punched."

I heard a slapping sound, and I thought he had actually hit him again, but Hypnos chuckled.

Thaos said in a more relaxed, maybe even humorous, tone, "Don't touch me. Your soul is disturbing." I realized Hypnos had most likely clapped him on the shoulder.

"I think that might be the first joke you've made in like six centuries. Now I am concerned."

"Little do you know I wasn't joking."

I heard a snort of laughter from both of them.

"Seriously, though," Hypnos said. "What are we going to do to save our Sleeping Beauty?"

"We'll figure it out in the morning. Right now—"

"Yeah, yeah, I don't want to know. It's torture as I'm practically celibate. Just go."

I scrambled and launched myself to the bed. Diving under the covers, I tried to make my breathing appear deep and constant. The next second I heard the door and then the shuffling of clothes before I felt the bed dip beside me.

I turned to him, and he pulled me into his chest until our bodies meshed together.

"I thought you'd left," I mumbled, wincing at how horribly needy the words sounded.

He frowned and pushed my hair behind my ear. "Of course not. I had to talk to Hypnos."

"About Apollo? We're in trouble now, aren't we?"

"Yes. He'll want you delivered to him, and I'll be expected to comply."

Dread poured into my soul and spread, making my heartbeat quicken. "He'll kill me. He was furious with me."

"No, he won't. The Pythia is too valuable. But he would make you suffer for rejecting him."

If that was an attempt at comfort, it didn't have the intended effect. "He's obsessed. Why can't he just leave me alone?"

He ran his hand up and down my arm, provoking light tingles of sensation that danced on my skin. "When he has the Pythia, Apollo is more powerful. People do favors and give him things to see the Oracle. Plus, he would never let another God have what he believes is his. That would make him appear weak. I also wouldn't be surprised if he sensed the same thing I did—that you're unique."

"He did," I confirmed. "He said so. Now what do we do?"

He kissed my forehead. "I don't know. But I'll figure something out. He won't have you."

"You seemed confident you could kill him," I mumbled, and then quickly added, "Not that I'm asking you to."

Smirking, he said, "I would beat him, but it wouldn't be easy. I'm older, but his skill set is the exact opposite of mine. Shadows and sun offset each other, making it hard for either of us to seize the upper hand."

I turned my face up and kissed him. My hands rested on his cheeks, and I pulled him closer to me, pressing my body suggestively against his. A laugh rumbled in his chest.

"You should sleep."

"I don't want to," I whispered, a small slice of panic cutting through me. "What if this is the only time we get to do this?"

The humor disappeared from his face. "I selfishly hope that's not true."

"We don't know what's going to happen. Tomorrow isn't even a guarantee."

His head dipped again and found my lips, and a heated kiss followed. My skin jumped at his hand traveling down my left side until it rested on my thigh. He lifted my leg and draped it over his hip, pushing against me. Breaking the kiss, he stopped and looked at me with concern.

"How are you? Don't you need to rest?"

His thoughtfulness, and how he claimed to be dark when I only saw light made my heart surge.

"I'm okay. I heal faster than humans do."

He smiled, kissing me again. After a brief moment, he tensed and lifted his head. His eyes glazed over for several seconds. I waved my hand in front of his face, but he didn't react.

"Thaos?"

I touched his face, and then he relaxed, his eyes squeezing shut.

"What was that?"

He sighed. "Zeus has summoned me. The Pythian Games that are overdue are to take place tomorrow in the realm of Apollo and I'm to attend. I'm to bring the Pythia to her rightful place."

"Oh."

I wasn't sure what else to say.

"If I don't take you, it will cause a lot of problems for Hades. He will want me to hand you over to avoid any conflict in his weakened state."

I sighed. "When? First thing in the morning?"

"I have to have you there at noon."

He pressed his forehead to mine, and I felt even more desperate to enjoy this moment. I would go tomorrow to whatever awaited me at the hands of Apollo because I would not let people get hurt over me. There was no way I was going to allow some kind of war to start between the realms. Especially when everything else was already so chaotic with the undead, the plague, and the death of one of the Fates.

"We can worry about it in the morning then."

He stared down at me. "You should be afraid."

"I am," I admitted. "I'm terrified, but that doesn't change what is going to happen. Trust me, I know better than anyone that fate always finds a way."

I dropped the walls in my mind, gazing at him, but I only saw blackness. What a worthless gift.

"Did you just read me?" He sounded unimpressed.

"I tried. I saw nothing."

"Good. Don't read me."

"Why?"

He sighed and brushed his lips over mine. "Because I know I don't get to have you forever and I don't want to know when this ends."

CHAPTER TWENTY-SIX

I woke in a tangle of limbs, Thaos' body draped around mine. He was already awake, his hand traveling up and down my arm. I twisted to him, noticing fine lines of tension bracketing his mouth and eyes. He placed an easy kiss on my lips and another on my forehead. Unwrapping himself from me, he rose and started pulling on his clothes.

"Where are you going?"

"To visit my mother."

His mother was Nyx, Goddess of Night. She was ancient, older than Zeus and the other Olympians. Known as a Protogenoi, it was said she was there at the beginning of creation itself.

"Why?"

"If she'll help us, I can keep you protected in her domain. Not even Zeus would dare enter."

"Do you think she'll help?"

His frown deepened. "No, but right now it's the only idea I have."

"Even if she does, it will still cause strife between the realms. I don't want anyone hurt because of me. I will go before I allow that to happen."

He sighed. "I don't doubt that, because I don't want you to, and you seem to thrive on doing the opposite of what I ask."

I snorted a dry laugh but couldn't argue the truth. He turned back to me, grabbing his scythe. His eyes heated when they fell on me, and I realized the sheet only covered the bottom half of my naked body.

I pulled it up, and he looked offended, then a small boyish grin appeared. "That was rude. But charming. As if my hands and eyes don't already know what's under that sheet."

I blushed, meeting his gaze and thinking I wouldn't mind if he just got back in bed with me.

He arched an eyebrow and then murmured, "Don't look at me like that."

I offered him a coy smile in return. "Like what?"

"You know exactly what you're doing. And I wish I could remain in that bed with you all day, but I'll be back soon."

After he left, I showered and then went down to find Hypnos at the table, looking more stressed than I'd ever seen him.

He sat up when I strode in, peering behind me. "Where is he?"

"He went to talk to your mother."

"Well, I doubt that will get him anywhere. She doesn't concern herself with matters she finds irrelevant. Which is everything. You might think we're old and apathetic, but the Protogenoi are in a league of their own."

"He thinks so, too, but it's the only idea he has."

"He got the summons as well, I'm guessing."

"Yes, you did too?"

"I did. Apollo will want my head because I hit him with that candlestick. And Zeus never got over that whole thing where I helped Hera put him to sleep so she could try to kill Hercules. He is not my biggest fan, either."

"I'm sorry." I was, too. If I hadn't made him take me last night, we wouldn't be here.

Curious, I gazed at him and dropped the walls in my mind.

"Are you reading me?"

There was nothing screaming in my head. Just one soft whisper floated to the forefront.

"Don't grieve your heart, Sleep. Sloth will salvage it."

Hypnos grinned down at his breakfast. The smile was so broad I worried it might crack his face.

"Are you going to tell me what it means?" I asked.

"Aergia, my sweet Goddess of Sloth. We were a thing once."

"What about your wife?"

He shook his head, pushing out a breath. "Last week I confronted her about being a traitor. I wanted to know whether or not she played a role in bringing those undead to town while you were there. She was deeply offended that I accused her of such a thing. She said she didn't want to see me, and in her eyes we are no longer married. As you saw last night, she means it. She seems to be enjoying her life as a single woman."

"I'm sorry," I mumbled. "It wasn't her fault or yours after all, it was the imposter Aeryn that told them we'd be in town."

He shrugged. "It's not like there was a lot of love between us to lose. If it hadn't been that, she would've soon found another reason to end it. But I knew I might see her at the festival acting that way, which is why I decided not to go. I tried to prepare myself, but it still got to me, and I left you alone. Now we're in this mess."

"You deserve better than her," I said, jutting my chin out. "You're amazing."

He smirked but didn't answer.

Thaos dropped into the room from the void, and his face suggested he was unsuccessful.

Hypnos cleared his throat. "How'd it go? How was dear old mom?"

"Stubborn. She says she *can't* help. Not that she won't. Actually, she told me to deliver Cere to Apollo, and to stop being an obstinate fool."

"Shocking," Hypnos said, his head resting against his hand in a depressed slouch.

"Now what?" I asked. It was already just past ten o'clock, and the second hand looked to be ticking faster than normal today.

He sat next to me, forcing out a breath. "I don't know."

"Well, they summoned me and Hades as well," Hypnos said.

Thaos frowned deeper and then opened his mouth to say something, but the door opening cut him off. A woman and a man I didn't know entered.

I studied her first, taking in her deep sepia colored skin and the jumble of midnight curls so wild I didn't know if it had ever been conquered. Her eyes were blue like Hypnos', creating a striking contrast with the dark hue of her face. She was tall and wore black tights with a lengthy golden blouse. On the inside of her wrist, I spotted the image of an apple tattoo and I wondered what it represented.

The man wore all black and had the insignia of a closed eye on his shirt. He had chalky skin, sunken cheeks, and dark circles under his silver eyes. Well, his eye, I guess. His listless white hair was long and straight, hanging forward in his face, so only one of his eyes was visible.

The woman was grinning like a wolf, but the man had a drawn morbid expression.

Hypnos sighed. "As if we didn't have enough trouble to endure. What are you two doing here?"

"Mom sent us," the woman said, her curls bouncing as she spoke. "She says our older brother is pretty pissy with her and we need to make sure he doesn't get himself killed over a mortal woman."

"So she sends us Chaos and Doom? That doesn't seem helpful at all."

"It's not," the man said, his expression and tone flatter than the table we sat at. "We're fucked."

Hypnos pinched the bridge of his nose and exhaled. "Thank you Moros, very helpful."

The woman's eyes set on me, and she grinned. It was a broad and vicious smile that disturbed me.

"Is this her? The mortal that has our brother so agitated?"

"Yes, this is Cere. The Pythia," Hypnos answered. "Cere, this is our sister Eris, Goddess of Chaos and Strife, and our brother Moros, God of Doom."

"My mother's name is Eris," I blurted.

"Well, your grandparents had great taste in names then," the woman praised.

There was a blinking flash, similar to what happened when Hypnos traveled, and two more women stood in the room. One looked like she just finished teaching kindergarten at the local elementary school, with light brown hair, soft chocolate eyes rimmed by large circle glasses, and a warm smile. She wore a floral button up blouse and khaki pants.

The other was a stark opposite, brandishing a scythe similar to Thaos'. Her skin was ebony, and she had terrifying, piercing onyx eyes. The way she studied the room reminded me of an eagle, and her vast black wings reinforced that image. They were not made of shadow like Thaos', but full and feathered. She cut her hair short in a sharp-angled bob, colored silver with black streaks scattered throughout. Her clothes were all black leather, hugging the sumptuous curves of her body.

"Now here's some actual help," Hypnos said.

Eris glared at her brother, but he ignored her.

"And what does mother expect you all to do?" Thaos asked.

"Persuade you to take her to Apollo, and then go with you and stay to help," the tender looking one explained. "She says it's the only way."

"It's still going to be nothing but a catastrophe," Moros chimed in, sounding solemn. I suspected he couldn't sound any other way.

Thaos was defiant in his refusal. "No. That's not happening."

The other reaper looked at me with a curled lip. "Why? She's a mortal. We'll just get you a new one."

"Watch your tongue, Keres," he spat.

"Or what? You don't scare me, Death. I'm Death, too."

"Now," the nice goddess said. "Let's all get along." The air saturated with a scent like fresh summer air, and the desire to be best friends with all of them overtook me.

I rose, intent on hugging every person in this room. Thaos grabbed my arm, encouraging me to return to my seat. Overwhelmed by this odd sensation, I threw my arms around his neck and hugged him, practically crawling into his lap. His lips tilted and he wrapped his arm around my waist.

"Don't do that Phil," Hypnos said, shaking his head to clear the fog. "I despise that."

They all scowled at her, and she shrugged, a timid grin crossing her delicate features.

"What just happened?" I asked, trying to fight through the haze in my mind.

"Cere, this is our baby sister Philotes, Goddess of Friendship and Affection. She just tried to compel us to be chummy, which never works." He glared at Philotes again and then nodded towards the winged woman. "Keres is the Goddess of Violent death. She likes war."

I glanced around at all of them, and a dry laugh escaped me. "Let me get this straight. Nyx spawned Sleep, Death, Death again, Chaos, Doom, and then, for some reason, Friendship?"

"Yeah, weird right?" Eris said. "Poor Phil."

"You can all leave," Thaos said, his tone dark and forceful. "She's not going."

Moros shook his head. "It will start a war. There will be a lot of suffering."

"On second thought, that doesn't sound so bad," Keres mumbled.

Thaos stood, pulling me up with him since my arms still held his neck. "I have to go see Hades. You all should not be here when I get back."

He grabbed his scythe, and to a room full of shocked gasps, he leaned down and kissed me. It was the first time he'd ever shown me affection like this in front of other people, and it was not a friendly peck, either.

I tensed, not expecting it, and then closed my eyes and kissed him back. I knew what I was about to do, so I cherished it. He broke away and lingered at my lips for just a moment longer.

"Oh, this is bad," Moros said. "Bad, bad, bad."

Hypnos answered, "For once I agree."

"I was going to leave you here," Thaos said, ignoring them. "But I have a suspicion you're going to do something reckless."

My eyes widened. I had been planning to ask his siblings to take me to Delphi.

He read my expression and narrowed his eyes. "I knew it."

"You should let me go," I whispered. "I don't want anyone to get hurt because of me."

"Apollo won't have you. I still have time to figure this out."

"Mother says she has to go," Philotes interjected, her voice still soft and reassuring.

"She is not going." Thaos seemed relaxed, but the blackness had clouded his eyes.

I didn't understand what was happening or why the entire atmosphere of the room had shifted with those words. I stared at Thaos but detected a subtle movement out of the corner of my eye.

Bedlam erupted as he spun, wielding his scythe, and blocked a strike from Keres, who was standing on the table. They started exchanging rapid blows and Thaos stepped in front of me. The smell of summer air filled the room again, soothing my confusion and worry. It did nothing to stop the fight between Thaos and his sister.

Keres cursed after a vicious blow slashed her face. "What is your problem, Thanatos? Pull yourself together. She is a mortal woman!"

I heard Hypnos yelling something and then Eris answered him, cackling, "Mom said we have to get her there no matter what."

Shadows filled the room, and I wasn't sure if it was from Keres or Thaos or both of them. Then Philotes appeared next to me.

"I would never make you go against your will," she said, extending her hand. "But I will take you."

"People will get hurt if I stay, won't they?"

"Eventually, yes. I trust my mother when she says this is the only way. She knows things that others do not."

I looked at her hand, already knowing what I was going to do. I reached for it—

"Cere."

I glanced over to Thaos, who was now being restrained by both Keres and Moros. He had been resisting them but stopped. His chest was rising and falling as he stared into my eyes.

"Don't go. Apollo, the things he'll do, it will steal your light. I can't lose you." He sounded so woeful it took my breath away. His furious eyes turned to Moros, the black cracks erupting on his face. "Get your hands off me, Doom, before I rip your heart out. You're putting things in my head."

Moros shook his head. "We both know that's not how it works. Your dark thoughts are your own, I just aggravate them."

Thaos growled, trying to grab him.

"I'll be okay." I cut in, sounding about as confident about that as I felt. "But I can't let anyone get hurt because of me. I've already caused so much suffering."

His eyes whipped back to me. "Then don't go because I'm asking you to stay. Please."

His siblings stared at him, a silent shock enveloping the room. Hypnos was the only one who didn't look surprised, his expression set in a pensive frown.

"He's lost his damn mind," Eris laughed. "I love it!"

My heart wrenched, and a different raw ache opened in my chest. He wasn't suggesting I could stay—he was asking me to stay. I was the one who'd convinced myself there was a distinction between those two things after I'd left his room that first night we'd kissed.

And I was correct. They were two utterly different things. I could see in his face this was about more than saving me from Apollo and that alarmed me more than anything else.

She'll have your heart, Death, for it belongs with her. But, once it's surrendered, the son will steal your life.

Even though my heart lurched in protest, I knew I needed to get away from him, for his sake.

I swallowed the knot in my throat. "I want to stay. But I should go."

"Cere—"

"I'm sorry."

Grabbing Philotes' hand before he could convince me otherwise, I closed my eyes, and the world shifted around me.

When the blurring stopped, I found I didn't want to stop clutching her hand. She allowed me to, not appearing bothered by the contact. We were standing in the open doorway of an immense white marble temple.

The walls were open, creating an airy space with an abundance of light. The weather here was bright and beautiful, the sky a soft blue dotted by fluffy white clouds. I felt the sun on my skin and loved it. It had been awhile.

We were walking towards a giant statue of Apollo, and I recognized its inspiration sitting at the base on a throne that looked to be chiseled out of pearl.

Standing next to him was a man I knew had to be Zeus himself. I recognized him from the vision I had in the dungeon. He'd been fighting the half serpent creature that emerged from Tartarus. He was the same behemoth size as Hades, but his tanned skin glowed like gold and produced a powerful aura around him. His long hair hung in soft, white waves down to his waist, framing a broad, stern face that watched us with cunning eyes as we approached. When we stopped in front of them, he frowned.

"I am glad to see the Pythia," Zeus said. His voice resounded like a thunderclap, echoing in the open chamber. "But I specifically summoned Sleep, Death, and my brother as well."

"They'll be here, Your Highness," Philotes answered, inclining her head. "Any moment I'm sure."

A woman stepped from behind the throne, and I felt an instant pull to her. Her hair was spun gold like Apollo's and pulled back in several intricate braids. They shared the same sapphire blue eyes and round, pink lips. She wore a short white robe over leather leggings and had a gleaming silver bow strapped to her back.

"You're Artemis," I said. I had read enough about Apollo in these last weeks to recognize this was his twin sister.

"Yes," she acknowledged. Her voice was smoky and wild, her scent strong like pine. A piece of my soul called to her. "And you're one of my children."

I found a loose thread on my shirt and rolled it in my fingers. Feeling shy, I nodded. "My parents are wolf shifters. I never got my wolf though."

She approached me, and I considered bowing or dropping to my knees. Her presence overwhelmed me, and I gawked at her, star struck. This was Artemis, my mother Goddess that I'd prayed to a thousand times. She startled me by pressing her thumb to my forehead and closing her eyes.

After a moment, she removed it. "You're right, your wolf couldn't fully develop because of your other powers. There just wasn't enough room. But she's there. She makes herself known as much as she can."

"I heal faster than humans, and I'm stronger and more agile, too," I offered, thinking that's what she meant.

"Yes," she said, laughing. The sound was rich and husky. "But I was talking about this." She put her finger on the bite mark Thaos had left on me the night before and I felt heat rise in my face. "She thinks she's found her fated mate, *and* she got him to mark her. Your wolf is more active in your decisions than you think."

My hand flew to the two little scabs. I thought of how I'd blurted yes last night when Thaos had brushed that spot. The outburst had astonished me. The corner of my mouth tilted. That had been my wolf driving me.

Tears stung my eyes as emotion overwhelmed me. That explained my immediate intense attraction to him and my inability to resist being with him. It also revealed why I didn't fear him when everyone else did.

"He's my mate? How?"

Apollo shifted in his seat behind her. "Oh, who cares? It doesn't matter if she's one of yours, and I couldn't care less about fated mates. You're mine. The Pythia is always mine. Why is everybody suddenly struggling to understand that?"

My eyes darted to him, and he viewed me with obvious malice. Irritation flared when I noticed that he had my Mastix dagger secured at his waist.

He caught my stare and his hand fell to it, a sneer curling his lip. Squaring my shoulders, I looked him in the eye. "That's mine. I'd like it back."

Apollo barked out a laugh, his fingers strumming the handle. "You want it? What will you do for it?"

I scowled at him, and he stood. He glided down the stairs until he was in my face. "I can't wait to teach you respect." His blue eyes were amused but sharp.

I thought of the overseer and his discipline. His never-ending quest to make me behave. "You wouldn't be the first to try. Good luck."

Artemis chuckled, but her eyes widened in disappointment when he raised his hand. I squeezed my eyes shut, waiting for the blow to land, but a breeze of cool air enveloped me instead.

Opening my eyes again, I found Thaos had caught his hand. Shadows billowed around us, icing the air. He glared at Apollo with black eyes full of intense hatred, a look that was mirrored back to him.

"You will never strike her again."

Apollo's answer was instant, "I will do as I please. She is *mine*."

There was stunned silence, and then pandemonium erupted. Thaos punched Apollo in the ribs, making him blow out a breath of rough air. They started grappling, and I felt someone grab my arm and pull me back away from the fight.

Screams of excitement erupted around me from Thaos' siblings, who had arrived alongside Hades. The King of the Underworld looked like he might need to sit down before he collapsed.

I heard Eris say, "I knew this was going to be good." She took a long deep breath, like she could actually smell the chaos in the air.

Next to me, Keres slammed the end of her scythe against the floor and roared with aggression, "*Kill* him, Thaos!"

She sounded so terrifying that I took a cautious step away from her. I was a bit confused. Weren't they just fighting? It was obvious the lines of their loyalties to each other were blurred, even if they were siblings.

Thaos and Apollo were on the ground, blows landing with such quick ferocity my eyes struggled to follow. As far as I could tell, neither one of them had a solid advantage.

Shadows poured out of Thaos' mouth, and I knew it was what Ulther had called the kiss of death. But this opponent wasn't the overseer, he was the God of Sun. Beams erupted from Apollo, so blinding that I had to squint to see what was happening.

The beams held the shadows at bay, the light and dark seeming to block each other from advancing any further towards either man. Apollo kicked Thaos off of him and they both rolled to their feet with unnatural grace.

I recognized the slide of a sword being unsheathed, and Apollo wielded the blade of fire he'd had the night before.

Thaos pulled his scythe from its spot on his back and twirled it with expert skill that the shameless part of me found impossibly alluring.

They raised their weapons, this grapple about to turn into a fight to the death.

"Enough!" Zeus' voice shook the entire temple. It was so loud I was sure my ear drums had burst. I clamped my hands over the sides of my head.

Apollo and Thaos stopped, their chests heaving with rage and exertion. They glared at each other with untethered hostility while their muscles quivered, as if they were coiling to attack again.

After such anarchy, the silence was overwhelming. Everyone looked shocked, eyes on Zeus.

"Death?" Zeus said, confused. "What is this? You've never been a troublemaker. You just keep to yourself and do your duty. You're not like the others." He glared at the group of siblings, in particular Hypnos and Eris, who looked sheepish.

"He wants her," Apollo spat. "I told you there's something special about this one and he knows it, too. But the Pythia is always mine. She belongs to me."

"She belongs to no one," Thaos said coolly.

Apollo barked out a dry laugh, but my heart danced a swirling waltz at the words. I wondered again what Apollo meant by something special, and Thaos had said something similar last night regarding my soul. Plus, the strange way my gift was developing—what could it mean?

"Are you sure? I smell you all over her, and her on you. And the bite marks on her neck are yours. How *dare* you?" Apollo snarled.

"They are," Thaos said, smirking. "And she asked me to. Unlike some, I don't have to force myself on women to get what I want."

The siblings cackled like a murder of crows, their raucous laughter echoing around us. Zeus frowned in disapproval. I hadn't forgotten what I'd learned of his actions with Laurenth, and a fresh wave of hatred swept through me.

Apollo stepped towards Thaos, intent on fighting him again.

"I said enough," Zeus warned, stepping forward. "Thanatos, I sympathize with you, but the Pythia belongs here with Apollo at Delphi. We're having the games, long overdue, and she has to be here. After that, she'll stay. As it's always been. That's my decision."

Apollo looked smug, turning and winking at me. I bristled, glowering at him in response.

"Why do we even have the games?" Keres complained. "Apollo always wins anyway."

The God of Sun smiled at her, his arrogance untethered.

"Of course he does," Hypnos muttered. "He was a coward and picked events specific to his skill set so he'd never lose."

Apollo's smile morphed into fury. "I've got a score to settle with you, too, Sleep."

Hypnos blanched and stepped behind Keres, who rolled her eyes.

"I challenge you then," Thaos said. "I'll compete against you in the games and the winner gets her."

My heart melted in my chest, and I stared at the God of Death. My fated mate if Artemis was to be believed.

There were a few gasps of surprise, and Apollo laughed. "You? You think you can defeat me at my own games?"

"If you're so sure, then accept the deal."

Apollo hesitated, probably surprised by Thaos' confidence. He glanced at Zeus, who looked intrigued.

"He's issued a challenge. What you do is up to you, God of Sun." Zeus' tone suggested to me that he would think less of his son if he declined.

Still, Apollo didn't have to accept, but he was too arrogant and proud. I knew he would.

After a moment, his cocky demeanor returned. "Fine. I accept. Winner keeps the Pythia."

I dropped the walls in my mind and looked at Apollo.

He smirked at me. "Trying to read me? The Pythia can't unless I want her to, but nice try."

"I challenge you, too," Artemis said, speaking up. "She's one of mine. She belongs with me."

Apollo looked like she'd slapped him. "What? Sister—"

"It's decided then," Zeus said, clapping his hands once. "It's been awhile since we had a real challenger, and now we have two. This is going to be fun to watch for once."

Thaos walked to me, and in the pandemonium, no one seemed to notice. Apollo was arguing with his sister, who looked bored with the conversation, and the siblings of Death were in a fit of chatter with each other, excitement filling the room. Hades just looked tired, staring off into space as if he had bigger problems. Which he certainly did.

Thaos had a trickle of blood at the corner of his mouth, but other than that, he seemed fine.

He wiped it away and ran his hands down my arms. "Are you okay?"

I nodded. "Are you mad?"

"I was, but now I think this worked out better than expected. I'll just win these trivial games, and then you won't have to worry about hiding anymore." He stared down at me, clicking his tongue. "Did you really think I would give up so easily?"

"Thaos—" I closed my mouth, unsure of what to say. I wanted to tell him what Artemis had just said. I wanted to ask him what he was doing or why he would do this for a mortal woman he could never love. But no words came out.

He stepped closer to me and brushed his lips over my cheek. "I will win."

It was a promise built of steel resolve and I believed him.

Artemis appeared next to him. I glanced around her and saw that Apollo was now complaining to Zeus about her late entry. Zeus appeared to care little for the argument.

"Okay, Death. The winner is the best of the four events," Artemis said. "I can take the archery event from him because you'll never beat him. He'll win the chariot race, no doubt. I hope you have a fast horse because you must win the single rider race."

Thaos reached into his robe and pulled out the coin that hosted Nychta. "I do," he said, eyeing her suspiciously.

"That leaves boxing and that's all up to you."

"I planned to win those two events, anyway."

Her eyebrows lifted, and a smile played at her lips. "And force the tiebreaker? You know what the tiebreaker is, right?"

"Yes, and I would've won."

She scoffed. "Now I wish I would've let it happen because, *that*, I want to see. But I'll spare you the tiebreaker."

I looked between them. "What's the tiebreaker?"

"Apollo is the God of the Sun, but also many other things, including music," Artemis explained. "The tiebreaker involves playing a lute and singing."

My mouth opened, but I didn't know what to say. I stared at Thaos, trying to suppress a giggle. The image of him strumming the chords of a lute and serenading an audience was as hilarious as it was unsettling.

He gave me a sly look. "I would've won, too. And I'm grateful for your help, Artemis. But why?

She looked at me with a soft, loving smile that made me want to faint or scream like some crazed fan. "Because she is one of mine. And the thought of a little wolf without her mate breaks my heart."

My eyes widened at the same time as his. I wasn't sure if I was ready to have that conversation, but now it looked like I had mere seconds to prepare. My gaze flicked to Thaos, terrified to know what he would think. He was my mate, but that didn't mean I was his. He wasn't a wolf, so he would have to choose me without the influence of the mate bond driving his decision. I knew he felt things for me, but he had stated several times we weren't to be together.

He watched her walk away, and then his gaze slid back to my face. Then down to my neck, realization dawning. He must know enough about shifter culture to understand what it meant. The mark was the last step. It signified the completion of the bond. I was connected to him for the rest of my life.

"Did you know?"

Finding I couldn't speak past the nervous lump in my throat, I shook my head no.

He stared at the mark for a moment longer and then reached up and touched it. Even that simple contact sent a shiver straight through me. I watched his features, trying to discern what he could be thinking.

"This explains some things. Like how you can stand to be in my presence and endure my touch."

I frowned, feeling annoyed. "I don't *endure* your touch...I enjoy it."

His voice lowered so only I could hear him, and it was full of teasing desire. "It also explains why you're such a naughty little mortal, enjoying my bite the way you do."

I blinked twice, my face doing as it had done so much these last few weeks and flaring to life. I gaped at him, shocked by words I never expected to hear from him, and I glanced around to make sure no one else was listening.

"Gods," I whispered, suppressing the stupid smile that was trying to break my lips. "Shut up."

He looked amused, the corner of his mouth turned up. "I'm glad for this," he said, shocking me again by leaning down and brushing the mark with his lips. "I shouldn't be, but that's what I am."

Smiling, a rush of warm relief coursed through me. It was accompanied by a twinge of shyness at his open affection. He drifted up to my lips and kissed me. My heart skipped with joy and then dipped in despair. I may be naïve, but this was feeling an awful lot like how I imagined love would be.

Apollo's voice topped the rest. "That's not fair. Since she technically belongs to no one right now, he shouldn't get to be all over her like that. I don't want him spoiling her any further before I have her."

Thaos was looking at me, but his jaw flexed in anger. I put my hand on his cheek and kissed him again, earning a furious gasp from the God of Sun.

"I agree," Zeus said, looking at me. "Come here, child, you'll stay with me today. And you, big brother, you'll join me as well. We have much to discuss after the tragic events at your festival last night."

Hades looked as excited as I felt.

"Yeah, Mom is not happy about that," Keres said. "She wants someone to answer for Clotho's death."

Hades and Zeus both tensed at the mention of Nyx. They glanced at each other, unable to hide the small flashes of nervous anticipation.

"We'll give everyone time to get here," Zeus said, clearing his throat. A broad smile painted his face. "And then we'll begin."

CHAPTER TWENTY-SEVEN

"Friends!" Zeus boomed. "Welcome to the long overdue Pythian Games! You'll all be pleased to know that our Pythia of Delphi has been rescued and returned to her rightful place!"

There were cheers, and I might've heard them if my eardrums weren't ringing from being in front of Zeus while he bellowed his introduction. People packed the expansive stadium, sitting in white marble bleachers above an oval racetrack. An archery field covered the grass in the center of the track. I had the best spot in the house, looking out over everything from a luxurious seating box.

I was among the Olympians, next to a beast of a man that spilled out of his seat and into mine. He seemed jolly, but everyone else around me looked bored, like they didn't care to be here.

"I love the games," the man next to me said, leaning over and grinning. His voice was a deep, rumbling baritone. "I'm so glad they found you."

In true Hypnos fashion, I offered him a withering glare. "I'm not."

His grin widened, and then he barked out a laugh. Not the reaction I expected.

Turning away from him, I saw Apollo and Artemis were now on the field with Thaos. They were all carrying bows and arrows for the event.

Zeus continued his assault on my ears. "We are here to celebrate the triumph by my son Apollo, who defeated the python and claimed this sacred ground!"

"Apollo! Apollo!" The crowd chanted, and he waved as he flashed a million-dollar smile. I wanted to vomit, but the stadium went wild, a frenzy of screams and whistles.

"This year we have some very able contestants," Zeus continued.

"Hercules! Hercules!" the crowd returned.

The giant on my left stood and waved to a riot of cheers. His chest was bare, his bottom half covered by a leather kilt decorated with silver discs. On his shoulders, he wore an enormous pelt from a slain lion.

Zeus chuckled a belly laugh, "No, Hercules is taking the year off. But we have another Olympian—Artemis!"

The crowd erupted again, and she waved, beaming with pride and confidence. The cheers were different, and it took me a moment to recognize some of the crowd were howling like wolves.

"And, finally," Zeus said, excited. "An Underworld challenger we've never seen before, Death himself, Thanatos!"

The stadium fell silent, it was so quiet I could hear the gentle breeze whistling through the flags at the top of the wall behind me. No cheers, but no one foolhardy enough to boo, either. Thaos stood stoically, his posture bored, and his face masked by his hood.

After a few seconds, a small ruckus of cheers erupted from a section of the crowd. I looked to find Eris and Keres shouting vulgar things like, "Rip their godsdamned throats out!"

Moros sat with his arms crossed, looking sullen, while Hypnos clapped at a slow, sarcastic pace. Philotes looked bright, beaming and clapping in a tiny little burst. I noted that all the closest sections around them were empty despite the packed stadium. Gods, I wished I were sitting with them instead of here. Hypnos caught my stare and gestured with a subtle wave, which I returned.

I looked out over the field, seeing there were targets at various distances in a line. As they progressed, the target grew smaller. The last target was the size of a silver dollar, positioned behind a line of swinging axes with holes in the center of the blades. As they swung, the holes only lined up for a fraction of a second. To me, it was an impossible shot.

"The Odysseus challenge is first! Normally it's a head-to-head shoot out, but with three contestants we have changed it to a timed event. Whoever can hit the bullseye on every target in the fastest time is the winner! Begin!"

Artemis and Thaos stepped away, giving Apollo the first turn. Cheers erupted, and he waved, looking confident. He stood at a starting line with his golden bow in his hand. A horn blared, and he moved with speed so incredible my eyes had trouble keeping track of him.

I heard the soft thwack of arrows sinking into the targets as he ran at full speed across the field, not missing a single shot. He paused for just a brief second at the last target, waiting for the axes to line up, and then released a straight shot through. From my count, it took him about nine seconds to finish the entire course. I was stunned. Such a feat would've taken me minutes to complete.

The crowd cheered their love for him, and he waved, looking smug. Field attendants started moving, removing the arrows from the targets, and resetting the course.

"He's not bad is he?" a voice said next to me, making me jump in surprise. I'd been so engrossed in the event I hadn't even realized someone had taken the seat on my right. "Artemis will beat him, though," he added.

I glanced over at him. "I hope so."

He grinned and held out his hand. I stared at it and then looked at his face. He retracted it, understanding I wasn't going to take it. His confidence wasn't diminished in the slightest.

"Dionysus, God of Wine and Fertility," he said with a sultry wink.

One of the Olympians, another son of Zeus.

He was, of course, incredibly handsome with dark bronze colored skin and long hair the color of ripe plums. His eyes were like lilacs, and he wore a one shoulder robe in black that rested loosely on his body, revealing most of it. A wreath made of green and purple grapes rested off-center on his head, and he wore a cape made from the skin of a fawn. The glass of wine he held in his right hand was so full I didn't understand how he hadn't spilled a drop. His other hand gripped a staff wrapped in ivy and topped with a jeweled pinecone that glistened with some kind of sticky substance—it looked like honey.

I studied him, trying to find his motive. "I'm Cere."

"I had to come meet the woman that pulled Death out of Hades to compete in this pointless event. Not that I hate the games. It's an excuse to party and make questionable choices, of which I'm definitely a fan. I mean, I perfected it."

"You know him? Thanatos?"

A sly smirk pulled at his lips, and he took a sip of the wine. "We all know each other. You can't exist for millennia in the same world and not meet everyone. But he's *not* a fan of mine. I stole my mother's soul back from the Underworld a long time ago. We had words about it. When Death was younger, he was quite unyielding in his job." He beamed and waved. I followed his gaze to find Hypnos watching us closely. Sleep returned the gesture, waving to the God of Wine. "I've partied with Hypnos though. The God of Poppies they should call him. He grows the best ones."

I made a mental note to ask Hypnos about Dionysus and why he liked his poppies so much.

"But it's surprising that Thanatos is here," he continued. "He doesn't usually mingle. Although, I've heard you're a special little mortal."

The hair on my neck prickled. I wondered how he heard such things. From Apollo? Maybe Zeus?

"You heard wrong," I said. "I'm a normal *little mortal*."

Thaos could call me that, but I didn't like it when this man did.

"Well, I don't believe that," he said, running his finger up my arm. I tensed at the contact. His touch was strange, making me feel dizzy as a wave of unexpected heat coursed through me. Arousal stirred in my stomach, and the overwhelming need to take off my clothes struck me. I realized he had to be using some kind of mind manipulation.

"What are you doing?" I asked, breathless. I squeezed the arms of the chair, determined I would not be stripping here in front of the entire stadium.

He answered my question with one of his own. "I see why Death is here. What are you?"

"Keep touching me, and I'll cut your arm off," I hissed, reaching for my dagger that wasn't there. I cursed Apollo again for taking it.

I glanced over at Hercules who watched the exchange with an unreadable expression.

The God of Wine snickered, enjoying this strange torment he was inflicting. "I love it. A mortal that threatens a God. How fun."

I jumped at Zeus' scolding tone behind us. "Dionysus, you degenerate, leave the woman alone. You have plenty."

He sighed and pulled his hand away. As soon as his finger stopped touching me, the sensation vanished.

"Of course, Father," he said, rolling his eyes and smirking at me like we were sharing a joke. I glared at him, unsettled by the power he wielded with only a brush of his hand.

He got up and moved to his seat, and I realized Zeus wasn't exaggerating. There were at least a dozen gorgeous women there waiting to throw themselves at him.

The horn blared, and I whipped my eyes back to the field where Artemis started her run. Thoughts of the God of Wine were pushed away as I followed her silver bow. It glinted like fine jewelry in the sunlight as she made her way down the course. She moved with more animal grace than anyone I'd ever seen before.

Gods, it was going to be close.

She was just as fast as Apollo as I counted her run in my head. On the last target, she pulled, knocked, and fired two arrows, both of them squeezing through the small circle and finding the bullseye. An impossible shot that had my chin in my lap.

The crowd erupted, and I clapped like I'd lost my mind. She was amazing, and I was so proud to be one of her children. The howls from the crowd started. Maybe I *had* lost my mind, because I surprised everybody by throwing my head back and joining. Hercules, who was closest to me, laughed in a deep timbre. My cheeks heated, but I was grinning. I hadn't been able to help myself.

I'd counted her run at nine seconds, too. Anxiety pulled me to the edge of my seat. If I wasn't sitting amongst the Olympians, I might have gotten up and paced in an attempt to settle my nerves.

The course was reset again and Thaos took his place, his posture still bored. My pulse thrummed. It seemed like he and Artemis were sure he didn't have a chance at winning this event. The horn blared, and he didn't run like the others. He strolled casually down the line of targets, knocking and releasing arrows that thwacked into each bullseye as he passed. The crowd was quiet, with whispers and snickers the only thing I could hear. He stood at the last target and lined up the shot, making it.

Apollo was at the edge of the arena talking to a group of swooning women. One was extending him a beautiful red rose. He took it, flashing her a smoldering smile that once again drew acid into my throat. As he pulled it away, I heard the twang of an arrow being fired. The rose was in Apollo's hand one moment, and then pinned to the arena wall the next.

There were gasps of surprise and I glanced back at Thaos, who lowered the bow and then handed it to a stadium attendant that looked like they might keel over from fright just having to stand so close to Death.

The crowd's gasps turned to giggles and then laughter. Thaos' siblings led the charge and heckled Apollo.

Eris was the loudest, yelling, "Are you sure you're a sun and not a black hole? Because you *suck*!"

It was a cheesy insult, but I put my hand over my mouth to cover a smile. Laurenth brought me a magazine once that talked about what happened to a dying sun, so I actually understood the joke.

The God of Sun's face contorted with rage, and he glared daggers at them, which made them all laugh harder. Thaos went to stand by Artemis, who was hiding a smile behind her hand. She said something to him, but I couldn't tell if he answered because of his hood.

"How exciting!" Zeus boomed like a megaphone behind me, making me turn to look at him in shock. How could one person be so loud?

Another God appeared next to him in a blink. He wore a helmet with golden wings over the reddest hair I'd ever seen. It looked like a fire was blazing atop his head. In his hand he held a staff decorated by two winding snakes, which caught my eye. Was he part of The Cause?

"Thank you, Hermes," Zeus said as he accepted a small piece of paper. Reading it, the king chuckled, shaking his head.

"The results are in! We have Apollo with a time of nine point eight two seconds." The crowd cheered, but Zeus held up his hand. "And Artemis, with a time of nine point *four* two seconds!"

My heart leapt in excitement, the noise deafening as a frenzy of whistles and howls began. Even the surrounding Olympians, who had looked unimpressed during the event, started clapping and laughing.

"Is that the first time he's lost that one?" Hercules asked Zeus, looking thrilled.

"Yes. Maybe we should rethink who we call the Archer in this family," Zeus said, chuckling.

I found the God of Sun on the field, who looked like he was near combustion.

"He'll win the next one, though," Hercules said to me. "The chariot race. If he doesn't, I'll never let him forget it."

I leveled him with a gaze I hoped projected the animosity I felt. "I hope he wrecks."

Hercules looked at me with arched brows and then busted up with another deep belly laugh.

Zeus announced a thirty-minute intermission, and I watched Thaos walk next to Apollo and Artemis until they disappeared into a massive door directly underneath where I sat. I could see Apollo jeering at him the entire way, and Thaos' head turned as if he were talking back. It was hard to tell because of his hood, but I wondered what they were saying.

The other Olympians all started shuffling away, trailing Dionysus, who was inviting everyone to try the new wine he brought for the event.

Hades and Zeus didn't move, and they seemed to forget I was there as they started speaking in hushed voices.

"It is foolish to hold this event the day after mine was sabotaged," Hades hissed.

"Don't insult me. I know how to keep my people safe. I'm sorry your realm apparently leaks like a sieve, and you can't keep your enemies at bay."

"This isn't your realm, it's Apollo's. I wouldn't be surprised if they showed up again here. And they've killed one of my Fates. The entire order of death is in a chaotic free fall. The mortal world is in ruins right now and the undead walk the earth, killing all of your precious humans. Yet, we're here holding a paltry sporting event."

"Then get a new Fate. And it's not my fault your lackey won't give my son what's his, so this is where we are."

I bristled at that, but Hades seemed unaffected.

Instead, he barked out a dry laugh. "Really? A new Fate? Would you like to be the one to enter the dominion of night and ask Nyx to produce us one?" Zeus was silent, and Hades chuckled darkly. "I thought not."

"It's your problem," Zeus hissed. "You're the one who allowed Clotho to be killed."

"It's all of our problem!" Hades growled. I jumped at the loud slap of his hand against the arm rest. "I'm weakening, and as much as it humors you to see that, it spells doom for us all. I'm losing control of the plagues of Pandora's box, and I can feel my grip loosening on Tartarus as we speak. It was bad enough before Clotho died, but without Fate, death doesn't work. Thanatos and Keres haven't been able to reap a soul since she died. I don't know if I can hold on for more than a week."

There was another stretch of silence and then Zeus uttered a flurry of curses. "You're telling me the Titans could walk free in a matter of days?"

"Yes, you fool. And I bet Mt. Olympus will be our father's first stop. Knowing him, he'll bring Typhon, your old friend, for a visit."

I had read about that, the war between the Olympians and the Titans. Zeus led the charge in overthrowing Cronus, the cruel father of several of the Olympians. Typhon, another Titan, almost defeated Zeus in a one-on-one battle.

Afterwards, Hades received the Underworld, Poseidon the oceans and seas, and Zeus became King of the Gods, residing in Olympus, and governing the sky. The mortal realm of earth was deemed neutral ground.

There was another heavy pause. "It's not just them. She saw Apollyon walk from the pit."

It took me a moment to understand I was "she."

"My, my, this is unacceptable. We will have to devise a plan," Zeus answered. I was stunned to hear sly humor in his tone. "Maybe I can take control of your realm and hold Tartarus myself."

There was a dead silence between them. I didn't even have to be looking to feel the waves of rage rolling off of Hades.

"You can do that brother, after I'm dead."

CHAPTER TWENTY-EIGHT

The others filed back in and took their seats, ending the icy conversation between the brothers. My mind whirled at what I'd just heard, and it did make this tournament seem meaningless. In the grand scheme of things it was, but for me it was the most significant event of my life.

The Olympians seemed happier now, all holding cups of wine that even I had to admit smelled decadent.

"Would you like some, Pythia?" Hercules asked, offering me his goblet.

"My name is Cere," I said, stunning him by seizing it and drinking what remained before passing it back to him. I coughed a little, thinking it tasted somewhat like vinegar. "And thanks."

"You're welcome." He chuckled with lifted brows. He called out to Dionysus, who had been observing us with an amused expression. The God of Wine snapped his fingers and the goblet in Hercules' hand swelled to the brim. He sipped at it, so it didn't spill over.

"Do you want more, Cere?" Hercules asked, beaming.

I shook my head, smiling like a fool as the drink I'd had was already making my body tingle and my mind hazy. I felt less anxious though, so that was nice.

A horn blared again and the exit doors the contenders used earlier opened again. Apollo emerged on a chariot of shining gold pulled by four of the most magnificent horses I'd ever seen. They were blood red, with manes the color of summer sun. Flames licked at their hooves, as well as the two wheels of the golden chariot he rode.

He himself had donned a golden suit of armor and a helmet with a crest of red. The God of Sun rode a lap around the oblong track, waving like a celebrity as the crowd encouraged him on. The wheels of his chariot and the strikes of the horses' hooves left a trail of burned dirt in their wake.

When his lap concluded, he took a place at the starting line. Artemis emerged from the tunnel next. I gasped in delight because her team was not horses, but four splendid snow-white stags with pink noses. Her chariot was silver, like her bow, as was the armor she'd put on. Her blonde hair was free of its braid and whipped behind her as she drove her team for her introductory lap. It was all very grand and spectacular, the crowd in a constant state of excitement. She pulled up to the left of her brother, taking the inside lane.

The crowd hushed, curious as I was to see what team the God of Death would drive. There were gasps as the spectators across from me caught the first glimpse. I leaned over the railing, straining to see. The team emerged, and I heard a mischievous chuckle from Hades behind me.

"I knew he would use the hellhounds," he said, sounding like a proud father. "My babies. Your son may be in trouble again."

Zeus huffed. "You are truly ill if you think the Mares of Helios will lose to those abominations."

Thaos drove a team of four creatures that struck a chord of terror in my chest. They were the size of Apollo's horses but were some kind of dog. Their patchy black skin stretched over long slender frames molded for speed. Flames licked out of their mouths and various random spots on their bodies where their skin was split. The gold and leather spiked bridles they wore glinted in the sun as two of the beasts started growling and then broke into a violent fight. Their snarls were one of the most unsettling sounds I'd ever heard, but Thaos shouted something, and they broke apart. The one on the right threw back its head and howled, causing the others to join in.

Fine hairs on my arms and neck rose at the eerie baying, and the crowd was silent, probably experiencing the same sensation. It sounded like death nipping at your heels, and I quelled the urge to get up and run. The horses and stags shifted, prancing away and throwing their heads, obviously not too keen on being around the hounds.

Thaos rode a black chariot with gold detailing and, to my surprise, had donned matching armor as well. The fact he had led me to conclude this event was going to be dangerous.

He forwent the introductory lap and pulled up to Apollo's right. The horses strayed away as a low growling sound left the hound closest to them and it snapped its teeth. Apollo steadied them and shouted something to Thaos. I could see Thaos turn and offer him a malevolent grin in response. I'd never seen him look so vicious, and it shocked me. The reckless part of me was thrilled by it.

Dread and anxiety burned alongside the wine in my stomach as Zeus stood behind me. I slouched in my seat to escape the direct line of his thundering voice.

"The chariot race, a fan favorite!"

The crowd reached a new level of frenzied passion, everyone on their feet in anticipation.

"I never win this one when I compete," Hercules said. "I think I'm too heavy."

He slapped his stomach and grinned at me. The wine had relaxed me, and I giggled, returning his smile.

"It's three laps and you all know the only rule," Zeus continued. "Stay on the track."

I tensed at the way he said it. His tone was full of wicked, foreboding excitement. That was the only rule? I swallowed, trying to settle my stomach.

There was a whistle, and the riders drew swords and then set themselves, reins held in one hand. The starting horn blew, and the teams lurched away from the line as the crowd came to life once more. The first lap seemed to be over in an instant with nothing too eventful occurring.

Artemis fell well behind, seeming to hold her team back and sticking to the inside of the track. The hellhounds and horses ran neck and neck, rounding the first sharp corner together. Apollo swung his sword and there was a clang as it collided with Thaos' blade.

A flurry of blows ensued, and I followed in amazement as they drove the teams with one hand and parried with the other. They were almost touching, the chariots mere inches apart, and fast approaching one of the pillars set in the middle of the track.

The crowd was shouting in hysteria, as it looked like both teams would crash. At the last possible second, they pulled apart, missing the pillar as the gold cap on Apollo's wheel scraped the stone. There was a collective gasp, and a relieved sigh from the crowd, followed by more cheers. I wanted to stand, leaning forward and gripping the railing with my sweaty hands.

They crossed the line again, signifying the final lap, and the sparring between them became more violent. The chariots clashed together, and the hellhound on the left bit at the closest horse, snarling with malicious intent.

Apollo, showcasing his immense skill, took the reins in his mouth and produced a long whip. I thought he was going to use it on his team, but he whipped Thaos across the exposed skin on the back of his neck.

The Gods and Goddesses around me laughed in delight, clapping. Thaos jerked his chariot away, causing it to rock. My heart skipped, and I stood, following with wide eyes. The action had given Apollo a slight lead. Thaos snapped the reins twice, and the hellhounds responded by lurching forward. They closed some of the gap, and I didn't know if it could be any tighter as they rounded the last corner and flew up the final straight.

Apollo whipped again, and the crowd gasped when Thaos caught it with his hand this time and ripped the weapon away from his opponent. Cheers erupted with elation as he cast it aside. The swords started clashing again, and I thought Thaos might win as the hounds pulled a snout ahead.

Apollo brought his sword back, and instead of striking at his opponent, he drove it between the rungs of Thaos' wheel and into the wood of the chariot. The timing and speed required to achieve such a feat made my head spin.

Things happened in slow motion as the wheel splintered against the sudden obstruction. Thaos leapt from the chariot, using his sword to slice the tether between it and the team as he landed on the yolk. He kicked at the connection, breaking the team free so the hellhounds wouldn't be harmed.

His chariot spun out of control, splintering into a chaos of broken pieces on the track. The wooden yolk fell to the dirt, creating significant drag that slowed the hellhounds in the last ten yards of the race.

Apollo and his horses crossed the line first to a flurry of excited cheers. Thaos hopped down from the yolk and petted the hellhound closest to him. The terrifying beast leaned into his hand like a lovable puppy. I saw shocked faces in the crowd and around me. The race was closer than anyone had predicted.

The way Thaos had freed the chariot and surfed on the yolk—yeah, he'd lost, but my blood still heated with desire as I gazed down at him.

"That was incredible!" Hercules said, jabbing me in the ribs with his elbow. I huffed out a breath, sure he'd broken one, and he looked at me with an apologetic smile.

I wasn't the only one who found appeal in Thaos' performance. A woman's steamy, breathy voice drawled out behind me. "I don't remember Death being quite so alluring."

Another woman answered, her voice a stern whip. "Here we go. Leave it alone, Aphrodite."

I shot a glance over my right shoulder and spied the pair. One was a hardened warrior, the side of her head shaved, and the rest of her long ashen hair twisted in a collection of intricate braids. She wore full armor, silver embellished with a gold pattern shaped like an olive tree. Her skin was a dark caramel, smooth and beautiful, but her lips were set in a stern line. The gray of her eyes was an odd, unsettling color, and they gave her a wise, regal appearance. A helmet sat on her knee, the design of a snake covering the side. *Another snake.* Could she be an ally of The Cause?

"Oh quiet, Athena, just because you choose to be a virgin Goddess, it doesn't mean the rest of us have to," the other, who I assumed was Aphrodite, commented.

"We all know that's the truth," Athena said. "You are far from it."

Aphrodite laughed. The sound was so sweet and charming I was sure it was the most beautiful thing I'd ever heard. It suited her because I'd never looked at anyone more enchanting. Her skin was like porcelain, a lovely contrast with her rosy cheeks and crimson lips. Long waves of chestnut colored hair hung down her chest, covering what I realized were her bare breasts.

She wore a short white skirt around her waist, leaving little to the imagination. An intricate hair piece crowned the back of her head, making it appear as though the sun were rising behind her. I blushed, stunned by her brazen nakedness and unparalleled beauty.

Zeus' voice boomed out over the crowd. "To no one's surprise, Apollo wins! But, thank you Death, it was an exciting race." The crowd agreed with another raucous cheer. "We'll return tomorrow morning with the single rider race. Until then, enjoy the activities and the wine, provided by Dionysus, of course, and have fun!"

The God of Wine smiled and extended a lazy wave to a crescendo of shrieks from crazed women. And men.

"I'm going to see if the God of Death is busy," Aphrodite said, standing. "I think I'd like an autograph."

Athena scoffed, "Really? And where do you keep your autograph book? Between your legs?"

Aphrodite only giggled, flouncing away down a set of stairs.

A hot, thick bubble of jealousy popped in my chest. I didn't have time to process the feelings because a feverish grip on my arm made me jump. Apollo smirked down at me. His hand made my skin crawl, and traumatic memories of the night before flashed in my mind.

"Let me show you to your quarters, my Pythia."

I looked for Zeus, as if he would help me, and found his seat empty. I ripped my arm from Apollo's grasp as I stood.

"Don't touch me."

His eyes danced with a dangerous fury. Glancing around, I realized we were being observed by several of the others, including Hercules. Apollo put his hand on the back of my neck and squeezed, nudging me forward and down a set of stairs.

I wasn't surprised when he led me to a row of cells and pushed me into one. The walls were gray stone and there was one door and one small, barred window. The only things present were a bucket, which made me feel sick, and a grimy mattress. Seeing it, my heart seized, then kicked into a panicked tempo. I expected him to attack me as he had the night before.

He seemed to read that in my expression and smiled. Walking to me, I was once again backed against a wall with him in front of me.

His eyebrows furrowed. "Why Death and not me?"

I stared up at him, shocked, because he sounded genuine in his confusion.

"He is my mate," I said plainly, as if he were an idiot.

His eyes widened in indignation, but maybe he was trying to exercise some self-control because he didn't strike me like I thought he would. Instead, he ran his hand up my arm. I recoiled in disgust, once again reliving the night before. My stomach twisted, and I wondered if he'd leave me alone if I vomited that wine in his face.

"I know I was rash last night," he purred. "I was stunned to find you. You should give me a chance."

His words appalled me. *Rash?*

"Are you seriously trying to seduce me in the prison cell you're about to lock me in?"

He smiled, the same sultry grin he'd offered the woman from the crowd. "You can come to my room if you ask nicely."

"If that's the case I will die in this cell. I will never ask you to touch me."

He frowned again, still looking confused and frustrated.

"Did you know him? The man in the garden yesterday?" I asked, both for the benefit of stalling and curiosity.

He tilted his head. "Why do you care?"

I hesitated. He had to know about the plague and the undead. But the effect it was having on Hades and the potential fall of Tartarus, I wasn't sure. I didn't want to reveal anything to him he could use against the Underworld. Against Thaos.

"He is the one who kidnapped me," I said, hoping that would be sufficient explanation to pull an answer from him. "I was in his possession for ten years. He pretended to be you. Last night in the garden he said he hated you."

That seemed to interest him, and his eyes drifted to the side like he was trying to remember. "I think I know him. But only his scent. I've never seen him before, and I'm struggling to place the scent. Earth and cinder. It's possible if I think about it long enough, I will figure it out, but I've had other things on my mind. Like you in the arms of Death."

"You need to remember," I insisted. "It's important."

"To whom?"

I frowned, biting my lip. "At least talk to Zeus about it."

He looked intrigued, studying my face. "You've seen something, haven't you? Tell me."

"Just talk to Zeus."

He glared in irritation and stepped somehow closer to me. "You are audacious. Ordering me to do things like you're not a mortal and I'm not the God of Sun. Do you not value your life?"

Fear still flooded my veins, but I had to strangle a maniacal giggle that was clawing its way up my throat. Thaos had asked me the same thing once.

"I don't fear for my life, as no one wants to kill me. They want to use me. That gives me leeway to voice my opinion."

He contemplated that, tilting his head again. "I could always kill you. The Pythia would be reborn with your death and in just a few short years, I could have a docile woman instead of you."

I hadn't considered that, but I schooled my face in a calm expression. I felt he was bluffing, especially if the Gods were as bored by immortality as Hypnos believed.

"If submission is what you crave, then I suppose you enjoy living a dull life. If that's truly what you want, you should just kill me now because I will never be *docile*."

Never again anyway.

No one would ever hold me with rules and walls like they had at the temple. I would rather die.

"Clever," he said, amusement dancing in the endless blue of his eyes. "Docile is so ordinary, and you're right, it is not what I want. I want you."

Studying his face, I tried to appeal to reason. "I only desire my mate."

"Then you'll reject him. Break the bond and you can join the rest of the sane world and see Death for what he really is. Repulsive." His answer was quick, as if he'd had it prepared for some time. Like it was a simple solution to all of his problems.

Anger blazed through my veins at the suggestion, burning away the cold fear and loosening my tongue. "I assure you that will never happen. And Death is a better man than you could ever hope to be. Even if I rejected him, I would never want you."

His eyes flared, and he gripped my chin, digging his thumb into my bruised jaw. He looked like he wanted to force his lips on me but thought twice about it. Wise of him, I would bite him again.

"I will have you," he promised, pushing his body against me. "If you haven't noticed, your precious God of Death is losing. I will win."

"Even if you do, I will never submit."

He smirked. "Yes, I know. I'm looking forward to breaking you." He dipped his head, and I knew he would kiss me then, so I strengthened my jaw.

"Brother," a voice said from the door.

We both jumped. Hercules stood in the entrance, looking less than impressed.

"I'm busy," Apollo said, grinding his teeth in annoyance.

"Father would like a word." Hercules glanced at me. "Now."

The God of Sun clicked his tongue, scowling down at me like he couldn't understand how I kept getting so lucky. "Fine." He skimmed his lips over my forehead. "But I'll be back."

His words terrified me, but I tried to still my beating heart and keep the evidence of that fear from showing on my face. Hercules stepped to the side and let Apollo pass, then offered me a subtle, slanted smile. Had he made that up about Zeus to save me?

When the door closed behind them, I slid to the floor and clutched my knees to my chest. Outside, I could hear the sounds of laughter, music and a wild party starting as the sun went down and darkness took over the cell.

My thoughts flew to Thaos. About where he was and who he was with. I knew Aphrodite must have powers of persuasion at her advantage, and I thought of my earlier reaction to Dionysus' touch. If it was anything like that, I doubted many said no to her. My chest and gut burned from the thoughts, so I tried to shove them away.

Resting my head on my knees, I shivered. It was cold in the cell, and I wondered if Apollo made it so, because the rest of the realm seemed to boast a perfect temperature.

I must've dozed off, because I woke up with a start when I heard the key working in the lock of the wooden door. I stood, sure Apollo had come back for me and knowing there wasn't any way I could stop him if he had. I balled my fists. That didn't mean I wouldn't fight with everything I possessed.

CHAPTER TWENTY-NINE

The figure that entered was taller than Apollo, and I saw the indistinguishable outline of a tattered black robe. I gasped and ran to him, feeling his arms open and then close around me.

I looked up at his face. The glow from some kind of fire outside provided just enough light that I could barely see him.

"I had to see you," he said. Glancing around at my cell, his mouth turned down into a furious frown. "I swear I'll make him suffer."

He looked down at me, concerned. "I was trying to get to you first, but someone distracted me, and I didn't know where he'd taken you. I was worried. I thought he'd gotten you alone."

"Hercules saved me," I said, but the actual words I wanted to say came out, too. "Aphrodite? She's the one who distracted you?" I cringed at how devastated I sounded.

"Yes," he answered, furrowing his brow.

Several thoughts and emotions traveled through me. None of them were pleasant.

His eyes widened. "How can you think what you just thought?"

I blushed, looking away. "She's the most beautiful woman I've ever seen."

"She is not. If you saw people the way I do, you would know she certainly is not."

"I'm sorry," I whispered. "I was sure she possessed many powers of seduction. Dionysus touched me earlier, and if it was anything like that, I wasn't sure what would happen."

"She does, and she tried them all," he confirmed, his hand brushing over my cheekbone. "But I only want you."

I turned my face back to him, my heart fluttering in my chest. He looked annoyed, flexing his jaw. "And apparently everyone else does, too. First Apollo, now Hercules and Dionysus. See how incredibly alluring you are?"

"Dionysus maybe, but I think Hercules is just nice."

His brows dropped, darkening his features. "No one is just nice. Trust no one."

"What about you?"

His lips kicked up. "Well, me, yes. But no one else."

"What about Hypnos?"

"I would normally say yes, but his recent life choices have me questioning his sanity."

I sighed.

"I promise I'll win, and this will all be over tomorrow," he said, exuding a cool confidence that comforted me.

Except Apollo had been as sure of his own victory.

I opened my walls and tried to read him. Once again, I was met with only blackness.

His eyebrows shot up, realizing what I was doing. "Not losing faith in me, are you? Today's events weren't my strong suit, but I'll be better tomorrow. I promise." A mischievous smile spread across his lips. "I have to admit I wanted to win that chariot race, though."

I snorted a giggle and put my hand on his smooth cheek. "It was very intense. I thought I might have a heart attack." I moved my fingers to his neck where he'd been whipped, expecting to find a welt.

"It's already healed, don't worry."

"What was he saying to you? When you walked out of the stadium to get your teams Apollo was jeering at you. What did he say?"

He scowled, shadows erupting in his irises. So it was that bad.

"Don't worry about that."

"Tell me."

"Why do you want to know?"

I struggled to answer the question because I wasn't sure why. "I just do. Please."

Thaos' jaw flexed, but he answered me. "He was telling me all of the things he will do to you when he wins. In graphic detail."

I sighed, assuming it was something like that. "What did you say?"

"That I never cared much for sports, but I couldn't wait for the boxing event. I'm going to make him sorry for every word he uttered. I'm going to make him sorry for many things."

I nodded, believing him.

Running his thumb over my cheek he said, "I don't have long. I couldn't enter this cell through the void, so I gave the guard a diamond the size of my fist, but he is nervous."

My eyes widened, and I wondered if he was joking. "The size of your fist?"

"I'd give him every jewel in the Underworld if that's what it took. My next option was to convince Hypnos to make him sleep." The way he gazed down at me made my chest constrict. "I just couldn't stay away."

His head dipped, and he pushed his lips against mine. I greeted him, and our tongues met. The kiss was devouring, and heat blossomed in my body, pushing away the cold of the cell and the disgust that still lingered from my earlier confrontation with Apollo. Desire coiled to life, hot and wanting, and settled as an ache between my legs.

It was not the time nor the place for such things, but I breathed against his lips, "I want you."

He grinned. That genuine smile of his was rare, and it took my breath away. I watched him glance around, the smile disappearing as he glowered at the cell. "I feel horrible to have you in such an awful place."

"This place is awful no matter what," I reasoned, pushing my lips against his again. "But we can make it *not* awful while you're here. You can help me forget." After a second, I added, "Please," knowing he was weak to it.

I felt his smile return at my kiss, and he nipped at my bottom lip.

"One night together seems to have cured you of any hesitation," he said, a throaty chuckle accompanying the words.

Smiling, I bit my lip. I couldn't deny his words. I couldn't muster up an ounce of shyness at the thought of being with him.

"Is that acceptable?"

His hand pulled at my shirt and then traveled up my bare stomach to my breast. "I'm not sure. I already find it hard to tell you no in any regard and now you're asking me to *please* fuck you. I fear I'll never be able to deny you anything ever again."

The heat in his voice made me shudder, and he squeezed the bud of my breast between his thumb and forefinger, pulling a sharp breath from me. "Although if these are the kinds of requests you're going to make of me, I'm not complaining."

I arched my back into his touch, and a small moan escaped me. His lips traveled down my face to my neck where his mark was. The bite that carried more meaning than either of us realized when he'd placed it there. In shifter culture, it signified a lifelong bond.

What that meant between the two of us, I didn't know. I was a mortal, and he wasn't, and I didn't know if that had ever happened before.

Thaos kissed the spot with tender lips, and as if he was riding the same train of thought he whispered, "I know we should talk more about this." He pressed his lips to the spot again. "But right now we don't have enough time."

He sucked the sensitive flesh into his mouth with a heady pull, and electric sparks of pleasure cascaded through me. I moaned and wrapped my arms around him until my fingers fisted the material of his shirt.

I pushed my hips forward and tried to mold my body into his. His hands fell to my waist and pulled me flush against him. The friction between our bodies caused us both to moan. I looked up at him, finding his heated gaze, and then my eyes slid to the disgusting mattress.

He turned over his shoulder to follow my look and then he whipped back towards me with a frown. "I would never."

My eyebrows knitted together. "Then, how?"

Thaos turned me around and lifted my hands with his, pushing my palms flat against the wall. His arm snaked around me and unfastened my pants, which he pulled down to my ankles. I stepped out of one leg, and then he stood. He shoved his boot between my feet and pushed my legs apart. The action combined with the cool air that kissed my skin made me tremble with anticipation.

He pulled my underwear to the side, and I felt his hand between us unbuttoning his pants. His fingers brushed up the slit of my aching core, and he moaned, saying, "To find you so slick already... I cannot wait to have you."

The strained words were the only brief warning I received before he fisted the material of my shirt and found my center, pushing into me with a soft groan. My fingers dug into the stone on the wall and my toes curled. There was only a small twinge of discomfort this time and a sharp cry broke from me, followed by uneven breaths as I adjusted to the sudden fullness.

As soon as he was moving against me, hot pleasure erupted. My body cried out in relief as the tension of desire turned into the heat of building release. His right hand covered mine, lacing our fingers as his chest molded against my back. His other hand moved to my hip, holding me and moving me back as he pushed forward.

The sounds of my needy moans, his choppy breathing, and our bodies meeting filled the cell, and I forgot for a moment where we were and why. It was just the two of us in this world that was our own.

His hand left mine and rested against the side of my neck and shoulder. I felt one of his fingers under my chin, and another fall against my cheek. My head dropped back, and my lower back arched more, causing that coil of pleasure to tighten further. I turned my head and pulled the finger that was on my cheek into my mouth, sucking on it.

He tensed in surprise, and a long, rough groan left him. His hand tightened on my hip and the rhythm of his thrusts changed, becoming slower and deeper. The hand moved, snaking around and finding the most sensitive spot on my body.

"That wasn't only inappropriate," he said, his voice heavy and teasing. "That was just naughty."

I would've smiled, but the way his hand was moving and the friction this position was creating had me in a torture vise of pleasure. My hand left the wall, and I squeezed his forearm, my nails digging in. The sensations of release started their slow tormenting build and then finally peaked, holding me on the edge for a moment.

I cried his name, loud, and he answered by slamming his hips forward. I came undone at the seams, sharp slices of pleasure crashing through me. His arm tightened around my waist to keep me from falling as my knees knocked together, turning to soft rubber. I shuddered against him, riding the release as long as it lasted.

I was still boneless as he turned me and picked me up. My legs wrapped around him, and I felt the smooth stone push against my back. He spread my legs wider, hooking his arms under my knees and pressing me into the wall with his body. With a soft growl, he was back inside me again, his pace quickening. The intense fullness left me gasping for air, my fingers digging into his shoulders.

Our lips collided, and I laced my hands around his neck to hold myself closer to him. He ripped his mouth from mine, his erratic breaths brushing my cheek. I could feel his body tensing, telling me he was close. I kissed down his neck, my moans a choppy rhythm as they followed his thrusts.

When I reached the sensitive spot where his shoulder meets his neck, a new sensation overcame me. The need to mark him overwhelmed me, and something happened that never had before. My teeth hurt, burning for a moment, and then I felt them scrape my bottom lip. For the first time in my life, I had a physical representation that my wolf was present—*fangs*. I knew I should ask him permission or at the very least warn him, but my mind was on an instinctual autopilot, and I sunk my teeth into his flesh.

He hissed in a surprised breath, and I felt the sharp squeeze of his hands on my back where he held me. He moaned my name as he buried himself inside me, shuddering. His skin was so quick to heal that only a drop of blood escaped, and I moaned with him. The taste wasn't metallic like I was expecting, but rich like the sweet rum I'd tried at the festival, tasting similar to his kiss.

The fangs stayed, and I wasn't sure how to get them to go back. I hoped they would just retract by themselves, although if Apollo tried to touch me again, I'd like to bite him with these.

Thaos was breathing hard against my shoulder, kissing me on the spot that bore his own mark.

"That was unexpected. When did you get those? How much blood did you drink?"

He sounded worried, and guilt crashed through me. I knew I should've asked. "Just one drop. It just happened. I'm so sorry I couldn't stop myself."

"Don't be sorry." He kissed me roughly, pushing my mouth open and then feeling the tip of one of them with his tongue. He groaned. "Just when I thought you couldn't possibly be any more bewitching."

He set me down, and we pulled our clothes back on. A loud knock sounded on the door, signifying that the guard's diamond-bought patience had expired.

"Thaos," I whispered, gripping his arms.

I wasn't even sure what I wanted to say. If he didn't win tomorrow, I didn't know if I would ever have the chance. I wanted to tell him my true feelings. But fear held my tongue. Part of me was nervous he didn't feel the same and the other part of me was terrified that he did.

"I will win," he assured me, but his tone was dark and venomous. "I'll kill Apollo during the boxing match if Zeus doesn't stop me. If he intervenes, I'll kill him soon enough. He will never touch you again." His eyes had blackened, and sharp promise dripped from his tone. "Then you'll be free."

My eyebrows shot up. "Free? What about Hades?"

He looked surprised, and the black faded until I was gazing once again into pools of violet. "Yes, free. You can decide your own path. I'm not competing in this pointless tournament for the

Underworld to possess you. I'm competing for your freedom." He paused and his fiery gaze held mine. "Although if you choose to stay with me, that would make me... happy." He said the word like it sounded strange on his tongue, as if he never thought he'd speak about himself in that regard.

I was stunned. He'd made it very clear we wouldn't be together many times. Even when he spoke to Hypnos last night he had said I wouldn't be able to stay with him much longer.

"You want me to stay with you? What changed?"

He frowned and wrapped his hand around the nape of my neck. Pulling me towards him, he kissed my forehead. "You left me yesterday, and I wanted you back. It was like someone stole away the only light I've discovered in thousands of years, and I was standing alone in the dark again. I want you with me as long as you'll stay. I would protect you from Apollo and anyone else that would like to keep you. You wouldn't have to do another reading for the rest of your life if you don't want to."

Emotion choked me, making it hard to draw breath. He was willing to let me go, to let me be free. He truly wasn't interested in my sight at all. But, he wanted me to stay with him. Tears filled my eyes, and I blinked them away.

He continued melting my heart as he added, "If you don't want to stay, I would help you get somewhere out of their reach. Maybe Poseidon's realm under the ocean. That's where people go to disappear."

"Why are you so kind to me?" The words were a choked whisper, and it surprised me I could push them around the lump in my throat.

He gazed down at me, his expression soft, but he didn't seem to have an answer. Instead, he kissed me again, tender and sweet, and I felt the spike of panic in my chest again. Was this love? He had promised he wouldn't, *couldn't*, love me, but Hypnos wasn't convinced the night before on the balcony.

The knock sounded at the door again, and Thaos hissed in annoyance. He hadn't put his robe back on, and he wrapped it around my shoulders.

I sighed. "You should go."

He offered a sad smile and brushed his thumb over my cheek. "But I don't want to."

He lingered just a second longer before kissing my forehead. "I won't be far, the God of Sun will not come back in this room."

With that, he pulled himself away from me and out the door.

CHAPTER THIRTY

The next morning, Zeus came to retrieve me, and to my surprise, the three challengers, Thaos, Apollo, and Artemis, accompanied him. My teeth had returned to normal after an hour, and despite my best efforts, I couldn't summon the fangs voluntarily.

As I stepped out of the cell, Artemis was scolding Apollo for keeping me down here.

"If I would've known I would've never let you—"

"She deserved it," he sneered. "She tried to stab me in the heart. With Mastix steel."

"I can't imagine why she would do that if you weren't doing something to warrant it," she grumbled.

"I wasn't doing anything she wouldn't have liked."

My eyes were on Thaos, whose face remained placid except for a muscle that jumped in his jaw. Apollo was grinning, but then his eyes fell on me. I still had the black robe on my shoulders. His eyes widened in fury, and he whirled on Thaos, checking to see if he had his robe, as if anyone else would've loaned me one in the middle of the night.

"I'm going to kill that guard," Apollo spat.

My heart sank, and I looked at Thaos. I hadn't even considered the guard could get in trouble.

"Good luck," Thaos said. "He's the newest citizen of the Underworld and I understand he just came into a lot of money."

Apollo stepped towards him. "We agreed—"

"I agreed to nothing," Thaos cut in, blackness swirling into the purple in his eyes. "Not that you were intent on honoring it, either."

I thought they might fight again, but Zeus pinched the bridge of his nose like an exasperated parent. "I'm going to let this go Death because I drank a lot of wine last night and I'm not in the mood to deal with it."

"*What?*" Apollo shouted.

Artemis rolled her eyes at her brother. "Oh, shut up, Apollo."

He scowled at her and then at everyone else before storming back down the hallway. I took the robe off of my shoulders and handed it to its owner. He took it, his fingers brushing over mine as he did.

Zeus regarded me, wrinkling his nose at my appearance. "Pythia, you will bathe and then you need to put on a red dress. The Pythia always wears red, especially to the games. I let it go yesterday, but today we need to put on a good show for the crowd and assure them that everything is fine and normal."

And not let them suspect that Titans and plagues are days away from breaking free of the Underworld, I finished in my head.

I wondered if Artemis knew. If she did, her expression revealed nothing.

I nodded to Zeus, knowing that fighting would get me nowhere. I was escorted to a bathing chamber and left alone with a golden tub already full of bubbles. Glancing in the mirror, I noticed the bruising on my face was gone. Healed by one tiny drop of blood. I was grateful for the bath after the night in the cell and I sighed when I lowered myself into the water.

Afterwards, I was dressed in an over-the-top crimson ball gown that was made with more tulle than I had ever seen in my life. The giant skirt made it hard to move, and the ladies cinched the bodice too tight. The wendigo might as well be standing on my chest again. I felt uncomfortable in it, the neckline dipping lower than anything I'd ever worn and revealing cleavage that I didn't even know I possessed.

A nice human woman painted make-up onto my face like Keilah used to, making my heart pinch, and then she curled my hair and styled it. I tensed when she wove a crown of laurel leaves into the strands. It was not my favorite plant.

She talked the entire time about the excitement of the games, but I could only offer her the smallest of acknowledgments. My nerves worked in overdrive, tying my stomach into a chain of painful knots. A foreboding, tense feeling invaded every fiber of my being. I knew this was the most important day of my life.

Finally, they handed me a mustard-colored sash for my shoulders. All of that had been true, then. These were the Pythia's colors, and I was expected to possess the laurel branch. The master and the overseer had mixed some truth with the lies. It was the most effective way to make someone believe.

She escorted me to a different arena this time, alongside two guards in gold and red armor. The track here was larger, and there was a sand fighting pit in the middle surrounded by bleachers.

I moved to my seat next to Hercules and in front of Zeus. A woman that hadn't been present yesterday sat next to the king.

Her intricate diadem, pure gold adorned with sapphires and emeralds, made me believe she was the Queen of Gods, Hera. Her hair was the same color as mine, a dark amber, and she wore a gown of deep royal blue. On her shoulders sat a small cape of peacock feathers that glistened in the morning sun. Lips the color of red roses were pulled straight in a serious line, bridged by a soft, round nose and hard green eyes.

She inclined her head to me, and I offered her a stiff bow, unsure of how to act. I took my seat, glancing at Hercules. He was his normal, cheery self. From my reading, I knew Hera hated him. Zeus favored him even though Hercules was conceived with a mortal woman and not his wife.

I searched the crowd and found Hypnos, who was looking at me. I waved again, and he smiled, but I didn't like the nervous tension shadowing his face.

"If everyone wants to return to their seats," Zeus boomed. "The single man race will start momentarily."

People did as he asked, settling in for the event. The last Olympians shuffled in as well. There were more of them here today.

I heard Athena ask Aphrodite, "So how was it? Your tryst with Death?"

"Oh, it was unbelievable. I assure you he's very much alive."

My eyebrows furrowed, and I wondered what she was talking about.

I heard a snort of a laugh. "You know, I do find that unbelievable. From what I heard he said, and I quote, 'Your soul makes me want to vomit,' when you propositioned him."

I looked over to see it was Dionysus who had said it, and he wore a devilish grin. He noticed me and winked. Everyone in earshot started snickering, and I smirked.

Aphrodite gasped in anger. "I demand to know who said that!"

"I can't reveal my sources," Dionysus said, flipping his hand in a dismissive gesture.

Aphrodite huffed in annoyance, and I heard another exasperated sigh from Zeus before he continued his announcements.

"Let's begin today's events! The single rider race. It's three laps, same rules as the chariot race."

"Death better win," Hercules said. "I want to see him in the boxing event."

"He will," I said. He had to. If he lost he would be eliminated, and my only hope would be for Artemis to somehow win the boxing match and tie Apollo. It would force the tiebreaker, which she would also have to win.

But, Thaos would not lose.

I wrung my hands together as anxiety boiled hot in my chest. I heard the gates open, and the crowd perked up and started cheering. They weren't as loud as yesterday, but I imagined if the King of Gods had a hangover, a lot of them did, too.

The contestants entered together this time, riding a starting lap at a smooth gallop. Apollo rode one of his red horses, Artemis a massive white stag, and Thaos was on Nychta.

They took to the starting line, Apollo on the inside, Thaos in the middle, and Artemis on the outside. The whistle blew, and they readied, waiting for the horn. As soon as it sounded, they burst across the line.

Same as yesterday, Artemis entered a slow trot. Nychta and the red horse were taking full strides, eating up the track at an incredible rate.

I couldn't believe it was only three laps as they already rounded the first corner and entered the opposite side straight stretch. The riders drew swords again and were fighting. The metal clashed so aggressively that small sparks radiated from the points of impact.

I rolled the tulle of my dress between my fingers. Why did it have to be so close? Nychta and the red mare kept a solid pace with each other, unaffected as the battle raged on their backs. Neither one could manage to pull even a hair's width ahead.

Before I knew it, they were rounding the corner and entering the last stretch on the final lap. Everyone stood, except Dionysus, who continued to recline casually. I gripped the wooden rail, my nails scraping against it.

Hercules was bellowing in excitement next to me, cheering against his own brother for Death to win.

Thaos dropped the reins against Nychta's neck, but she didn't react, continuing her stride. He deflected an attack from Apollo and then used his free hand to punch him across the jaw. I knew there was noise all around me, but I couldn't hear it. I couldn't hear anything except my deafening heartbeat.

Apollo had dropped his reins as well, and the riders locked together in a furious fight. The horses were only inches away from each other, and the flames of the sun mare were licking up its legs to hold the shadow of Nychta's left wing at bay. Neither mount faltered, and I had to admire their icy resolve.

Thaos punched Apollo across the face again and the sound of the bone smacking snapped through the rush of blood in my ears. Several sympathetic murmurs rippled through the crowd, but excited cheers followed them.

Apollo faltered and then Thaos stuck his sword straight through his gut. There were gasps of surprise and horror from the crowd. Thaos held his opponent's shoulder, driving the sword in as deeply as he could and then giving it a vicious twist.

They pushed apart, and Apollo fell back, catching himself at the last second by grabbing the reins. His horse veered left at the pull, running off course and almost crashing through one section of bleachers in the middle of the track.

Thaos picked the reins back up and slowed Nychta to a casual lope across the finish line. The crowd was wild, cheering either for Thaos or because the two would now be facing off in the next event. Apollo was red faced, ripping the sword from his stomach in a way that made me cringe. I was sure they were regular steel, but it still had to hurt.

Hercules laughed, his meaty hands producing the loudest claps I'd ever heard. He smacked me on the back in excitement and I struggled for breath after the blow. I sat back down, relief weakening my knees, and I was sure my nerves would never recover.

Thaos turned, and even though his hood was up again, I knew his eyes were on me. I imagined he boasted that boyish grin in the obscurity of his hood and I waved, blushing.

"Death is the winner!" Zeus shouted to more cheers. "We'll take an intermission so Apollo can heal and then we will move to the pit for the finale!"

I thought we would move, but Hercules grabbed me and hauled me like a child to the seat on Zeus' left. Hercules sat on my other side.

"I know you're an oracle," Zeus said quickly. "But utter a single spoiler about the games and I swear I'll take your voice and keep it forever. I hate spoilers."

"Then what do you want?"

"Hercules is my successor in the unlikely event I'm ever deposed, and my most trusted advisor. We were discussing the issue at hand with the rebellion. *With Hades.*" He whispered the last part, not wanting others to hear.

"Why him?" I asked, surprised to hear this is who Zeus had chosen as his heir.

Hera giggled at my blunt question, obviously eavesdropping, but said nothing.

Hercules looked offended, but I didn't mean it to be. It was just that there were others I would expect to be chosen before him. Athena was the first to come to mind, or any of the other Olympians.

Hercules wasn't an Olympian, although he'd been ascended after his mortal death and now lived on Mt. Olympus with his father.

I thought of the blood sign hanging at the festival in Hades' house. *The True Heir Will Rise.* Maybe some weren't thrilled about Zeus' choice.

"Because he's the best fit for the job," Zeus hissed, giving me a look that told me he was tired of answering that question. "Hades tells me the ones that held you before Death found you are the ones causing all of this trouble. Tell us everything about them. No detail is too small."

"Why? Apollo knows who the leader is." Zeus looked bewildered by the revelation, and I wrinkled my brow. "I told him to talk to you about it."

Zeus was furious. "All he has talked about is *you.*"

"Well, ask him. I don't know where his priorities are, but I would think that talking to you about that would be more important than this."

"I plan to as soon as he wins this and gets his head back on straight." I glared at him and he, like Apollo, looked surprised by it. Hercules looked amused. Zeus apparently held his temper better than his son though because he didn't move to strike me. Instead, he stood, saying, "Let's get down to the other arena. I like to watch this event from a closer seat."

People were cheering as we walked across the dirt racing track towards the fighting pit in the center of the field. I realized they were looking at me as well as the King of Gods. I glanced at Zeus, who answered the question in my eyes. "People of Delphi. They're pleased to have their Pythia home at last."

A strike of guilt shot through me because I didn't want to be here, and I didn't plan on staying at Delphi, no matter what happened during the next event. My heart quickened as I recalled my freedom was at stake today. My life was about to be determined by a contest I had no control over, and I felt nauseous thinking about it.

I scanned the crowd, finding Hypnos. He waved with a small, confident smile on his lips. He must've been nervous about the horse race, but now he seemed sure Thaos would win the boxing match.

I noticed Ulther sat with the rest of the siblings now, and he waved when he saw me look at him. My heart broke as the smile he gave me failed to reach his eyes. He had to be devastated about Aeryn.

I raised my hand, too nervous to return their smiles. The gates across from me opened and Thaos, Apollo and Artemis emerged. Cheers erupted from the grandstands and the surrounding bleachers. Down here on the ground, the sound was even more deafening.

The men were shirtless. More than that. They wore only their underwear and had oil all over their bodies. I blushed, swooning a little as I watched Thaos.

"Why are they oiled?" I asked Hercules.

"It makes it more difficult to get your hands on your opponent. It makes everything more difficult. We call this a boxing match, but it's really not. It's an outright fight. Oftentimes, wrestling is involved."

Artemis wore her normal attire and stepped forward when the crowd quieted.

"Father, I concede the match."

No one looked surprised after how she'd treated the last two events.

"Very well," Zeus answered, waving her away.

Apollo glared at her, but she ignored him. She came over and sat on the right of Athena, and I noticed Aphrodite frown in disapproval. There must not be much love there. In fact, I felt that all the Olympians barely tolerated each other despite being related. The loyalties of the gods and goddesses were confusing.

The two fighters entered the pit, and Hercules leaned over. "I always win this one when I play in the games. Apollo hates it."

I smiled despite my nerves, feeling glad Thaos wasn't fighting him. "I don't doubt that."

I leaned forward in my seat, too restless to sit still. The edge of the ring was only about twenty feet from where I sat, but Thaos didn't look my way. He focused on Apollo. The hatred between them was tangible, buzzing around them like a swarm of angry bees.

"Let's have a good fight!" Zeus shouted behind me. The crowd went wild, the sound crashing down in a frenzy of yells and whistles. "This is a physical fight only. No weapons. No shadows or light of dawn."

"Light of dawn?" I asked Hercules.

"One of Apollo's powers," he answered, sounding amused. "He gets really shiny."

I nodded in understanding. "I saw it yesterday when they were fighting."

The whistle blew, and then the horn. The fight started where it had left off in Apollo's temple yesterday. It was a riot of fury and anger, fists connecting with sickening cracks that would kill any mortal.

The sand flew as their bodies rolled. Hercules wasn't lying. It's not like I knew the exact rules of boxing, but I knew there *were* rules. There seemed to be no order to this fight. It was just violent madness, and I winced every time Apollo landed a strike.

Thaos had Apollo in a headlock under his arm and landed three vicious blows to his face. Hercules whistled and then chuckled next to me. Apollo hit him hard in the gut and then broke free, punching him in the face.

Thaos' jaw knocked, and he stumbled back. They glared at each other for a moment, both of them bleeding and breathless.

They were as evenly matched as Thaos had warned, and I felt sick as my knotted stomach twisted again.

"You, girl," a voice said behind me. I turned to find Aphrodite was addressing me. "How does it feel to have two men fight over you? Fun, right?"

I didn't think this was anywhere near fun. One was fighting to own me.

"Not particularly," I muttered.

She looked affronted by my answer, but Artemis grinned, and Athena looked amused. I turned back to the fight, astounded at how casual everyone else was when this was my life on the line. I wondered about being a Goddess, and if I would grow as indifferent as them after centuries of being alive if I were one.

The grappling continued, both men breathing hard, until Thaos grabbed Apollo by the back of the hair and pulled his face down towards his upcoming knee. The crack of bone against bone resounded across the arena. Everyone around me made sounds of sympathetic pain, and Apollo fell on his back. My heart quickened with excitement.

I glanced up at Hypnos again, surrounded by his excited siblings. He was still sitting, his shoulders relaxed in a casual pose and his fingers steepled, but his face held an evil, knowing smirk. I'd never seen the God of Sleep look so wicked. He caught my gaze and winked, making me grin.

Turning back to the fight, I saw the blackness take over Thaos' eyes as he jumped on Apollo, his knees pinning the God of Sun's arms to the sand. His wings were full and churning with an emotion that could only be interpreted as rage.

The shocked crowd quieted as he unleashed a series of savage blows, beating his opponent's face in a dramatic show of overkill. Blood spurted from Apollo's mouth, staining the surrounding sand in a pool of shining gold. Anyone other than a god would be dead. Thaos wrapped his hands around the God of

Sun's throat. I knew then that he was serious, he would kill him if—

"Death! Enough!" Zeus bellowed.

Thaos stilled, staring down in fury at his defeated opponent. After a moment he stood and kicked Apollo in the face.

"I said enough!" Zeus raged behind me, his voice shaking the entire stadium.

I thought he would hit him again, but he restrained himself.

He leaned down and whispered something only the God of Sun could hear, and then spit blood dangerously close to Apollo's face.

The crowd was in a shocked frenzy. Many booed, but others cheered in excitement. Hercules was bellowing congratulatory things to Thaos, and he grinned over at me and winked.

Zeus stood, thundering, "The winner! Death!"

Thaos turned, black eyes searching for me, and a devilish smirk on his lips. Gods, this was real. My heart was wild, skipping the happiest beat it ever had. He'd won, and I was going back to the glass castle.

Thaos approached me and I beamed, but a movement behind him caught my eye. Apollo, swift despite his bloodied face, pulled a bow from the sand and knocked an arrow. Thaos stuck his hands out to me, unaware of what was transpiring behind him. Time slowed, and my own words echoed in my head.

She'll have your heart, Death, for it belongs with her. But, once it's surrendered, the son will steal your life.

In the next heartbeat, I understood I'd misinterpreted my own prophecy. That's why I hated my gift, true meanings often hid behind riddles. It wasn't the *son* as in someone's child. It was the *Sun*. More specifically, the God of Sun.

"Thaos!" I shouted, launching myself over the rail with minor consideration for anything aside from my need to save my mate.

The cumbersome dress made it difficult, tripping me, and I crashed into his arms with less force than I was hoping. My momentum turned us, though I'd wanted to move him out of the line of fire or tackle him to the ground.

I sucked in a breath, but it didn't go anywhere, and I thought for a moment someone had punched me in the back. Pain seared as I tried to draw another and failed. I looked at Thaos, my eyebrows knitted in confusion. His eyes were wide with disbelief, stark shock filling them.

"Cere?" he whispered.

I glanced down, stunned to find the rainbow glint of a Mastix arrow meant for him protruding from my chest. Blood seeped, the perfect color to blend with the crimson red of my dress. My knees gave out, and he dropped with me to the ground. I couldn't hear anything in the stadium, and cold tendrils of ice crept up my legs.

Hypnos appeared, his eyes wide and his hands clasped on his head.

"You coward!" he screamed at Apollo. I heard his voice next to me and felt his hand on my shoulder. "Oh no. Not like this. You're okay, Sleeping Beauty. Do something. Can't you stop it? You're Death. You can stop it, right?"

"Why, Cere? Why did you do that?" Thaos said, desperation coloring his words as he covered the wound with his hand. The cold shadows flowed and tried to stanch the blood loss. I groaned in pain when he applied firm pressure.

I repeated the prophecy to him, my voice a choppy rasp. *"She'll have your... heart, Death, for it belongs with her. But... once it's... surrendered, the Sun will... steal your life."*

His eyebrows furrowed, and his panicked gaze darted over mine.

"You said… you wouldn't fall in love," I said, my voice broken into gasps. "You… promised."

"I can't," he protested. But his expression twisted into understanding and sorrow. He pressed a kiss to my lips. "Is that what this is? I'm so sorry."

"I'm not sorry," I choked, putting my hand on his cheek. "At least… he didn't steal your life."

He closed his eyes and put his forehead against mine. "That's not true, my *Vasilissa*. He certainly has."

My heart twisted at those words, and I tried to speak more, but hot liquid filled my mouth and spilled over my lips. I just wanted to say the words *I love you* before it was too late. My lungs burned, and I tried to cough for air, but nothing seemed to work as it should. I felt the fresh blood flow from my mouth and pool in my ears.

"Don't go," he pleaded, taking my hand, and kissing my wrist. His voice sounded strange, like he was drifting away from me. "Don't leave me in the dark again."

It broke my heart that I couldn't listen, but at least the pain had ceased. My body was numb, and I stopped trying to breathe through the liquid in my throat. The butterflies appeared around him, and my eyes floated to them. Their soft, weightless beauty comforted me. Thaos saw them too, and a devastated breath rushed from him.

The last thing I watched was the change in his eyes, going black as the dark fissures erupted from them and spread across his face.

Blackness filled my vision, too, and I had no choice but to surrender.

CHAPTER THIRTY-ONE

I didn't expect to feel anything after death, but I did. My body was in a lazy drift, like I was floating through water. Opening my eyes, I found the blackness of the void surrounding me. My hair floated around me, and I was naked. An unusual sensation seized me, and I was suddenly being pulled in a sure direction.

I stopped, and my bare feet greeted cold stone. In front of me, a woman sat on an ivory throne. Looking closer, I recognized it was not ivory, but bone. Human bone. Her hand rested on the curve of a skull that made up the top of the armrest, her long black nails clicking against it in an impatient thrum.

It was just darkness around us, a section of stairs leading up to the dais her throne sat on being the only other things present.

I stared at her in confusion, reaching for the spot on my chest where the wound should be. It wasn't there, the skin was smooth and whole.

Was I alive or dead?

"I've been waiting," she said. Her voice was deep and robust. It sank to the depths of my bones, chilling me. The icy terror that had taken me in the forest when I'd faced the wendigo threatened to overtake me just from standing in her presence.

She wore all black, a dress that reminded me of Nychta's skin. It moved like swirling, dripping oil. Two curling horns sprouted from her head, reaching towards the sky like high pointed spires that reminded me of the glass castle. The midnight hue of her clothing played a dark contrast against alabaster skin, and I recognized the same violet eyes as the God of Death. Her face looked strange, boasting cheekbones higher and more pronounced than any I'd ever seen, and generous lips painted black.

Not even knowing why, I fell to my knees. Her aura was smothering, crushing me into the floor, and I just felt like I should. This woman was true power.

"Do you know who I am?"

"I think you're Nyx, Goddess of Night. Mother of Death."

"Correct." Waving her hand to indicate I should rise, she added, "As you were, dear." I stood on shaky legs and watched her inky lips pull smoke from a long tube that held some kind of cigarette at the end.

I tried not to think about how odd it was to be called dear by the most intimidating person I'd ever met.

"Why am I here?" I asked. "I think I died. Am I here because souls can't travel through the iron gates right now?"

"You did die. But it's all part of the plan."

"What plan?"

"You met Clotho? My daughter, the Spinner of Fate."

"Yes, twice, but only briefly. I'm sorry for your loss."

She looked at me, maybe curious, but her expression barely changed to show her feelings. "Thank you, dear. When my children find the one who slid the blade through her heart, they are to bring that person to me. I will pull their spine from their body while they squeal like the little pig they are."

I shuddered, the power and sincerity of her words sliding like ice chips against my skin. She had sounded casual, like deboning people was a routine occurrence in the dominion of Night. I was certainly glad not to be that particular little pig.

She took another drag and exhaled the smoke. "Several years ago, Clotho came to me, having seen the end of times. The Fates cannot reveal anything about what they see, but she went against the rule and shared pieces of her plan with me. She told me I had an important role to play if the end of the entire mortal realm was to be stopped."

I stared, uncertain, then asked, "She said she chose me. What does that mean?"

"The only way to save the mortal realm would lead to her death, so she selected you. When you were still an unborn babe, she placed a piece of her power in you. You are not just the Pythia. That identity is how she hid your true nature. You are, in fact, a daughter of Fate. The piece of Fate you carry is also why my son Death is so attracted to you. Death and Fate are as intrinsically intertwined as two things can be. It's also why Apollo, God of Prophecy, boasts an insatiable hunger for you. I know you've only seen the worst of him, but he is not usually this irrational. Not that it excuses his actions."

"That's why my sight differs from Pythias of the past."

She clicked long, pointed black nails—claws?—against the arm of her chair and then smiled, but it was more disconcerting than her scowl. The black paint on her lips highlighted the brilliant white of her teeth. Where the other gods and goddesses had two fangs, she possessed a mouth full of razor-sharp teeth.

"Yes, it is. You are the next Spinner of Fate. Clotho chose you as her replacement."

"Why?" I breathed. "Why me?"

"I don't have a detailed answer for you, as she did not share that information. She must've recognized something in you. Being a Fate is not for the weak of heart. I have faith in her choice. I also trust the judgment of my son. Death would not choose a frail woman."

"I don't understand. I'm dead. How can I be the next anything?"

"That is where I come in. I am a Protogenoi. I can ascend demigods. Do you know what ascension is?"

"Yes. Hercules ascended after he died."

Her head dipped in a sharp nod. "We don't use it often. In fact, I never have. But Clotho instructed me to offer you ascension with the condition I make sure you understand that the life of a Fate is not pleasant."

My mouth fell ajar. "You want to make me a goddess? How? I'm not a demigod."

"Yes. If you accept." She flicked the tube, and a dying ember of ash broke free from the cigarette, drifting to the stone floor beside her chair. "And you're close enough to a demigod to be ascended with her shred of power in you."

I stared at her, my mouth still open.

"You are to understand, though, The Fates know the futures of every sentient soul, but may not speak about what they see. No more prophecies. You must let Fate take its course. Events can still change it, people have free will, but you can't be the direct catalyst that stimulates that change."

"What about Thaos?"

A shadow of a smile pulled at the corner of her mouth. "You may act however you please with the God of Death.

"Gods," I mumbled, "if I have Clotho's power, am I his sister?" Feeling mortified about the possibility, I had to ask.

She laughed around the black tube in her mouth, puffs of smoke passing her lips as she did. The bright sound caught me off guard, considering who it was coming from.

"Not that it matters in the world of the Gods, but no, you are not his sister. You have a piece of the power of Fate inside of you, that is all."

"Okay," I said, relief crashing through me. "I will do it then."

"Are you sure? You will see the deaths of those you love and be able to do little to stop it."

"Well, I'm not ready to die. I just started to live. I just learned what love is. And if this is Clotho's plan, then I have to honor that and save the mortal realm. I have to save my family. It's always been about them."

"Good choice. I would've been so disappointed if my daughter had died for nothing. It wouldn't have gone well for you, dear."

The not-so-subtle threat laid against my skin like an itchy wool blanket.

"But it is decided. I will return you to your body and partially ascend you. However, before you enter the Pavilion of the Fates beyond the iron gate and seal your destiny, you have one more prophecy to deliver. It is to one of my followers, a race you know as dark elves that live deep beneath the Earth. You must find a prince named Keiwren. He is the next piece in a sequence of events that must occur to save the mortal realm. Thanatos will take you to him."

"Okay."

"Once you enter the Pavilion of the Fates, there will be no going back. However, if you don't, I will revoke the ascension and you will die. Do you understand?"

"I understand. Return to my body, find the prince, enter the Pavilion of the Fates."

"Good. Now I will take you back before my son kills everyone in Delphi and rips the God of Sun to pieces."

She stood and flowed down the steps of the dais with regal grace. Shadow danced around her feet the entire way until she stood right next to me. She was almost as tall as her son, and my heart clenched with fright as I stared up into her sharp features. I held my breath, as if that would help mitigate the stifling pressure of being this close to her.

Was this how others felt around Thaos?

She gripped my wrist, and her hand was like donning a bracelet of ice. Using one of her nails, she tore a rip in the fabric of reality in the same fashion as Thaos did with his scythe. We stepped through and plummeted into the darkness.

The arena materialized around me, and I was back in my body, opening my eyes to stare up at Hypnos. Who, if I didn't know better, looked like he'd shed some tears. He was cradling me in his lap.

I choked on the liquid in my lungs, and he jumped in astonishment, nearly tossing me to the ground. "Fuck!" His eyes grew wide, his mouth opening and closing twice. "Cere? How?"

She materialized then, Nyx, and thick, black shadows billowed across the ground level of the stadium. I looked at the Olympians and watched with humor as they all blanched at the tendrils of darkness surrounding them. Even Dionysus, who had maintained a calm, confident demeanor throughout the games, shifted in obvious discomfort.

Some blinked like they were trying to flash, but the shadows held them in their seats. Zeus, who had been yelling, dropped the lightning bolt he was holding and paled in surprise. He sat heavily in his chair and glanced at Hercules, who maintained a stoic look. I noticed his knuckles were white where he held the arms of his chair, giving away his true feelings.

Only two people hadn't seemed to notice her arrival. Thaos was in a rage, his own shadows erupting and forming a black fog. Some people were trying to leave, wisely attempting to get away from the immortal fight that could easily spill over into the marble bleachers. Others stood in shock, watching as the shadows of the Underworld battled the light of dawn.

Thaos was on the offensive. He held the arrow he must have pulled from my chest, intent on killing the God of Sun with it. In his other hand, he wielded his scythe. All of his visible skin looked like that cracked marble, shadows leaking from the dark fissures of his skin and rolling around him in waves.

Apollo was glowing so brilliantly that it was impossible to see him. He was the personification of light, the blinding rays cutting through the shadow and holding them at bay. He must've also held his weapon because I heard the clang of metal as they fought.

They were both still in their underwear, which made me want to giggle.

I grasped at my chest, feeling that the wound had already closed and healed. Turning on my side, I spit out the thick, cooled blood that had congealed in my mouth, coughing and sputtering to free my lungs of the obstruction.

I felt different. My vision was sharp. I could make out the finest features of everyone in the arena, even those sitting in the highest seats. I also heard so much random noise that it overwhelmed my ears. The softest whispers from the crowd to the blood rushing through Hypnos' body invaded my head. I focused, trying to get my bearings in the sensory overload.

"She ascended you," Hypnos whispered.

I nodded, clutching my head.

"Death, my son. The God of Sun has a role to play regarding the future of the mortal world," Nyx called, her voice the gentle coo of a mother. "You cannot kill him yet."

At her voice, everything quieted, and the whispers died away. A scent permeated the air, acrid and bitter on my tongue. It was fear. I could smell the terror of everyone in this stadium.

Thaos whirled on her, the cracks in his face so wide his skin was nearly all darkness and glared like he might attack her next. She chuckled and took a long drag from her cigarette.

I sat up, and his eyes tracked to me.

I smiled through tears and teased him. "You're so vicious."

His face softened, and in a heartbeat, he was kneeling next to me.

"My job is done. For now," Nyx sighed, setting her gaze on me. "Don't dawdle, dear. You have things to do."

"I won't," I promised.

She looked over to the Olympians. Some shrank back in their seats as she approached. One of her fingernails dug into the railing in front of them, and she walked, dragging the sharp claw. A curl of wood twisted free in her wake. She stopped in front of the King of Gods.

"Zeus. Always good to see you."

"Nyx," he said, his tone as flat as his stare. "You look well."

"I hope you're prepared."

He maintained his stoic expression. "What for?"

"War."

Anger flashed across his features like a lightning strike. "Is that a threat?"

Nyx grinned, and I saw the Queen, Hera, pale. "A warning. How much do you trust those who sit around you?"

His eyes widened in shock, and then she disappeared in a plume of black shadow. No one had time to recover as events continued to unfold into chaos.

A bellow of rage traveled across the arena. "Apollo!"

Everyone's attention was drawn to a figure standing at the top of the arena where the Olympians and I had sat this morning. It took me less than a second to understand who it was. The one I had called master.

He continued to yell, his voice echoing. "Your retribution is at hand!"

I heard the first shrieks before the doors opened, twisting to see several dozen undead creatures pour out from the area where the horses had emerged from earlier. Their unnatural gait ate up the expanse of the field, but they ignored us in the center of the arena and headed straight for the stadium bleachers. They were only interested in mortals.

The God of Sun was on the move, his face already healed from the boxing match. Finding his bow again, he barked orders at the crowd. "Run! Get out!"

Screams erupted as people tried to do as he instructed. The mortals, most of whom were citizens of Apollo's realm, were stampeding, moving in mass toward the exits as the undead crawled the walls of the arena like insects and started tearing people apart. Most of the minor gods and goddesses in the crowd flashed away, not willing to stay and fight.

"Enjoy the rest of the Pythian Games!" The master said with a cackling laugh.

I was looking around the arena in horror and pushing to my feet. But a cool arm laced around my waist and pulled me back. I pressed into Thaos, his chin resting against my ear.

"I need something," I yelled to him over the screams. "I need my dagger!"

But I didn't hear or see anything else because I was falling through the void. Heavy boots smacked against a wood floor, and I gasped in surprise. We were back at the black glass castle.

I whirled, stunned. "What are you doing? We need to help!"

But his expression caught me by surprise. The vulnerability of his features as he gazed down at me was so unexpected that my heart halted its excited tempo. He brought my wrist to his mouth and kissed it, taking a deep breath as his eyes drifted shut.

"I'm okay," I whispered.

"I'm not."

A lump formed in my throat, and I put my hand on his cheek. "You promised."

"I shouldn't love you. I don't even understand how it's possible," he breathed. "But my heart is yours."

I pressed up on my toes and found his lips, placing a soft kiss there. "And mine is yours."

"You're ascended."

"Partially, yes. This was all planned by your sister, Clotho. But it's a lot to explain. First, we need to go back and help."

He didn't move, and our lips found each other again. After several moments, he walked across the room to his wooden chest.

"What are you doing?"

"You need a weapon."

He shifted things around and then produced a short sword forged of Mastix steel. It boasted a pommel adorned with an enormous diamond that was encircled by amethysts and seated atop a handle of gold.

It was the most breathtaking weapon I'd ever seen, and I sucked in a sharp, awed breath. "It's so beautiful."

"It is," he agreed. "And it deserves to be wielded by its equal."

He handed it to me, along with a leather scabbard. While I strapped it on he hurried to find clothes. When he was dressed, he grabbed me around the waist again.

Pulling me flush against him, he pressed his lips to my ear and purred, "If people weren't dying, I swear we wouldn't be leaving this room for at least a week."

I shook my head and giggled.

He lifted a brow. "You think I'm joking?"

Falling through the void, we returned to the arena in Delphi. We landed in the booth where my former captor had just been standing.

There were screams of horrific agony from every direction. The white marble bleachers ran red with blood, the poor souls unlucky enough to be caught by the creatures quickly becoming piles of viscera as the undead ate their fill. The monsters shrieked and howled, their unholy sounds mixing with the cries from their victims.

My stomach turned in horror, and I covered my mouth with my hand, feeling sick. I didn't expect the smell. With my heightened senses, the heavy scent of iron and death hung in the air, while the screams blasted my sensitive new ears.

In the middle of the field, Apollo engaged in furious combat with the white-robed figure. His hood was pushed back, revealing the off-putting translucent skin I'd seen up close in the garden.

"Who is he?" I asked in frustration.

As if to answer my question, the master threw back his head and roared. The bellow overtook the rest of the chaos, and everyone paused. Above him, his creatures answered with excited shrieks and returned to the slaughter with new fervor.

The master, I realized, was shifting. His body was contorting and growing. The human skin he wore tore away and white scales blossomed in its stead. They looked to be made of pearl with soft tones of blues and pinks shifting in the sunlight. I thought of Apollo's throne, as it had to be crafted from these scales. The smell of earth and cinder permeated my nostrils, and it took me back to that first night when he stole me from my family home.

"It's Python," Thaos explained.

"Who?"

"Python is the monster that Apollo defeated at Delphi. Mythology wasn't correct in calling him a python. He is a son of

Gaia and the father of dragons. He is the first dragon. As the son of a Protogenoi, he is as powerful as a god."

I gritted my teeth. I'd known the answer all along, since the first day I'd visited the library at the glass house. I didn't even pay the story much attention. I thought the beast was dead.

"That's why Apollo only recognized the scent," I muttered. "I bet he never saw him in his human form."

Python finished his shift. A colossal white dragon stood before us, his claws digging into the earth as he launched himself at the God of Sun. He had to weigh at least eight tons, but he was quick, faster than anything that size should be.

Apollo was holding his own, moving with the grace and agility of a feline. He fired arrows at an impossible pace, and I saw he was trying to shoot the beast in the heart. It was the only place in his pearly armor that was exposed, and I watched the orange glow of his heart pulse behind translucent white skin.

Python was no fool, though, blocking the arrows with his tail or turning just enough to deflect them away. His jaws snapped at the God of Sun, almost crushing him between razor sharp white teeth. In the mythology book I'd read, it said that it took Apollo a hundred arrows to slay the beast the first time. I believed it and thought it was a near impossible shot. The hole over his heart was only the size of a dinner roll.

"I thought he was dead? I thought Apollo killed him and buried him under the original temple in the earth realm?"

"So did I," Thaos said. "Maybe his mother re-birthed him."

My eyebrows raised. "How is that possible?"

He shrugged. "Dionysus' mother was killed while pregnant with him. Zeus sewed his fetal son into his thigh, where he survived and was reborn. And that's not the only time the God of Wine was resurrected."

I gaped at him, both horrified and awed. "That can't be true."

"You'd be surprised. Immortal beings are hard to kill. Many times they don't stay dead."

"What do we do?"

"I suppose I should go help him," he hissed through clenched teeth. "Although I'd like to let that beast tear him to pieces."

I wrinkled my nose. "We have to be on his team now?"

"It works that way in the world of the Gods. Everyone is your enemy, and on rare occasions, your ally."

I assumed he was going to tell me to stay here, and I started planning how I could get down to help the mortals without him seeing me. He turned to me. "You go help in the stands."

"Aren't you worried about me?"

His lips turned up. "Of course I am, but I'm much more worried about any enemies that cross your path."

I smiled at that. "You sure know how to flatter a woman, Death."

"Yes, when they're vicious little creatures," he muttered, still smirking. "Besides, we both know you wouldn't listen if I asked you to stay."

"I was already planning how to get out there without you knowing," I admitted, shrugging one shoulder.

Thaos laughed, and it was a deep smoky sound that made my heart flutter. I realized it was the first time I'd heard anything past a chuckle from him, and I hoped he would do that more often.

He was trusting me to fight by myself. I didn't know why it was such a big deal to me, but I beamed at him. "I may like you a little bit."

I went to step and frowned. Bending, I ripped at the skirt of the ridiculous dress. The amount of fabric I tore away could have been used to craft a new, separate gown.

I turned my back to him, "Can you loosen this? I can hardly breathe in this thing."

He did as I asked, quickly yanking at the ribbon of the bodice until I could draw a comfortable breath. I wiggled my body in the dress, satisfied that I could at least move now.

I faced him, stunned to see the unmistakable burn of desire in his eyes.

"Gods, I don't even want to know what you're thinking," I said, lifting one brow.

"I'm thinking I'll go kill this beast myself if it means getting you home quicker."

I blinked at him, my cheeks reddening.

He grinned and brushed his thumb over my cheekbone before lifting his hood and abruptly leaping from the balcony. It was at least four stories and I gasped in astonishment, looking over as his robe billowed around him and he landed in a graceful crouch.

Peeking over the edge, I felt my stomach flip-flop. I was technically a goddess. Could I do that now? I didn't have wings like him, so I didn't know. Pushing away, I chose not to test it right now, or maybe ever.

I looked across the field at one of the undead creatures and my heart sank. It had a young woman cornered, and I knew there was no way I could help in time. If I could just get over to that spot—

The world blurred around me, and I was standing exactly where I wanted to be. Shock crashed through me, but I couldn't dwell on it. I had just flashed myself face to face with an undead. It reached for me, and I turned the sword, severing both of its arms and then spinning and slicing its head clean off.

My own movements shocked me, excitement welling in my chest. Gods, I was fast. A wild, inappropriate giggle ripped through me, and I set to work, cutting through the crowd and relieving as many undead creatures of their heads as I could.

At one point, I ran into Ulther and beamed. I'd missed him. He returned the sentiment, but I still saw that dark sadness in his gaze.

"I'm so sorry, Ulther." He knew what I meant.

"I'm glad you're alive, Cere." He looked closer at me. "And you're ascended."

I nodded, and he sighed. "Well, I suppose you'll be whipping me good during training from now on."

"Would you rather I took it easy on you?"

He scoffed and grinned. "Gods, no."

We worked together after that, clearing this entire section of bleachers of the undead and brown coats, many of whom were dryads like the red-haired one I'd seen Thaos fight the day he took me to reap souls.

Some looked similar to that dryad, while some were less human. I parried a blow from a man that appeared to be covered in bark. His skin was a deep brown, with cracks running through it. He didn't have tendrils of hair, but spiky needles of a pine tree that stuck straight out of his head. This creature did not wield a sword, but a wooden spear boasting a Mastix tip. His skill was nothing to laugh about, and I was sure he would have defeated me before my ascension.

He made a move that opened his body too much, shifting the balance in my favor. I blocked the spear and kicked him in the side of his knee. The joint popped, snapping, and he yelled in pain. The shout died with him, though. My next immediate strike plummeted past his upraised arm and through the side of his neck. I pulled the blade free and noticed with intrigue that his blood was gold, like the gods'. I almost expected it to be green.

While Ulther and I fought in the stands, roars of aggression and fury sounded from the field below. Thaos was helping Apollo fight the dragon, and now Artemis was joining as well. It was a strange twist of irony as the competitors of the games were forced to work together. It would be an exciting conclusion if the spectators weren't all running for their lives.

I focused on the orange glow in the dragon's chest where it needed to be pierced by Mastix steel to be killed. I was still in awe of its speed, as it turned and blasted a torrent of blue fire at Artemis.

Scanning the bleachers, I found the siblings of Death had stayed, following the instructions from their mother to help. My eyes fell to Moros. He did not wield a weapon, but stayed close to Eris, who held a large machete. Chaos giggled like a maniac, chopping the undead to pieces, while Doom walked through the pandemonium and brushed his fingers over people. At his simple touch, some of the brown coats would seize their weapons and drive them through their own heart. Others scrambled to the top of the stadium wall and threw themselves off, plummeting to the ground on the other side. I shuddered. That was an unsettling ability.

Hypnos was fighting a brown coat and losing. Gods, he really wasn't a good fighter. They pinned him, intending to stab him in the heart. I was about to flash to his aid when a woman with short brown hair appeared first. She held a large rock and bashed the brown coat over the head with it. It was an odd scene to watch unfold, and I almost laughed.

Hypnos stared up at her and then grinned. The heat of desire in his eyes made me avert my gaze for a moment, and blush. He stood, grabbing her and dipping her like they did in the movies.

They kissed with such passion that Eris yelled, "Get a room!"

I shook my head, glancing at another section. Hercules moved through enemies like he was rowing wheat. He wielded an enormous club that boasted barbs of Mastix steel. A direct blow from the brutish weapon resulted in a sickening skull explosion. That section would soon be covered in a thick layer of brain matter.

It did not surprise me to find him here fighting. He was the people's god, born to a mortal woman, and ascended after he died. I thought maybe Zeus hadn't made a terrible choice in him as his successor. Hercules cared more for the mortal realm than all the other gods combined.

Athena was the only other Olympian remaining as far as I could tell and she, too, fought to save those who couldn't escape. I wasn't sure of her motives. Maybe she just refused to run away from a battle.

"Why aren't the other Olympians helping?" I asked Ulther.

"They went to secure their own realms," Ulther answered. "They couldn't care less about Apollo's realm if there is a potential threat to their own."

"Even Zeus?"

"Especially Zeus."

"Well, well, if it isn't the love of my life," a voice crooned behind us.

We both whipped around to find Aeryn standing up the stairs from us.

"Aeryn," Ulther gasped, making a move to walk to her.

The relief in his tone shattered my heart as I grabbed his arm. "She is not Aeryn."

CHAPTER THIRTY-TWO

Ulther knitted his eyebrows together, but the woman cackled, and I watched her drop another of Aeryn's blonde hairs. Her skin rippled and started changing until the dark-haired woman with red eyes and mossy skin stood before us.

I didn't expect to see her but guessed her heart or spine must need to be pierced to cause her death. Apollo had only gutted her.

"My name is Zaehyla, love," she cooed at Ulther. "And I must admit I truly enjoyed all of those special moments we spent together… the way your body felt pressed against mine and all the romantic things you whispered to me afterwards." She clicked her tongue. "You are so sweet."

My stomach dropped, and I glanced at Ulther, whose face burned a deep crimson with shame and disgust. He raised his sword. "Is Aeryn dead?"

"Maybe," she answered. "If she isn't, she wishes she was."

"I'll kill you," he hissed, stepping towards her. She drew her own sword with a wicked grin.

I lifted my blade as well. I didn't care what she was, she didn't stand a chance between the two of us.

"Cere," a familiar voice said, just out of my field of vision. "Talk to me."

I turned with my sword up. "We have nothing to talk about, Laurenth. You're allied with murderers. With monsters." Emotion choked me. "You let him turn Keilah into that thing. And I had to end her." The last sentence came out as a whisper, a fat tear rolling down my cheek.

"Keilah was a good woman. I liked her. She chose to join The Cause. Like me, she wanted to devote herself to a brighter future."

"Why would she do that?" I snapped, interrupting her.

"She lost her family in a malicious act of cruelty by her patron God. A husband and two daughters were taken from her, just like that." She snapped her fingers, "Because Ares was throwing a temper tantrum."

I swallowed. Poor Keilah. This world had been so cruel to her. At least I could understand why my sweet handmaid was aligned with such evil people.

Laurenth continued, tapping the pommel of her sword with a fingernail. "Do you think anyone cared? Do you think he was punished? We're stuck in this vicious wheel of destruction at the hands of the ruling gods, and someone has to stop it."

"Well, that's hypocrisy considering you've caused the downfall of the entire human world."

"Sometimes innocent blood has to be shed in order to initiate change. That's just how it is. It's naïve of you to think otherwise. As long as we achieve our goal, it will all be worth it."

"Well, I am a bit naïve having been locked away most of my life. Which you knew was wrong, that's why you brought me things. Books and magazines."

She shrugged, frowning. "I'm sorry for the sacrifices you had to make. But the hierarchy must fall. There are monsters on both sides. Zeus is a monster. As you found out, Apollo is no better."

"Thaos told me what happened to you and I'm sorry. Truly. Maybe it is time for a change, but to sacrifice the entire mortal realm? It is not an option I'm willing to consider. There's got to be another way."

"It's too late now. The plague is spreading. Nothing can stop it. Zeus will lose all of his precious humans. Hades will weaken to the point he can't hold the Titans back anymore and the true heir will rise."

"Who is the true heir? You mean him?" I indicated over my shoulder to where Python fought Apollo and the others.

She laughed, and my heart broke. How could her laugh sound the same? I thought it should be different. It should sound evil to match the betrayal I felt.

"Python is the mastermind behind your abduction and the beasts. He was promised his chance to best Apollo and kill as many humans as possible and he accepted, but he is certainly not the one I serve. Our true leader has earned my love and my trust."

"Who is it?"

She shook her head and pulled her lips into a thin line. "It is too soon for his identity to be revealed. This is only the first chapter in our journey to overthrow the King of Gods and usher in a new era."

"Well, I suppose the one you love and trust will be happy to rule over the ashes," I spat. "Over the blood-soaked earth crawling with undead. And you'll be happy too? You'll have your revenge at the expense of innocent people. Of my family."

She looked saddened but determined. "I can't allow you to help them. You need to come with me. We need to know more about the baby of shadow and sun."

"Why? So you can kill it, too?"

I hadn't been serious, only speaking from spite, but the look on her face horrified me. They would. They would kill an innocent baby in the cradle if that's what it took.

"Monsters," I hissed. "I will do everything in my power to stop you."

She lunged at me, stabbing out with her sword. I quickly blocked and moved away. Somehow, it still shocked me despite everything she'd already done. "You would kill me?"

"Hoping to incapacitate you and take you with me. But if killing you is the only way to stop you from working against us, then so be it."

It stung, the realization that she would rather have me die, by her own hand no less, than let me live free.

Grinding my teeth together, I glared at her. "I'll never be a prisoner again. I am not a possession."

This time I lunged at her, delivering a series of offensive attacks that she'd taught me. She grinned, recognizing the move, and for a strange, fleeting moment, it was just us and the blades again. Like we were before Death showed up and whisked me away. Before I learned the love I felt for her was built on a foundation of lies.

But this wasn't a practice match, it was fatally real. A truth she reminded me of when she compounded her defensive move with an explosive offensive one. I moved enough to avoid serious injury but still received a small knick on my left thigh.

It was my first time being cut with Mastix steel and it burned like an army of bees had stung me. A drop of gold blood slid down my leg from the wound.

"I loved you," I said through gritted teeth and blurry eyes.

"I still love you, Cere," she answered.

That angered me. She didn't deserve to love me. No one who would allow me to experience the life they'd forced on me could claim love. I stopped holding back after that, unleashing my newly gained strength and speed.

It surprised her, and I saw a beat of nervous determination flash in her eyes.

Blocking her next attack, I exposed her chest. I kicked her hard, sending her flying back into the stone steps of the bleachers. I was on her the next moment, and I punched her as hard as I could, making her face snap to the side.

I punched her twice more and then lifted my sword to her neck. She stared at me, but I saw no fear in her eyes.

"Kill me," she goaded. "Don't you dare let Zeus have me."

I tensed, my grip tightening on the sword. Could I do it? Kill Laurenth? I understood her sentiment about Zeus. I wouldn't want to know what he'd have planned for her. For a moment, I wondered if I was fighting for the wrong side. Should I ally with Zeus? He wasn't a good man.

"I won't let him have you," I promised, standing and stepping off of her. I looked away, unable to gaze at her for a moment longer through the tears that burned my eyes. "Just go."

I turned and heard a shuffle of movement behind me. I wasn't sure how I knew she was going to stab me in the back, but I just did. With speed and precision that awed even me, I turned and plunged my blade into her chest as she rushed me. It pierced her heart and her eyes widened.

"Damn, Cere," she whispered with a bloody grin. "You may be a warrior after all."

It was one of the last things she'd said to me before Thaos took me from the temple. A quiet sob broke my lips. "I told you to go."

"Still you cry for me after everything? I would've stabbed you in the back."

"I loved you," I repeated. "I *love* you. Thank you for teaching me how to protect myself, Laurenth. I'll always be grateful for knowing you, no matter what else you've done."

She opened her mouth to say more, but red blood bubbled out of her mouth and down her chin. She coughed, and I closed my eyes as the expulsion misted my face with a sheen of crimson. I sobbed with her in my arms and held her until I knew she was dead.

I wasn't sure how long I sat there with her, but the clang of metal pulled my attention. Ulther was still fighting the skinwalker, Zaehyla, but she had the upper hand. They both had several nicks and bruises, showing the battle had been well fought.

I moved in behind her, but Ulther shouted at me. "No! Take her alive. We have to find Aeryn!"

My heart pinched for him. I thought it was very unlikely that Aeryn was alive.

Zaehyla cackled. "You'll never find her."

He pushed forward again, allowing his anger to cloud his judgment, and left himself open to an attack. She seized the opportunity.

"Ulther!" I yelled, willing myself to be there.

My blade sliced through her wrist just as her sword entered Ulther's right rib cage. I sighed in relief. It wasn't a fatal wound. Her eyes widened in fury as a screech of pain sounded from her throat. The severed hand thumped to the bleachers, but she recovered quickly and grabbed her blade, pulling it from Ulther and blocking my next swing.

"You're ascended," she hissed.

"Yes, and I'm going to kill you."

"Don't you need me alive?" she teased with a wicked grin.

"Aeryn is dead."

"Are you sure?"

We exchanged a flurry of blows, and she was better than I was expecting. I wondered how old this creature was.

"Are you the last skinwalker?"

A beat of surprise crossed her features before the pinch of fury took over. "Of course not. Python and his mother have saved many species thought to be extinct since humans swarmed the earth like destructive rats."

"Where are they all hiding?"

She laughed, a sweet, delicate giggle as she slid her blade across the back of my calf. "Wouldn't you like to know?"

I frowned, spinning away before the blade could inflict serious damage. "Well, yes, that's why I asked."

She paused, offering me a curious look. Ulther moved behind her, but I trained my eyes on her, not wanting to give him away. He deserved this kill, and I wouldn't take it from him.

He raised his sword and struck her across the back of the head with the pommel. She crumpled and lay still before him.

"We should kill her," I warned.

"No," he looked at me with pleading eyes. "If there's a chance Aeryn is alive, we have to question her."

"Ulther—" I started but stopped myself. I would do the same if I was in his situation. "We better restrain her then."

CHAPTER THIRTY-THREE

Glancing around, the battle was waning, but the bleachers were more red than white now. Hercules, Athena, and the siblings of Death were all still fighting. Almost all the creatures were dead now, but the brown coats were more adept and proved harder to defeat.

The heart of the field was where the action was, with the dragon still holding off Thaos and the twins. Its vast wings flapped twice, and its feet started lifting off of the ground.

"Don't let him go!" Apollo yelled. "We'll never catch him in the sky."

The God of Sun turned, running up and topping the twenty-foot wall to the bleachers with an effortless jump. Climbing to a higher vantage point, he knocked an arrow and took aim.

Ulther and I watched slack-jawed as Artemis said something to Thaos before backing away from him and running full speed back to him. He laced his fingers, and she stepped in them. Lifting at the same time she jumped, the momentum rocketed her straight up towards the dragon and she landed in a graceful crouch on its back.

Thaos used his wings to leap to the side of the arena and then jump, flapping them once and joining her. Python roared in frustration and turned his head over his shoulder. A burst of fire erupted from his maw, barreling down his back towards them. Artemis ducked and rolled, standing just out of the way on the joint of its wing.

A scream built in my throat as Thaos didn't move, and the fire seemed to consume him. When it died down, there was a churning ball of shadow in his place. The darkness dispersed, and he stood untouched, still somehow looking bored. Glancing at Ulther, I shoved out a breath of relief and smiled.

"Everyone is going to be so jealous that I got to see this," Ulther muttered in amazement.

My heart was thumping as the dragon continued its climb. Artemis moved with unparalleled grace, balancing and hopping on the tiny peaks of the pointed spikes on the dragon's back. When she stood at the head, she knocked two arrows and fired them at the base of the dragon's neck. The scaled armor was too strong, and the arrows fell away, flipping through the air and burying themselves into the dirt track.

With unrealistic speed, the dragon snapped at her and snatched her by the ankle. I gasped, covering my mouth with my hands in dismay. She shouted out in pain as he pulled her off of his back and shook her as if she was nothing but a rag doll.

Thaos moved, leaping to the shoulders of the beast. In one swift motion, he spun the scythe and split the thin flesh of one of its wings.

The dragon screamed in agony, and Artemis fell from his mouth. I followed her fall in dramatic slow motion. I didn't think such a thing would kill her, an immortal, and especially an Olympian, but I couldn't watch her smash into the ground.

Without a second thought, I flashed to her, capturing her in my arms when she was about twenty feet from impact. We landed on the dirt track of the arena, the height of the fall and her weight offering no challenge for me.

She was in dreadful shape, so I flashed back to Ulther and set her down by him, where he could at least guard her body while she healed.

I whipped back around to see the dragon's fleshy wing had healed, and he was seeking to shake the God of Death from his back as he circled the arena. He rolled in the air, diving, and Thaos crouched on his back, holding fast to one spike. Frustrated, the dragon turned and blew another stream of blue fire at him.

I crumpled my brow. That had been the perfect opportunity for Apollo to take a shot at the heart. I looked where he'd been in the bleachers.

"That's not good," Ulther said, following my gaze.

Apollo was in trouble. No less than twenty of those brown coat fighters had besieged the God of Sun and his sword of fire. Even with his immense skill, he was mostly on the defensive as they attacked in sync around him.

They were fighting at the top of a marble staircase and my eyes caught on a glint of gold at the bottom. He'd dropped his bow, and it had skittered down to the base of the stairs.

I glanced back at the dragon, still in the air. He was trying to fly higher, but Thaos cut his wing again.

Making a quick, possibly reckless, decision, I turned to Ulther and pulled a handful of silver arrows from the quiver on Artemis' back.

"Good luck," Ulther said, with a tilt at the corner of his lip. "Don't die. Again."

I smirked and turned around, focusing on the golden bow and flashing to it. I picked it up, running my hand over the warm metal. Python focused on Apollo now, and I ducked out of instinct as he flew just feet over my head, trying to swoop down and grab The God of Sun between his jaws. He almost succeeded, Apollo ducking as he made slow progress in his fight.

I knocked an arrow as the dragon banked in the air, positioning to make another loop. My hands shook with nervous energy, and I tried to steady them. I was efficient with a bow, but I was no Apollo or Artemis.

Hiding from sight, I ducked behind the marble railing and half wall that bordered the spectator area. If Python hadn't seen me, I could ambush him and maybe pierce his heart.

Thaos was moving up the dragon's back, having fallen back toward his tail at one point. He rested now on the shoulders of the beast. I wasn't sure if he had noticed me, either.

Python started his next descent and even though he was heading for the God of Sun, I felt like he was aiming right at me. I rose and lined up the shot as he drew near, my focus on the orange pulsing flesh at the center of his chest. My sight was sharp, my movements quick. I could tell the bow string had a heavy pull, but I drew it back with ease, still in awe of my new strength.

Taking a deep breath, I loosed the arrow, but I underestimated the dragon. He had seen my intention and tilted away from the shot.

The way he did pulled a small yelp from me, because he'd angled himself so the arrow now soared straight towards Thaos. Python was clever, attempting to use me to rid himself of the God of Death. My arrow buried itself deep in Thaos' thigh and I heard him hiss in pain.

I thought about throwing the bow and feigning innocence, but his eyes flared, and he looked for the source, settling on me. I offered him an apologetic smile while his eyebrows shot up in surprise.

"Whoops," I whispered. I doubted I would ever live this one down. He was only just getting over the stabbing incident.

His eyes flared with what I thought was amusement as he gripped the arrow and pulled it from his leg. They buzzed just over my head, and he dropped it to me. I snagged it out of the air, still slick with his blood, and knocked it again.

Python dove at Apollo, who in a ruthless move lifted and threw one of the brown coat fighters into the maw of the dragon in his place. The dragon's jaws snapped shut and severed the shrieking woman in two. He roared in frustration when he realized it was not the God of Sun.

The dragon turned, flying around the arena once more. His nostrils flared, blowing smoke as he puffed out a breath and set his sights once again on Apollo, the object of his obsession.

I didn't know how I would make the shot now that Python was aware of me. He was quick and clever. Unless something distracted him, I would never be able to take him down.

I heard a grunt behind me and turned to see the God of Sun had taken a sword through the gut but was still fighting despite the injury. The brown coats swarmed him and hoisted his struggling form like some sort of offering to the dragon.

If I didn't make this shot, it was the probable end of Apollo. While that prospect appealed to me, I remembered Nyx claimed he still had a role to play.

I turned, taking aim at the one I'd known as my master. The one who'd stolen me from my family and locked me away with a psychopath, lied to me, and used me to bring immeasurable suffering to the world.

It dawned on me that this was a gift. I was going to have revenge. For myself, for Keilah, and for everyone else he had harmed. Clotho twisted the threads of fate in my favor. She was handing me his icy heart and, now, I would crush it.

My head cleared, and I breathed, willing my heart to slow just as I'd been taught. Python saw me and snorted again, bellowing a roar. I saw blue flame well in his throat and I hesitated, not too keen on being roasted.

Thaos moved atop of him, running up the spines of his back like Artemis had. He made a heartbeat's moment of eye contact with me, and I readied my aim. He swung his scythe over the head of the beast.

The curved blade buried itself into the dragon's eye and Thaos pulled with incredible strength. Python roared in pain, his head snapping back with the force. The blue flame erupted, spewing straight into the air.

Well, I couldn't ask for a better distraction than that.

I sucked in a breath, holding it, and released the arrow. It flew straight, seeking its target as a flash of silver death.

I watched with satisfaction as it pierced the translucent flesh of his chest, plunging deep into his beating heart. Fire erupted from his mouth alongside a roar of fury and defeat. Behind me, I heard wails of agony and sorrow from the brown coats as they watched their savior fall to my arrow.

Thaos pulled his blade from the dragon's eye as the beast stopped using its wings and dove into a dramatic plummet, turning in the air.

My eyes widened when I realized if I didn't move, his falling body would crush me. I flashed away from the spot, astonished at what I'd done. The entire stadium shook as the dragon crashed headfirst into the marble bleachers.

The God of Death moved with beautiful grace, stepping to keep his balance even as the dragon crashed with immense force. He jumped down from its back when it finally settled, half its body on the bleachers, the other half hanging over the side and onto the track.

I wondered if a more attractive man had ever lived, and then quickly answered my own question.

No, one had not.

I flashed to him, appearing right next to him where he stood. His hand found my waist and pulled me to him.

He placed a kiss at my temple, but I heard a soft chuckle from him as he murmured against my ear, "You've stabbed me and now you've shot me. Do you still deny that you're vicious?"

I smiled sheepishly. "It wasn't intentional this time."

"I don't know if I believe that."

My eyes narrowed. "I can show what it would look like if I were actually trying to shoot you. Since you're obviously confused."

He laughed, the sound rumbling through him, and he placed another kiss at my temple.

Ulther appeared next to us, helping a conscious but limping Artemis. Her leg had looked akin to ground beef when I'd left her, but it seemed to be healing well. She grinned at me, and I offered her the other two arrows I still held. They were hers.

She shook her head, smiling with pride. "Keep them, they're yours. You may not have a fully developed wolf, but you're certainly one of mine."

I beamed, clutching them to my chest. Would it be too much to ask her to autograph one?

Ulther helped her sit and then turned to me. For a moment, the sadness left his eyes. He was gushing in excitement, "Gods! You just killed the first dragon with Apollo's bow and Artemis' arrow, and I got to be here for it. That was incredible! Legendary!"

Ulther and I shared the excitement of being young and having not seen as much as the others. Many of those present here had been alive to see things much more incredible than slaying a dragon. Hercules alone had done about a million things more impressive. But to us, it was still amazing. I had killed Python, my oppressor, and I felt powerful satisfaction.

I should be humble.

But it was so hard.

I squealed in agreement. "I know!"

Jumping away from Thaos, I hugged Ulther. He stilled, his eyes widening and traveling to the God of Death as if Thaos might cleave his head from his shoulders just for touching me.

"Oh, don't worry about him," I said, glancing over my shoulder. "I can hug whoever I wish."

Thaos snorted behind me. "Yes, I wouldn't want to be shot again, and she's still holding that bow."

Ulther's eyes widened and then he sighed, now convinced I was insane, but he returned the hug. His arms tightened around me, and I felt his mood shift, the sorrow returning. I tried to push all of my good feelings toward him. I wanted so badly to bring back his joy, but I couldn't imagine what my life would be if I was in his position.

I patted his back. "If Aeryn is alive, Ulther, we will find her."

There was a throat clearing sound, and I turned to see the God of Sun, as well as Hercules and Athena had joined us.

Apollo and Thaos looked at each other. It was a glare of pure malice despite their temporary alliance. Murderous tension filled the air and my hand instinctively fell to the handle of my sword in response.

Apollo's lip curled, and he defended his actions, "The Pythia is always mine. I didn't want to shoot *her*. It's your fault as much as mine for what happened."

Thaos' grip on the handle of his scythe whitened. "Coward. You tried to shoot me in the back. I should kill you just for that."

Apollo frowned, angry at being called a coward. His sword erupted in flame again. "Try it, Death."

Thaos shook his head, his eyes blackening as he sneered, "I'm patient. I can wait. You say she's yours? I disagree. I beat you at your own game, and she is no longer the Pythia. She is a Goddess of Fate. And I promise you that someday, when this is all over, I will reap your soul. Then you'll understand what it's like to belong to someone, because you'll be *mine*."

The God of Sun's face tightened in a furious scowl. I suspected there may be another fight, but he didn't make a move.

"See, that's terrifying," Ulther muttered to me.

Gods, I was swooning. "I find it attractive," I answered, earning me a raised brow look.

Apollo set his gaze on me, his scowl shifting to unbridled longing. Gods, Nyx hadn't been exaggerating. He was *obsessed*. I bristled, glaring at him.

Thaos stepped in front of me, and the shadows swirled around me, seeming to hold me in a protective embrace. He clicked his tongue in annoyance.

"You're testing my patience, God of Sun."

"My bow," Apollo hissed through gritted teeth.

I looked down at the golden weapon and stepped around Thaos to give it back. But on second thought, I snapped it away, holding it against me.

"I want my dagger. Or I'm keeping the bow."

He glared at me, but flashed away and returned, holding my dagger and sheath. Tossing it to Thaos, he then held out an expectant hand.

Maybe I was petty, but I threw his precious bow to the marble at his feet. Apollo winced when it clanged against the stone, and by the look he served me, I knew if I hadn't been standing by the God of Death, he would have attacked me.

He bent stiffly and picked it up, turning and kneeling next to Artemis to check on her.

When it seemed the tension had settled, Hercules, Athena, and the siblings of Death all converged around us.

"Wow, that was fucking crazy from start to finish. I live for it," Eris said, clapping her hands.

"I knew mother was right," Philotes said to me, taking my hand. "She ascended you, didn't she?"

"Yes. She said it was a plan put in place by Clotho before I was born."

"She chose her own replacement," Hypnos reasoned, his fingers laced with Aergia's, who leaned her head against his shoulder.

I nodded. "But I'm supposed to do Nyx a favor before I finish the ascension. Well, not really a favor. The next step in the series of events that must occur to save the mortal realm."

CHAPTER THIRTY-FOUR

Hypnos whispered something into Aergia's ear, and she giggled, then he turned to everyone else. "Well, thanks for the good times, everyone, but my fun card is punched. Apollo, wonderful games. It was such a joy to watch you lose."

Apollo's face burned with anger, but Hypnos was already gone. The siblings cackled and then started leaving.

"What about the skinwalker?" I asked Ulther. I'd completely forgotten.

He frowned in distaste. "Hypnos took her to Hades' dungeon for me."

I nodded, and he called out to Philotes, "Can I get a ride home?"

She held out her hand, and he took it, both of them disappearing.

"I'll talk to Hades," Thaos said to Hercules and Athena. "He and Zeus can figure out a strategy. Maybe Poseidon if he decides to help."

"He won't," Hercules said. "Poseidon won't get involved unless he has to. He'll stay in his golden palace beneath the sea and ignore the chaos of the surface world, like he often does. The humans don't respect his oceans, so he is glad to see them suffer. He and Zeus already had a volatile discussion about it. Notice he wasn't in attendance for this event."

Thaos nodded and then used his scythe to enter the void. We arrived in his bedroom at the black castle, our feet hitting the ground at the same time.

I felt him kiss the top of my head as his arms folded around me in a tight embrace.

"What does my mother want from you?"

"I have to find a dark elf prince named Keiwren and deliver a prophecy to him. Afterwards, I have to enter the Pavilion of the Fates and take Clotho's place as the Spinner. If I don't, the ascension will be revoked, and I'll die. Clotho planned my whole life to lead me to this point."

"We will go find this prince then," he said. "But it might be better if you're not covered in the reeking blood of the undead."

I looked down at myself, still wearing what was left of the ridiculous red dress. "Some of it is Laurenth's," I whispered. "She tried to kill me."

"I'm sorry. I know you cared for her."

His hand laced around my back, pulling at the ribbon of the bodice. I pushed away the thoughts of Laurenth and the fact that I'd been the one to end her life. It was something I couldn't deal with right now.

I resorted to deflecting with humor. "Are you sure you aren't just looking for an excuse to undress me?"

But Thaos wasn't in a joking mood. His expression was drawn. "I hate this dress," he muttered. "I never want to see it again."

His tone was dark and deadly. Something else was laced in it though, too, sadness or grief.

"I hate it too. I never want to wear red again."

"Then you never will. I can't believe that fool almost took you from me for something so trivial."

He paused and touched the rip in the front of the dress, the hole where the arrow had pierced the material, as if to confirm it really had happened.

"Your mother told me he's obsessed with me because he's the God of Prophecy, and he is drawn to the fact I hold a shred of Fate. But my death was all part of the plan," I reminded him.

"That doesn't make it acceptable."

He pushed the dress down my body, past my waist and hips. I stepped out of it and kicked it away, standing in my bra and underwear like it was completely normal. I rolled a loose thread of his shirt between my fingers and looked up at him.

"This means I'm immortal now."

His gaze softened. "I know."

"And," I added.

"And? Have you decided what you would like to do?"

I stared up at him in surprise. My gaze searched the eyes of the man who stole me away from my miserable life as the scarlet bird in the golden cage. The man who competed to break me from the chains of my identity and win my freedom.

"Did you think I wouldn't choose you?"

"I was cautiously optimistic that you would."

"You're my fated mate," I said.

"Is that the only reason you choose me?"

The corners of my lips curled. "I told you. I might like you a little bit."

He brushed his thumb over my cheek, muttering, "I like you more than a little bit."

I was opening my mouth to answer when his eyes glazed over like they had when Zeus summoned him.

He looked frustrated when his gaze snapped back to me. "Hades wants to see us."

A beat of apprehension shot through me. "What's wrong? Is it bad?"

"No." He leaned down and brushed his lips against mine. "But I was looking forward to washing that blood off of you. I planned on being very thorough."

My body flushed with heat. "We're supposed to go see the prince and then to the Pavilion of the Fates."

"I'm finding it hard to care. I told you your irresponsibility is rubbing off on me," he said against my ear, grabbing the lobe with his teeth.

"Your mother said she would revoke the ascension if I didn't," I said, gasping at the tingles that traveled through me.

"She won't."

"How do you know?"

"I'm her favorite."

"I should ask Hypnos if that's true."

"Do it," he chuckled. "He won't deny it."

His lips found mine, pushing my mouth open with his. The kiss was aggressive, devouring, and my body burned with need for him. His hands found the curve of my bottom with a rough squeeze, and a deep rumble of desire vibrated through him.

He broke the kiss with a grin. "And now that you aren't a fragile mortal, I don't have to be gentle."

I tensed in irritation. "*Fragile*?!" But the rest of the sentence was dawning on me, and my heart skittered. "You were being gentle?"

His eyes were bright with humor and lust, bridging a wicked smile. "Of course, I was. It wasn't easy either."

A shiver of anticipation rolled through me as I wondered about *not* being gentle. His eyelashes dipped, and he gazed down at me. "You're doing it again."

"Doing what?"

"Looking at me like you want things from me."

"I do," I admitted, my voice rough.

His eyes flashed, and then he closed them, sighing in exasperation. "Why does the world have to be ending right now?"

"So I should shower by myself?"

"That would be the most responsible choice. Let's get this over with so we can have a moment of peace."

I returned to my room and showered. Wrapping myself in a towel, I entered the bedroom to use the wardrobe. My thoughts were so distracting, I didn't notice Thaos was sitting in a chair in front of the fireplace.

Sighing, he said, "I am disappointed for all time and eternity that I didn't get to wash that blood off of you."

I jumped in surprise and blushed. "What are you doing?"

His hair was damp, and he wore fresh clothes. He arched an eyebrow at me. "Waiting for you. We're supposed to be in a hurry, remember? The fate of the mortal realm and all that."

I sensed a tone of teasing admonishment. Was he suggesting I was taking too long?

I offered him a smile crafted of artificial sugar. "It will just be a moment."

Dropping the towel, I spun to the wardrobe.

He sucked in a stunned breath, and I wished I was bold enough to turn and see the look on his face.

"I thought you wanted to save the mortal realm. Are you trying to doom them?" he asked.

"I don't know what you mean," I said, acting coy as I selected pants and a shirt. I could feel his gaze searing into my back.

"You still overestimate my ability to control myself."

I smirked, making sure to bend over more than necessary as I dressed. When I turned to him, his hands were gripping the chair with such intensity I worried the wood was moments away from snapping.

"Ready?" I asked, the fake sugar still lacing my tone.

He stood and walked to me, wrapping his arm around my waist. "You dare tease me so shamelessly?"

I straightened his robe and smoothed his shirt, running my hands across his chest. "Maybe. What are you going to do about it?"

His brows lifted as his lip curled on one side. "I promise you'll find out soon enough." His voice was laced with smoky assurance that made the butterflies dance a waltz in my stomach.

We traveled through the void, landing outside of Hades' palace. As I stared up at the black doors, a beat of anxiety pulsed through me at being summoned. We started up the steps, and I felt Thaos' cool hand push into mine and lace our fingers.

I offered him a lifted brow, and his bright eyes gazed back at me with a hint of amusement. "I want to hold your hand, and I'm not worrying about should and shouldn't anymore."

I stared at him as my heart melted through my rib cage and pooled in my stomach. "You're quite the romantic, Death."

He smirked at that and led me up the stairs. We found Hades in an expansive dining room. Persephone was there. She was stunning, her fox-red hair braided into an intricate updo. The dress she wore was dusty pink and hugged the sumptuous curves of her body.

I grinned when I saw Hypnos was present as well. However, he was without Aergia and looked sullen because of it. I noticed there was food on the table, but no one was eating.

I didn't think Hades could keep anything down, even if he wanted to eat. He looked violently ill. His eyes were sunken, and his lips were chapped. The deep cocoa of his skin had taken on a greenish tint.

"Finally," Hypnos said, rolling his eyes. "What took you so long?" His eyes fell to our joined hands and his eyebrows lifted. "On second thought, I don't want to know."

My face flushed at his implication, but it wasn't far from the truth. I went to sit in my own seat, but a strong arm wrapped around me, and I gasped as I was pulled back to sit in Thaos' lap. My already red face flamed to the next degree.

"Oh, no, he's finally accepted it," Hypnos said, sighing. "This is going to be weird."

"I agree," Hades mumbled, eyeing us.

The queen offered me a sweet smile. "I think it's lovely."

I shyly returned her gesture and wondered if I was expected to bow or curtsy. Thaos hadn't, but she seemed so regal.

Hades cleared his throat. "We have more important things to worry about than Death's love life." His gaze fell on me. "I'm told we are saved, that you are our next Fate?"

"Yes. Clotho planned it when she saw the end of times. Nyx requires me to enter the mortal realm and find a dark elf prince before I become a Fate and can no longer reveal the future."

"Read me," Hades ordered. "One more time before you can't anymore."

Thaos tensed beneath me. "You don't have to if you don't want to, Cere. I promised you wouldn't have to."

My heart stuttered at the words, and I couldn't help but smile. Hades looked affronted by his insubordination, but I cut in. "It's okay."

I dropped the walls in my mind and gazed at him. Images appeared from his point of view. He looked out over his own soldiers, a vast army of black and gold armor. Several battalions of the Gods were poised for war at the base of a mountain I recognized as Mt. Olympus in Zeus' realm.

I relayed the images I saw, and then the prophecy pushed its way past my lips.

"If the brothers three fall, a new order will rise. Peace lies with the babe of sun and shadow. The child will sow salvation at the cradle of life."

He stared at me with wide, furious eyes. Hypnos sat with his mouth hanging open, and Persephone had placed a hand on her chest in shock.

"Civil war?" Hypnos asked.

"The three brothers have to be you, Poseidon, and Zeus," Thaos said.

"That's the second time I've prophesied about the baby," I added. "Whoever it is, they are extremely important."

"Sun and shadow? What does that mean?" Hades asked. To my surprise, his eyes fell to my stomach as if he was trying to sense if I carried this baby. My hand reflexively covered where his gaze perused. I was sure my own eyes were as wide as the empty dinner plates sitting in front of everyone.

"It's not my child," I squeaked, even though I understood his suspicions. Thaos could be shadow, but I didn't understand how I could be sun.

"Of course not," Hypnos said with a scolding tone. "Because we're all responsible people here who don't have unprotected sex. Right, brother?"

My breath hitched, but Thaos said nothing in response. Hypnos inferred from that and sat back in his chair. "I can't believe you ever had the audacity to call me a fool. You don't want kids. They're awful. They eat all of your food and still always prefer their mother."

Thaos shrugged as if he wasn't worried at all and brushed a strand of my hair behind my ear. "I would prefer her over me if I were them."

Hypnos scrunched his nose, but I saw a smile tugging at his lips. "Seeing you in love is incredibly disturbing for me."

Hades sat back and rubbed his temples. "So I guess Python was only the tip of the so-called apocalyptic iceberg?"

I cleared my throat, thankful he was changing the subject. "Yes, before Laurenth—died—she suggested as much. That he was interested in revenge against Apollo and against the humans for desecrating Gaia. But he is not the mastermind of the entire movement."

"Then who else is involved?"

"It has to be an Olympian or someone more powerful than one," Thaos answered. "The realm Cere was kept in could've only been created and maintained by someone of immense power."

"Then who—" Hades broke out in a violent coughing fit and I sank back against Thaos at the sudden outburst. Persephone put her hand on her husband's shoulder with a worried look drawing her features.

"We should go," Thaos said. "We need Cere to restore Fate so we can reap souls. The mortals that turn may still chip away at your power over time, but if we don't collect the ones we can for you, our part in this war will be over before it begins."

Hades nodded but didn't answer, wiping his mouth. A tiny strip of gold colored his cracked lips, and I realized he'd been coughing up blood.

Thaos stood and set me down, grabbing my hand again and leading me out of the front door. Hypnos joined us and I recalled there was no magic travel inside the Palace of Hades for security reasons.

When we were on the steps, Hypnos looked at me. "I'm glad you're alive. I wouldn't know what to do if I didn't have odd questions to answer over breakfast anymore."

"I know you love me," I said with a grin. "You don't have to hide it."

He arched an eyebrow. "I've been beaten up more than once because of you."

"But you have to admit things haven't been boring."

He laughed. "They certainly have not."

I threw my arms around his neck, surprising him. I guess I was becoming quite fond of hugging now that I could.

"Thank you," I said against his shoulder. "For your friendship. And I'm sorry about your wife. I just want you to be happy."

"*Happy*? I haven't considered what it's like to be that in a long time. But maybe I could be. Look at Death standing here smiling like he found a cookie in his pocket."

I glanced at Thaos, who wore a soft, amused expression.

Hypnos looked distracted, his eyes staring through me. He was thinking of someone else, and I knew it was the Goddess of Sloth. After a moment he cleared his throat. "I'll see you at *home*, Cere Goddess of Fate."

I nodded and he winked, flashing away.

Thaos wrapped his arm around me. He leaned down and kissed me, and the intensity of his passion made me breathless.

"Do you think Hades is mad that you disobeyed his order? That you told me I didn't have to deliver the prophecy?" I didn't want him to be in trouble.

"As if I care if he is. I promised you wouldn't have to. Obviously it's a matter of life and death that you deliver the one my mother assigned to you, but if you hadn't wanted to read Hades, you wouldn't have done it."

My eyes widened. "He's the king."

He shrugged. "I am older than him. Despite what *some* people believe, I am not his minion. Hades does not control me. We work together to oversee death and the dead. If I don't want to do something, I won't do it. It's that simple."

"What about Zeus? You're older than him."

His lips tightened in a firm line. "I could never stand against Zeus. He is the supreme. Hades and I together couldn't defeat him. If Poseidon came up from the ocean and helped, the three of us together could not. All the Olympians working together could not. He is too powerful. Although, the world would never want the three brothers to engage in a serious battle. All of them unleashing their true power would certainly spell the end of the mortal realm. They could destroy the entire planet. Zeus avoids conflict whenever he can, and despite his shortcomings as a ruler, he can be reasoned with in most instances. He is a diplomat. While he could exercise ultimate power over anyone at any time, he allows Fate to guide the world." A muscle in his jaw flexed. "If I hadn't challenged Apollo to the games, Zeus would have forced me to hand you over, and I wouldn't have been able to stop it." He paused, gazing down at me with a soft emotion that made my heart flutter. "Not that I wouldn't have tried."

We stared at each other for a moment. There was an intensity between us that had followed on the heels of acknowledgment. Admitting our feelings for one another was so powerful. He pulled my hand up to his mouth, kissing the center of my palm and then my wrist.

Finally, he finished his thought. Although I'd almost forgotten we were discussing anything at all. "But Zeus allowed us the leeway to resolve the situation ourselves. He doesn't want to fight with his brothers or anyone else."

"What about your mother?"

"She could have defeated him at one point. But I don't know if she could even stand against him now. However, I doubt he is keen on testing it. She is wicked."

"What do you mean now?"

He furrowed his brow, searching for words. "Zeus was always powerful. But he gained the ultimate enhancement when he swallowed a primordial egg. It contains the very essence of the universe, a potent substance called chaos. The egg makes him indestructible and unbeatable. Zeus can appear invisible, rain down lightning and ice from the sky, and an armor-like, indestructible aura surrounds him. As long as he holds the primordial egg in his gut, no one will ever overthrow him."

"Ulther told me they almost succeeded once. Laurenth was part of it."

"They did. The Queen of Gods led that rebellion, but one of Zeus' allies betrayed her. That is another factor of his power. The King of Gods has many powerful friends to call upon."

"His own wife tried to overthrow him?" I gasped, eyes wide.

He nodded. "I told you there is little love in marriage when it comes to the gods. Zeus hung her from the sky for her betrayal, where she wept endlessly. Apparently, it kept him up at night, so he eventually let her down. They have been distrustful of each other ever since."

"Hera did not seem happy earlier at the games."

"She isn't. Now, we must hurry. You need to deliver your last prophecy so you can become our next Fate."

"Do you know where to go?" I asked.

"I believe so."

CHAPTER THIRTY-FIVE

We dropped through the void and landed in a sub-level throne room. The walls, floor, and ceilings were carved out of dark stone, and it smelled like deep earth. Black banners depicting a ruby red crescent moon and six stars hung from the ceiling. It was the crest of Nyx's most devoted followers. Wolf shifters did not have a friendly relationship with them, and I tried to recall everything I'd ever learned about dark elves.

It looked like some kind of court was being held as people gathered around a dais where a dignified woman sat. Her black and red gown pooled around the base of her throne as she appeared to be giving stern instructions to a small group of people in front of her.

Alarmed shouts erupted when we dropped into the room, and the guards produced weapons, threatening us. I peered around at the scowling faces. There were torches lit, but the light was low. The elves had evolved for darkness and required little light to live by. If I remembered correctly, they could even see in infrared if they wanted to.

Their irises and hair were solid black, and their skin was a light bluish gray color. All of their features changed after generations of time in the underground. They needed little, if any, sunlight to survive.

Like their surface-dwelling cousins the fae, they had tall, pointed ears. However, the fae had intermingled with other species over time. The elves were purists. To produce offspring with another species was illegal and punishable by death for everyone involved, even the baby.

"Who are you?" a guard demanded in a gruff voice, pushing a sword towards us.

My hand traveled to where my new weapon rested at my waist. The gold handle was cool to my touch, and I gripped it, ready to fight if necessary.

"Don't," Thaos told them, his tone flat and unforgiving. "You don't want to do that."

His wings were full, and the shadow flowed around us, crawling up my body in a protective embrace. He still held me to his side, probably not planning to let me go.

"Stop!" a woman's voice shouted. It was full of authority. The guards stilled but didn't lower their weapons.

"That is the God of Death," she hissed. "Drop your weapons, you fools."

The guards stepped back in fright, and shocked expressions spread through the crowd. Weapons clanged to the floor, and everyone dropped to one knee, bowing and placing open palms over their hearts. I glanced at Thaos, but he didn't seem surprised by the gesture.

The woman rose from the red jeweled throne at the front of the room and knelt as well. "Please, ancient ones, I am sorry for my guards. Why are you here? What is happening?"

I almost chuckled at the moniker of "ancient one" as I had to be one of the youngest people in the room. "I need to speak with Prince Keiwren. Please."

Her face blanched, a nervous frown pulling her beautiful features. "I am his mother, Empress Raysan. Death is here for him? Has he done something wrong?"

I heard someone in the crowd whisper, "They want the Blood Prince."

I spoke in a gentle tone to ease her anxiety. "I am the Oracle to the Gods. I am here to deliver him a prophecy."

She nodded and snapped her fingers at a man close to her. "Get the prince. The rest of you, out!"

When the room was empty aside from us, the empress, and two guards behind her throne, she turned to us.

"It's this plague, isn't it? It's destroying our people. Nyx has answered our prayers and sent you, hasn't she?"

"I am the son of Nyx," Thaos replied. An answer that wasn't really an answer.

Empress Raysan nodded, looking both wary and hopeful at the same time. "I know."

"The plague is a result of unrest among the Gods," I explained. "I'm sorry."

I didn't understand how it even worked its way down here. They were a private species.

"It infiltrated our people through a human slave we acquired from the surface." She pushed out a dry, humorless laugh. "A human girl barely past her first blood has brought the last of our people to its knees. It's spread like wildfire. If we don't stop it, the end of our race is fast approaching."

Elves were one of the supernatural species to still possess human slaves. Vampires, dragons, and dark witches did as well.

The doors banged open, and two guards escorted a young, fierce looking dark elf. He looked no older than me, and his eyes darted to us filled with wary confusion. A ruby encrusted silver circlet donned his head, matching the dramatic headdress worn by his mother.

I stared at him curiously. Maybe it was my newly ascended status, but I sensed he was not purely mortal.

Keiwren's hand drifted absentmindedly to one of two swords sheathed at his waist when his eyes set on Thaos. I couldn't blame him, although he wouldn't stand a chance.

"What is this?" he demanded, his voice carrying a similar authority to his mother's. "They won't tell me anything."

"I am the Oracle of the Gods. I was sent by the Goddess Nyx to bring you a prophecy, Prince Keiwren. Time is of the essence."

He knelt as the others had, placing his palm over his heart. "I am honored. What do you require from me?"

"Nothing," I replied, dropping my walls.

There were no images, only whispers. They surged, becoming too loud all at once, and I winced. The voices were excited, as if they'd waited our whole life to deliver this prophecy.

"The prince of darkness seeks the beauty of gold that sees through forest and ocean. Wed her and take her heart at the Crow of Nyx. You will be rewarded with what can save the mortal realm. Closely guard your prize, for many wish to destroy it."

"Wed her?" he said hesitantly, as if that was the only part he'd heard.

The empress clicked her tongue in annoyance at him, then looked at me. "My lady, what does it mean?"

I opened my mouth to answer that I didn't know, but Thaos spoke first.

"The Crow of Nyx is an altar in my mother's realm. Your people have made blood sacrifices there before, but it's been a long time since you've ventured into the dominion of Night."

The empress nodded. "I've heard something about that."

Keiwren stood, seeming to have recovered from his shock that he was to be wed soon. "How do we get to Nyx's realm? Once I find this woman?"

"Our ancestors wrote of an entrance to the dominion of Night deep under the mountain, but no one alive knows where it is. Plus, it's dangerous to venture that deep into the tunnels and suicidal to travel in the Night realm. We only tell of it as tales to scare naughty children," the empress answered, pausing with a thoughtful, determined expression. "Is that what we're supposed to do? Sacrifice this woman at the Crow of Nyx?"

That seemed awful, but I thought of Nyx's throne crafted of bone and offered my honest answer. "Possibly. I don't know."

After a moment, Thaos looked at the young prince, who winced under his gaze but did not cower. "I suggest you start searching. Today. Good luck."

The empress looked surprised, yelling, "Wait!"

At the same time, her son asked, "Where?"

Thaos didn't offer an answer, and I didn't have one for them.

Swinging the scythe, we entered the void. I saw their shocked faces gaping at us, and then blackness surrounded me.

We landed at the iron gate of Hades. My heart thudded against my rib cage. I would enter here to find the Pavilion of the Fates.

"After you do this, you'll no longer be able to share the future with anyone," Thaos reminded me. "It's going to be a heavy burden. You may see your own fate. Your family's. The world's. Even mine."

"I know. But it's my destiny. If I don't, Hades will fall, and everything will descend too quickly into chaos. Keiwren won't have a chance to find the beauty of gold and save the mortal realm. Clotho worked hard to give me this chance and I can't disrespect her by not taking it. Not to mention if I don't, I'll die." I looked up at him, putting my hand on his cheek. "And I'm not ready to leave you. Will I still be able to stay at the glass castle?"

Thaos nodded, leaning into my touch. "As far as I know, that shouldn't be a problem. I expect they will give you something like this." He indicated the hourglass on his scythe. "That way you can manipulate time, so you aren't always spinning fate. The extra time you can spend however you want."

I grinned. "Well, I have some ideas."

He arched an eyebrow, and a small smile turned his lips. "Let's hurry this up then."

I laughed as he picked me up and carried me to the gates. They parted, revealing a grand hall of black and gold laying beyond the blinding light. It was empty, filled only with eerie silence. His boots thudded across the granite floor, echoing in the massive chamber.

"This hallway is usually full of waiting souls. But neither Keres nor I have been able to reap any since Clotho died."

"Where are they?"

"Stuck on Earth in their physical bodies."

"Oh...Gods. And they know that this is their fate?"

"I can't know for sure."

That made me feel sick. To be stuck in your dead body buried in the ground or trapped in an urn of ashes after being cremated. What a nightmare.

We passed an area with three empty golden chairs.

"The judges sit there, studying the life of each soul and passing a decision on where they will spend eternity," Thaos explained.

A large wooden door opened for us and allowed us through. We emerged on a dock resting against a river that looked like a flow of black ink.

A figure in a rickety two-person boat waited, leaning back in his seat as if he were sleeping. When he heard the door, he sat up in anticipation, but when he saw Thaos, his face soured.

"Death. Damn you. I thought we were back in business."

"Sorry, Charon. We are not."

I wondered if the image of this man was whom mortals confused with Thanatos when they depicted death. He was much closer to the frightening figure I expected that first day when Thaos' hood fell back.

Charon's face was the only part of his body I could see aside from his hands, and both were gaunt and skeletal. A large-brimmed black hat sat atop his head and the band of it jingled with dozens of small bronze coins. He wore a long, black, tattered robe with a wide belt that boasted hundreds more of the same coins.

When he stood, the money jingled, and he took a long drag off of a black pipe. I knew he wasn't smoking tobacco because when he exhaled, the smoke was a strange color of purple, like fading lilacs.

"But we may be in just a few minutes," Thaos said, tightening his arms around me. "This is the Fate that will replace Clotho."

Charon's entire demeanor changed, and he readied himself with a long pole. "Well, why didn't you say so? Come on, young lady. You can't cross the Acheron and Styx rivers without the Ferryman."

Thaos set me down, and I climbed into the boat, balancing as it rocked and plopping into the seat before I could fall out. I didn't think a dip in the onyx depths of this river would be pleasant.

"I'll see you on the other side," Thaos said when I was settled.

My fingers clenched on the cool, clammy edge of the boat. "You're not coming?"

He shook his head.

"Not even Death enters this part of the Underworld," Charon explained. "Only myself, the Fates, and Hades can see the rivers, the meadow, Tartarus, and the gates of Elysium."

"I see." I calmed my heart and nodded at Charon. "Then let's go."

I looked at Thaos, waving to him. His mouth lifted in a reassuring smile. "I'll be waiting."

I looked back at the Ferryman, whose expression was curious.

"What is it, Charon?"

"Nothing," he said, tilting his head and eyeing me. "I've just never seen my brother smile before."

Another sibling of Death?

I glanced back over my shoulder at Thaos, but the dock was empty.

CHAPTER THIRTY-SIX

Charon hummed an eerie tune as he guided us down the still river. We entered a pitch-black tunnel, but I could still see his outline as we traveled through. I couldn't help but wonder how frightening this would be for a mortal entering the afterlife.

When the darkness broke, we entered an enormous valley. I gasped in surprise at the unexpected expanse of space that traveled as far as the eye could see.

"Since it's your first time, I'll try to explain everything," Charon said suddenly, making me jump. "This is the river Acheron. It is the only way into the core of the Underworld."

I looked over the edge into the inky water and swallowed a lump of fear forming in my throat. Up ahead, I saw the river forked into three distinct branches.

Charon continued as we stayed in the center. "Taking the middle path, we've now crossed over into the river Styx. If we had veered right, we would have entered the river of Phlegethon, or fire. It flows slowly, and eventually, into Tartarus. It is where I would give souls deemed evil a nice little shove out of the boat. They burn for centuries in the river and then find themselves under the rule of the Titans in Tartarus. Not a good time for them."

"Thaos sent the one I called the overseer there," I commented. I looked at that branch of the river and it was no exaggeration. Flames licked the surface of the slow-moving, molten liquid. Shrieks of agony rose from it and occasionally I could see a blistered hand reach forth from the fire.

"Yes. I escorted him." Charon wheezed out a dark laugh. "He begged like a coward."

My lips curled in a vicious sneer. "Good."

The ferryman liked that answer, giving me a look of stark approval.

"If we had veered left," he continued, waving towards the green river on that side. "We would've entered the river of Lethe, or forgetfulness. The souls delivered to the Meadows of Asphodel drink from that river and forget their previous lives. They must drink in order to be reincarnated and try again to live the life that grants you entrance into Elysium. The Lethe river eventually empties into the Marsh of Lethe, which borders the Cave of Hypnos."

"The black glass castle," I said. "I've been there."

"Yes, I imagine you have as Death lives there as well."

I looked out beyond the river of Lethe and saw an expansive grassland with rolling green hills. I thought I would see souls there, but I didn't. "So those are the Meadows of Asphodel?"

"Yes."

"Where is Elysium?"

"It's up the river a piece. Particularly brave, kind, or righteous people are awarded eternity there. The last soul I escorted was delivered there. My sister, Clotho." He cleared his throat. "However, we'll pass the Pavilion of the Fates first and that's where you'll be getting off."

"Do you come get me when I'm done? How do I get out of here?"

"You know how to flash, don't you?"

I nodded. "Kind of."

"Once you're officially a Fate you'll be able to come and go as you please."

I watched the branches of the river grow further and further apart. Far in the distance beyond the Phlegethon river, I saw black clouds looming over mountains with treacherous peaks. I supposed that was the entrance to Tartarus.

Up ahead, a grand pavilion of black and gold came into view. Charon pushed the boat to the dock. "This is it."

Down the river, I saw white fluffy clouds atop a gate of pure gold. Elysium.

I hopped out of the boat. "Thank you, Charon."

"Hurry now," he answered with a wink. "We need to get back to work."

I nodded and bounded up the dock to a set of black cobblestone stairs. At the top, I entered the pavilion to find two women waiting for me. I tensed as I passed through the open doorway, expecting something to suggest my future was now sealed as a Fate.

Nothing happened, and I paused in confusion, staring ahead at the women.

"Come now," one rasped. "Our new Spinner."

I stepped forward, my body rigid with nervous tension. The two sat beside an enormous pile of unruly golden yarn. Behind them were infinite rows of golden threads hanging on rods. The threads seemed to be in a constant state of shifting, lengthening and shortening on their own.

As I got closer, their appearances came into focus. One was a beautiful elderly woman wearing a gown of gold. Her pale skin was wrinkled and spotted, but her features were still lovely. Piercing blue eyes watched me approach, and I felt like a child under the stern gaze of a respected teacher. A long white braid traveled down the length of her entire back and pooled on the floor around her seat.

In her hand, she held a pair of black scissors. They hummed with immense energy. I could feel the magical power pouring off of them and vibrating the air around them.

"I am Atropos," she said, and I knew the raspy voice belonged to her. "I cut the threads of Fate."

The woman next to her, in the middle of the three seats, spoke next and held what looked like a black measuring tape. It vibrated with power, too. "I am Lachesis. I measure the threads of Fate."

This woman was middle-aged, with deep onyx hair and skin. The strands at her temples were graying, and I saw the first appearances of lines and wrinkles around her eyes and mouth. She, too, wore a golden dress and long braid that gathered around her feet.

I looked at the last chair and recognized some kind of spindle resting there.

Atropos leveled me with a stern gaze. "You will take Clotho's place and spin the threads of Fate. You will never speak to anyone about what you see here, and you will do nothing to change Fate. If you do, it will inevitably lead to your own death, as it did for your predecessor."

"She caused her own death?" I asked, surprised.

"Several years ago, before you were born, we noticed everyone's Fate ending because of this plague or the subsequent war. Clotho knew revealing Fate to our mother was the only way to intervene. In doing so, she doomed herself. She accepted the cost and selected you to take her place."

My wide eyes regarded them with awe. "That was very noble of her."

"It was. She rests in Elysium for all time and eternity for her sacrifice."

A silence fell, and I felt like they were staring into my soul.

"If you're ready," Lachesis said softly, "pick up the distaff and spindle. Once you do, your ascension, and your future, are sealed. You will become the Spinner of Fate."

I stared at the spindle, cold dread settling in my chest. It thrummed with energy. The power called to me, pulling me towards my destiny. "I can still leave, right? I can live with Thaos and Hypnos?"

The older woman laughed, and the sound was dry and raspy like her voice. "Do you think we live here?"

I glanced around. I kind of had thought that.

"You can be Death's *Vasilissa* if you so choose."

I scrunched my nose. "*Vasilissa*?" I remembered Thaos had called me that while I was dying, but in the chaos of everything I'd forgotten.

"It means queen," Lachesis clarified. "You would be the Spinner of Fate and the Queen of Death."

"What about Persephone?"

"She is the Queen of the Dead. There's a difference."

"Okay," I answered. I didn't really understand, but I didn't want to seem foolish.

I wrung my fingers, unsure of what else to say.

"When you're ready," Atropos said, indicating my seat.

I nodded. Time was of the essence. I pushed out a breath and reached for the distaff and spindle.

My head exploded with pain when my fingers closed around it, and I fell to my knees. I heard agonized screaming.

Gods, it was me making that sound.

I clutched my head, surprised to feel that it was not physically splitting apart under my fingers like the pain suggested it was.

The enhanced sight was not what I was expecting. I didn't understand how Clotho made any sense of it. Everything blurred together in a mass of alternative realities. The element of freewill muddled the lines of what would happen. There were some events that were sure, set in stone, but most were just a blur of infinite possibilities.

The pain finally ebbed, and I looked up at the other two Fates with wide eyes. Glancing down at myself, I saw I now wore a golden gown identical to theirs. When did that happen?

"Now we begin," Atropos said, her voice steady, as if I hadn't just had a complete breakdown on the floor.

I looked at the chaos of gold yarn in front of me and grabbed a bundle. I somehow knew exactly what to do. Using the distaff and spindle like a seasoned professional, I weaved my first life. A human girl named Carrie. I handed the thread to Lachesis, who, to my horror, only measured a life of four years.

"That's all?" I whispered, looking at her.

Lachesis nodded solemnly. "Many of the lives you bring forth will die young. The human world is destined to descend into an apocalyptic wasteland. No matter what we did, it could not be saved. If we're successful, if Clotho's bold plan is realized, humans will go on, but they will be a decimated population."

She handed Carrie's thread to Atropos, who hung it next to her on a rod that held thousands of others. While I spun, she had been rapidly snipping at many of them, ending those lives.

I swallowed as a wave of raw grief passed through me.

CHAPTER THIRTY-SEVEN

The work was constant—unending. But they assured me that like Thaos' hourglass, the pavilion manipulated time, so only mere minutes had passed outside.

After what felt like days, Atropos set her scissors down, looking relieved. "We're caught up for now. Let's take some time."

Without another word, they both stood, setting their instruments down, and flashing away. I sat there in a daze, still shell shocked by the insight that now swamped my mind.

I didn't know precisely how the flashing thing worked when I wasn't standing in the same area that I was trying to go to. I closed my eyes and pictured Thaos. Wherever he was, I just wished to be with him.

The world pulled around me and I opened my eyes to a forest of golden trees adorned with white leaves. The grass was emerald green and rippled in a gentle breeze. Thaos sat in front of me on an iron bench, staring up at me with curiosity.

I was pleased to discover that when I left the Pavilion of the Fates, the images of the future calmed.

"Was I gone long?"

"I don't think so. I had to reap many souls, so I'm not sure. It will surprise you how immortality seems to render time worthless. Most often I don't even know what year it is."

A small smile formed on my lips. "So it worked?"

"Yes. Hades is already regaining strength. We pushed the end of times back for now."

He held his hands out to me, and I took them, thinking he wanted help standing up. A surprised giggle left me when he pulled me forward, and I sat sideways in his lap. His thumb swept over my cheekbone and his gaze was attentive and searching.

"Where are we?" I asked, taking in the stunning beauty surrounding us.

"The Ivory Forest. One of the most spectacular parts of Hades. It's suggested that these trees pour out of Elysium, but no one can find a way through. It just seems to go on forever. No one can fly over either, the clouds are too thick."

"It's magnificent," I said, watching the leaves twist. "No wendigo, I'm guessing?"

"No," he promised. "Nothing lives in this forest. I hoped you would like it."

"I do." The love I felt for him and the beauty of the forest were so profound that I felt emotion gather in my throat.

He swept his lips over my forehead. "How are you?"

"I'm okay," I sighed. "Overwhelmed."

"I know you can't tell me about it and I'm sorry."

I acknowledged him with a nod and felt a burn at the back of my eyes, thinking of the first thread I'd spun. A tiny life of only four years.

Although many had advised me of the miseries, being a Fate was more than I could've prepared myself to endure. "I'll get used to it. The others, Atropos and Lachesis, reassured me it would get easier."

Thaos nodded.

I leaned against his chest and kissed the contour of his jaw.

His face spread in a devilish grin. "Do you want to go home? I may not be able to help you with your life as a Fate, but I know a few ways to help you forget."

A faint smile turned my lips. "*Home.* I have a home."

"You do. At the glass castle… and with me. Here."

He held my hand and placed it against his chest, where I could feel his rapid heartbeat. It seemed even faster than normal.

I looked down at where my hand rested. "Who knew Death was such a romantic?"

"Only for you my *Vasilissa.*"

My eyes flitted back up to his, and I found him smiling at me. I put my hand against his cheek, and he turned into it, kissing me on the wrist.

"Don't you want to know what that means?" he asked, looking at me with a gaze so heated a flush of warmth traveled through me.

I already knew, but I wanted to hear him say it. "What does it mean?"

"Queen. *Vasilissa tou Thanatou.* Queen of Death. Or that's what you will officially be if you marry me. You're still my *Vasilissa*, regardless."

A soft blush colored my cheeks. It was all so bizarre. Not long ago, I was a mortal, an Oracle, but still a mortal woman. Today I was a goddess and a future queen.

I kissed his jaw again, asking, "Do you wish to marry me?"

"If you'll have me."

"Are you asking?"

He grinned, his head still resting against my hand. "If you want me to beg, I will."

"I *would* like to see that," I teased.

"Okay," he said simply, reaching into his robe and producing a ring box. It was black wood, a golden gillylily inlaid on the top.

"Gods," I whispered. "You were serious."

"I am very serious," he said, his gaze reinforcing his words. "Couldn't you feel my heart thundering? I've never been so nervous in my life."

I nodded, giggling and struggling to blink away blossoming tears.

He pulled me closer, "Please, please, Cere Goddess of Fate, Former Pythia of Delphi, Wild Daughter of Artemis, Slayer of the First Dragon, The Most Vicious—"

I gasped, cutting him off with a laugh as a single tear escaped.

He grinned, kissing my cheek. "And my light—my warmth, will you honor me by becoming my queen, my *Vasilissa*?"

I knew it was all happening quickly, but I didn't care. It didn't matter to me if it had been weeks or years. In the culture I grew up in, people often mated and married within days of finding each other. There was no point in putting it off. Your mate is your destiny. And Thaos was mine. I hadn't known he would do this today, but I had seen many pieces of our future together. Some thrilled me, and some terrified me.

He shifted beneath me, his grip tightening on my thigh. I hadn't answered yet, and his head tilted as his curious violet eyes tried to read me.

A small giggle left me, squeezing around the emotion that gathered in my throat. "I will."

A breath left him, and it occurred to me he had been holding it. "Are you sure?" he asked. "I haven't even shown you the ring."

"I'm sure. I don't care what's in that box. Unless it's the wendigo's maggots, then I change my answer to no."

He chuckled, shaking his head. Opening the box, he presented it to me.

I laughed, staring down through tears at a breathtaking ring. "It matches my sword."

The band was gold, hoisting a beautiful round diamond encircled by amethysts. It looked just like the pommel of the sword he'd gifted me. Studying its immense size, I wondered if it was as heavy, too.

"I thought you'd like that," he said, plucking it from the box and sliding it on my finger.

"I do," I whispered.

He turned and found my lips, kissing me as though he aimed to steal the breath from my lungs. As though my taste alone was the only thing he needed to survive.

My other hand found his cheek, and I pulled him to me, our tongues clashing together in a desperate need for one another.

I shifted, straddling him and draping my arms around his neck. Shameless as ever, I moved against him like we weren't in a potentially public place. I didn't know if people visited the forest often, but the bench suggested as much.

Thaos' hands swept up my bare thighs, pushing under the dress until he clutched my hips and groaned into the space between our kiss.

He broke away and pressed his lips to my ear. "You should flash us home unless you've turned into an exhibitionist and want me to take you here on this bench."

"That would be inappropriate," I breathed, the throaty grate of my voice catching me off guard.

"So I can feel confident in the assumption you'd like it? Every time you tell me something is inappropriate you end up liking it very much," he teased me, humor playing across his features. "You're much naughtier than I expected from someone intended to lead a life of abstinence. Do I have that well-read romance novel to thank?"

I scoffed, blushing. "It's moments like these I'm glad I stabbed you. And shot you."

He laughed, and it was the rich, smoky laugh that made my heart swell.

"I dislike you," I grumbled, struggling to hide the smile that was trying to turn my lips.

"You are still a terrible liar."

His head dipped, and he kissed my neck and collarbone, and then the spot that bore his mark.

I sucked in a breath and closed my eyes, picturing home and willing us both to be there. I thought a moment too late that I should've probably been more specific.

And I was right.

Dishes clattered noisily to the floor as we ended up flashing onto the dining room table with me still straddling his lap. My dress was pushed up to my hips, but Thaos' body was thankfully blocking me.

I heard Hypnos shout a shocked curse and then burst into laughter.

"Oops," I whispered, looking down at Thaos, who was chuckling, his eyebrows raised.

"You could've just told me if you were hungry," he said, grinning wider.

I glared at him. "I didn't mean to flash to the dining room. You were distracting me."

I looked around him to the God of Sleep, horrified to see that Aergia was there as well, sitting on his lap. She looked amused and offered me a lazy wave.

I gave her a sheepish grin in return. "Hi."

"Well, hello," Hypnos snickered. "My goodness, what are you two up to?"

"Nothing."

"That doesn't look like nothing, that looks like foreplay."

I gasped at his forwardness, my face somehow burning hotter than it already was. I snatched a piece of garlic bread and threw it at him. My ascension had vastly improved my speed and aim. With the way Aergia sat on him, he didn't have a chance at catching it. I smirked as it hit him on the forehead with a crispy thump.

"What is it with you and throwing bread?" he asked, holding it up.

Aergia took it from him and bit into it, grinning. "Thanks. I wanted one, but I was too lazy to get up and grab it."

"You're welcome," I mumbled, wishing our official first time meeting hadn't been quite so humiliating. "Nice to meet you."

I closed my eyes and thought of my bed, willing us there. The world blurred and my knees met a much softer surface as we arrived in the correct place.

I was still dying of embarrassment while Thaos watched me with an amused expression. His hands still rested on my hips and his right thumb ran up and down the crease between my hip and thigh. He leaned forward and pulled his scythe from his back, setting it next to the bed.

When he sat back, he pulled me closer to his chest. "I made you a promise earlier. Do you remember?"

I furrowed my brow, taking a moment to recall what he was talking about. The time spent in the pavilion made it seem like days ago. My blood heated when I remembered. "That I would find out what happens when I *shamelessly tease you*."

The last words came out like I was issuing a challenge, and he ran his tongue over his top lip, his eyebrows lifting.

He chuckled darkly, running his finger down my chest into the valley of my breasts. "You don't believe me, *Vasilissa*? Or are you just provoking me?"

"We both know I am reckless," I whispered, losing some of my bravado as my body shivered at the cool touch of his finger.

I bit my lip, looking down at him. The familiar curl of desire made itself known, twisting to life in my stomach and answering his caress.

"Bold of you when you quiver like a leaf at a simple brush of my finger."

I thought to say something else, but he claimed my lips with a ferocity that took my breath and the words riding on it. The curl in my stomach spun tighter, and a damp heat followed as he turned his head to deepen the kiss.

"This is a nice dress," he said against my lips, and I thought he sounded—apologetic?

I don't know what else I was expecting, but I still gasped when I felt his hand at the vee of the golden gown and heard the sharp tear. I couldn't bring myself to care. In fact, another beat of arousal pulsed through me.

I felt him pushing the sleeves of the ruined dress down my arms and I helped him slide it off. The kiss pressed deeper, and he hissed in a breath when my new sharpened canine, another addition of my ascension, nicked his lip.

I tasted him, the rich sweet rum flavor, and I couldn't suppress a moan. It was different this time. The essence of his blood flashed through my veins, lighting every nerve in my body on fire. Was this what gods always experienced?

"I'm sorry," I breathed. "I'm not used to them."

A low rumble sounded in his throat, and he rocked forward, changing our positions with one effortless motion until my back pressed against the bed and he was over me. He discarded his robe and shirt, gazing down at me through dense, lustful lashes.

I admired his body for the work of art that it was, running my hands over the dips of his powerful physique. If I had any talent with a paint brush, I would be honored to commit such perfection to canvas.

The shadow from his full wings fell around us, cooling the air and making my skin prickle with goosebumps. Dark tendrils of hair fell across his forehead, and I reached up, smoothing them back and gazing into his eyes. My eyes traced the sharp bridge of his nose, The high rise of his cheekbones, and the firm line of his jaw.

"You are so beautiful," I gushed, then snapped my mouth shut with a blush.

I thought he would tease me, but when I looked back at his face, he seemed to be rendered speechless.

Had no one ever told him of his beauty?

His wings pulsed with strong feeling, the shadows now cascading around us like a dam had burst. The tendrils brushed over me like they were caressing me, too.

He looked at me for several moments, with that strange emotion dancing in his eyes. Finally, he muttered a quiet, "Thank you." His head dipped, and he kissed my collarbone. "But I still find I am not worthy of your beauty. Of your light."

"I disagree," I gasped as his mouth traveled lower, closing over the pink peak of my breast.

"You disagree? What a surprise," he answered after a long moment, the light teasing tone back in his voice. "But you're wrong this time *Vasilissa*, no one is worthy of you."

"Then I guess I'll spend the rest of our lives convincing you."

His eyes snapped up to mine with a grin, both of us still reeling from the idea that the rest of our lives meant forever. He held my gaze as his lips traveled from my breast and kissed the valley between them before closing over the other.

I sucked in a breath, watching him, and then moaned when I felt the soft slide of his fang over the sensitive flesh. A cascade of heat traveled down my body and my hips lifted.

His eyes glimmered with surprise and lust as he released the hold of his mouth. "You are naughty. You would like that, wouldn't you? If I sink my teeth into you here?" He pressed his lips to the curve of my breast to show where he was talking about.

I swallowed, and another wanton wave of desire coursed through me at the thought. He clicked his tongue and smirked, but to my shameless disappointment, he did not do as he said.

Instead, his lips wandered down the plane of my stomach, my muscles jumping at each soft caress. My core ached for his touch and my hips were lifting of their own accord each time his mouth brushed my skin.

Leaning up, he grabbed the tattered remains of my dress and the flimsy undergarment beneath, dragging them down my legs and tossing them aside. He laid on his side next to me and I looked at him in a daze of arousal and confusion.

"What? Did you want something from me?" he asked, feigning innocence as his hand traveled down my stomach and stopped just above where I was in desperate need of it. His fingers started swirling circles around my navel. The maddening movement made my skin tingle with desire.

I glared at him. "You know I do. Tease."

"Not so fun when you're on the receiving end, is it?"

His hand moved like it would dip lower and my hips rose to meet him, but he hesitated again. He watched me, his eyes lustful and shimmering with amusement. "You do like my fingers inside you, don't you?"

My eyes narrowed, already tired of his game. "Mine will do just fine."

I ran my hand down my stomach, underneath his hand, and thrust my fingers against my own swollen flesh. It was more pleasurable than I was expecting, and I moaned, my head dropping back against the bed.

Thaos hissed in a disbelieving breath, accompanied by a thick laugh. "Exactly what kind of romance novel was that?"

A breathless giggle left me, and I opened my eyes, seeing that he was watching what my hand was doing beneath his own. I shuddered at the erotic sight, biting my lip.

His fingers squeezed around mine, stopping me. I watched wide-eyed as he brought my still wet fingers to his lips and took them in his mouth, tasting me.

I quivered again, and he leveled me with a heated gaze. "*That* is my job."

"Then do it," I retorted before I could catch the words.

His pupils dilated, and a wicked smile formed on his lips. He moved so fast that before I took another breath, his broad shoulders were driving my legs apart and his mouth was on me. The first flick of his tongue pulled a strangled moan from me.

Thoughts and words abandoned me, my hips raising to meet him. His left hand and forearm clamped down across my stomach, shoving me back down to the bed. His mouth closed over the apex of my nerves, sucking with blazing intensity. A broad finger pushed inside of me, and I once again tried to lift my hips, determined to move and relieve some of the unbelievable tension he was creating.

He held me and I thought I felt a wicked chuckle rumble through him. Moans of surrender poured from my mouth as both of my hands found the forearm that held me in place, and I dug my nails into his flesh. I writhed as much as I could, the coil of desire twisting and turning until it threatened to undo me.

"Thaos," I moaned, more of a plea, and my voice was so rough I barely recognized it as mine.

I glanced down at the same time his lashes swept open. Our eyes locked, and he finally moved his arm. My hips lifted, grinding into his touch. His tongue didn't cease, swirling circles as a second finger joined the first. The release was quick and devastating, as I spent hardly any time in that beautifully cruel suspension before the fall. I came apart, crying out his name and pulling at his hair as I broke through the first tidal wave of pleasure. He pulled the climax out as long as possible, not ceasing his movements until I stopped shuddering.

My eyes were closed for several seconds as I tried to calm the rise and fall of my chest. He pulled away, his hair sliding from my hands. His lips fell over mine again and I felt him pushing his pants down and away. My hands wrapped around his back, and he tensed as I brushed over what felt like a giant scab.

"What's that?" I asked, concern forcing my eyes open.

"Nothing. I came across some undead while reaping and one scratched me."

I felt gently down his back. There were three more similar gashes. "You're hurt."

"I'm fine, I promise. They're already healing."

I thought of when he'd given me his blood after the wendigo scratched me. Technically, I had god's blood now, too. A slice of fervent desire shot through me. I was growing concerned over how badly I wanted him to bite me.

"You should take some of my blood," I blurted. "It will heal you faster."

"*Maybe* I will," he teased, knowing I had my own incentives.

I felt his hands on my waist, and he sat back against the pillows, pulling me on top of him. With us both naked, I moaned as hard arousal pressed against me.

"Do you remember what I told you that night on the beach?"

He'd told me a lot of things that night. I hadn't forgotten a word.

"Which part?"

He lifted me, his hand snaking between us and positioning himself at my center.

"I told you I wanted you to ride me like you were riding my hand. I've been thinking of it ever since."

My eyes widened. "I-I don't know how."

He barked out a short laugh. "I have faith that you'll learn quickly."

His hand that had been lifting me disappeared, moving to my hip and easing me down. I sucked in a quick breath that left me as a long moan. Gravity and the soft pressure from his hand slid the length of him inside me.

When my body was shockingly flush with his, I cried out while he moaned, his head falling back against the pillows. This was—I didn't even know. Fresh, wicked jolts of pleasure ripped through me as my body clamored, trying to adjust to the fullness that was almost too much.

He looked up at me, his chest moving as erratically as mine. His free hand found my other hip, and he lifted and then lowered me again, both of us moaning.

"Like that," he rasped, watching me.

I copied the movement, crying out again as the same intense spike of pleasure rippled through me. My toes curled, and I realized I still wore the strappy gold heels that had come with the dress.

I moved with a sort of rhythm. He looked between us, at where our bodies connected, and a deep rumbling groan traveled through him.

Understanding the movement, I increased my speed. "Like this?"

He squeezed my hips. "Yes," he hissed. "Everything you do is perfect."

My eyes closed, and my head fell back, my moans filling the emptiness of the room. I could feel his gaze burning into me. I knew he watched my face, my breasts, and where we were joined. His hands followed his eyes, roaming over my body. He ran them up my arms, resting them on my shoulders and pushing me down against him as I moved.

After a moment, they floated down to my breasts and kneaded them roughly. I said his name several times, repeating it between moans like a prayer. Finally, I felt a tug at the bottom of my long braid, and he sat up, pulling the hair free. We shared a rough kiss as he did, but my movements didn't falter.

He laid back again, and I put my hands on his chest, leaning forward so my loose hair fell around us like a curtain. The angle of the position shifted and—

Oh, my.

A surprised moan ripped from my lips as the spikes of pleasure turned into shards, cutting through me. His hand moved between us, finding the bud at my center, and moving against it. It was too much, and I was so close. My movements started stalling as I tried to succumb to the bliss.

Thaos' cool, calloused hand clamped onto my waist, and he thrust his hips for the first time, mercilessly pushing me down against him as he did. He repeated the motion, moving faster and rougher than I had been. I said many unintelligible things; most of it was begging him not to stop.

He didn't.

When the tension exploded, the release shattered me. My wild cries bounced off the walls, and my nails dug into his forearms where I clung to him. Ecstasy sliced through my quaking body, cutting me into a million tiny pieces, and I wasn't sure if I would ever recover enough to stitch myself back together.

When the waves ceased, I could still sense his gaze on my face. My eyes opened, expecting to see pools of violet staring back at me, but glimpsing onyx instead. His eyes had blackened, cracks of darkness branching from them. Maybe I was truly crazy because all that did was elicit a new shudder of excitement.

He rolled us so I was underneath him, hooking one of my legs in the crook of his elbow. He unleashed with a fierceness that showed me he had let his control slip away.

His mouth found mine, the kiss a desperate frenzy of brazen lust. I felt his fingers lace into the hair at the nape of my neck and pull my head back, exposing my throat. I gasped, a sharp pang of desire and arousal thundering through me.

His lips found my neck, and I pushed it to him, threading my fingers into his hair.

"No, that's not what you wanted," he reminded me. His voice was dark and lustful, as thick with pleasure as I'd ever heard from him.

He sucked on the spot that bore his mark before dipping his head lower. I felt his lips on the swell of my breast and then the brush of his fangs, followed by a sudden sharp pinch. Crying out, I clung to him, tensing. The pain quickly evaporated, and I felt nothing but hot, overwhelming pleasure.

The draw of his mouth and the simultaneous thrust of his hips made the world melt away. My eyes closed, stars twinkling behind the cover of my lids. His arm laced around my waist, holding me tightly as he devoured me, claiming me in a way I didn't know existed.

The sensations engulfed me, proving to be too much, and I cried his name, coming apart beneath him. He kissed me, pressing hard against me once more, as I caught his hoarse shout with my lips.

We stayed like that for a long time, his head resting against my shoulder. I ran my hands over the ropes of muscle in his back, realizing after several moments the skin where the deep scratches had been was smooth. Completely healed.

"That's incredible," I whispered.

"You're welcome," he said, looking up at me with a crooked smile.

I arched my brow. "I was talking about the scratches."

"Are you sure? Because I would consider all of that incredible."

I smiled, putting my hand on his cheek. "I suppose it will do."

He laughed and leaned back, looking down with a groan of approval. "You are... just flawless." His cool lips pressed against the tender marked flesh of my breast. "This is the most erotic thing I've ever seen."

My eyes widened when I realized what I was feeling against my thigh. That was an impressive recovery time. I felt like I'd just started breathing again.

"Gods, you're insatiable." I giggled.

Heated eyes and a mischievous smile locked my gaze. "I knew you thought I was joking when I said we wouldn't be leaving this room for at least a week."

I watched his expression change, shifting to a more serious stare. "*Vasilissa?*"

"Yes?"

He brushed his thumb over my cheekbone and appeared to be in deep thought. After several moments, the side of his mouth curled slightly. "I love you."

Love. That was the first time he'd told me that word outright. The way he said it still conveyed his own shock, his own belief that it wasn't possible that he ever would.

My heart swelled. "I love you, too."

"What do you know of love?" he teased. It was a question he'd once asked me when I knew nothing on the subject.

"I know you."

He looked pleased with that answer as he drifted forward and kissed me again.

When he leaned back, his eyebrows furrowed, but he held my gaze. "I forgot to drink that damn prevention draft again. Hypnos was right, it is incredibly irresponsible and selfish of me. You are very young, and this has all happened so quickly."

It took me a moment to realize he was referring to some kind of birth control. My heart leapt. I knew this conversation would happen, but I just didn't expect it so soon. "I am not so naïve that I don't know where babies come from. The blame lies with both of us."

I was young, especially in his eyes, but I now knew and understood things he didn't. Everything had happened quickly between us, but that was all part of our destiny, our fate, and it didn't make our love any less real.

He ran his hand through his hair, pushing it back. I could see he wanted to argue with me and insist he was at fault, but it didn't matter either way. I struggled with forming the words, not knowing how much I could say.

"It doesn't matter," I whispered.

I opened my mouth to tell him more, but the words stuck in my throat. Not only was I oath-bound as a Fate not to say them, it seemed I physically couldn't. I thought of that day when Clotho stopped me in the Woods of Woe, and the strain on her face. I wondered how she ever shared her plan with Nyx.

He watched me curiously. I tried again, but the words died before they ever passed my lips.

"I want to tell you, but I can't," I mumbled, feeling frustrated.

"Is it too late for the prevention draft?" he asked, eyebrows lifting.

I shook my head. "Not yet. But we shouldn't use it."

It surprised me that I could tell him that much.

He contemplated that for a moment, and then concern crossed his features. "Our child is the babe of sun and shadow? Like you foretold?"

I shook my head again, and he looked relieved. "But our child still has a role to play?"

I nodded. The anxiety of that role pulsed through my veins. Thaos and I had already played an important part, but it was only the first step towards the bigger picture that would decide the future of all the realms, both earthly and godly. Our child didn't even exist yet and so much already depended on them.

"And we're to produce this child, when? As soon as possible?"

My heart fluttered at the thought of being a mother, but I nodded warily. I was nervous about how he'd feel about that. I didn't know exactly how I felt about it.

Weeks ago, I expected to remain pure. Children weren't even a possibility I'd allowed myself to consider. Now it was essential that I have one. The dramatic change in such a short amount of time stirred profound feelings of nervousness and fear in my chest.

Thaos pushed out a breath and ran his hand through his hair again.

"You're upset," I said, twisting the sheet with my fingers.

"I'm just sorry. I feel you're being forced to carry my child when I wish we were making that choice ourselves."

Despite his concerns, his words actually comforted me. He didn't say he didn't want the child, which would've been much harder to hear.

"Don't worry about that," I answered, putting my hand on his cheek. "It is obviously sooner than I was expecting, but the only thing that makes it less terrifying is the fact that it's happening with you." Maybe it was easier for me to accept because I had seen glimpses of the future. I had seen this child and who they would be, and I loved them already. "I want this."

His eyes were bright and soft when he looked at me, leveling me with an intense expression that I didn't quite know how to read.

"Since we have already established on multiple occasions that I am selfish when it comes to you, I'll admit that even when we spoke about it at the palace, I felt nothing but satisfaction at the thought of you carrying my child. You are the only woman I would ever desire this with. I never—*never*—thought I would be a father, but the thought of being one alongside you makes me... excited."

His smile was crooked, and he once again spoke of the emotion like he couldn't believe it.

I sighed at the cool relief his words brought. "I love you."

"I love you, *Vasilissa*," he said. "And our future sweet prince or princess."

My lip curled on one side. "*Sweet* is probably not the correct word."

His eyebrows shot up. "You know what they will be, then? They will be a god or goddess, of course. And you already know of what?"

"I do."

"I'm jealous," he admitted, but to my surprise, he gave me a sultry look that made me giggle.

"Well," he drew the word out as he leaned back down to kiss me, settling himself between my legs. "If the fate of the world is depending on us, we best not let them down."

EPILOGUE

I sat at the dining room table with Hypnos, Aergia, Thaos and Ulther. They were making small talk, but I was pushing my food around my plate. Ulther was doing the same, and although I didn't need a guard anymore, he still stayed here. I think it helped him deal with his sorrow. He had changed, growing more drawn and serious every day since finding out about Aeryn.

The skinwalker had revealed very little, despite intense questioning at the hands of Hades—something Thaos assured me I didn't want to see. But she had told him that Aeryn had been a gift for the vampire that had helped create the undead. If she wasn't already dead, she had been turned or was being used as a feeder.

I already knew all the possible conclusions of Ulther and Aeryn's story, but I couldn't reveal that to him.

I toyed with the edge of my napkin as my thoughts drifted back to myself.

Today was the day. I had been waiting so long, all these years, and knew it was time. This was the first time I could go see them without endangering their lives or my own. This brief peace wouldn't last, so I had to go while I could.

That was the strange thing about being a Fate. Some events were sure and clear in my mind. Others weren't. I couldn't know how my family would react to seeing me today, and I honestly tried not to focus too hard on the prospects.

So much had happened that sometimes I didn't feel like that was ever my life. There were times I even thought maybe I'd dreamed those first years.

But it was real. They were there, and I was going to see them.

I had revealed to Thaos that my name was actually Ceres, but I still wanted to be Cere to him, and to the world. It was hard to explain, but Cere was the person who I saw myself as. She was the person who'd overcome the obstacles of this life and carved happiness out of the darkness. Ceres was still a special part of my heart. She was those first happy years of my life, the ones that kept me going all those endless days at the temple.

A cool hand rested on my leg, and I turned to find Thaos studying me with concern. He agreed it was important I see my family again, but insisted he wanted to come with me. I was more than happy that he did. I didn't know how my parents were going to react to their daughter's engagement to the God of Death, but I wanted him to meet them.

I gave him a small, unconvincing smile. "I want to go. I can't stand another second of wondering about it."

"Then we'll go."

He held out his hand, and I took it, standing with him. I wore a golden gown. I often did now, with it being the color of the Fates. Besides, I thought it struck a handsome contrast with his black attire when we stood together.

"Do you want to flash us there?"

I nodded and closed my eyes before I could have one more second thought. I pictured my mother, wanting to see her first.

The world moved, and our feet landed on a carpeted floor. I kept my eyes closed as my stomach churned with too many emotions. My eyes already burned with tears at the smell of the room. We were in their bedroom. I knew it without opening my eyes. I remembered how it smelled, their familiar scents mixing.

A shocked gasp traveled across the room, and my eyes flew open. A small sob broke my lips when I saw her. She was sitting in the lounge area with her legs curled under her, a book in her hand. Her long blonde hair cascaded around her, framing a face that bore so many similarities to mine.

Despite over a decade going by, she didn't appear much older. Wolf shifters may not be immortal, but they aged slower than humans. I looked into her eyes, the ones I'd inherited from her, and tears flowed down my cheeks.

She paled, staring at me as if I was a ghost. Blinking several times, she seemed to convince herself I was real.

"Ceres?"

Another sob left me. "Mother."

"Is this another dream?" she asked, looking unconvinced. Her eyes shifted warily to Thaos, who still held my hand.

I shook my head. "It's me."

She jolted to her feet. The book was forgotten as it thumped to the floor. "Oh, my baby!" she sobbed, her own tears breaking free as she ran to me.

I caught her, holding her weight as her knees seemed to give out. Her sobs were so violent that they were soundless against my chest, and her body quaked with them.

"Mother." I wept into her shoulder. "I can't believe it's you."

The door burst open behind us, but I couldn't let her go.

"Eris!" It was my father's breathless voice, and I could hear his intense concern. "Are you okay? I felt—" He must have rounded the corner into the sitting area and stopped.

My parents were true fated mates, able to sense each other's emotions, and I was sure her sudden burst of intense feeling had caught him off guard.

She didn't offer him an answer, but I assumed she told him what was happening through their bond because he gasped in surprise.

I felt him next to us and his arms encased us both. "It can't be."

I'd never seen my father cry, but I felt his body shuddering with sobs, which only made me near hysterical. He grabbed my head and pulled it gently against his chest, under his chin, and held me close. I sobbed into his shirt, unable to find a shred of emotional control.

It felt like a small eternity that we stood there, holding each other and soaking each other in tears. Finally, my mother pushed away, cupping my cheeks and wiping at the tears there.

"Ceres, Ceres. My girl. My baby, where have you been?"

"It's a very long story," I answered, laughing through thick tears.

"We searched for you," my father promised, guilt spilling over in his words. "We never stopped looking, I swear. I would've torn the entire world apart. We never stopped hoping."

"You still wouldn't have found me," I whispered. "There is nothing you could've done."

He nodded, fighting a fresh wave of emotion that gathered in his expression and threatened to erupt.

"You are not a wolf," my mother said curiously. "At least that's not what your aura feels like. You seem much more powerful than that."

"I am and I am not."

"She is many things," Thaos said, and they both jumped in surprise, having somehow forgotten he was there despite his stifling presence. "She is a daughter of Artemis, the former Pythia of Apollo, and the Slayer of the First Dragon. She is a Goddess of Fate and my *Vasilissa*—the future Queen of Death."

The pride in his voice made my heart swell, but the way my father's arms tightened around me made it pinch at the same time.

"Is this who stole you from us?" His tone was murderous. I knew he could sense the power of Thaos, but I also knew he would fight for me, with no chance of victory.

"No, this is who saved me. He helped me kill the one who stole me from you. This is my fated mate, Thanatos, the God of Death."

Their faces conveyed several emotions. Gratitude, then pride, followed by disbelief and awe.

"I would like to marry your daughter," Thaos added. My cheeks flushed. We hadn't discussed that he would bring that up.

My mother spoke, a tone of disbelief. "Are you asking us? The God of Death is… asking us for permission?"

"Traditionally I would be, but the only permission I need is hers," he said, gazing at me in such a way that it left little doubt of his feelings for me. "However, I am asking for your blessing."

I returned his look, the unquestionable love I already held for him blooming and digging its roots deeper into my chest.

My parents both watched me. I saw my father's hazel eyes track down my face and find Thaos' mark. He smiled. "This is what you want?"

I nodded. "It is."

"Then you have my blessing."

"And mine," my mother added, tears clouding her voice again. "This is all so overwhelming. Ceres… a goddess. Returned to us."

She started weeping again, and my father held her close to his side.

"I brought you something," I said.

Thaos reached into his robe and held it out to me.

Grabbing it, I turned it in my hand and offered them the feathered fletching.

"You brought us an arrow?" my father asked, eyes glowing with curiosity.

Nodding, I grinned. "I brought you an arrow of Artemis. I pulled it from her quiver and used its sister to pierce the heart of the First Dragon."

Their mouths fell open, and I extended it to them. My mother took it, holding it protectively against her chest like it was her greatest treasure.

From the open door, I heard a voice calling, and my soul sang in recognition.

"Dad? What's happening? Someone came to my office and said you hurried away to find Mom. That you were in a panic. Is she—"

He stopped, taking in the scene with a confused expression. It was like looking at a mirror image of my father, only younger. Much older than I remembered him, though. He wasn't the freckled-faced boy I'd pictured every morning for the last ten years. He was a man.

I gasped in delight, more tears threatening to spill over.

"Gods. Henry."

After I cried on my brother's shoulder, the day flew by in a flurry of teary faces. Aunts, uncles, and cousins that I never dared hope to see again. My brother found his mate young, when they were both eighteen, and they already had three children. His first daughter he called Ceres, which made me cry even more.

We were all in the yard, and I was playing with the children. I could feel my cheeks were flushed from the exertion, but I didn't want to stop. A sad piece of me was in shock, mourning the life I'd missed here with them. The time I could never get back.

But I had to stop because head spun unexpectedly when I stood up. I rubbed my forehead and called to the others, "I've gotta sit for a second."

Thaos was there, asking, "Are you okay?" His hand was resting on my lower back and we walked towards a bench.

"Yeah. It was weird. I just got a little dizzy..."

My head snapped up to look at him. We both knew what it meant and watched the realization play out on each other's faces. There was a wild stir of emotions exchanged in that glance.

Love. Fear. Excitement. Dread.

"You carry our child, don't you?" He pressed his hand flat against my stomach, and I watched his pupils dilate. "Yes. You do." I put my hand over his, and I could sense what he did. A tiny little life.

I was fighting tears, but Thaos' demeanor shifted, and his eyes darted around the yard. "I know you want to linger. But we should go."

My heart pinched, and I looked back over my shoulder. Mother watched us. She hadn't taken her eyes off me since I'd arrived. A sad smile spread her lips, and I knew she understood.

"Can't they come with us?" I asked, looking back at him.

"Of course. Anytime they wish. But I don't think they will go now. They lead your people, don't they?"

"Yes."

She knew he was right. Her family would not abandon the pack.

"But if it gets too bad up here, we can get them?"

He nodded.

"Okay. I'd like to say goodbye. I didn't get to do that last time."

Thaos arched an eyebrow, frowning at the reminder of my kidnapping and subsequent imprisonment. "Well, you are the Queen of Death this time. You get to do as you please."

Smiling, I cupped his cheeks, and pushed up on my toes to kiss him.

Against his lips, I breathed, "I love you, Death."

"And I love you, Cere. Forever."

THE MEN OF SHADOWS TRILOGY

Follow the paths of three different women as fate weaves its web, intertwining their destinies to save the world.

The story continues with Cere's prophecy, and the beauty of gold sought by the prince of darkness.

COMING SOON! Book Two: KISSED BY SUN

Lati, a distinguished member of the Fae Queen's Guard, is determined to live out the rest of her life doing what she does best.

Killing and maiming.

More recently, she spends her time disposing of the undead creatures pouring across the border from the human world.

Lati has her life figured out. Kill things, get promoted, be the best soldier she can be, and live happily ever after. *Alone*, because people let you down, and swords don't.

Her routine is her comfort until one night when a dark elf prince steps out of the treeline.

Their swords cross, and he whispers, "It's you."

Let's Stay in Touch!

Thank you so much for reading Loved by Fate. I am a self-published author, so if you have time and would like to leave a review on the site you purchased this book from, please do! It is the best way you can help me on this journey, and I appreciate it beyond words.

If you enjoyed my work and want to be updated when I release the next title, Kissed by Sun, please follow me on social media or subscribe to my newsletter via my website.

Printed in Great Britain
by Amazon